SARA'S MOON

MOONS OF MYSTERY BOOK 1

S BOLANOS

MOONS OF MYSTERY

Sara's Moon

Charline's Solstice

Diana's Eclipse
(Coming Soon)

CONTENTS

*To my incredible husband who believed in me when I couldn't.
You'll always be my werewolf.*

**No, for the last time, the love interest is not named after you.*

1

SWEET FREEDOM

I opened my eyes to the macabre array of tubes and wires pulling unpleasantly at my arm. I clenched my jaw to keep the frustrated sound at bay lest it provoke another round of sedation. Yes, the wires pinched. Yes, my arm hurt something fierce. And yes, the pain in my leg bordered on mind numbing. But I was freaking done with lying around in a hospital bed.

I shifted my focus from my mottled arm to the optimistic kittens decorating the door. The calendar was likely meant to inspire cheer and hope. While it was pleasant in a forced sort of way, all I cared about was the date written in large green numbers.

Friday. Finally.

Excitement at my pending release surged through me, simultaneously waking me the rest of the way up and painfully drawing my attention to my restrictions. I scowled when I stretched my legs and only one bothered to comply, the other currently wrapped in so much gauze that it could have belonged to a stuffed animal rather than a human.

I drew in a deep breath as I pushed past the fuzzy pain and forced the miserable thing to move. Along with the breath came the tantalizing smell of baked goods so strong I could almost taste the promised sugar. It definitely wasn't an allergy conscious hospital treat either, but the gooey decadence of something with way too many calories.

Did someone bring real *cookies?*

I rolled carefully onto my back, mindful of the bandaged leg. The wrappings itched like poison oak, but the nurses, doctor, and anyone else I tried to ask about removing them, insisted they were necessary despite my argument to the contrary. The smell of cookies got stronger as I shifted to my other side in order to face the window and the likely source of the delicious smell.

Please be chocolate chip.

My pupils contracted painfully at the bright glare from the open curtains and I let out a strangled squeal of pain that sounded remarkably like my neighbor Mrs. Oliver's ornery cat. By the time I managed to blink the world back into focus, a shadow fell over me, obscuring the intense sunlight.

"I can't believe I fell asleep. Some friend I am."

I squinted at the figure hovering above me and was rewarded with a glowing halo of red. It took a half second longer than it should have for my brain to finish making the connection.

Charline.

She's here. She's, like, actually here.

I really am going home.

A quick look around revealed she'd brought a clean stack of clothes as well as a polka-dotted balloon, a rainbow bouquet of flowers, and a big teddy bear card.

How long has she been here?

She glanced down and her eyes widened. "Oh, sweetie, you're awake!" Her natural southern accent added a twang to the words and helped soften the pitch.

"I am now," I mumbled as I carefully maneuvered to sit up. Charline did what she could to assist me, then gave me a fresh glass of water. I sipped at it gratefully, despite the fact that it was bitterly cold.

"It's about time." She flounced back into her seat, causing her yellow, polka dotted dress to puff up. I envied the way the material accentuated her figure; no dress would ever be able to create those kinds of curves on me. She absently smoothed it back down and returned her intense focus to me. "I swear those nurses intentionally upped your meds so you'd always be asleep when I came by." She flapped a dismissive hand. "Oh well. You're alive and well, plus it gave me plenty of time to get to know that doctor of yours. Isn't he a treat? Shame I'm already taken," she added with a dramatic sigh.

I chuckled softly. Charline was a fantastic friend, if a bit high strung. "God it's good to hear your voice."

"It's good to hear yours. When I got the call, I totally freaked and came right over. Of course, I only got to see you for a moment before they whisked you off to more surgery and then you were asleep *forever*," she said, rolling her eyes for emphasis. "Pretty sure the nurses got tired of me asking if you were in a coma. That yummy doctor though—"

"Dr. Chandler," I supplied.

"Dr. Chandler," she repeated with a wink which made me suspect she's known his name the whole time, "assured me that all of the sleeping was normal and good for the healing process. But man, that dog really did a number on you."

I didn't have the heart to tell her I didn't remember anything about the supposed attack. Not when the hospital staff had asked, not when the officer had come by, and definitely not when I'd tried so hard that I'd given myself a migraine. I must've frowned or something, because Charline reached out a hand and placed it gently on my shoulder.

"You're looking much better now though, almost can't even tell."

"Thanks. I think." The ice clinked hollowly in the glass, while beads of condensation dripped onto the sheet, and the soft whisper of air filled the room.

I blinked and a flash of amber burned behind my eyes. A sound like tearing sheets echoed in my ears. Cold battled with the warmth saturating my arm.

I shook my head to clear the indistinct visions and inexplicable sense of fear that came with them.

"Sara, honey, are you okay?"

I nodded absently and returned the glass to her with a shaking hand.

"You sure? You spaced out a minute."

"Yeah. It was...a memory," I answered vaguely.

"About that night?" A touch of awe mixed with Charline's concern.

I nodded again. "Dr. Chandler said that things would start coming back, fuzzy at first, then with more clarity." Assuming they came back at all. The mind was funny like that. I shifted and fidgeted with the sheet, uncomfortable with Charline's gaze. "Hey, did you bring cookies?"

Her face clouded over in confusion. "No. I made some this morning, but they're at the house." She plucked at her dress as if she was going to sniff it and let out a huff. "I knew I should've changed."

"You cook in a dress?"

"Don't you? Though technically it was bakin' and that doesn't count," she added with a flourish.

I rolled my eyes and smiled. "First off, we both know I can't cook, and even if I could, I wouldn't do it in a dress. Secondly, you do know it's winter, right?"

"Of course I know it's winter. What do you think that's for?" She jerked her thumb at an over-the-top coat lying next to the ridiculously large card. The outerwear was a fluffy, PETA-approved, nightmare of fake fur that would hang to her knees and make it look like an actual bear was trying to absorb her body.

"Oh, I get it. You didn't dress for the weather, you dressed for the doctor," I teased.

"Hush you."

Just then, the nurse came in. If I remembered correctly, her name was Katelyn. Thankfully, she was not one of the nurses I remembered having to restrain me. I hadn't seen any of them since the night I'd been admitted.

"Excellent, you're already awake," she said, walking over to check my vitals. "Good to see you again, Miss Montgomery."

"You as well."

"And how is our patient doing this morning?" Nurse Katelyn asked.

"Not too bad. A little groggy," I responded honestly.

She nodded and peered at the IV bag hanging by the bed, then moved on to inspect the bandages holding me hostage. "And how's the leg?"

"Stiff, but otherwise alright." Nurse Katelyn raised her eyebrows and gave a slight shake of her head, but otherwise didn't comment on my assessment. I spared a glance at Charline who shrugged back at me. "Should be good to go home..." I ventured. The nurse chuckled and tucked the chart back at the end of the bed.

"In that case, I have very good news."

"Woo!" Charline cheered and threw both hands up like she was on a roller coaster. I tossed the covers aside and made to hop out of the bed, heedless of popping my nearly healed stitches.

"Easy there. We have to go over a few things first," Katelyn said, effectively dampening the mood. I scowled and fell back into the pillows while she rattled off a thorough list of instructions that I didn't have a prayer of remembering. "Lastly, we'll be sending you home with crutches to help you stay off that leg in addition to the medications and antibiotics. Any questions?"

"No?" A glance at Charline showed that she was equally overwhelmed at all of the information.

Nurse Katelyn gave a small laugh. "Not to worry, I have the instructions already printed out for you. I'll give them to Miss Montgomery. Feel free to call the doctor's office if you have questions or you start to feel worse. The number is with your instructions."

"Yes ma'am," I said as Charline took the page and slipped it into her purse.

"We'll finish up your discharge paperwork and you'll officially be ready to go."

"Thank God!" I exclaimed. She smiled knowingly at my enthusiastic appreciation and set to task.

In hardly any time at all, she'd taken my blood pressure one last time, shaking her head as she did so, liberated me from the excess of wires and tubes, then left us to gather everything and make our escape.

As soon as the door clicked shut behind her, I turned to Charline. "Can I go home now?"

She positively beamed. "You better believe it! We'll get you fixed up right and you can read your card when we get you settled in back at the house." Like a force of nature, Charline immediately began the bustle of organizing my things, which mostly consisted of everything she'd brought.

"Anything I can do to help?" I asked as I gingerly swung my legs over the side of the bed.

She scowled at me, then promptly shoved a stack of

folded clothes into my arms. "You can get dressed. I'll take care of this, hon."

I leveraged the bed in order to comply. The process was slow going and only added to my eagerness to be free of this place. The bandages already felt excessive. At least at home there wouldn't be an army of nurses to stop me from ditching them. I pulled my brown hair into a ponytail, finished tugging the cotton sweater into place, and sat hard on the mattress exhausted.

Maybe I'm not as "good to go" as I think.

"You ready?" Charline asked from behind a wheelchair. My brows pulled together as I eyed the vehicle with no small amount of trepidation. She wiggled the chair and I winced at the screech of wheels on linoleum.

"I am *not* riding in that."

"Oh, yes you are."

"What about the crutches? The nurse said something about crutches," I protested. Crutches at least were dignified.

"Right, almost forgot." Charline promptly snatched a pair that had been unobtrusively leaning on the wall and stacked them with the rest of the goodies. "Come on!" she encouraged me. "We both know getting dressed completely wiped you out. If it makes you feel better, you'll have to use the crutches when we get to your place. This'll never make it up those death traps you call steps."

I groaned and sagged my shoulders in defeat. She flashed a victorious smile and wheeled the chair closer so I could hobble awkwardly into it.

"This is completely unnecessary. And demoralizing. Everyone is going to stare at me."

"Quit your bellyaching. We're in a hospital, lots of people are in wheelchairs," she scolded and promptly rolled us out of the room.

2

HOME AT LAST

I stared at the front of my one-bedroom rental as Charline put the SUV in park. The bungalow style was prominent on Sycamore and though it was smaller than the three-story Victorian I'd grown up in, it was cozy—and affordable. Nothing about the faded blue paint, white columns, or shuttered windows hinted at any sort of past violence. Even the cobbled street boasted the serene quiet of established suburbia. The only thing even remotely amiss was the streetlight standing opposite my walkway that had yet to be repaired in the two years I'd lived here.

"Ready?"

I turned my gaze from the unassuming facade to meet the hopeful optimism of Charline. "As I'll ever be."

"Then let's do this thing." Knowing full well that I would deny any assistance she offered, Charline swung around to the trunk. She propped the crutches within easy reach for me and returned to unloading the plethora of goodies. "You sure you don't want your coat?" she hollered through the vehicle.

"No, I'm good."

She scoffed and pulled her own cream monstrosity

tighter. Truthfully, I'd started sweating through my arguably thin sweater almost the minute I'd put the damn thing on.

I braced myself on the door and heaved my battered body out of the car. The nurse's warning not to put too much weight on the leg or I'd end up back in her care rang loud in my ears. It took a few tries to get the crutches settled comfortably under my arms and I sent up a silent thanks for whoever had had the foresight to adjust the height beforehand.

Charline walked past me laden with gifts as I trudged my way slowly towards the front door. My gaze caught on an odd discoloration on the walkway. It spread out in a large circle that threatened to envelope an entire square of concrete. Distantly, I recognized the brown stain was what remained from a pool of blood left to sit for too long.

Funny, you'd think the rain would have washed it away.

I tried to take another step and one crutch caught on a loose piece of gravel. Any hope that I'd adjust perfectly to life with one leg went right out the window as I struggled to get my bearings and prevent my face from meeting rudely with the ground. I winced as the staples in my arm pulled at newly healed flesh. Balance restored, I carefully relaxed my death grip on the crutches and resumed my trek.

"You coming?"

I glanced up. Charline stood there, naked concern in her eyes, keys dangling from her hand. I wanted more than anything to be on the other side of the blue door behind her, but all the will in the world couldn't get my feet to move.

"Sara?" The soft click of the door latch shifting pierced the inexplicable bubble of panic that had consumed me.

I shook my head to dispel the fog clouding my thoughts. "I'm coming. Must be dazed from the meds."

I continued forward with stubborn determination until

my journey came to another abrupt halt at the stairs. My body froze mid stride. My heartbeat pounded in my ears. Sweat coated my palms, causing my grip on the crutches to slip slightly. The sheer weight of my clothes was the only thing that held me in place in the face of the inexplicable need to run.

You're fine, nothing is happening to you.

Despite the reassurance, my breathing remained heavy and the world was in serious danger of sliding right past its current alarming angle.

"Charline?" I squeaked out with the little air remaining in my lungs.

"Yes?" She turned to see me frozen once more. "Oh, goodness! I'm so sorry. I can be such an addle-brained ninny sometimes." She immediately came to my aid and helped me up the steps. "I told you these rickety things are a death trap."

I sighed with relief and leaned into her when she looped an arm under my shoulders. "Yeah, yeah. It's a rental, it's not like I own the place."

Charline gave a rather unladylike snort and released me safely on the landing. "The offer stands. You could come live with me. It'd be fun. We could have girls' nights all the time, I could teach you to cook..."

"I wouldn't want to get between you and Ted."

She rolled her eyes and pushed the door open. "Please. Ted and I are solid as a rock."

"Because that's how every relationship wants to be defined—sharp and pointy."

Her mouth fell open then twisted into a scowl. "Smarty pants," she teased and gave me a playful shove then cursed when I stumbled backwards.

Time seemed to slow as I careened towards the steps. Charline's fingers passed through empty air as she made a grab for my shirt and missed. Crutches forgotten, my bad leg caught the full weight of my fall and I came to a complete stop at the edge of the landing with only a minimal twinge of pain. I blinked back at Charline whose face seemed to reflect my own astonishment.

"Are you okay?" she asked.

I shifted the crutches back into position and moved away from the precarious ledge. "Yeah?"

Her eyebrows furrowed in skepticism, but she didn't call me out on the lackluster answer and instead turned to finish opening the door. It swung inward on silent hinges, beckoning me to the sanctuary that I'd been dreaming about since I'd woken in the hospital. She placed the items inside and returned to retrieve me. "Here, let me help."

"No." The sharp reply took her aback. I softened my tone and met her worried green eyes, "No. I mean, *I* need to do this."

She nodded and stepped back, staying close enough to intervene if needed, but far enough to give me room. I took a deep breath. The familiar smells of Chinese take-out, lemon-scented dish soap, and the spruce candle I loved wafted through the open door and dispelled my lingering anxiety. Balancing on my good leg, I positioned the base of my crutches inside and cleared the threshold in one hop.

Home at last.

Now that my symbolic move had been accomplished, Charline rushed to help me the rest of the way to comfort. I plopped down on the couch and the cushion sank as if trying to embrace me in some form of upholstered welcome. Tension leached out of me while I watched Charline heap everything from the hospital on the narrow island, obscuring the aged blue tile. My gaze slid past her flurry of organizing to the stack of framed pictures leaning against the far wall waiting to be hung. I frowned at the dejected art. It had been waiting two years now.

Like that, my relief at being home turned bitter. Why couldn't I pursue anything permanent? The art remained unhung, because it would put holes in the wall. I rarely cooked at home, opting instead for delivery. Hell, I'd even bought most of my furniture at a secondhand store. I kept meaning to refurbish most of it, but I...didn't.

Maybe I should *take Charline up on her offer.*

"I went ahead and put a few groceries in the fridge for you." Charline gave me a pointed look as she joined me. "Just a few things while you adjust."

"I seriously doubt it's a few," I said, giving her a look in return. "You shouldn't have. I can easily order something. Delivery is a thing, you know."

She looked properly scandalized at such a suggestion. "It was nothing. Besides, fresh food is exactly what you need after a stint in the hospital."

"Charline, you really shouldn't have. You have to let me pay you back."

"Never you mind, I wanted to. And how many times have I told you, you've got to stop eating junk? Don't think I didn't see all the takeout containers." Despite the teasing, the smile on her face was genuine. "You sure I can't convince you to stay with me, just for a little while? There's nothing here that can't easily be moved."

The truth of her words smacked me solidly in the chest. Once more, I seriously considered taking her up on the offer. It wasn't that I didn't like the idea of living with Charline. Truthfully, I imagined it'd be the exact grand adventure she claimed it would be, but that wasn't why I'd moved to the city. How would I prove to myself and to my parents that I could make it on my own if I ended up relying on her generosity?

Bumping into her on my first day at Raleigh Marketing Services had been the break I hadn't known I'd needed. She was fun, bright, and made me challenge my perspectives on a near daily basis. Despite the fact that I was an extreme introvert and she was obviously an exuberant extrovert, we'd somehow clicked. I was eternally grateful for our friendship, even if I didn't understand it, and was loath to do anything that might jeopardize it.

"You really do too much," I said and gently poked her leg with a crutch. She chuckled and rolled her eyes.

My gaze was drawn to the fridge, which was now undoubtedly packed with food I didn't have a clue how to cook. I was about to commend Charline on her craftiness when I spotted the calendar hung on the door of my microscopic pantry.

"Shit," I hissed at spying the vibrant red declaration of my parents' annual vacation that ended the day before.

"What's the matter?" Charline asked, glancing about in confusion.

"Think you could grab my phone? It should be plugged in on the counter."

"Sure thing." She immediately hopped up to retrieve the small device from the blue-tiled counter top. "Is everything alright? Who do you need to call?" she asked when she passed me the phone that I'd never be able to afford on my own and the lone symbol of compromise with my parents who were probably worried sick.

"My dads. They go to Paris every year for their anniversary and would have freaked at coming home to a message from the hospital. With any luck, they haven't left the house yet." I flipped open the phone and sure enough, a dozen messages and a full voice mailbox. The groan slipped out even as I dialed the number by heart. It only rang once.

"Sara! Sweetheart, is that you?" Despite the worry in his

voice, the low timbre of Peter Sheppard's voice soothed something inside me.

"Hey, Dad. Yeah, it's me."

"Is that her?" a higher pitched voice called in the background. "Is she okay? Tell her we're packing now. We should be there in a few hours."

"That's not necessary," I immediately countered.

"Like hell it's not!" Tom's screech came loud and clear, suggesting he'd picked up the other line.

"No, seriously, I'm fine. I don't know what exactly the hospital told you, but I'm fine. Charline picked me up today. We're at the house."

"Tom and I are coming," Peter insisted in that no-nonsense dad tone.

"Please don't. It's a long drive and you two just got back. I promise, I'm okay. I'm not even in a cast."

"Sara, honey, a few hours on the road is hardly the sacrifice," Peter countered.

"What if I have Charline vouch for me? Would you consider at least waiting to drive halfway across the state?" I didn't wait for a response before passing the phone to a wide-eyed Charline.

"Uh...Mr. and Mr. Sheppard? Hi, this is Charline. It's true, Sara's in great shape. A picture? Um, I guess." She put her hand over the phone though the move would do nothing to block the sound. "Does your phone take pictures?"

I nodded. Phones with cameras were relatively new and expensive as hell, but right then I was more than grateful for the splurge. Charline removed her hand.

"Okay, we'll send the pic asap. Did you want to talk to Sara again?"

Unsurprisingly, she passed back the phone. "Hey, I'll email it to you in a few, okay?"

"If we're not convinced, we're coming anyway," Tom threatened.

"Understood. Now I should go so I can eat something. I'm starving."

"Peter, she's not eating," Tom said to his partner through the shared line.

"I am too eating," I interjected before they could start feeding each other's over-protective paranoia. "I love you both and I'll call again tomorrow." I finally ended the call, but not before another demand to send photographic proof of my well-being. The phone bounced on the cushion as I let out a sigh.

"Your parents sound nice."

"They are. They worry, but sometimes they worry too much. There's a reason I moved four hours away. Come on," I said, shifting to stand up, "let's get this over with."

I passed her back the phone with the camera already pulled up. She snapped a couple and helped me hook it up to the computer. I picked the one that did the best job of downplaying the injuries and sent it off, though in hindsight, I probably should have ditched all the gauze first. Mission complete, we adjourned to the kitchen where Charline performed a daunting feat of culinary mastery.

After dinner, we gossiped a bit about what I'd missed at work and she helped me get my medications in order. I was surprised to find an anti-anxiety prescription amid the rest. I continued to stare at the prescription bottle wondering why it had been included. Eventually, I set it down with the others on the counter.

"That about does it. Thank you again for dinner," I said.

"Stop making such a fuss. Any excuse to cook is a good one." Charline gathered her purse and stepped toward the door. I vacated my seat and followed after her. She paused and turned back to look at me. "Are you sure you don't want me to at least stay the night? It's really no trouble. I have more than enough vacation time."

"That's because you never take a vacation. And, yes, I'm sure. How am I supposed to become self-sufficient if you insist on coddling me?" She looked doubtful. "I'll. Be. Fine," I said, emphasizing each word.

"Okay...But call if you need anything. I can be here in a flash." The door opened and the chill night air wafted into the snug house.

"I know. Phone will be right by the bed."

"Did you take your antibiotic?"

"You watched me."

"Oh, right." She stepped across the threshold at last and almost immediately spun back around.

"I'll be fine," I interjected before she could start in on the list again. "Go home, get some rest. I've got leftovers if I get hungry, supplies for breakfast, and I'll call if I need help."

Her shoulders slumped and she begrudgingly made her way to the silver crossover. "Don't forget to lock the door!" she shouted back.

"I know, I know."

She gave me one last look as if hoping I'd change my mind before giving it up as a lost cause. I stood in the doorway waving her goodbye and trying not to second guess my decision to send her home.

When Charline's car rolled out of view, I turned back into the house and shut the door. I let out a slow breath as the silence of night filled me with a sort of peace that had been elusive in the hospital.

A small metallic noise like a penny bouncing on pavement shattered the quiet. My chest tightened and I held my breath as I pressed my ear against the cool door and strained to hear any other movement. The soft sounds of crickets chirping outside the window raked at my nerves.

The hairs on the back of my neck craned in protest at the hollow sound of wind whistling through the eaves.

Never in my life had I been terrified of being alone at night, but that didn't stop my hand from shaking as I scrambled to lock the door. The heavy thunk of the deadbolt striking home was at once comforting and nauseating. My breath came in short bursts. I backed away from the door while my heart thundered and blood roared in my ears. I wiped slick palms on my overly warm sweater and swallowed thickly.

You're being paranoid. There's nothing out there.

I glanced around the empty space devoid of personality.

There's nothing in here either.

The draft leaching through the sliding glass door to the backyard filled the room with an eerie chill, making my sanctuary feel more like a tomb.

I should call Charline, tell her I changed my mind.

I instantly squashed the thought. *No. I can make it a whole night on my own.*

I shuffled back to my room, put on my coziest pajamas, then curled up on the bed. My hope that pursuing normalcy would help banish the sudden ache of loneliness or irrepressible bout of fear shriveled in the dark.

I knew I would regret sending Charline home.

Even the admission felt selfish.

I'm an adult and can take care of myself.

I curled around my pillow with only my stubbornness to keep me company.

3

———

MEAT CUTE

"Hey, girl."

"Nice to see you about."

"How are you doing?"

"Is it true..."

"What was..."

"You'll be on your feet in..."

I pushed past the throng of well-wishers and at last emerged in the relative safety of my cubicle.

"Thanks, everyone, I appreciate it...I really should start getting back to work... I've had my holiday..." I said as I propped my crutches against the fabric wall.

My words failed to appease the masses. I wiped sweaty palms on my slacks and endured the suffocating press of bodies in silence. When it seemed my forced smile couldn't take a moment more of fake cheer, they dispersed. I let out a relieved sigh and turned to face my desk, eager for the monotonous chore of work, or at least I was until I saw what awaited me.

As I stared dumbfounded at the mass of paper on my desk, a folder slid off the mountain to land with a ruffled thump next to several of its fellows already on the ground.

How many times do I have to tell Bob? This is not my job.

I scowled at the insulting heap and grabbed the chair with enough force to make the plastic creak in protest. No longer looking forward to my mind-numbing task, I plopped down into the swivel chair which promptly rolled out from beneath me. I landed with an undignified "Oof" amid the rebellious folders.

The death glare I gave the chair should have burst the damn thing into flames. Instead, it sat there mocking me, remaining perfectly untouched. I pulled myself up, mindful of applying too much pressure to either my arm or leg. This time when I sat down, I made sure the chair was truly captive. It gave a small squeak of challenge, but nothing more. My miserable groan filled the tiny cubicle as I rolled up to the monitor and yet another folder plunked to the ground.

Today is going to be awful.

The door immediately opposite my workspace clicked open. I closed my eyes and awaited the inevitable.

"Sheppard. Take these down to Marketing."

I turned to face the opening of my cubicle and the source of the demand. Robert Hargrave hung half in my cubicle, the object of his request clutched in a pudgy hand. Per usual, his button down seemed half a size too small and his thinning hair was combed over in a style that easily made him appear ten years older. He thrust the big stack of folders in my direction, his perpetually sour expression stamped on his face.

I stared blankly at him.

He can't be serious. How the hell does he expect me to carry all of that?

He waved the stack impatiently. "Today, Sheppard."

This is what Hell looks like.

Bob raised his eyebrows expectantly when I didn't move.

Unable to come up with an excuse he'd hear, I grabbed a crutch and hoisted myself upright. Bob, of course, offered zero assistance, nor did he acknowledge my injuries.

He dropped the stack into my waiting arm, then turned back into his office without so much as a thank you. I winced at the sharp smack of blinds hitting the slammed door.

Stupid pig of a man.

I took a moment to balance the stack, mildly amazed at how much lighter it was then I'd anticipated.

Maybe the crutches are building my upper body strength.

I took a hesitant step out of the relative safety of my cubicle. Off to the left, the walkway stretched before me with its wall of pale gray on one side and beige cubicles on the other.

How am I going to navigate three hallways and overt potential disaster?

I took a fortifying breath, shifted the stack to a more comfortable position, and set out. With the speed of a snail, I crept out of the PR department, snuck past the major juncture that would take me straight to Accounting, and didn't die when an office door opened unexpectedly in my face. Hope swelled in my chest as I eyed the final stretch.

I'm going to make it.

I inched around the last corner, wary of unseen people.

Just a little farther.

The path spread out before me, miraculously clear of people. I quickly moved to take advantage of the rare opening before it could disappear. The rubber tip of my crutch caught on a snag in the carpet. My heart leapt to my throat while adrenaline shot icy cold down my spine. All semblance of coordination abandoned me. Fragments of paper and lint embedded in the carpet fibers leapt into focus as my face raced to meet the spotted, sand-colored floor and the promise of rug burn that was undoubtedly in my future.

Then, it wasn't. Rather than the questionable carpet, my face slammed into navy broadcloth while an exceptionally warm arm slid around my back to steady me. The owner of the arm smelled of a deep, woodsy scent reminiscent of the forests I'd played in growing up. I relaxed into the comforting smell, then it clicked that I was resting on a muscular chest and I pushed away. The bracing arm was replaced with a firm hand under my elbow.

I swallowed my mortification and looked up to thank my rescuer—that's when my hormones betrayed me. Michael Howell, resident office hottie and notorious flirt held onto me as my heart landed in my stomach with a sickening thud.

This isn't happening.

I stared up into deep brown eyes framed by equally dark hair that seemed to twinkle with amusement. My focus was drawn to his mouth as his lips curved into a good-humored smile.

"It's good to see you back, Sara."

Holy shit. He knows my name.

"You alright?"

"Uh…" I repositioned my crutch to give my brain a chance to reboot. My rebellious gaze left his face and traveled over his strong fingers wrapped around my arm, to the smooth back of his exceptionally tan hand. Then to his own arm where the muscles were clearly straining against the confines of his dark blue button down.

Small wonder he was able to stop my fall mere inches from the ground.

"Thanks," I managed.

So much for being eloquent.

"You're welcome. Should you really be carrying all of this while you're healing?"

"I've got it," I grumbled.

"Please, let me give you a hand," he insisted. I blinked as I realized he already had everything. His voice brought my attention back from the folders he held to him. "Now, where were you headed?" He wore a broad smile, his eyes dancing with the hint of levity I'd detected earlier.

"You... I mean marketing." I stamped down the pending blush, determined not to make any more of an ass out of myself.

"Are these the analytics reports about the new proposed focus group?"

I nodded, unable to find my voice.

"Perfect. Max has been waiting for those. I'm headed that way already. I can walk with you."

I reluctantly began to move as I realized he wasn't going to give me back the folders. We'd only gone a few steps when he spoke again.

"Your hair is down."

I had a clear vision of someone who'd been left out in a windstorm. "I must've forgotten to pull it back this morning." It was a small fib. I hadn't forgotten anything; I'd simply been too tired to try.

"It looks nice."

Mildly shocked, I kept my gaze forward, thankful to find we were at Max's office so I could be done with this painfully awkward encounter. Instead of leaving me and the reports to face Max on our own, Michael opened the door and stepped inside.

"Hey, Max, this is Sara from PR with those reports you wanted," Michael casually proclaimed, placing his stolen stack on the already covered desk.

How does he know I'm from PR? Half the office doesn't even know we have a PR department.

"It's about time." Max grabbed the folders and immediately started flipping through them. I caught Michael's nod toward the door, took the hint, and hobbled back out.

Outside of Max's office, Michael tried to assure me. "Don't mind Max. It's the end of the quarter and accounting is breathing down our necks about the budget." Before I could formulate a response, he asked, "Are you doing anything for lunch?"

"Not really." The honesty slipped out before the implications had a chance to take hold.

God, he's gonna think I'm like the rest of the office floozies throwing myself at him.

"Perfect, then how about you meet me and some of the department at the deli across the street at one?"

"Okay."

What am I doing?

"Great, I'll see you later." Someone called his name and he turned to address them. I seized the advantage and toddled away as fast as I could.

Charline is never going to believe this. I barely believe this.

The sounds of bustling downtown Raleigh dwindled to a muted roar as the deli door swung shut behind me. I took in the red vinyl booths and quaint tables, amazed that I'd never been here before.

I really need to get out more.

The bell over the door dinged again, announcing the arrival of another patron while I perused the occupants for a familiar face. I shook my head when I came up wanting.

Should have known better. People like Michael Howell don't talk to people like me.

"You made it."

My whole body erupted in goosebumps. "Yeah," I replied awkwardly as I glanced behind him. "Where's everyone else?"

"They bailed." He shrugged his substantial shoulders, then led the way to the counter. "Have you been here before?" I shook my head. "In that case, you have to try the roast beef. It's the best in town."

"I was thinking more like the turkey club," I said, not sure if it was possible to sound blander.

Michael's face crumpled into a confused scowl. "I feel duty-bound as a regular to inform you that you'd be making a terrible mistake."

"But—"

"Romero is known for his roast beef. It'd be an insult to the man not to at least try it," he finished.

"Fine," I said with a defeated huff and a radiant grin instantly stretched across his face. I mentally rolled my eyes at how quickly I'd caved while he turned to the counter to order.

"Two roast beefs...rare...with everything," he said to the man in a white apron behind the counter.

"No onions on mine," I spoke up. Michael flashed me a satisfied smirk before turning back to the man.

"One with no onions, please," he added, the undercurrent of amusement undeniable. "Thanks, Bill." Order made, he promptly paid for both and steered me to a table.

"You didn't need to do that," I protested, gesturing ineffectually at the purse slung across my body.

"My treat," he said and took a seat. "Consider it a welcome back to the office." He smiled as I slumped into my own wooden chair unsure how to respond to his generosity.

Within minutes, our food arrived. Michael glanced at his plate then at mine. Before I could ask, he leaned over and switched our trays.

"That's better," he said, then took a sizable chomp that liberated several slices of onion.

The plate in front of me contained a masterpiece of a sandwich that boasted piled slices of the supposedly famous roast beef as well as lettuce, tomatoes, some kind of suspect sauce, and side of chips.

How does he expect me to eat this monstrosity?

I grappled with the heaping sandwich and raised it to my mouth, then took a hesitant bite, followed by a more enthusiastic one.

"Your thoughts on Ramero's beef?"

"It's great!" I took another huge bite while he chuckled into his water.

"Told you it was the best."

"Mm, you don't understand, I don't even like roast beef," I admitted and snatched a napkin in time to rescue my blouse from the dripping juices.

"I guess that's changing."

"Absolutely," I agreed.

"Glad it *meats* your approval," he said with a twinkle in his eye.

I snorted and rolled my eyes. "You're one of those people that can make a pun out of anything, aren't you?"

He shrugged and leaned back in his chair. "I have my moments. I'd be happy to supply more *hefty* puns for your amusement."

"No, please, spare me." I wiped my mouth then placed the used napkin on my crumb-free plate.

"It kind of works out that the others bailed, it gives us a chance to catch up. I feel like we never talk," he said as he polished off the last chip.

Probably because until earlier, I didn't know you even knew my name.

He leaned forward to rest his forearms on the small table and I resisted the urge to mirror him. "Tell me, do y'all have the same problems with Accounting that we do?"

I snatched at the topic with the desperation of a drowning person for a life raft. "Absolutely. And as if that isn't bad enough, I get to hear all about the budget problems from Charline's boyfriend."

I can't believe how easy this is. I can almost imagine that lunch dates are something we do all the time.

Date? What am I thinking? This is a pity lunch, nothing more.

"She's dating—what's his name? Ted." He snapped his fingers as it came to him and I gave a small jump. "Talk about no reprieve."

"No kidding. If I'd wanted to be that involved in numbers, I would've become an accountant myself." He laughed and I smiled.

Casual, I can do casual. Besides, it isn't like he can hear my heart pounding, no matter how loud it sounds to me.

"So, Max seemed really stressed," I prodded.

"He has been since our last projections were off."

"I didn't hear anything about that."

"We like to keep department mistakes inside the department," he said with a wink.

"I could see how that would be beneficial."

I'm the picture of ease. Now if only my stupid heart would stop fluttering every time he looks at me.

"It keeps the rumor mill down." I snorted at the mention of the mill. No doubt it had been running full force since I'd told Charline about my lunch plans. "That's right. Your friend is the unofficial Chief of the Busybodies. To be honest, I'm a little surprised she's with Ted. She's so..."

"Beautiful?" I supplied. My deluded heart sank. So much for my be-nice-to-the-injured-girl theory.

"Animated. He's kind of a stick in the mud." To be fair, I'd said as much to Charline myself. Maybe this wasn't some ploy to get closer to my best friend. "Today's your first day back, right?" He asked unexpectedly.

All of my ease sprouted wings and flew right out the door. "Yeah..." Talking about work was one thing, talking about myself was another, even dealing with a possible romantic interest in my friend would be preferable.

"You don't look half as roughed up as everyone said you were." The openness of his face did nothing to ease the tension now running rife through my body.

"I guess that's a good thing. The doctor says I'm healing quickly," I added. Sweat coated my hands. I wiped them on my slacks beneath the table.

"I'm glad. I heard it was a stray dog. That true or another product of the rumor mill?" He laughed like he knew it had to be the latter.

My unease ratcheted up another level. Pieces of my discarded napkin came away in tiny bits beneath my restless fingers. "Actually, it was, so that's one thing they got right."

His smile faltered. "Sorry, I didn't mean to pry. It can be difficult separating truth from gossip sometimes." He glanced down at his wrist. "It's almost two. We should probably start heading back. I'm sure Max has gone through enough of those reports by now. He'll be looking for me."

"Does that happen often?" I asked, pouncing on the change in topic.

"Nearly every day. I swear, there are weeks I've done the exact same work for him four or five times. Oh well, what can you do?" He pushed back from the table and stood.

Back in shallow waters, the tension drained out of me and my breath came easier. I followed his lead and continued the conversation as we crossed back to the office together. "I know what you mean. Sometimes when I give a report, I feel like I might as well be talking to myself." We reached the elevator and he stopped. "You coming?" I asked.

He gestured over his shoulder. "I have another errand to run. But what do you say we meet up for lunch again in a couple of days? Say Thursday? There's a burger joint around the corner I think you'll like."

"I like burgers." I mentally clapped a hand over my mouth. Once again, it had run ahead of my brain. I'd barely survived lunch today, what made me think I'd do any better a second time?

For the love of God, Sara, think before you speak.

"Perfect. See you around." The elevator arrived and I stepped inside. An awkward beat went by where we stared at each other in silence. The doors closed and my calm evaporated into a full-on freak out.

4

STORM MOON

"Look at you! No crutches!" Charline exclaimed as I pushed past several people in the living room to pop free in her kitchen.

"I gave those up days ago." Truth be told, the incident with Michael had convinced me to immediately abandon the pretense of needing them. Four days later, I was happy to report I did not regret that decision. "Now, where do you want this?" I waved a bottle of her favorite Malbec.

"Um..." She spun in place, assessing the cluttered kitchen. "You could try to make some room on the counter, or...you could stack it on top of the fridge." She tapped her lip thoughtfully, then her gaze snapped back to me. "Hey! You're wearing the outfit I picked out."

I did a brief swish in the blue cocktail dress that I'd literally only worn because I knew it would make her happy. It was subtle enough that I didn't feel too self-conscious, but with enough glitz to appease even the glamorous Charline. Of course, it didn't hold a candle to the flamenco-inspired red number wrapped around her hourglass figure. She did a swish of her own and her frills threatened to overturn some precariously placed hors d'oeuvres. There was enough food in here to feed an army and there wasn't a doubt in my mind that she'd made every last bit of it from scratch.

"It seemed appropriate given the occasion. I'll take care of this. You get back to your guests. And who knows, if we don't get to it tonight, we can have our own little party later."

"Damn straight," she said before sweeping out of the kitchen and into the crowd that had amassed in her living room. I peered after her, more than a little daunted by the press of bodies and unfamiliar faces.

She really went all out with this party.

I glanced at the counter where I'd been told to make room. An impossible task, as it was currently dominated by an array of miniature quiches and deviled eggs waiting to refill the table in the other room.

She must've been up all night getting this together.

I swiped an egg, placed the bottle on top of the fridge, then considered my options. Parties may not have been my thing, but I wasn't here for me, I was here for Charline. I took a deep breath and launched myself into the swirl of colorfully dressed people.

After a bit of searching, I caught sight of some of my acquaintances from HR that I really only knew through Charline, as well as a handful of familiar faces from other departments.

Should have invited Michael.

I blinked, a little surprised at the wayward thought.

We've had lunch once and now I'm considering inviting him places? Way to put the cart before the horse, Sara.

I tossed back the last of my wine and ventured back into the kitchen to pour another glass and enjoy a brief reprieve from the press of bodies. Only my refuge seemed to have been invaded by an overflow of party guests. Rather than jockey for personal space, I found a vacant corner of the formal dining space to the side of the living room and resumed my people watching.

I spotted a few more familiar faces, but none worth braving the horde. Someone guffawed loudly, drawing the ire of a cluster of women dressed to kill in stilettos that looked like skyscrapers and skirts that aspired to the same heights. I plucked absently at the chiffon of my own dress.

Perhaps it's best I didn't invite Michael. Definitely can't compete with that.

I pushed away from my perch, eager to find a different source of entertainment. The entire world tilted and I stumbled forward. I pressed a shaking hand to my temple as if that could somehow make the room hold still and took a few, deep breaths until the colors stopped swimming. My gaze fixed on the half-empty wine glass in my hand.

I could've sworn I've only had two of these.

I looked around at the myriad of curious faces as I discarded the glass. It rocked dangerously on the dining table then settled.

Why am I here? These are all Charline's friends, or at least people pretending to be.

I searched the room for any sign of my friend. Colors and faces blurred together and I swayed once again. My nails scraped on the wallpaper as I sought to steady myself. I blinked past the haze and dragged in another deep breath.

Definitely time to go. Now where is Charline?

I found her chatting animatedly with some coworkers and gripping Ted's arm as though she feared he'd bolt if she let go. Judging by the look on his face, that seemed a very real probability. I didn't understand what she saw in him. He never smiled, laughed, or even went to lunch with us. If I didn't belong here, he belonged even less.

I took a step towards Charline and had to push through a sudden cluster of people that materialized in my path. By the time I was clear of them, Ted had vanished. As had Charline.

Good grief. Now what am I supposed to do? She'll kill me if I leave without saying goodbye.

I sighed heavily and scanned the crowd for literally anyone to talk to while I waited for her to reappear. It came as no surprise, that once again, I came up empty.

Could always sneak outside and call my dads back.

Maybe if I call while surrounded by people, it will lend more believability when I say I'm fine.

The more I thought about it, the more going outside seemed like the best idea. Between the wine and oppressive mass of people, my head was pulsing as if my heart was up *there* rather than in my chest. I desperately scanned the horde for the hostess and was rewarded with Charline's distinct copper waves bobbing through the crowd. A sigh of relief trailed after me as I made a beeline for her.

"Having fun?" she asked, grooving in time to the music.

"Yeah," I lied. "Where's Ted?"

"Oh, he and some of his buddies got caught up talking about some depreciating something or other, so I left them to it. Hey, you alright?"

I closed my eyes against a wave of nausea. "Sorry, I'm not feeling well all of a sudden." I pressed a hand against my stomach in a vain attempt to steady it.

Charline's face clouded with concern. "Let's step outside. Get some fresh air."

I nodded in agreement and let her navigate the sea of people. The back door stood like a beacon before us when Ted called out to Charline.

"It's nothing, sweetie!" she responded over her shoulder. "Sara's not feeling well."

"He going to be alright without you?" I asked as we emerged into the cool night. The noise from inside diminished to a muted cacophony and the chill breeze felt like a kiss on my flushed skin. Twinkle lights sparkled around the small patio adding an ambiance lost to the chaos inside.

I should have come out here sooner.

"Don't fret. He can survive a few minutes on his own." She glanced back towards the house. "You're not the only one the crowd bothers," she added with a conspiratorial wink.

We walked off a short distance to get away from the handful of people that had spilled outdoors. I took a deep breath and looked up at a night sky spotted with stars. "Where's the moon?" I asked.

"I guess it hasn't risen yet. It's supposed to be a full moon." Her hair shone copper in the twinkle lights as she leaned back to stare up at the sky. "I think it's either called a Snow Moon or a Storm Moon. I prefer Snow Moon personally." She let out a wistful sigh and returned her attention to me. "Can you believe Ted and I have been dating for six months? I think this might really go somewhere. You know?" The hope in her voice was telling. Charline didn't have a good track record where her romantic life was concerned.

"Yeah, that's gre—" My gut wrenching violently cut me short.

"Sara?"

"I'm sorry Charline, I think...I think I'm going to have to call it a night." An abdominal cramp forced me nearly double and I gasped at the pain.

"No worries, dear, you go right on home and get some rest. Give me a sec, I'll get someone to grab your things." Without another word, she abandoned me to my heavy panting.

I focused on deep steady breaths while I waited for her

return. The effort was wasted, as each and every attempt caught in my throat and made my chest spasm.

"Okay, Jenny is grabbing your purse, but I couldn't find your jacket," Charline said beside me once more.

"Think I left it...in the car," I managed through gritted teeth. Twinkle lights ran together in streaks of white and yellow. My head spun and even the ground seemed to be pitching beneath me, though I'd yet to move. "Need to go."

Please don't let me pass out in her backyard.

"Are you going to be okay to drive?" Charline gave me another concerned look as she wrapped a steadying arm around my waist.

"Yeah, I...I just need to go home." She didn't look convinced. "Seriously, Charline, I think it's just too many people after what happened."

Her mouth pulled down in a half scowl. "Okay, but I expect you to call me the minute you get home."

"Sure thing," I wheezed.

She shook her head, but didn't argue. "Come on, we'll go around the side." I could've cried with gratitude. Leave it to Charline to be the perfect hostess even when I was being a subpar guest. "You make yourself a nice, hot cup of tea and lie down. That'll fix you right up," Charline said as we approached my car. A person who must have been the promised Jenny, manifested with my things as Charline helped me into the driver's seat.

"I'm really sorry," I said again.

"Not another word. I'll talk to you later. And don't forget to call." She gave me a quick side hug and stepped back. I managed a small salute before closing the door.

It took every ounce of concentration I had to pay attention to the road. Like the twinkle lights in the backyard, all of the lights seemed exceptionally bright, surrounded by star bursts that streaked together in nearly indistinguishable blurs. I squinted in an attempt to bring the lights of my fellow drivers into better focus.

Does everyone have their high beams on tonight?

I sailed blindly through another intersection.

Was that light red or green?

The road seemed to roll up and down and my stomach lurched in time with the perceived hills. Finally, I pulled into my driveway. Shaky fingers fumbled with my phone as I shot off a text to Charline. It wasn't until I went to unbuckle that I realized I never had. I shook my head, which proved to be a huge mistake, and stumbled out of the car and into the house.

The door clicked shut behind me as I kicked off my shoes and tossed aside my purse. It landed with a clatter that sent my phone skittering across the floor. I stared at it dumbly before another spasm in my stomach set my feet moving again.

I can't be drunk; I didn't drink nearly enough for that.

Pain lanced sharp and unforgiving through my side.

Tea be damned. I'm drinking a gallon of water and going to bed.

I stumbled toward the fridge, but came to an abrupt stop when I slammed into something. I looked down at the island with its glistening blue tile.

Who put that there?

A series of spasms ripped through my midsection. I gasped as agonizing pain washed over me. My nails dug into the fabric of my dress as I doubled over and nearly careened off of the counter.

What's wrong with me? It's too early to be my cycle.

My sweaty hand slipped on the slick tile as I tried to brace myself. The flimsy material of my dress clung to my equally sweat-coated skin.

It's hot. How did it get so hot?

Outside. I need to be outside. Fresh air will help.

I staggered to the sliding glass door and managed to push it open and barely remembered to close it before trying to lean against it. Cold air filled my lungs and burned my nose. Fog billowed before my eyes with each gasped breath. Slowly, I looked up at the pitch-black sky studded with white. And there, in the middle of it all, was the full moon Charline had promised.

A pain unlike anything I'd ever known brought me to the ground. My hands and knees burned where unforgiving concrete scraped the skin clean off. I choked on a cry as my back arched unnaturally. My arm spasmed and sent me sprawling. The awful popping of my joints rang in my ears like fireworks and brought its own fresh wave of pain. I panted heavily, dragging burning cold into my lungs. My right leg kicked out of its own accord. It hit the glass and the impact radiated through my foot.

What precious little balance I had retained vanished. Hot blood dripped down my legs as my knees skidded along the grit covered ground. I desperately dragged myself away from the door. The move catapulted my stomach into my throat. A sharp prickling sensation spread like fire across my body. I scratched violently at my clothes, eager for some modicum of relief from the incessant burn. Another wave of acute agony rolled over me and sent me crashing face first into the ground as my vision narrowed.

I squeezed my eyes tight against the pain and sobbed through lungs made of fire past bleeding lips. Then everything went black.

5

LOST IN SUBURBIA

I blinked to clear the grit from my bleary-eyed view. Street-lights pierced the clear night, their halos bright and painful. Scenery leapt out of the darkness in lurid detail. I closed my eyes against the weird sharpness for fear of being sick and focused on getting up. A groan drifted out of me to vibrate dully between my ears.

Come on, one foot in front of the other. You've got this.

I straightened my legs and my stomach lurched in protest. Once it settled again, I was aware that my brain at least believed I was fully upright.

That's not right.

I dropped my head to look down at my feet and instantly regretted the decision. The world swam violently, my stomach clenched in retribution, and I gave up the endeavor to focus on taking a shaky breath.

Why am I on my hands? Am I on my hands?

The discordant thoughts tumbled one on top of the other.

I could use some tea.

I swayed in the general direction of the sliding door and bumped into it with my face. Pain rippled through me, starting at the point of impact then spreading like a wave to encompass my entire body.

What the hell?

Remembering my earlier quick movements, I slowly lifted my neck back up to search for the handle. My focus zeroed in on the ephemeral image of a large canine standing on the other side of the glass. I jolted backward, backpedaling as fast as my abused body would allow, aches and pains forgotten in the panic. My foot caught on an edge of concrete and veered out from under me. The world went wrong side up and I tumbled even farther back.

Fear swallowed reason and squeezed the breath from my lungs. Aching muscles tensed to the point of agony as I waited for the final snap that would end me.

The neighborhood cat yowled houses down. Cars honked on the main thoroughfare a couple streets over. Mr. Phillips and his wife argued louder than ever. A sprinkler ticked away in the distance, even though it was much too early in the season for that. My ears strained in the darkness for sounds I didn't hear: no nails on concrete, no sinister growl, no shuffling body.

Slowly, I uncurled myself, forcing paralyzed muscles to move. My body protested the continued mistreatment, but I kept going. Then, in an amazing moment of bravery, I cracked an eye. Unfortunately, the first thing in my field of vision was my hand, which was supposed to be steadying me, except it wasn't a hand—*that* was definitely a paw.

Positive that I had a concussion of some sort, I tried to look at my other hand and found in its place another paw nearly the size of my face. Thoroughly freaked out, I hurried closer to the reflective door. The glass revealed the same light-brown canine with a long muzzle and a remarkably bushy tail I'd caught a glimpse of earlier. I blinked hard, willing myself to wake up from the obviously liquor-induced nightmare.

It's not real. It's a dream. I'll wake up.

Despite my insistence, the image remained unchanged.

Maybe I'm dead.

I shut down that line of thought.

This isn't happening. It's not possible. I've lost my mind. Maybe I fell again, only now I'm in a coma.

There was only one way to know for sure: standard dream test. Gathering myself, I rushed the door. My head collided with the unforgiving pane hard enough to make a loud thud and shake the door. I stumbled back.

Great, now I'm hallucinating and *I have a headache.*

I gazed intently at the reflection. The sleek brown fur shone beneath the light of the moon high overhead. A gentle breeze drifted through my hair, but the chill didn't touch me.

This has to be the strangest dream. But what could have brought it on?

The large canine before me tilted its head. As it was, I stood taller than I would have if I'd been on my hands and knees. Even my head was slightly larger than an average human one once the extra bits like the extended muzzle and pointed ears were taken into account. Truthfully, I'd never so much as seen a picture of a dog that kind of looked like this.

I let out a frustrated huff. At the same time, I felt and saw my ears swivel forward. I laid them down and perked them up. Then I picked up my hand and my entire body adjusted. Interestingly enough the tail—my tail—caught my attention as it too moved to compensate for balance. I willed it to wag and was rewarded with a satisfying swishing motion.

That's not weird at all...

The reality of my predicament was getting harder to ignore.

All the nope. Time to go inside.

I took a step forward and a fresh horror arose.

How am I supposed to open the door without opposable thumbs?

I scratched at the point where glass met the wall in the vague hope it was at least cracked to no avail. If it wasn't shut all the way before, it definitely was now. My despair deepened and I snatched at another plan of attack.

The latch isn't complicated. I can totally manage without thumbs.

I briefly considered the simple mechanism, then attempted to work at it. The screech of nails sent a shiver down my spine and every hair along my back stood on end as if I'd been electrocuted.

Determined to persevere despite what was proving to be a very thorough dream, I pushed past the ear-piercing sound and tried again. After several frustrating minutes, I resorted to my teeth, earning myself a sore muzzle and a scratched frame.

No no no. I'm going to be stuck out here until I wake up.

Or return to normal, my mind offered unhelpfully.

Not inclined to believe any of this, I didn't appreciate my subconscious blindly accepting the fantastical situation.

Maybe I can make myself normal. In dreams and movies, it's a matter of willing something right? I can do that.

I braced myself and squeezed my eyes tightly shut. A feeling deep in my gut manifested. I focused harder. The pressure intensified.

That's it, it's working.

I let out a soft burp and hung my head in defeat.

This isn't real, it can't be.

A distant noise infiltrated my bubble of self-pity. My ears

rotated forward and I froze. A shiver of fear swept through me. I barely dared to breathe as I listened harder. A shrill cry rose into the quiet night and a bone-deep chill washed over me. People could still die in their dreams and that sound was definitely getting closer.

I glanced around, taking in the privacy fence circling the small yard, but the thin, wooden boards had lost their illusion of safety. What should have offered protection was now a six-foot-tall cage.

I swiveled around frantically searching for a means of escape. By the back gate, I spied a stack of neglected pots for plants I'd never gotten around to buying. They were stacked in a pyramid against the fence so they wouldn't fall over.

Before I could second guess the audacity of what I was about to attempt, I sprinted across the yard. I hit the stack at a dead run and jumped on top without a thought for whether or not they could actually hold me. The pyramid teetered and swayed, but it was too late to change course now.

I launched up with all of my strength. Pots clattered behind me, shattering as they smashed to ground. My right leg hit the top of the fence. I tumbled over and landed in a bruised heap on the other side. The pain scarcely registered as another howl pierced the night. The nearness of it sent me back into motion. I lurched blindly in the opposite direction of the approaching sound. Ms. Oliver's cat yowled as I bolted past it and the haze clouding my mind solidified. All rational thought departed, replaced with one, singular drive: run.

Cars blared as I appeared in their path. I veered away and kept going. There was no time, no logic, only darkness filled with fear and streaking lights as I became lost in my nightmare.

I stumbled as my run slowed and panted for air. The

world tilted as I swayed. I took a step to steady myself and my injured leg buckled. At a loss for what else to do, I crawled behind a line of shrubs, determined to sleep out the rest of this awful dream.

I blinked to find light in dappled patches all around me.

Morning already?

It was difficult to tell what had woken me up—my thirst or the persistent ache dominating my entire body. I rolled over and came face-to-face with small, round leaves. I closed my eyes and desperately prayed that when I reopened them it would be to see a bland white wall and not dense green foliage. No such luck.

I whimpered and fought to keep from completely melting down.

Why am I dreaming this? Why can't I wake up?

The raucous call of a bird startled me out of my spiraling depression. Dream or not, there were some basic necessities that needed to be tended to. At the top of that list was finding water. I poked my head out of the bushes to take a look around, the sound of dry leaves crackling outrageously loud in my ears.

How do animals put up with this nonsense?

My breath misted in front of me as I let out a heavy sigh.

That's one plus, at least I'm not cold.

I stuck one hand out.

Foot, I mentally corrected. A flash of stubbornness surged through me.

There's still a chance I'm actually in a coma and none of this is real.

The hope grew dim as I stepped into the bright light of morning. I recognized the fact that my refuge was a row of bushes by an abandoned house and that I was clearly in a suburban neighborhood.

Why does everything look funny?

I squinted against the sharp detail of the world that seemed to have become brighter and more vibrant while I slept.

I don't even have a name for most of these shades.

At least there aren't any people around.

There was no telling how someone would react to seeing something like me on their neighborhood street. Try to catch it? Call animal control? Scream in terror?

I erred on the side of caution and stuck closely to the houses, keeping a wary eye out for cars and the casual passerby as I looked for water. A few streets later, a birdbath sitting in the front lawn of a modest colonial caught my attention. The simple shallow bowl on a pedestal was nothing spectacular decoration-wise, but at that moment I'd never seen a more beautiful piece of yard art. I checked the area then darted across the narrow street. Just because I couldn't see anyone, didn't mean anyone couldn't see me. Once there, I eyed the water skeptically.

That's definitely not filtered.

I braced my front paws on the rim and tentatively dipped my tongue into the questionable liquid. All pretense of caution vanished the moment my body registered water. My tongue scraped concrete as I greedily lapped up every drop the shallow basin had to offer. The winter air made the liquid almost sweet with cold.

Thirst at least partially satiated, I sought some more shrubs to hide in while I considered my plight. The indisputable detail of everything made it harder and harder to believe I was asleep; not even the most lucid dreams were this thorough. I slumped into the dirt then let out a violent sneeze at the cloud of dust the move created...and didn't wake up.

Fuck my life. This is real.

I had no idea how it had happened, how to undo it, or even if it could be undone.

Will I be stuck like this forever?

I shook off the depressing thoughts and focused on what I could control. Before I could even begin to make a list, my stomach growled. Without thought, I ran my tongue over the points of my teeth.

Those are definitely bad news. There goes all hope of begging for scraps and handouts. What am I going to eat? How am I going to eat?

A garbage bin nestled beside a house caught my eye. Even from this distance, the pungent smell of rotting food made my nose twitch. Like the sounds and colors, the smell held infinitely more dimension, details woven into a pattern layered with intricacies—all of which were absolutely revolting.

Grumbling to myself in a near perfect echo of my gnawing hunger, I abandoned my shelter. I trotted past another cul-de-sac and my steps slowed as the tantalizing smell of charcoal and meat filled my nostrils. I lifted my nose to the air and breathed deep, savoring the delicate balance of paprika, garlic, and salt.

A loud bark rang out across the suburban landscape effectively breaking my concentration. I quickly dropped my head and scanned the area.

When I looked up to check my surroundings and get my bearings, I realized my hunger had driven me from the cover of the houses around me. A bark came again and I flinched. As the barking continued, my feet tangled up beneath me with conflicting signals to bolt and to stand my ground.

Ten feet away, a Labrador gave up barking and lowered

his head in a threatening growl. He advanced slowly, head hung low, teeth flashing. Behind him emerged the people I'd been trying to avoid. The dog's growl deepened. A part of my brain demanded me to growl back. I ignored the signal as my focus darted between the dangers.

"Buster, what is it?" a woman asked, then screamed as her gaze fell on me.

Immediately a man ran to her side. "What is it?"

"What is that!" she shrieked. Buster took another step closer.

My feet finally obeyed my desperate plea to move. I spun and bolted down the wide, empty street. Buster's furious barks and the people's screams chased me as I raced past house after house. The burning in my lungs returned as the bright light of day faded to dusk. Shadows stretched along the ground tripping my tired feet. Through the fog of exhaustion, I realized that silence dominated the world around me.

I stumbled to a jerky halt, dead on my feet. All around me lay close-cropped grass and expertly cultivated trees. Nose in the air, I walked in a slow circle. No sense of danger sprung to the forefront, but something crystal and pure did —water. Saliva flooded my mouth at the promise. Safe in the knowledge that I was alone, or at least not in any immediate danger, I took a step towards the source and found no purchase.

Paws skidded out in front of me as I went careening forward and down head over tail. Rocks smashed into my ribs, legs, and shoulders as I bounced down the incline. Each painful thump let loose a fresh shower of dirt and small stones that rained down on me when I finally landed in a splayed heap at the bottom.

Bruised and aching, I stumbled over to the pond, the only consolation to my relentless bad luck. Tendrils of mist curled off the placid water, my fuzzy reflection barely visible in the dim light. I hung my head and debris slipped free of my fur to land in hollow plinks that created tiny ripples in the otherwise smooth water. Before I could second guess myself, I plunged my head into the icy cold. The wet shock slithered past the protective layer of hair to freeze along my scalp. With a gasp, I yanked free in a spectacular spay of water.

Note to self: water in your ears bad in any reality.

I gave my head a thorough shake that spread down my spine and up my tail. The move took with it the last of the silt and the last of my energy. Beyond exhausted, I collapsed at the edge of the pool not even caring enough to seek shelter.

6

A FAMILIAR FACE

A persistent honking that would not be ignored threaded through my sleep. I cracked heavy lids to glare at my possessed alarm and instead found a gaggle of geese holding what appeared to be a morning meeting.

Oh, right. This.

Grumbling to myself, I shifted slightly and lapped at the water. The small movement effectively startled the group into alarmed chaos. A handful took flight in a flurry of gray feathers. The vast majority however, proceeded to honk in rapid stream as if they'd been personally insulted by my audacity to move.

I remained still, less than eager to give them a reason to attack. Gradually, they returned to their waddling and chatting, and a few brave ones even dared to swim within reach to investigate. Once they all seemed sufficiently satisfied that I intended no harm, I got up and glanced around.

The little pond stretched twenty feet across, surrounded by green grass that defied the season. Another thirty feet past that stood a ring of trees encircling the area on three sides. The last side, the one behind me, rose up in a steep incline.

I eyed the hill that had almost killed me the night before. Rather than dwell on the improbability of surviving the nearly sixty-degree incline virtually unscathed, I ventured out to explore the small clearing.

Far as I could tell, nothing about my predicament had changed. I was alone, lost, and—judging by the geese's reactions—not dreaming.

The sun set while I contemplated what to do next. Despite the encroaching dark, however, sleep eluded me. As I lay there, my ears swiveled to catch each new sound. Small splashes of tiny things entering and exiting the pond. The slight rustle of dry leaves as a breeze stirred the distant canopy. A faint humming in the distance too indistinct to be of any real concern.

My ear twitched as the same breeze reached down to tickle it, then resumed its incessant swivel. I rested my head on my paws and stared out across the serene water. The geese had long since settled for the evening and the moon rose to sit fat and heavy in the sky. I rolled onto my back and stared up at stars that were at once brighter and duller.

Light pollution. I can see light pollution.

That was nearly as depressing as inexplicably being turned into an animal with no hope of turning back.

Hours later, the only thing that had changed was the stars gave way to a cloudless day. The hollowness of my stomach emphasized a hunger I'd never experienced before. I eyed the geese warily, but before I could decide if I was up to the task, a branch snapped. I tilted my head, ears swiveling to inspect the source of the noise.

People?

It was possible, though I was torn whether that was a good thing or not. I took a deep whiff of the late morning air as the breeze shifted and adrenaline rocketed through every nerve ending. I scrambled to my feet while I scoured the tree line for the source of my sudden, inexplicable anxiety. Details leapt into focus, clear as if seen through binoculars, but nothing out of the ordinary stood out. Then my gaze caught on movement and I froze.

A massive wolf strode towards the pond from the edge of the wood. The mottled gray and brown of his coat helped him to blend in as he slunk closer, intently sniffing the ground.

I fought the primal impulse to bolt while crippling fear clawed at my insides. Shaking overtook my body as I stood rooted to the spot. The wolf was lean and distinctly larger than myself. It glided across the lawn towards the water's edge with a grace that contradicted its size. The geese panicked when they finally noticed the wolf's approach and took flight in a cacophony of wings and honks. The wolf snapped at one that flew too close. The sharp clack of its teeth as it missed ricocheted in the small oasis.

No amount of logic could hold back the tide of liquid fear that instantly fueled my limbs. Instinct took over with a vengeance and propelled me forward. In a heartbeat, I'd crossed the clearing and was crashing haphazardly through the underbrush with little care to how much noise I was making.

A growl sounded behind me and my panic took on new heights. I surged forward. Scattered trees merged into a crowded forest. Low-hanging branches whipped across my face. Thorns snagged on my fur. Dried leaves and twigs crunched beneath my feet while the echoing crash of the wolf behind me urged me on faster.

Time slipped by in a haze until I blinked to find that the sky was bleeding magenta and orange. I slowed, my sides heaving as I panted for breath, the sounds of pursuit having faded at some point.

A sharp howl rose up over the trees. My body instinctively lurched forward. In defiance of my overwhelming exhaustion, I picked up speed and resumed crashing through the underbrush once again. Abruptly, the trees gave way and the leaf-riddled ground morphed into unforgiving asphalt. My nails scraped across the black tar, carrying me further onto the road despite my desperate attempts to turn around.

My body obeyed the command to stop just in time to be bathed in the twin yellow glow of headlights. The blare of a horn accompanied an ungodly screech of tires.

Stars burst behind my eyes as the bright yellow jeep slammed into my frozen body and sent me skidding across the asphalt. Despite the nauseating pain radiating across my left side, I attempted to stand. A whimper of hopelessness escaped me as I crashed back to the unforgiving ground.

Not safe. Have to keep moving.

My ears strained to hear the howl of inevitable pursuit, but there was only ringing. I shook my head and groaned. With a level of determination I didn't know I possessed, I attempted to stand again. I pulled my front right leg in to take the weight and pushed up, but my paw found no purchase on the slick ground and I crumpled back down with an agonized whine.

"Oh shit," a deep voice said above me.

I rolled my eyes in pursuit of its owner, but couldn't make out much more than a dark silhouette against the backdrop of lights.

"Okay. I can fix this. Sweet moon, you came out of nowhere. What are you doing all the way up here?"

My eyelids fluttered and gray encroached on the yellow. The ringing in my ears faded to be replaced with a rushing sound that muffled the man's footsteps as he approached me. A paw twitched as my body tried unsuccessfully to run once more. But I had nothing left. My entire left side was officially numb and whatever strength had powered me before had fled.

The man crouched down making soft shushing noises that blended with the ringing. He reached out a hand and I whimpered again. "Shh, shh, you're going to be alright."

I wanted so much to believe that, but if the last couple days had taught me anything, it was that I was far from alright. I was lost, injured, being chased by a nightmare. Despair threatened to crush what was left of me into dust, then his voice came again.

"I want to check you for injuries before I pick you up," he said as he reached out. "Please don't bite me."

I closed my eyes in anticipation of the pain that would likely erupt the moment pressure was put on my ribs. Yet when his hand came down, it was on my head and it was so gentle, I almost didn't feel it.

"I'm so sorry. If you'll let me, I'd like to help," he said, his voice soft and sincere as he brushed a thumb across my cheek.

I wanted to respond, to agree, to desperately accept the help so kindly being offered. All that came out though was a whimper followed by another and another until my aching side was heaving with them. My mind was numb with over-saturation of fear, body beaten and abused past its limits.

An extreme sense of deja vu pierced the fog dulling my senses as I was lifted straight into the air. I blinked my eyes back open, not sure when they'd closed. Where I expected to see flashing red and blue lights however, there was only a steady yellow getting brighter with each jolting step. My head rolled to the side and immediately met resistance. The deep smell of the woods wrapped around me like a cloak. I drank up the scent of home and let it carry my mind away from the pain.

My dad led me through the woods, pointing out maples and

magpies as we ventured deeper into the forest. School had let out early and I'd gotten almost perfect grades. As a reward, we were headed to his favorite place: the lake at the heart of the forest. There, Tom would be waiting for us, probably with a picnic basket full of treats. And if I was lucky, we'd stay out late, swimming until I was so tired I had to be carried home.

The sound of an engine roaring to life shattered the peaceful image. I opened my eyes once more to find myself in a car wrapped in a jacket. A cautious glance over showed my rescuer in the seat beside me. From my current angle it was nearly impossible to discern his features. I gave up trying and settled back down. Outside my bubble, the world rushed by unconcerned. Lights blurred past in streaks of red, green, and yellow.

I sighed heavily, regaining the attention of the driver.

"We're almost there, I promise."

True to his word, mere minutes later the soft squeak of brakes filled the air and we came to a stop. He unbuckled and walked around to my side of the car. For a brief moment, the headlights illuminated him, but they dimmed before I could make out much more than wide shoulders and dark hair. Then he was standing by my door, once again backlit by another light and reaching towards me through the open cabin.

I flinched away from the touch and let out a small whine.

"Okay," he said, taking a step back, both of his hands raised so I could clearly see them. "In your own time." He took another step backwards and the glow from the porch touched him. Even in the dim light, I could make out brown eyes to match equally dark hair, a square jaw and an open face.

I know you...

Michael?

I sat upright, not sure if I trusted what my eyes were telling me. Given my last thirty-six hours and the fact that I'd been hit by a truck, it wouldn't be wholly outside the realm of possibility that they were starting to play tricks on me.

"No need to rush. I'm not going anywhere."

Contrary to his words, he stepped towards the house and didn't stop until he reached the door. The key clicked in the lock, then the red door swung open. He leaned inside and flicked a switch all while remaining in view. Instantly, a warm glow emanated from the previously dark recesses of the home. Then he calmly walked back to his previous position in the middle of the front yard, leaving me a clear path to the door.

I glanced from him to the standard Craftsman and back again.

"You must be tired and we really should get you cleaned up. Maybe something to eat?"

At the mention of food, my ears perked up.

Do I trust this?

Given my recent misfortunes, that was a decided no. But could I afford not to? I was bone-weary, hopelessly lost, and couldn't even remember the last thing I'd eaten. Another glance at the open door and the safety it promised decided me.

The coat fell to the floorboards as I stood up. I looked over the door to gauge the distance to the ground. While standing had barely triggered a twinge in my side, I seriously doubted that a four-foot leap would be as forgiving. A glance up at Michael showed that he'd yet to move. I shifted from foot to foot as I considered the drop again.

I can do this.

My front paws landed with a muted thud quickly followed by my rear ones. A minuscule spasm twisted my side, but nothing more. I stood for a minute totally dumbfounded at the lack of body-wracking pain. Then my state of exposure registered. I eyed Michael as I warily made my way past him towards the inviting door. To my surprise, he stayed put, allowing me to pass unhindered.

Once at the threshold, I hesitated. Inside was warmth, food, and safety. But inside, I couldn't run. If something happened, there would be nowhere to go. And to top it all off, this wasn't just anyone's home, it was Michael's, a man I hardly knew.

Don't be such a wuss. You have teeth and claws now. You can either go inside and probably be safe or take your chances out here where you'll definitely starve.

I took a deep breath, picked up my tattered courage, and stepped into the glow.

I can do this. I'm fine.

Lifting a trembling paw, I set one foot inside, then the other. The first thing I noticed about Michael's house was the scent. Strong wafts of pine and ash hit me, followed by the woodsy scent that I'd picked up on before, interwoven with the subtle undertones of musk and body wash.

Taking a deeper step into the house, I glanced around. At the far side, a large glass sliding door offered a view of the backyard. To the left of it, the kitchen opened up, dominated by a large peninsula that was probably great for entertaining. Big windows with views of the side yard covered the wall to my far left, and on the wall immediately to my right was the fireplace and sitting area. Feeling a bit safer, I stepped all the way inside.

That's when Michael shut the door behind me. Every instinct I had rebelled at being confined with nowhere to go. I spun to approach the door and let myself out, then I remembered I had no thumbs to open it anyway. I peered around, my pulse fluttering like a hummingbird's wings.

I glanced around the room again, only to find the walls were much closer than they'd seemed only a few moments ago. Even the ceiling felt like it might drop on my head at any moment. Everything closed tighter around me. My lungs fought against the pressure, straining through the panic for my next breath.

I stood in the entryway and trembled.

"Whoa there, it's okay." He walked closer. "You're safe here."

Safe? I didn't feel safe. Michael reached out as if to restrain me. I wrenched away, my nails clicking and sliding on the hardwood floors as I scrambled to move out of reach. My back pressing against the couch in the middle of the room brought me up short. I whined my distress as my eyes continued to roll, searching for an escape that wasn't there.

Michael let out a sigh and took a step towards me. I stiffened and he stopped. His shoulders slumped and he ran a hand over his face. "I'm not going to hurt you, but I don't expect you to believe me. Not after what you've been through."

Like hitting me with your car?

The angry thought did its job in grounding me. My claustrophobia took a back seat while I glared at him.

"You have no idea how sorry I am and I'm going to do everything I can to help. But first, I need to get out of these clothes. The blood smell is starting to get to me." It wasn't until he pointed it out that I realized that almost the entire front of his blue tee was covered with red blood, there was even some on his jeans.

Is that mine?

"We should probably get you cleaned up too, but one thing at a time. You wait here, I'll be right back." Without another word, he turned on his heel and made his way down a short hallway to my left. His form continued to recede until it disappeared into a room at the far end. The moment he was out of sight, I found my footing and booked it to the back door.

Beyond the glass, the sky was stained a deep purple. I made out the shadows of trees looming in the darkness as if the forest itself had declared war on his backyard. I swallowed and took a step back to inspect the handle. Like my own, there was no way to open it without thumbs.

I hung my head and sat heavily on the floor. Inside the house was almost perfectly quiet, but so close to the door, I could hear the soft sounds of night coming to life. An owl hooted, cars passed on the street, the wind whistled softly through the exposed rafters.

A stronger breeze rustled the trees and sent shadows darting around the yard. My heart skipped, convinced that the inky patches belonged to the monster hunting me. Even though my mind knew better, I backed away from the scene and went in search of my other would-be-killer. Along the way, I discovered a guest room and bath to match, then finally the main bedroom. Which was where I found Michael doing exactly as he said he would—changing.

Walking in on Michael had not been my intent. Yet, I found myself staring transfixed, soaking in the vision of a tanned, naked Michael.

"Now, where on earth did I put... Aha, there you are," he exclaimed triumphantly as he snatched a pair of sweats and turned to find me sitting like a total peeping Jane in his doorway. "Oh, hey," he said with a smile that made his eyes crinkle. I cocked my head to the side. "Didn't want to be out there by yourself, I take it?" he asked, standing there with the sweats in his hand.

I glanced behind me down the hall and back at him. That was a solid nope.

He continued to stare at me and my tail gradually began

wagging of its own accord, swishing lightly along the wood. All of a sudden, his eyes went wide and he quickly pulled on the pants promptly followed by a fresh tee that seemed to materialize out of thin air.

"So." He paused to clear his throat. "We should probably see about getting you cleaned up as well," he added, then promptly disappeared into what I assumed was the en suite bath. I leaned forward curious what he was up to, especially when I heard running water.

If he thinks he's giving me a bath, he's out of his damn mind. Animal or not, that's not happening.

The sound of water vanished and Michael reappeared holding two towels: one wet, one dry.

"This will probably be easier in the living room," he said and walked towards me.

I quickly stood up and backed out of the way until my tail rudely met the opposite wall. I gave a small yip and he chuckled quietly.

"Come on. Dried blood is harder to get out of fur." I narrowed my eyes at his receding form and stayed where I was. "I'm not cooking anything until you're clean." The threat drifted down the hall.

That got my feet moving. Besides, how dangerous could the office flirt really be? I'd technically worked in the same office as the man for two years and never heard anything truly untoward. With Charline as my friend, there wasn't a doubt in my mind I would've heard even the tiniest rumor of him being less than savory with any of his conquests.

Despite my conclusion, I hesitated at the edge of the hallway. I peered around the wall to sneak a peek into the room. Michael sat on the area rug between the overstuffed navy couch and the glass coffee table, wet towel in hand, dry one placed across his lap.

"You coming or not?" he encouraged me. I scowled at

him. But either that expression didn't translate to canine faces or he chose to ignore it, because he waved me over impatiently. "You're not the only one that's hungry and that blood isn't going to clean itself."

I took the last few fateful steps into the room and plopped down in front of him with a huff, prompting yet another chuckle.

"It really won't be that bad," he said, holding up the damp towel. I eyed it and wrinkled my nose. "If I may?" He met my eyes and for a brief second, it seemed like he knew me.

I dismissed the ridiculous fancy and dipped my head in what I hoped conveyed permission. My side flinched as the pressure of the warm towel passed over it.

"I really am sorry," he whispered as he methodically removed all evidence of the chaos that had consumed my reality the last two nights. "The last thing I expected was for you to come haring out of the woods. I'm glad I was able to slow down enough not to do more damage. This could've been much worse."

I let out a grateful sigh as he gently removed the dust from my face.

"Almost done." The words were more depressing than reassuring. Having someone take care of me was a welcome change from constantly being terrified for my life. "There. And I don't even think we need this." He gestured to the unused towel in his lap. "See, not so bad. There wasn't near as much blood as I feared. Must have gotten most of it on me." He smiled and slowly stood up. "Now, I believe I promised you something to eat. How does steak sound?"

My stomach growled as I tracked him to the kitchen. I drifted after him with only the faintest tick of nails to betray my presence. Once more I heard the sound of water, then he turned and placed a large bowl full of the stuff on the floor in front of me.

The last of my trepidation evaporated as I greedily lapped up the liquid, making a terrible mess. By the time I'd quenched my thirst, water soaked my face and droplets covered a radius of at least two feet around the bowl. I let out a whine and backed away, embarrassed at the spectacle I'd made.

"Hey, it's alright. No damage done." He walked back into the living room. When he returned, he had the dry towel. He held it up as if he was going to dry my face, but once again waited for permission.

I pushed my face into the waiting cloth and allowed him to clean me up yet again. Once I was dry, he mopped up the floor, refilled the bowl, and replaced it, this time, with the towel beneath it. Then without any other comment, he returned to the task of making dinner.

I took a seat on the cool floor as he adjusted a knob on the stove that already held a pan. Beside the burner sat a plate with two exceptionally large steaks. My stomach gave a savage growl.

"What do you think? On the fly?" he asked, turning to look at me. I cocked my head to the side, not sure what he meant. The image must have been amusing, because he let out his heartiest laugh yet. "Well, I think on the fly sounds perfect."

The steak sizzled deliciously when it hit the hot pan. My nose lifted into the air of its own accord to sample the irresistible smell wafting up. He waited awhile then flipped it. I whined impatiently.

"Give me a minute."

After a couple more minutes, he slid a plate in front of me. I eyed the pre-cut steak quizzically and looked back at him.

"What? I thought it would make it a little easier. I'll give you a minute to get acquainted," he said before walking past me.

Steam curled in my nostrils, tempting and teasing with promise while my mouth filled with saliva in eager anticipation. Without an ounce more of hesitation, I scarfed down the tender meat. Apparently, 'on the fly' meant bloody-but-seared. Rare had never been my preference, but I suspected, like many things, that had changed. Distantly, I heard a door open and a few seconds later close. My ear twitched, but I didn't pause to investigate.

I licked the plate clean and checked around it to make sure I hadn't dropped anything. Satisfied that the porcelain wasn't getting any cleaner, I stepped back in time to see Michael emerge from the hallway.

"All done?" My tail wagged appreciatively. "Excellent. If it's alright with you, I'm going to polish off my dinner as well. In the meantime, make yourself comfortable." He walked over to the peninsula where his own steak had cooled in his absence and took a seat on one of the bar stools.

Unsure what to do with myself, I remained seated where I was. In a time that rivaled mine, his plate clattered on the granite counter empty. Then he made his way back into the living room and plopped onto the couch with a loud whoosh of air.

Undecided about what to do with this unusual position I'd found myself in, I followed after. He glanced at me when I walked into his field of vision.

"It's kind of strange having someone else here. Especially a..." He trailed off, shaking his head. I took a nervous step towards him. "Don't mind me. Just the ramblings of a man who's been on his own for too long." He stared at me a moment. "I'm really glad you're okay. It would've been awful to maim you with my jeep."

I snorted.

"I said I'm sorry. Look, you're warm, clean, safe, and fed. What more do you want?" he asked, holding his arms out dramatically. I eyed the open cushion next to him, then steeled myself and jumped up. "Well, hello," he said, sounding surprised.

Thoroughly pleased with myself, I turned to face him. There was really only thing I wanted more than anything else, but was I brave enough to ask for it? Before I could second-guess myself, I took a shaky step towards him. The cushion sank beneath my paw and I stumbled forward slamming with all the grace of a new born giraffe into his chest. His arms wrapped around my back to steady me, careful of my side.

"You alright?"

In response, I let out a sigh and sank into the impromptu embrace. His hand faltered a moment then began rubbing my back. I tried to hum in appreciation, but it came out a soft whimper.

"Shh, everything is going to be okay. You're safe now."

The position wasn't the most comfortable, but I didn't care. This was all I wanted, someone to hold me and tell me everything was going to be okay, even though I knew it wouldn't be. Just for a little while, I wanted to believe the lie. I needed to believe, even if it was only for one night, that nothing was chasing me, that I hadn't almost died a million different ways, and that someday I would be able to hold someone the way Michael was holding me now.

While I lay in delusional bliss he talked about work, but I wasn't paying attention. I was finally at peace. I was safe.

7

RUMOR HAS IT

I yawned wide enough to crack my jaw and blinked open eyes crusted shut with sand. Warm sunlight poured through the glass doors lending the space a dreamlike quality. I looked around bleary eyed in search of my host before vaguely recalling hearing him getting ready for work.

Wonder if he left any food out.

My paws reached out before me as I stretched back. Incredibly, the pain in my side was completely gone. My bottom landed back on the cushion with an audible poof and I glanced around at the quiet, empty house. No obnoxious geese honking away, no monster chasing me until I collapsed. I sighed contentedly.

I could get used to this.

Partway through another indulgent yawn, my middle jerked. I stood and shook off the peculiar sensation. Mid shake, my body spasmed violently. My foot lost its purchase on the cushion and I tumbled to the floor where I landed with a thud. Pain blossomed in my hip to join the waves of agony washing over me, followed by a ripple that ran up my spine like someone forcing my fur the wrong way. My face crunched as if I'd run into a brick wall and something was horribly wrong with my tail. Sickening pops echoed in my ears and turned my stomach.

A memory of teeth scraping bone sparked. I pushed it away as I registered a different sharp pain in my side. The edge of the coffee table pressed mercilessly into the tender flesh, but my body refused to obey any commands to move. Hair fell all around my head and my toenails clenched in the center rug.

I lay panting in a pool of my own sweat as the pain finally began to ebb, every inch of my tortured body raw. Even the necessary act of breathing brought its own searing agony that threatened to send me back into convulsions. After a couple shakier breaths, I pushed myself back to all fours and tried to get my bearings. When I unclenched my eyes, I barked out a laugh at the sight of two hands complete with five normal fingers and nails to match.

"I can't believe it," I said in wonder as I proceeded to do a full pat-down inventory. "I'm all here and I'm all normal." Then another thought struck home. "And I'm all naked." I became obsessed with trying to remember if Michael had left. But in order to check, I needed to move.

Standing upright proved to be a challenge, but I managed. I stumbled around the couch, clinging to it for dear life to get a better look at the peninsula. His phone, keys, and wallet were gone or at least not readily visible. I glanced at the door and frowned. The distance seemed to stretch out before me.

I gritted my teeth, then began the arduous process of shuffling over, clinging to furniture, then walls in lieu of real balance. Cautiously, I peeked through the blinds. No jeep. The blinds snapped closed.

"He's gone. For now, at least." I leaned against the wall and let out a sigh of relief, then glanced around at the empty room. "What do I do now?"

With a human body came very real human problems. At the top of that growing list was the fact that I was standing naked in the middle of Michael Howell's living room.

First things first: clothes.

The house was familiar, though my perspective was off. Upon closer inspection the guest room and bath scarcely looked used. I dismissed them as not helpful and kept going until I reached Michael's room, my balance increasing with each step.

I quickly made my way to the bureau he'd been digging through the night before and did some digging of my own until I found a pair of sweatpants with a drawstring. I pulled it as tight as it would go and rolled up the legs so that I could walk. A worn t-shirt that smelled excessively like Michael completed the oversized ensemble. Decently clothed, I padded back to the kitchen where I promptly began raiding the fridge.

My stomach grumbled loudly. "I know, I know. I'm working on it." My gaze fell on a packaged ham steak. "Perfect."

I snatched it out of the fridge and tore into the plastic, eager to reach the contents. Watery juice spilled out of the ripped packaging to drip on the floor as I bit into the meat. Cold lanced through my teeth and I nearly spit out my bite.

Yeah, that's not gonna work.

I snagged the skillet Michael had used the night before. The meat barely had a chance to warm, before I flipped it to sear the other side. Confident that it was at least warm enough not to give me another toothache, I removed the thick piece of ham with my bare fingers not even bothering with a plate.

In less time than it took to get out the ham, it was gone. I shamelessly licked my fingers clean and looked down in search of the water bowl. It was still sitting on top of the towel filled to the brim with crystal clear water at the entrance to the kitchen. I took a step towards it then stopped.

"Way to go, dummy. You have hands again, use a glass." I rolled my eyes at myself and retrieved a glass from the cabinet. Meal devoured and thirst quenched, I cleaned the dishes and the rest of the mess I'd made. The dish towel flopped onto the counter and I placed my hands on my hips as I surveyed the room once more.

"Now what? I can't stay here. Speaking of which, where exactly is here?" I wandered over to a table that looked to be a sort of catch-all, covered in stacks of mail and other oddities. I held up a plastic bag with a scrap of filthy fabric in it. I promptly redeposited it on the table and picked up a stack of envelopes addressed to Michael Howell.

Surely just looking at the envelope isn't a felony.

To my amazement, behind the stack was an old phone. I quickly dropped the mail which scattered on the floor in favor of my new prize.

"I can't believe he has a landline!" My parents were the only people I knew who had one and that had more to do with the terrible reception where we lived than anything else.

Why does Michael have one? I quickly dismissed the trivial thought as a more pressing one took its place. *Does it work?*

I couldn't believe my luck as I followed the cord at the back of the phone to where it disappeared into the wall. Choking back a sob of joy, I quickly dialed one of the few numbers I knew by heart.

Beeps replaced the dial tone and then the most angelic voice I'd ever heard said, "Hello?"

"Charline—"

"Sara? Where have you been? I've been worried sick. Why haven't you been answering your phone? I've left like a million voicemails. You were supposed to call and tell me you made it home okay."

"I know. I'm sorry."

"Sorry my ass. Where have you been? Are you alright? You haven't been at your house. Ted and I have been scouring the city looking for you. I called hospitals, Sara!"

I pulled the phone away from my ear at the ungodly screech coming out of it.

"Look, I'm sorry I made you worry, Charline, but I need your help," I finally managed to get in. The last thing I needed was for Michael to come home to check on his new pet and find me instead.

The request effectively silenced her tide of worry. "What do you need?"

Now for the tricky part. "I need a ride."

"A ride?" she echoed. "Sure, doll. But where are you?"

"About that...how soon can you pick me up?" I asked, chewing on my bottom lip.

"I can leave now. I'll get Janice to cover for me."

"You're a life-saver, Charline."

"I know. But, Sara, *where* are you?" She repeated once more.

"Oh, I'm at..." I searched the mail fanned out on the floor. "One-eighty, Willow Way."

"What are you doing there?"

"I'll explain when you get here," I said and prayed she wouldn't press for details now.

"Okay, whatever you say. There, I've got the directions. Give me twenty minutes."

"Thanks again."

"It's nothing, but I better get a juicy explanation."

"Sure thing." The juicy part would be easy, it was the explanation that would be the problem.

The line went dead and I replaced it in the receiver.

Oh God, what am I going to tell her?

I took my time reorganizing the mail and making sure it was exactly the way I'd found it or as close to the same as I could manage. A final glance around Michael's house showed nothing out of place. With a resigned breath, I made my way out the back and looped around to the front to await my godsend of a friend.

It seemed my luck was finally on an upswing, because fifteen minutes later I was sitting in the front seat of Charline's crossover headed back to my house. I should have known it wouldn't last.

"Alright, spill. Where have you been and what have you been doing?" she asked with a twinkle in her eye. Considering the screech of concern from before, this note of mischief was unsettling.

"Well, um, that was Michael's house."

"I know."

"What? How?" Already my best explanations were ruined.

"I looked up the address, remember? So, what were *you* doing there?" Another sinister smile. I barely held back a groan of despair, because of course she didn't just look up directions, she'd checked the company database.

"Well, you see, um..." I faltered.

We stopped at a red light and she turned to me, all flippancy replaced with seriousness. "I know I give you a hard time about it, but I was really worried about you. If you're really interested in Michael that's okay, you can talk to me. Promise, mum's the word. Hell, even if it was a one-off, that's cool too. Just tell me it was all consensual."

"What? Of course it was!" I shouted, recalling the gentle way he'd cleaned the blood from my fur and how every move he'd made had been prefaced with a silent ask for permission. If he was that damn determined for assent with an animal, I couldn't even begin to fathom the levels he would go to for a human. Suddenly, I felt terrible for believing even half the rumors about him in the office. He clearly wasn't that person.

"Sara. Hello. You still there?" Charline asked, snapping me back to the present.

"Yeah, sorry."

"So, what happened?" she prodded.

I can do this.

"After the party, I drove back home," I started. She nodded along, none of this was news. "But I was so messed up that I couldn't open the door." She gave me a look out of the corner of her eye. "I'm serious," I responded defensively. "I was really out of it. I thought about going back to your place, but didn't trust myself to drive. Anyway, I sort of started to wander around, hoping that whatever it was would go away and I could get inside."

She made a face, but didn't interrupt.

"Look, it seemed like a good idea at the time. But I guess I was more disoriented than I thought, because I kind of got lost. Well, really lost. That's when Michael found me and insisted on taking care of me."

The story sounded even worse out loud and became feebler by the second as I realized how far we were from my house. I hadn't gone a couple of miles; I'd gone clear across town. At least parts of the tale had a little in common with the truth. The drive had been terrible. And I couldn't open the door at all, let alone try to steer a car with four paws instead of two hands. All in all, it wasn't that bad of a story, except I had no idea how I was going to get Michael to back it up.

"Really? He just stumbled across you and carted you off to his place?"

"Well, yeah."

She speared me with a look. "Why didn't he take you home?"

If she keeps punching holes in my story like this, there won't be a story left.

If I told her he'd technically hit me with his car, that was bound to lead to even worse questions. Also she worked in HR, so he'd probably get fired. There had to be a response that would satisfy her, but I couldn't think of one.

"I was in no shape to object, Charline," I countered weakly. "I already told you, I was pretty out of it."

"Uh-huh. I think you're lying—you're not very good at it. Something happened." Charline wiggled her eyebrows.

"Nothing happened!"

"If nothing happened, why did you ask me to come get you? Why not wait for him to get back?"

"Because I'm embarrassed." I slumped in my seat and stared out the window at a world once more passing me by.

"Well, that seems genuine enough. But what happened to your clothes?"

Crap.

"I must have forgotten them. He offered me these to sleep in."

"Sure he did. Well, I guess I'll find out the truth tomorrow at work."

"Work!" I slapped my head and instantly regretted it.

"Don't worry, when I didn't hear from you and you didn't show today, I covered for you. So, if anyone asks, you were really sick. Like really, really sick. And your phone broke."

"You're the best. What kind of sick? That way I know how to answer if people ask."

She spared me a quick look. "Best to fudge over the details. Tell them you don't really want to talk about it."

"Charline!"

"What! It had to be believable. Aside from that dog

attack, you never miss work." I sighed heavily and leaned back into the seat.

Eventually, we pulled up next to my faded green car.

Amazing how two nights of running full out only amounted to thirty minutes in driving time.

"Sorry I cost you your lunch," I said as I freed the seatbelt.

"No big. I'll sneak one in. But I should probably be getting back."

"Thanks again. I owe you," I added before I shut the car door.

She waved as she backed up. I watched her leave, grateful that she wouldn't see that I didn't have my keys. The gate creaked open and I padded through the shambles of pottery to the back door where my cocktail dress was a shredded, bloody mess. I hurriedly scraped up the ruined fabric and flicked the latch open, a much easier task now that I had opposable thumbs.

I groaned inwardly when I arrived at the office Wednesday and found Bob waiting to pounce.

"Sheppard, where have you been?" he demanded before I could even sit down.

"Sorry, Mr. Hargrave, I thought you would've been notified. I was out sick," I said in the mildest tone I could manage.

He scowled at me as if he didn't believe a word of it. "I heard HR's excuse, but any reasonable person would have called in. It's behavior like this that prevents you from moving up in the company, Sheppard. If you can't take yourself seriously, why should anyone else?"

My jaw fell. "Excuse me, sir?"

"You heard me, Sheppard. Now enough chit chat. Have you seen the Sanderson Report? I could have sworn I gave it to Kyle, but neither he nor Quinn have seen it."

I stood there staring at him in disbelief.

Who treats people like this?

"Well, Sheppard, have you, or haven't you?"

My jaw finally closed with an audible snap as I spun to pull out a drawer behind me. I pulled out the cherry red folder and practically threw it at him. "There's your Sanderson Report. It has triplicates of graphs and alternate strategies depending on how aggressively they want to pursue things. And don't worry, it's been proofed as well."

He stared down at the folder as if he couldn't understand what he was seeing or what I was saying. "You did the Sanderson Report?"

My indignant fury fizzled. "Yes."

His jowls wiggled as he glared at the glossy cover another moment then gave an aggravated huff. "It's too late to have one of the guys look it over, the presentation is this afternoon. I'll have to do it myself. Fetch me a coffee so I can get started." He turned on his heel to disappear back into his office, then stopped and turned back to me. "For your sake, Sheppard, this had better be good," he said, waving the folder for emphasis.

I swallowed, instantly anxious in the face of the blatant threat. He didn't wait for me to find my tongue, simply vanished behind his office door, the crash of blinds echoing in his wake. The breath I was holding burst forth and I clutched a hand to my racing heart. I'd only wanted to prove myself. I never thought I'd get fired over it.

At that moment, one of my coworkers popped their head up a couple cubicles down. "You're back, huh?" Kelly asked, making her way towards me. "Was starting to think you were done with this place." She blatantly eyed me from head to toe. Kelly was one of those women with perpetual resting bitch face, so it was difficult to tell if she was about to be exceptionally nasty or compliment my blouse.

I dropped my hand back to my side, refusing to be intimidated by a woman who believed that sleeping your way through the office was the only way to get ahead. "Yeah, I'm back."

"You're not contagious, are you?" She borderline sneered, once again looking me over. Whatever illness Charline had concocted must've been truly impressive.

"No, I'm not contagious," I answered without going into details. She continued to stand there staring at me and the awkward tinge in the air intensified. "Can I help you with something?" I asked when she didn't leave.

"You've got some nerve taking that Sanderson Report. Robert has been looking for that thing for days."

I refused to cower before her. "Well, it's done now, so he doesn't need to worry about it."

She raised a penciled brow, no doubt surprised at my uncharacteristic hostility. That made two of us. "At any rate, I'd get that coffee if I was you." She spared me one last condescending look, then turned and walked back to her own cubicle.

What is going on with me? I never confront Kelly.

With a shake of my head, I made my way to the coffee station. As much as I disliked Kelly, she was right about one thing, it wouldn't hurt to get the brute his coffee. I turned the corner and ran smack into the last person I wanted to see. Or more appropriately, he ran into me.

At least he didn't hit me with a car this time.

"H-hi, Michael," I stuttered.

"Hey, Sara, I've been wanting to talk with you," he said, his expression serious.

Blood rose to my face as my stomach sank to my feet.

Oh no, Charline told everyone the real story. No wonder Kelly was giving me a strange look. She thinks someone like me slept with Michael Freaking Howell.

"I never did get a hold of you last week," he added when I didn't say anything.

Okay, maybe Charline didn't tell anyone about finding me at his place. The reassuring thought was quickly forgotten as the rest of his words sunk in. *Crap, I totally forgot we were going to hit up that burger joint last Thursday. He probably thinks I stood him up.*

"Right. Not sure if you heard, but I was a bit under the weather." I sent up a silent prayer that he'd accept the lame excuse.

"I did. I'm glad to see you're doing better," he said, leaning against the wall and preventing me from going any further. A couple of co-workers walked past. He spared them a smile and a wave, then returned his full attention to me. "In all seriousness though, there is something I've been wanting to talk with you about. Think you could meet me in the parking garage after work?"

That's definitely not lunch.

I cast a nervous glance at another pair of coworkers eying us, not fully convinced that everyone hadn't heard some version of the lie I'd told Charline.

"Uh, sure, I guess. But why the parking deck?"

"Perfect. See you then," he said and promptly walked off without answering my question.

It wasn't until I was pouring the cream in Bob's coffee that it dawned on me what Michael might want to talk about.

8

WEREWOLVES ARE REAL

Five o'clock rolled around, but my palms had started sweating at four. It took me searching two different parking levels to find the right one. Michael's yellow jeep stood out in blaring contrast to the gray concrete surrounding us. He stood, leaning against the hood, arms crossed, scowling at the ground.

I wiped my hands on my slacks and approached. *How do I explain any of this? He's probably totally pissed that I've ruined his reputation by sullying his standards. What must people have said to him?*

I fought the increasing urge to run the other way as fast as I could. I'd find a new job somewhere else, hopefully somewhere that genuinely appreciated me. Starting over might not be so bad.

I wonder how far I'd get before he noticed.

My shoe scuffed the concrete and I winced at the betraying sound. Unsurprisingly, Michael looked up.

"Great, you made it!" His enthusiasm caught me off guard and it took me a moment to formulate a response.

"Of course I made it. So, what's this thing you've been trying to talk to me about?" I asked, playing coy while I mentally crossed my fingers. *Please don't be about how I was supposedly at your house.*

He glanced around then said, "Maybe we should talk about it somewhere more private."

Fuck. It's totally about that.

He pushed away from the hood. "We can go back to my place and I can make you dinner," he said, then opened the door of his jeep and started to get in without pausing for an answer.

"Wait a minute," I said, finally coming out of my stupor.

"What?" he asked innocently.

"I'm not following you home. I barely even know you."

His brow furrowed. It was a toss-up whether he was genuinely confused or just not used to hearing no. "Are you saying you don't trust me?"

"It's not about trust. I know we work together, but that doesn't mean I'm going to blindly follow you home. Until a week ago, I didn't even know you knew my name." So that was a little more honesty than I'd intended, but it didn't change the fact that he barely qualified as an office acquaintance.

His face fell at the onslaught. "What do your instincts tell you?"

"That I don't know you. I don't know anything about you. And you definitely don't know me," I said emphatically.

It was a little bit of a fib. He'd technically taken care of me—rather well in fact—and if he'd wanted to hurt me, he could have done it already. But that logic didn't do anything to shake my paranoia. Before, I'd been a stray dog. Now, I was a woman.

"And besides, why should we go to your house? There are plenty of other places we could go and talk." I gestured to the garage we were currently standing in.

"You're right, we haven't known each other long, but I bet

we have a lot more in common than you think. As for the house..." He paused looking anxious and glanced around the nearly empty deck. "What I want to say, I'd rather no one else overheard."

I was instantly doused in cold and at the same time my palms started sweating again in earnest.

Shit. It really is about the lie I told Charline.

Officially feeling guilty as hell, I caved. "Okay, you win. We'll go to your place."

His face visibly relaxed and my stomach rolled. "Great. I'll see you there," he said and resumed getting back in his jeep.

"Wait," I called out once again. "I don't know where you live."

Confusion flashed briefly across his face. Then he got out and walked towards me. I stiffened, not sure what to expect, and stood frozen as he took out a pen and scrawled on my hand. "There, that's the address, but I bet you could find it in the dark."

I blinked and frowned at him. He simply winked and walked back over to his jeep.

What the hell was that supposed to mean? Not everyone stalks you, you know.

"Michael, wait." He ignored the outburst. This was starting to feel like a bad idea. There was no way I could get to his house without looking like I already knew where I was going. "How about I follow you?" I suggested.

Again, no response.

"Seriously, wait a damn minute!"

He got into the Jeep despite my protests. My loud aggravated cry echoed back at me. His engine revved to life and the headlights flashed against the concrete wall. For a split second, I was back in the middle of the road, heart pounding, feet sliding on slick asphalt, about to get creamed by oncoming traffic. I blinked the vision away right as his tires started to roll back.

I scrambled back to my car as fast as I could, determined to at least appear to be following him.

Why the hell did I agree to this?

I screeched out of the space and hit the accelerator to catch up. Unfortunately, I lost him by the fifth light, but even with one wrong turn, I managed to pull up right after him.

I slammed the car door and stalked over to where he was propped casually against the blood red door. He looked back at me, the picture of innocence.

"You didn't exactly make it easy to follow," I huffed.

He simply snorted and unlocked the door. Inside, he tossed the keys on the peninsula and plopped down the same way he had the other night. For a moment, I feared he was going to pat the seat, but he leaned back instead.

I closed the door and chose the love seat adjacent to him. "Now what's this all about?" Some human-decorum part of my mind sent up all the red flags that I was entirely too comfortable in what was supposed to be a strange house.

"See, I told you you'd find the place no problem," he said with a smile.

I rolled my eyes and let out another huff.

Might as well get a handle on this now.

"About what people said at the office," I started, not wanting to assume what he'd heard.

He shrugged and leaned forward to rest his elbows on his knees. "They were all lies," he said matter of fact.

"Um, yeah."

Okay, so maybe this isn't what I thought it was.

"You weren't sick," he said with a straight face.

Like that, I was lost again.

I shouldn't have come here. Why did I come here?

"What did you want to talk to me about?" I asked, more nervous than ever about the answer.

Abruptly he stood up. "Do you want a drink? I could use a drink."

"No thanks."

"Suit yourself," he said, pouring himself a glass of amber liquid straight from a decorative bottle. The smell of whiskey filled the air and burned my nose. He downed the glass in one go and seriously seemed to be contemplating another. Both the glass and bottle scraped across the granite counter as he pushed them away.

"Okay, here goes nothing," he said, turning back to me. "Where were you Friday, Saturday, and Sunday night?"

I scoffed at the unexpected question in light of his demeanor. "What, you don't want to know where I was Monday night as well?" If this was supposed to be some roundabout way of calling me out for starting rumors, I didn't appreciate it.

"I know where you were Monday night."

The makings of a blush started to burn my cheeks. I pushed past it and fired back, "How could you possibly know that?"

"You were here," he said matter of fact without an ounce of accusation or insinuation.

I blanched.

Maybe he's mad about what Charline said. No doubt the tale has acquired some colorful details. Maybe this is all an elaborate ruse to get back at me for starting rumors.

"Look, Charline gets...interesting ideas sometimes. She clearly took the lunch too far," I tried to explain as my face heated more with each word.

"This has nothing to do with Charline or the rumor mill, which hasn't been turning nearly as much as I would have expected."

"Then what's this about?" I clutched the arms of the chair like it could somehow protect me from whatever was coming next. The fabric scraped against my fingers, which were turning raw with the pressure.

"Sara, you were here—not like that—but you were here." He gestured to my general human shape. "I know that you're a werewolf."

As my beloved friend would say, my cheese slid right off the cracker. All of the things I'd been too scared to think, rushed up to smack me in the face—hard.

Oh god, I think I'm going to faint.

I blinked and Michael was handing me a glass of water and urging me to sip slowly

"I wanted to talk to you about it last week. I was going to do it when we met for Thursday's lunch." He resumed his seat. "You shouldn't have had to go through your first change alone."

"Change? Werewolf? Michael, you don't honestly believe any of that?" I asked, struggling to grab hold of something concrete.

"It's not a question of belief."

"Why would you..."

He cut me off. "Because I'm one. I'm a werewolf, Sara."

My jaw dropped and I fought off another dizzy spell. No preamble, no cushion, just BAM.

"How..." I swallowed. "How did you know it was me? Assuming what you say is true." I needn't have bothered with the addition; we'd passed the realm of believability a few roads back.

He tapped his nose. "Just because you weren't human, doesn't mean you didn't smell the same."

I shook my head trying to dispel the confusion taking up residence. "Michael, this is ridiculous. You can't sit there and casually proclaim that you're a werewolf. Oh, and by the way, so am I. How am I supposed to believe any of this?"

"It's not about believing. Like it or not, this is your new reality. You were bitten and assuming you survived, you were changing that first full moon. I'm sorry I wasn't there for you."

This is a real conversation. I'm sitting in Michael Howell's living room talking about not just werewolves, but that he's one too.

"Sorry, I don't mean to be dense. This is a little out there," I said, waving my hand.

He nodded his head.

"So, you're telling me that werewolves are real, and I'm one... And so are you." I hesitated. "Did you bite me?"

"No! Stars, how could you think that?" He at least seemed genuinely affronted. "I've been trying to catch the *were* that attacked you."

"Oh."

"But I've been looking for *you* since the full moon," he added.

"Then it was you howling that night? What a load off." I looked up, a sigh of relief on my lips, but Michael's deadly serious expression made it catch. "That was you—wasn't it?"

"Sara, I'm sorry. It wasn't me. That's why I didn't find you that night. I figured you'd be safer if I went after him instead. I'm so sorry, I should have tried harder to tell you everything in the first place."

Black spots swam across my vision. The living room tilted sideways. I slumped in the chair and watched Michael float out of sight.

"Sara... Sara... Look at me..."

My eyelids fluttered erratically.

"Everything is okay. You're going to be fine. You're safe here. Sara, you're safe."

Safe?

The word floated out of reach.

Safe.

"Are you alright?"

My gaze finally focused on Michael.

Safe.

As my senses returned, I managed a nod and let Michael help me sit up.

"Take some deep breaths and try to relax." He passed me my water, then sat beside me. "I shouldn't have sprung that on you like that. I was surprised that you'd already thought about it and I didn't think..."

I held up a shaky hand to cut off his string of apologies. Mercifully, he took the hint. "Can I...can I have a minute? Please," I added when he remained rooted, a mix of doubt and concern playing on his face.

He stood slowly, hesitation written in every line of his body. "Sure. I'll, uh..." He glanced around the living room in search of an occupation and clearly unwilling to leave the room.

"Just a minute," I reiterated, suffusing the plea with all the assurance I could.

"Okay, yeah. I'll fix a drink and step out back."

"Thank you." I sat as still as I had by the lake as I waited for him to pour a fresh glass.

The clear glass door slid open and he stepped into the crisp evening. It whisked along its track behind him. No sooner did it snick shut, than I was out of my seat and making a beeline out the front door. Too late, I realized my keys were sitting on the side table. I quickly veered away from the parked cars and sprinted for all I was worth down the sidewalk.

The winter air burned in my lungs and the sound of my ballet flats hitting pavement rang down the street. My breath echoed loud and ragged in my ears. Distantly, I made out a curse and the unmistakable sound of a door hitting a wall. Panic blurred my sight and I willed my legs to move faster.

Pain twisted up my knee and my next step faltered. My arm shot out to break my fall as I tried desperately to keep my footing. I hissed against the burn of my palm being scraped raw. A heat that defied the season spread across my body. I managed two more lurching steps, then crumpled to the ground.

"Sara!" Michael skidded to a stop beside me, his eyes wide with the same panic strangling me. He squatted down beside my shaking form and I flinched away. "Shit." He reached for my arm and I yanked it away, nearly toppling over for my trouble. "Damn it, Sara, I won't hurt you."

"Go away. You're delusional." I lashed out with my injured hand and he caught my wrist. I struggled against the tight hold as he proceeded to crowd me.

"Do you believe me now?" He held up the captive appendage between us. To my horror, where there had once been nails, claws sprouted from my warped fingers. I opened my mouth to scream and he clamped a hand over it. "You have to calm down or you're going to force a change. Now, I want you to take a deep breath and calm down. I'm going to carry you back to the house."

Tears pooled as I stared back at him.

He let out a sigh and his face softened. "I promise, I'm not going to hurt you. Please, let me help." The quiet plea struck a chord and I nodded, setting loose tears to streak down my cheeks. "If I remove my hand, are you going to yell?" I shook my head, but he waited a moment before letting go.

"Why can't I walk?" I asked through the surprising rawness in my throat.

He glanced down at my legs twisted beneath me. "You should be able to, but if you try to run again, I can guarantee you won't get far."

I swallowed down a wave of anxiety and let him help me up. My legs ached and I seemed to have lost a shoe at some point. We gathered it as he led me back to the house with a firm hand on the small of my back. With each step, embarrassment took the place of my earlier panic until I was seated back on the couch in a mortified puddle.

"I'm sorry," I croaked.

"You have nothing to be sorry for." His compassion only humbled me further. A few minutes passed in silence.

"What time is it?" I finally asked.

"Um... it's about seven-thirty."

"You still good for that dinner?" He gave me a look. "I'll take that as a yes. Would you pass me my cell please? It's in the side pocket of my purse."

He snagged the bag and produced the requested item.

"Thanks. Oh, good grief," I said as the notifications listed in rapid succession. After my ill-conceived flight, this was the last thing I needed.

"What?"

"Nothing. Charline."

He smiled broadly. Charline was explanation enough. There were also two more voicemails undoubtedly from my parents, but he definitely didn't need to know about those.

"What did she say?" he asked.

"She sent me a text basically saying that she saw me with you this afternoon. No doubt that will fuel her idea that we're together," I bemoaned.

"What's wrong with that?"

I rolled my eyes. "Because, nothing is going on. I mean aside from the whole," I gestured back toward the door.

He mumbled something as he got up.

"What did you say?"

"Nothing. So how do you want your steak? On the fly?" His eyes sparkled and all of the pieces clicked together.

"Oh my God!" My face ignited in an altogether different kind of heat than the one that had dominated me outside while Michael's deep laugh rumbled only a few feet away. "You! You knew, and you let me do all of that anyway!"

"I didn't see any harm in letting you relax a little." He pulled out the same pan as before and it was official—I'd never been more mortified in my entire life. Michael continued to cook dinner, completely oblivious while I relocated to sit at the peninsula.

He set the plates on the bar and joined me in the adjoining stool. Thankfully, the steak was whole. I wasn't sure how much mortification I could take in one evening. We didn't say anything and quite frankly I wasn't sure if I was even capable of speech. Instead, I focused on the meal he'd prepared. The steak was even better now that I wasn't starving and the vegetables were a great compliment, though my embarrassment lent a certain tinge of awkwardness.

"Come on, Sara, you must be near to bursting with questions. You're a *were* now, there's no shyness in it."

I glowered at my empty plate.

"Ask away," he insisted as he gathered our dishes and ushered me back to the couch.

I took a deep breath and snagged a question out of the whirling millions. "Were you bitten too?"

He sat there a moment as if shocked by the question. Finally, he said, "Um, no. I was definitely born this way."

I glared at him, suspicious of the hesitation.

"Seriously, my first change happened with puberty and I was prepared for it, or as prepared as you can be." He leaned back and crossed his legs, resting his ankle on his knee. He made it all sound so perfectly natural, but none of what I'd experienced had felt natural in the least.

My mouth opened and closed soundlessly as I tried to wrap my head around it all. "So, you mean to tell me... I mean, so is your whole family...?" The question hung unfinished.

Michael glanced down at the fresh glass of whiskey in his hand and didn't answer for a second. He took a small sip and a deep breath before looking back at me.

"What?" I asked, warmth creeping across my cheeks. "Is that a rude question or something?"

"No. I told you—anything you want to know. Yes, most *were* communities consist of other werewolves. There are a few exceptions, but it's really no different from any other large family. Well, except for the part about changing into wolves every now and again," he finished with a playful grin.

"Does it hurt you too? You know, when you change?"

"Yes. I wish I could tell you it gets better, but that would be a lie."

My face fell.

"You do get used to it. Find ways to help the change instead of fight against it. But nothing stops it from feeling like every bone is being broken and reset. And before you ask, I don't have to change every full moon, but it's pretty hard not to." He took another sip while I took a second to process.

"Why? Will I only change during the full moon?" I added hopefully, despite what had happened not an hour before.

His smile turned sad. "No, Sara. Technically *weres*—including you—can change whenever they want. It's hard not to change during the moon, because we have such a strong connection, though the full moon is generally the only one strong enough to force a change. There are a few exceptions, but I don't think those are really relevant for you right now."

I was tempted to ask what these "exceptions" were, but he was still talking.

"Think of it like the pull of the tide. If you stay out of the light, you have a better chance of staving it off, but it takes serious will power if you're already outside. Not to mention if you're not outside, you'll instinctively seek it out—thus, the willpower," he clarified.

"Well, that's just great," I huffed. "Then how do I control it?"

"That part's a bit tricky. As far as I know, you should have changed back that first morning."

"What do you mean 'as far as you know'?"

He rubbed the back of his neck with his free hand and barely met my gaze. "Honestly, all of the *weres* I know were born that way. It's possible the reason you didn't change back once the moon passed is because you were bitten, but that's speculation on my part."

"How am I supposed to live if I have no control?"

"Don't worry, Sara, we'll figure it out. You're not alone." He wrapped an arm around my shoulders and pulled me closer in a half hug.

I sighed heavily into his shirt and took a deep breath. His musky scent flooded my senses and I became hyper aware of him slowly rubbing my arm. It held the same level of comfort it had when he rubbed my back the other night —*when I was a wolf.*

My head flew up, narrowly missing his chin. I quickly asked the first question that came to mind in an attempt to evade the awkwardness. "What do I smell like?" Heat bloomed across my face as he burst into laughter.

When he was finally able to catch his breath, he looked at me warmly. "Sara, you smell wonderful."

I didn't know whether to continue to be embarrassed or flattered.

It must have shown because he smiled and added, "You smell like a field of wildflowers in spring."

"Oh," I said, playing with the hem of my blouse.

"Don't be frightened of your new senses, get used to them," he encouraged. "Tomorrow at work, don't be so focused on appearing normal. Trust me, no one can tell what you are." I nodded absently. I hadn't even thought that far. "I mean it, Sara, when we go to lunch, I want you to tell me what at least three people smell like."

I opened my mouth to protest, but never got a syllable out.

He glanced out the back door at the darkening night beyond and gave a low whistle. "Wow, it's gotten late. It would probably be safer if you stayed here. You can have my room. I'm sure I have something that can be adjusted for you." He gave me an appraising once over and promptly stood.

"Excuse me?" I scrambled to my feet, but that too went unremarked. "Michael."

"What?" He turned back from the hall.

"I'm not staying the night."

"Of course you are," he said and continued toward the bedroom.

"Wait a minute," I stubbornly held out. "You can't boss me around like this. I'm a grown woman and perfectly capable of taking myself home." My scowl did nothing to deter him.

He gave me a stern look that sent tingles down my spine. "Sara, I'm not going to let you drive all the way back to your house this late at night. That maniac is out there and I won't put you in danger. I insist you stay here."

"No," I tried again. His face darkened at my blunt refusal

to comply. "You say you didn't bite me, but how do I know this isn't some sort of elaborate set up?" I asked, waving my arms to encompass most of the living room.

"What? That has to be the most ridiculous thing I've ever heard. Why would I—" The words clipped off. His eyes flared while his shoulders squared as if preparing to do battle.

My hackles rose in response.

"If I'd wanted to do something to you, there are easier ways to go about it." He wasn't wrong. "As if I would bite you," he mumbled under his breath, not quite low enough not to be heard. He took what appeared to be a deep breath and seemed to regather himself, then asked, "What do your instincts tell you?"

He had me there. I'd already followed him home, eaten dinner with him, and was entertaining the fairytale he'd spun. None of that changed the fact that if it'd been anyone else—if I hadn't literally been a wolf in his living room yesterday—then I would've already dialed 911 or at the very least tried to sneak out the back...again.

"What about work tomorrow? And besides, I can't take your bed."

"If you want, you can wake up early and drive home to change; being out at night isn't a smart thing for you right now. And yes, you can. It's the least I can do after hitting you with my car." Clearly finding his argument won, he turned and walked back to his room.

"But there's a guest room," I said to no one in particular.

I seriously contemplated making another break for it, but found myself still standing there when he returned. He wore his pants from the other night and was holding a t-shirt, but not wearing one himself. I was so determined not to stare at his broad, sculpted chest with its layer of fine hair, I basically did it anyway.

Damn it.

"I found this for you, but I couldn't seem to find mine," he stated with a curious look. I busied myself putting my cell away, thankful he hadn't noticed my blatant gawping. "And I couldn't find my sweats that looked like they'd fit you," he added, sounding more than a little perplexed.

"Oh! I brought back the pants I borrowed to get home."

"You *did* change here. I wondered about that," he mused aloud, rubbing the pronounced shadow on his square jaw.

"Where else would I have changed?"

His brow furrowed and I held up my hands and wiggled my thumbs for emphasis. As the implication sank in, his eyes widened with understanding, then rolled at the obviousness of it.

"I confess," he said, glancing at the coffee table, "I was really worried when I came back during lunch and you were gone. I smelled blood and thought something might have happened."

I vaguely recalled knocking the table.

"So, where are they?" Michael asked, bringing me out of the memory.

"Where are what?"

"The sweats," he prompted.

"Right. They're in the car. I'll go..." I managed all of two steps towards the door before Michael beat me to it. I was taken aback both by his proximity and his determination.

He held out his hand. "I'll get them."

"Don't you think this is a bit ridiculous? Honestly, it's bad enough that you're basically holding me hostage and now you won't even allow me to walk the thirty feet to my own car?" He raised an eyebrow and I bit down on my tongue.

"The fact that you're even asking that, proves that you should stay here tonight. You have no idea the danger you're in. This isn't something you can bark at and expect them to back down. The less time you spend exposed, the safer you'll be. I may not be able to do anything about what has already happened, but I can damn well make sure nothing else does," he said fiercely enough to make me take a step back.

"But you don't know any of that. You can't know I'm in as much danger as you say. And who gave you the right to be in charge?" I asked, my blood boiling with indignation and barely suppressed terror.

He ignored the query and grabbed the keys from my flailing hands. The door barely had time to close before he returned. "Here you go." He passed me the folded sweats and began rearranging the couch.

I glared at his back. He either didn't realize it or didn't care, because he continued to remove pillows and the back cushions from the couch. Rolling my eyes, I snatched the shirt from the table and went to change.

It would serve that bully right to have to sleep on the couch after this nonsense. Never in all my years has anyone manhandled me so much.

My angry thoughts were excellent company as I stripped down and put on the shirt. It was too hot for the sweats even after all of that, so I didn't bother with them.

I'll put them on in the morning.

"Everything okay in here?"

Startled, I pulled the shirt down as far as it would go. "Jesus, Michael!"

He shrugged. "I've seen plenty of naked women before. Besides, I think it's only fair."

My face burned, the comment adding insult to injury. Once I regained my wits, I stalked over and slammed the door shut.

Who does he think he is?

I switched off the lights then burrowed under the covers.

I hope he gets a crick in his neck from sleeping on the couch.

The malicious wish comforted me while I fought with the bedsheets. When I finally stopped moving, though, I realized the woody musk smell that was Michael's scent surrounded me.

Well shit. How the hell am I supposed to sleep like this?

A short, quiet knock broke the silence as the door swung open without waiting for a reply.

"What?" I asked harshly.

Michael stood in the doorway, barely more than a silhouette. I couldn't tell if it was a trick of the light or pure imagination, but his eyes seemed to glint yellow in the darkness. "I wanted to check if you needed anything."

"I'm fine, thank you." I started to regret wishing him ill in the face of his persistent kindness.

"Okay. Goodnight, Sara." The door closed silently and once again, I was alone.

9

———

TEST OF THE SENSES

Dawn found me groggy and miserable. Thanks to being wrapped in Michael's smell, when I wasn't dreaming of home, I was fending off hormone-fueled fancies. This wasn't some office romance; this was the waking nightmare that was now my life.

Michael did everything short of turning into a literal ray of sunshine to shake me out of my funk, including encouraging me to ask more questions. But I didn't have any and by five-thirty I was sliding into the driver's seat beneath his watchful eye. Truthfully, I'd half-expected him to insist on either driving me home or following me there. To my surprise, he did neither.

It's still possible I'm drugged beyond reason in the hospital, strapped to the bed, in the throes of a psychotic break.

I glanced up at Michael from behind the steering wheel. He gave a small wave and I turned my attention back to the road. Meandering to my place in a daze meant I had next to no time to get ready for work, but that didn't stop me from standing listless in the living room. Even after a year, the space didn't feel like home.

Sadness washed over me as I thought about calling my

parents. What would I even say, especially after last night's revelation? Convincing them I was fine was hard enough, but this...this was something else. Instead, I changed, pulled my hair back in a ponytail, and left for the office.

I parked the car in my usual spot, but it wasn't until I got out that I realized Michael's scent covered me from head to toe. Even the fresh clothes did next to nothing to diminish the cloud that seemed to encompass me. I pulled up a few strands of hair and sniffed them.

"I knew I should have taken a shower."

Someone walking past cast me a wary glance and scurried faster. I quickly dropped the offending strands that seemed to be saturated in Michael's scent.

"Great," I mumbled to myself and made my way to the elevators.

To my infinite surprise, Charline's boyfriend Ted held the door. "Hey," I said, then stalled out. I'd never really talked with Ted one-on-one; Charline had always been there as a buffer.

He pushed his glasses up his nose and slid his hands into his pockets. "You look like you're doing better."

"Did you come with Charline to the hospital?" I asked, confused as to how he could know I was looking better.

"She said you got sick," he stated blandly. Then again, everything about Ted was bland from his khakis and white button down to his brownish hair and eyes.

I so don't get what she sees in him.

It occurred to me that this was a perfect opportunity to test my new senses. There was one huge problem: all I could smell was Michael. It was like he'd seeped into every pore. I groaned to myself and slumped against the metal wall.

"You good?" Ted asked without any inflection of actual concern.

"Yeah, not looking forward to today," I responded

honestly. Before he could ask what was so miserable about today, I asked a question of my own. "So, how are you and Charline doing?"

His shoulders stiffened and his gaze slithered away from mine to stare at the closed doors. He shrugged, but the shift in body language spoke volumes. The elevator stopped and the doors opened onto our floor.

"Just don't hurt her, okay?" I said as he took a step out.

He turned and stared at me a long second, then walked away without a word.

That wasn't awkward or anything.

I quickly exited the elevator and made a beeline for the bathrooms to do whatever I could to eliminate some of the scent clinging to me. There was no way I'd be able to get anything done, let alone do the homework he'd assigned me, if I was walking around smelling like him. I scrubbed at my face and arms with enough soap to drown a mouse, then all but stuck my head under the faucet to give my hair similar treatment. I offered a tight smile to a woman who had the misfortune to witness my impromptu bathing. She took one look at the soaked paper towels I was using to wring the wet out and turned right back around.

I quickly finished up, re-tied my hair, then meandered my way to my own department. Despite what Michael had said, I couldn't help but feel like everyone knew, that they could see past the facade of normalcy to the new reality that had taken over my life. The people at the coffee bar gave me a wide berth. Kelly took one look at me and disappeared down a different hallway. Even in the confines of my cubicle, I could feel eyes on me.

The part of my brain refusing to accept any of this was convinced it was pure imagination, but I couldn't shake the sensation. No sooner had I signed into my computer, than Bob appeared from his office. He seemed to hesitate before plopping yet another excessive tower of papers and saying something about a report.

I marveled as the teetering stack lost a few pages to gravity, not really absorbing any of what he told me. He stood there as if he expected a response. When I offered none, he turned and left. It wasn't until the sound of his retreating steps disappeared that it occurred to me that I'd missed a prime opportunity to fulfill my homework assignment.

When did my life get so weird?

I buried my head in my hands and my wet hair slipped free of its band. The stubborn mess seemed even more rebellious, if that was possible. My nose twitched as a rich, buttery scent with hints of cinnamon and vanilla tickled the fine hairs.

Fresh cookies. Just what the doctor ordered.

"Hey, Charline," I said from behind my personal waterfall of misery.

"Oh! How did you know it was me?"

"That's easy, I could..." *Smell you.* "Hear you," I amended aloud.

Oh my god, I smelled Charline. How did I know it was her?

"Jeez, I didn't realize I made so much noise. Anyway, I was wondering if we were still on for lunch." She sat on my desk and waited expectantly, no doubt already anticipating what I was about to say.

"I already agreed to have lunch with Michael."

"Did you now?" There was something in that. I glanced up from wrangling my damp hair to find her smiling triumphantly.

"Charline," I groaned.

"Oh no. No, you go have your lunch and we'll talk all about it later." Ominous promise delivered, she traipsed out of my cubicle with a tangible air of smugness about her.

Great. Isn't it bad enough that I have to cope with being a mythical creature, but Charline too?

That train of thought brought me back to how I'd known the scent belonged to Charline in the first place. Without even trying, I'd correctly identified it was her. But how? What did she smell like? I sampled the air that she'd recently vacated. Beneath the assaulting cloud of sharp perfume was a distinct flavor of honey and chamomile and something else—a hint of cinnamon along with an undercurrent of baking that had led me to believe initially that someone had brought cookies.

This might not be as difficult as I thought.

A few hours later, I found myself sitting across the table from Michael in a secluded corner of yet another deli.

"You can stop staring at me like that. I did my homework."

"And? Was it as hard as you thought it would be?" he asked with a level of conceit that rivaled Charline.

I glared at him and gave a begrudging, "No."

He arched an eyebrow.

"You don't have to be so obnoxious about it."

He shook his head and laughed quietly to himself. "Sorry. It's just funny how hard you're fighting everything. Sooner than you think, this will all become second nature."

"That's easy for you to say, you were born with this. I'm still trying to figure out if I'm in a coma." The comment earned me a few curious looks. I sank deeper into my plastic chair and plucked at the wrapper that had held a BLT with more bacon than any sandwich had a right to.

"Fair point," he said, leaning forward and sliding the basket out of my reach. "Now who did you—?"

I quickly straightened back up. "Please, for the sake of what's left of my tenuous hold on reality, don't finish that sentence." He cleared his throat and I rolled my eyes at the not-so-subtle encouragement. "Of course, the easiest person to start with was Charline. I tried to start with Ted in the elevator, but couldn't smell a damn thing over—" I stopped mid-rant as I realized how that sentence would end. "Anyway, yeah, I started with Charline."

I paused, not really sure how to go on. At yet another encouraging gesture from him, I threw caution to the wind.

"She smells like cookies. There was honey and chamomile and maybe cinnamon. But definitely baking."

Michael's low laugh vibrated through the table. "Really?"

"Yes. Why? What does she smell like to you?"

"Charline smells like a massive assortment of spices to me. I'll have to keep a whiff out for honey though."

"She doesn't smell the same to you? If everyone smells different to everyone else, how are you supposed to know if I'm doing it right?"

"Slow down." He placed a warm hand over mine. "There are variances depending on how well you know someone, but the basis is always there and identifiable by anyone. You can't really do it wrong." He squeezed my hand and then released it. "Now who else?"

Michael and I had lunch together every other day during which he'd quiz me mercilessly about all things *were*. If he'd had it his way, it would have been every day, but there was only so much I could take. Thankfully, today was an off day which meant I got to have lunch with Charline instead.

As I joined her at the elevator, my stomach gave a loud

grumble. I was already ravenous despite the numerous snacks I'd taken to eating throughout the morning. She eyed me skeptically and it reminded me of the way Ted had looked at me the other day.

"Question for you," I started.

"Shoot," she said, pressing the button impatiently.

"How are you and Ted doing?"

Her brow furrowed and her happy demeanor dipped. "Okay, I guess." The response was almost the verbal equivalent to Ted's.

"You know you can talk to me. Granted, I'm not any kind of relationship expert, but I can listen." I might not be Ted's biggest fan, but that didn't mean I couldn't be a supportive friend. She gave me a warm smile, which I returned.

"So where will it be, doll?" she asked as the doors slid shut, completely evading my offer.

"There's a deli across the street that I think might even impress you," I said, and let it drop. If she wanted to talk to me about it, then she would.

She laughed. Impressing Charline with food was no easy task. "I'm glad you could pencil me in," she teased as the doors slid open on the ground floor.

I scoffed and led the way across the street. "You make it sound like you never see me."

"It certainly feels that way lately," she replied.

She placed her order for a salad while I debated getting two sandwiches instead of one, then we grabbed a table.

"Well, the service at least is impressive. But I thought you didn't like roast beef," she commented as I took a massive bite.

I shrugged. "Michael introduced me to it."

"Uh huh. You sure do seem to be spending a lot of time with him," she sing-songed, waving her fork like some kind of magic wand.

"I already told you, we're friends, that's it. Nothing more." I couldn't very well tell her the real reason we were spending so much time together. "People like Michael Howell are not interested in people like me."

She scoffed. She'd never be convinced of anything short of scandalous.

"I don't see why you have to be so down on yourself all of the time. You're very pretty, Sara."

I snorted.

She ignored my rude sound and went on. "Besides, nobody spends that much time with someone they only want to be friends with."

I rolled my eyes and skipped trying to convince her this wasn't some contrived romance or that Michael would never think of me that way.

10

PRACTICE MAKES PERFECT

After three weeks, I could identify anyone by smell and worked on waiting to address people until they entered the realm of normal human perception. Of course, I got the most practice with Charline as she routinely popped in to chat towards the end of each day.

Right on time, Charline sauntered into my sad little work space, preceded of course by smells that belonged more to a bakery than a person. I saved my current file and spun around to face her as she leaned against the wall.

"So, I talked Ted into taking me to that fancy new Italian place on Donahue, but now I can't figure out what to wear. What do you think?" she asked as she filed her nails.

"I think it's a miracle you get anything done when you're always over here," I poked.

"No, not about that, Sara. The dress?" she asked, her voice laced with exasperation.

"What about the red one with the slit skirt?"

"No. I think I'll wear that new green one," she mused to herself.

I shook my head.

I don't know why she even bothers asking.

At that moment, Michael popped his head in, his large frame effectively filling the doorway. I was a little surprised that I hadn't smelled him first, but then again, Charline's scent was a little all-encompassing.

"I think green would look great, Charline," he said, flashing her an award-winning smile.

"Why thank you, Michael, you're sweeter than a peach," she preened.

"You're welcome. Sara, are you busy tonight?" he asked, turning back to me.

Before I could answer, Charline's pointed toe found its way to the back of my calf. The gleam in Michael's eye made it obvious that he hadn't missed her well-meant encouragement. "No. Why?" I gritted through clenched teeth.

"I was hoping we could go out to dinner tonight."

"Oh, sure," I said without having to think about it.

Guess we're upping our smelling game from small places to big ones.

"Great, there's a new Italian place that I heard was really good. I'll pick you up at seven." With that, he sauntered off.

"Ah-ha!" she exclaimed triumphantly the second he vacated the immediate vicinity, waving her nail file in my face like she was brandishing a sword. "Sure, there's absolutely *nothing* going on between you two." The emphasis was a bit much, but there was no stopping her. "Sara's got a date," she crooned. "Ooh, maybe we could do a double! Wait, no, never mind. I think Ted and I are due for a more serious talk." Her happy expression melted into a frown that put a crease between her eyebrows.

"It's not a date," I snapped. Werewolf hearing aside, the last thing I wanted was to let her go on like this where the whole office could hear. I should have waited.

Michael rematerialized in the entry, scaring me half to death. "Of course it's a date, and I fully expect you to get all fancied up." And like that, he was gone again with as much warning as he'd arrived.

The look on Charline's face surpassed description. "I guess we should start worrying more about what you're going to wear," she said wiggling her eyebrows.

Someone, please shoot me now.

<hr>

Being picked up at seven was not exactly conducive to looking 'all fancied up' as Michael expected. Nonetheless, I raced home and took the fastest shower in recorded history. Consequently, I was done early and had a full half-hour in which to fret.

I ventured to the glass doors for want of a distraction. They offered a spectacular view of the sunset. A nearly transparent moon punctuated the shades of red and orange.

Why am I so worked up? It's not like I haven't been spending time with Michael almost every day.

I shifted my focus to the thin streams of clouds left in the wake of planes.

It's not that I don't enjoy his company. I do. It's just...

I glanced down at my bare feet. The toenails were unpainted and clipped short. The heels I'd daringly chosen sat beside the door waiting to be put on at the last minute. I dragged my gaze back up to the sky.

Why did he have to call it a date?

I groaned and rested my forehead on the glass. The winter air outside made it cool to the touch and it was actually helping to ease my anxiety, if only slightly.

Maybe it's not really a date-date and he's teasing me because of Charline. Curse that woman and her scheming.

I picked my head up and tried harder to lose myself in the nuances that I'd never noticed before, like the way the trees seemed to reach into the breeze or how the grass waved delicately. A lot of things had unexpectedly changed along with the obvious. The neighbors' fighting was louder than ever, the neighborhood cats avoided me like the plague, and even though the sun had been down for a while, I could see crystal clear.

I checked the sliding door again to make sure it was locked, then sighed heavily, letting my breath fog the glass. The white mist cleared and I saw two glowing orbs across the yard. A knock came from the front door and I jumped as every hair on my body stood on end. I raced across the house and yanked open the front door.

"Sara? Wh—"

"Something's out back."

Michael set his jaw and gave me a curt nod as he flowed past me, then out the back door. Some of my sense returned and I shut the door, bolting it for good measure. I stared at the knob as if any second it would start to twist. The back door clicking shut snapped me out of my trance.

"He's gone, but he was definitely there. Pack an overnight bag, you're staying with me tonight."

I quickly moved to comply, my overwhelming fear blinding me to the bossy nature of the command. He followed me to my messy bedroom where I dragged a duffle bag out from under the bed and started throwing things into it, not really registering what I was grabbing.

"Sara," a voice said right behind me.

"Jesus, Michael!" I punched his arm and glared at him.

"Ow, I was just trying to help," he said as he rubbed his arm. My flurry of movement continued unabated. "Sara, stop for a minute." It wasn't until his hand stayed mine that I realized I was shaking. "Put the brush down," he said quietly and drew me into a tight hug. His warmth banished the lingering terror and I loosened my grip on the hairbrush. "You're safe, I won't let anything happen to you."

I sighed all of my tension into his shoulder and for a brief moment, allowed myself to appreciate the small comfort. "Michael?"

"Hmm?" he responded absently as he continued to stroke my back.

"You're mussing up my dress."

"Oh." He released me and took stock. "You look beautiful, Sara," he said as he looked me over.

My cheeks heated. "Thanks. It's a shame it was for nothing."

"Why is that?" He frowned.

"You can't honestly want to go out?" He raised an eyebrow and I let out a huff. "There's a killer on the loose. Who was just here, in case you've forgotten."

"Why not? You need the distraction, I'm hungry, and you're going to stay at my place to be safe. Now let's try this again." He dumped out the oddities I'd been shoving in the bag. There was nearly nothing useful, except the hairbrush clutched in my hand.

While I focused on calming breaths, I grabbed the rest of my personal hygiene items. After I finished packing, Michael zipped the bag and swung it over his shoulder. Once outside, he slid an arm around my waist, the warmth of the contact a sharp contrast to the chill in the air.

"What are you doing?" I asked, unsure what to make of this latest development. First, he called this thing a date and now he had his arm around me like it actually was one.

He leaned closer to whisper in my ear. "Consider it a deterrent to...others."

I nearly giggled as the words tickled my ear, but they made sense too. The memory of being blanketed in his scent was still fresh. If it could somehow protect me from the monster hunting me, then I was all for it.

I leaned into the ruse and pretended that I wasn't enjoying the possessive feel as he pulled me closer.

"I hope you're hungry," he said as he helped me into my seat.

Quite frankly, after the scare I'd had, food was the last thing on my mind.

11

RESERVATIONS

"I realize we're a bit late for our reservation," Michael said, oozing charm. "But something unexpected came up and detained us." He flashed the hostess a smile that should have melted her where she stood. As it was, she did look a bit flushed. To her credit, she kept it together as well as anyone could expect.

"Uh, um, policy..." she stammered.

"We really would appreciate anything you could do to help," Michael implored in a low voice, giving me a slight squeeze as he did so.

"I'll see what I can do." The poor hostess attempted to subtly fan herself as she scanned the sheet before her.

"I didn't realize you made a reservation," I whispered.

"Looks like there was a cancellation. It'll just be a minute, Mr. Howell," she cooed, leaning forward slightly.

"Thank you, Rachael," Michael rumbled, and I swear the hostess got starry-eyed before darting away to make sure the table was ready. Then he turned back to me and answered my earlier question. "Of course I made a reservation, this place is nearly impossible to get into."

"When did you make it?" I asked, thinking about how Charline had spent weeks trying to get Ted to take her here.

"A week after it opened," he said, affecting an air of nonchalance.

"Your table is ready, Mr. Howell," the hostess said when she returned, sounding more than a little pleased with herself. Her gaze slid past Michael to me and what could only be envy flashed in her eyes.

I wanted to scream at her—*It's not what you think!*—but she was already turning to lead the way.

"Here we go," Michael said, applying gentle pressure at the small of my back to get me moving.

I followed after Rachel in a bit of a daze.

I wonder who he was originally planning to bring here.

We sat at the table and waters were brought as well as a small basket of bread. I fussed with my napkin and silverware becoming increasingly uncomfortable. This wasn't at all like our lunch meetings. This place was the kind of fancy you wanted when you were going to propose or got a killer new job, not one where you took a casual office acquaintance.

His real date is supposed to be sitting here, not me.

"What do you want to say?" Michael asked, taking a sip of water.

"What makes you think I want to say something?" I asked in turn, knotting the napkin in my hands.

He gave a small smile and leaned forward conspiratorially. "Because you always fidget when you want to say something."

I scowled and straightened the fork, then promptly realized I was fidgeting again.

Dang it.

"Out with it," he prompted.

I glanced back towards where the hostess was greeting another couple at her podium before responding. "That poor girl practically swooned when you started talking to her." He gave a small chuckle and took another drink. "I'm serious," I hissed. "Do you even know the effect you have on women?" The question was dangerously close to things I didn't want to admit to myself or to him, but it was too late to take it back.

Rather than laugh again like I expected, Michael gave a soft sigh and stared at his water glass. The lemon floated amidst the cubes as condensation ran down the perfectly clear glass. "Consider it another perk to...what we are," he finally said. When he looked up and caught my eye, there was something else in his gaze I couldn't quite place.

Nervousness? Resignation?

"You have the same effect on men," he added.

I snorted. "That'll be the day."

He frowned at the wry comment and sat up. His mouth opened to say something right as the waiter walked up to the table.

"Good evening. Would you like to start with any beverages tonight? Might I recommend the Cabernet Sauvignon or perhaps a more earthy Pinot Noir?"

Michael glanced at me and the waiter's focus shifted as well. I had a sneaking suspicion I was going to need a drink tonight and surely one couldn't hurt.

"I'll have a glass of Pinot, please."

"And it'll be the Cab for me," Michael said. Although the waiter had a pad, he made no note before disappearing.

We sat in awkward silence while we waited for the drinks to arrive. Michael seemed equally lost in his own thoughts as I was mine. By the time the wine arrived, I'd simmered long enough.

"Michael, what's all this really about?" I shuffled the

silverware around once more, then balled my fists in my lap to keep them from touching anything.

"What? I can't go out with a charming woman?"

I stared back at him. Charline could believe there was more to our interactions all she liked, but I knew better. He put up a good front, but eventually his persistent smile slipped and he sagged in his chair.

"Fine, I also need to speak with you about something." He glanced at where our server was currently taking another table's order. "But let's wait until the food gets here, so there is less of a chance we'll be interrupted."

"I knew there was something." I pointed an accusatory finger at him.

"Honestly, Sara, I don't see why you can't appreciate things for what they are."

"Because nothing is ever what it seems, there's always an ulterior motive," I countered.

"You've got that right," he mumbled almost so low I didn't catch it.

"What's that supposed to mean?"

"Nothing."

Before I could press, the waiter returned to take our orders and dashed off again. Once he was gone, Michael resumed our conversation albeit less enthusiastically.

He laced his fingers on the table and asked, "How have you been feeling?"

"Aside from knowing that something is wrong with me? I feel great—amazing actually." I hated to admit it, but I had more energy than I'd had in years.

"Nothing is wrong with you, you're just different," Michael admonished. "And the feeling of invincibility is to be expected."

"But I didn't say—"

He gave me a knowing look. "That'll change when you

start learning your limits. Don't get me wrong though, compared to the average person, we're pretty damn close."

"Is Max still breathing down your neck?" I asked, uncomfortable with the current line of conversation.

"No more than usual."

"Did he resolve the budget discrepancy?"

"Yes," he said bluntly. He clearly noticed the ploy and my cheeks colored.

This is going to be the most awkward dinner ever.

A little later, the food arrived and we were left in relative peace.

"Alright, what did you want to talk to me about?" I asked the second the waiter was out of earshot.

"Woman, you're insufferable. What's wrong with enjoying a nice meal first?" I shrugged and waited for him to get on with it. He gave me a sour look and took a dramatic bite. "Have it your way. Do you know what next week is?"

"No, does it have to do with something at work?"

"Not in the least. How long would you say it's been since your...incident?"

The sip of wine soured in my mouth. "I don't know, three weeks maybe."

"Which would mean that the next full moon is coming up."

"Yeah, so what? I mean it's not like..." I choked on my steak as his words finally struck home. "No, you can't mean...not again."

"You didn't really think it would only happen once?" he asked, his face stamped with disbelief. "We talked about this."

"No." But I'd hoped. "I thought that after I changed back the first time, I don't know, I'd be able to control it or something," I admitted.

"Sara, even with all the control in the world, it's nearly

impossible not to change during the full moon. And I hate to break it to you, but it takes years to acquire the kind of control you're talking about. For all intents and purposes, you could change at any time."

"Now you tell me this!" My fork and knife slammed into the table hard enough to rattle the dishes. The people around us turned to stare at the racket. I sank down in my chair beneath the weight of their collective gazes, but refused to give up my glare.

"You're right, I should have told you sooner. I was concerned that if you knew, you'd worry yourself into a change." His hand reached out to cover mine.

I stared at the appendage and recognized that he was aiming to make this look like a lover's tiff. A little abashed at my behavior, I played along. "I can't believe you didn't tell me, it's not like you haven't had ample opportunity," I said, somewhat calmer.

"I know, but you were adjusting to things so well and I didn't want to add to the situation." He sounded genuine enough, but that didn't excuse that he'd intentionally omitted pertinent information.

"Michael, as you have reminded me time and again, ignoring it won't change anything. How am I supposed to understand how I've changed if you don't tell me everything I need to know?"

He started to respond, but I cut him off.

"Wait. I think the rest of this conversation might be better held away from prying ears." I caught the eye of the woman who'd been whispering to her companion and she suddenly became very absorbed with her soup.

"You're right." He squeezed my hand before releasing it. "I wanted you to have a nice evening out before things got complicated again." Sadness swept across his face and my guilt returned.

"The evening *was* nice. And things were always complicated," I added with what I hoped was a reassuring smile. He lightly touched my hand on his arm, which seemed to have gotten there of its own accord. I quickly removed it. "We should be going before that woman chokes on her spoon."

He chuckled and nodded. In a matter of minutes, the bill was settled and we were getting up. As we walked to the exit, his arm once again slid around my waist. I looked up sharply.

"What? I told you it was a date," he said, calm as a stone. I shook my head, but left it alone.

The silence of the drive seemed to become a living thing as the tension between us increased the closer we got to his place. Once there, he disappeared almost immediately into the kitchen. When he returned, he was holding two glasses and a bottle of wine.

He caught my look and answered the unspoken question. "I don't know about you, but I could use a drink."

"I suppose one wouldn't hurt," I caved.

"Only one?"

"I'm a bit of a light weight," I admitted as the cushion sank beneath me.

He laughed, surprising me and relieving some of the tension. "Sara, you could probably drink a grown man under the table before you started to feel anything. Consider it another perk."

"Then what's the point?" I asked, not sure if I believed him.

"It's still nice." He passed me a glass and sat down. "Now, where were we?"

"You not telling me important information about being a werewolf."

"Sara, I said I'm sorry. I was wrong..." I held up a hand to stop the flow of apologies. His mouth snapped shut and he took a sip of his wine to hide the scowl growing on his face.

"It's frustrating. Every time I think I've got this figured out, something else surfaces." I looked down at my nearly full glass and rolled it between my hands before taking a sip. "You said I could change any time. How?"

He settled back into the couch and took another drink as if mulling over his answer. "Typically, it's when you feel like it. For instance, I could change now if I wanted. But you'll probably need more time before you can do that."

"Is that why you didn't say anything?"

"Not exactly. You still could, but I didn't want you to be so worried about it, that you accidentally triggered a change." He must have read something on my face, because he added, "Yes, that's a real probability. It doesn't happen very often, but it does happen. Kind of like trying so hard not to think about something, that you end up only thinking about that."

I eyed the contents of my glass which was now only half full and spared a glance at the bottle sitting on the coffee table. As if reading my thoughts, Michael reached forward to grab the bottle and topped off both of our glasses.

"Let's see," he began as he settled back cradling the delicate drinkware. "You know most of the obvious stuff already. What have I missed?" He glanced around the room and back at me. "How's your night vision faring?"

"I don't know. I'm not exactly taking midnight strolls right now." Bitterness coated the words and I took another sip in an attempt to wash it out.

"True, but I was talking about in here," he clarified.

"What do you mean?"

"The only light in this room is coming from the moon outside." Unnerved, I leaned over and turned on the lamp. "That's one of those things you'll have to look out for. We take it for granted, but it tends to seem unusual to everyone else."

"Kind of like the smell thing?"

"You could look at it that way. I'm sure you've also noticed that your body is running hotter than normal."

"Aha! It wasn't my imagination. And Charline thought I was weird for going without a jacket," I said to myself.

Michael gave a small laugh and polished off the remainder of his glass. "It would take a lot for you to feel cold now."

I took a congratulatory sip, pleased with myself for having figured out at least one thing on my own. "Okay, what else?"

"Well, if you've noticed the body-temp thing, then you've probably noticed increased sensitivity, especially in your hands, and that you heal a bit faster."

"Is that why you didn't take me to the vet after you hit me?"

He flinched. "I can't believe I basically ran you over. I'm supposed to be helping you, not making things worse. But yeah, once I realized most of the injury was superficial, I wasn't too worried."

I snorted and finished my glass, then placed it on the coffee table next to his. *Superficial my ass, that hurt like hell.*

"Alright, Miss Skeptical. There's also the tiny fact that you can't exactly take a werewolf to a hospital—animal or otherwise—without raising a few eyebrows." Michael's sass was comedic until I remembered my own stay at the hospital.

"About that. I'm not sure how relevant it is now, but I'm pretty sure I raised a few eyebrows during my recovery," I said sheepishly.

Michael groaned and tossed his head back on the couch. "This mutt is going to be the freaking end of me."

"I'm sorry. How was I supposed to know? This is all incredibly new, not to mention out in left field."

He lifted his head back up to meet my worried gaze. "No, it's not your fault. Things are ...complicated for me. I have to tread carefully with this or there could be serious consequences."

"Like the doctors conducting an inquisition?" I hazarded.

"That too. There's so much you don't know, things I take for granted." He stared back at me as if debating how far back to pull the curtain. "I realize all of this is probably a little overwhelming, but I promise, it's easier to adjust than you think. You'll get through this."

I tried to tell him that I really wasn't having that hard a time, but a huge yawn that cracked my jaw prevented me.

"Damn, I didn't realize how late it is." He glanced at the clock on the wall. "You've had a long day. And here I am keeping you awake with my own problems..." He shifted to get up.

"Michael, relax," I said, my hand on his arm.

He took a deep breath and let it out slowly. Clearly something in our conversation wasn't sitting well with him. "Alright," he said as he stood. "I'll get you set up." He grabbed my bag from the floor and headed down the hall, leaving me to catch up.

When I didn't find him in the first room, I moved down to the main bedroom.

Not this again.

"Michael, wait."

"Oh, here," he said and shoved a bundle of clothes into my arms without meeting my eye. "You go ahead and change." Message delivered, he whirled back around to continue cleaning, pointedly avoiding any eye contact.

Rather than stand there and argue, I gave him some

space. In the bathroom, I realized what he'd given me—the shirt I'd taken.

Crap. Now he knows that I took it and lied about it.

I shook my head and pulled it on anyway. The soft cotton hung off my shoulders, no less comfy for being too big. Determined not to make things any more awkward than they already were, I returned to find the room miraculously transformed.

"Michael, I'm not sleeping in your room," I said, doing my best to leave no room for argument.

"Yes, you are," he said as he fluffed a pillow. "It's the least I can do."

"I won't take your bed. It's yours, you sleep in it." *Not to mention, I doubt I could survive another night wrapped in your scent and keep my wits.*

"But you're a guest," he protested, looking thoroughly put out.

"So, I'll sleep in the guest room, that is what it's for. The bed just needs some sheets," I added.

He stared at the ceiling and let out a heavy breath, then finally met my gaze. There seemed to be a battle playing inside of him, but without him saying anything, I was at a loss for what it could be.

Is there some reason he doesn't want me in there?

"If you'll tell me where to find the sheets, I can take care of it."

My words seemed to propel him into motion. "No, I've got it. I don't know why I didn't think of that before. Suppose it has to do with the fact that I don't really have anyone stay the night. Most of the time, I forget I have the room altogether."

My cheeks burned slightly as I put two and two together as to how a man like Michael Howell could forget he had a second bedroom. I ducked my head to hide my blush as he walked past me to obtain the requested linens.

"Are you sure you wouldn't be more comfortable in the other room?" he asked for probably the fifth time.

"I'll be fine, this is great," I said, standing in the middle of the guest room. It was a decent space. Smaller than his, but that was to be expected, and the sheets were clean if a bit musty.

"Okay, but if you need anything, I'll be down the hall." He hesitated in the doorway as if he wanted to say more.

"I know, thank you. Goodnight, Michael," I said in an attempt to give him the out he so clearly needed.

To my surprise, he didn't immediately vanish. Instead, he stepped forward and moved a loose strand of hair out of my face, his hand lingering. My breath caught and I tried desperately to pretend my hormones weren't freaking out.

"Goodnight, Sara," he whispered.

I swallowed, unsure of how to respond or if I even could. "Goodnight," I said again, substantially more breathless.

His hand finally slipped away, trailing tingles in the wake of the intimate touch. I continued to stand there dazed well after he'd gone.

"Sara...Sara..."

I grumbled at the intrusion, not wanting to let go of my wonderfully fuzzy sleep. But it was too late, the damage was done. I cracked my eyelids. Deep brown eyes framed by long lashes stared back at me only inches away.

I screamed and scrambled backwards nearly falling off the other side of the bed. Between the harsh sound and heart-stopping scare, I was officially awake, though my brain was still struggling to catch up.

"Christ, Michael." My hand fisted in the fabric above my pounding heart. "Personal space much?"

Completely unphased, he sat on the bed. "You know you make noises in your sleep? It's kind of adorable."

"How long have you been here?" I screeched in violated outrage.

He shrugged casually in response and I smacked him as hard as I could in the arm, which I suspected was now actually quite hard. "Ow," he laughed, rubbing the appendage. "I'm sure breakfast should help make up for any grievance I may have caused."

Despite being in a completely human body, I could swear my ears perked forward. He laughed again and led the way. I followed his example and stayed in pajamas as I trailed after him and the promise of food.

"Where did you find grits?" I asked, sipping on my coffee and only a little disheartened that ham steak hadn't made the menu.

"I had a conference in Alabama a few years back and liked them so much that I brought some back. Now I keep 'em in stock. Why do you ask?"

"No reason, I just pegged you for an oatmeal kind of guy." As he laughed, something occurred to me. "Hey! You never mentioned anything about having an obscene appetite."

"I figured that was pretty self-explanatory," he said as he topped off his coffee.

"Yeah, but now I look like a cow when I go out and order mountains of food," I pouted. "Eventually, it's going to draw attention, not to mention the drain on my wallet."

"You look great, Sara," he said, leaning on the peninsula. "But if it really bothers you, most *weres* eat a full meal or snack before they go out so they can appear a little more normal."

"I suppose that could work," I grumbled, though it didn't solve the budget issue.

Michael sighed and looked into his steaming mug before bringing his gaze back to mine. "I can't even begin to imagine how much food it would take for a werewolf to put on weight."

"What do you mean?" I asked, intrigued despite myself.

"Our metabolism is incredibly high. It takes a lot of fuel to keep us running," he explained.

"Call it another perk?" I proffered.

He smiled. "Yeah, call it another perk."

"There seem to be a lot of those. I can't tell if you're just biased about being a werewolf or if you don't want to talk about the downsides."

His grin slipped. "There are a few downsides, but I don't expect them to be a problem for you." He hid a dire expression behind taking another sip and glanced out the sliding doors. "Look, it's a beautiful day. Why don't we hit up the park?"

I let the blatant shift stand unopposed. "You don't really expect me to believe that you just now came up with that. If I didn't know better, I'd think you'd planned a whole weekend."

"I can guarantee you this is not the weekend I had planned. Now go get changed so that we can get out of here." He followed his own advice by hastily rinsing his cup and walking around the peninsula dividing us.

"But I didn't even..."

"I'm sure there's something in there," he said and shuffled me off.

Sure enough, there were clothes for an outing to the park. I'd been joking earlier, but now I wasn't so sure. He could have easily planned everything out—though biting someone seemed a bit extreme.

I glanced towards the door and the living room beyond, where Michael was undoubtedly already waiting for me. Doubt and uncertainty warred in my mind. Whether he'd lied about biting me or not, he was definitely hiding something.

"Are you coming?" he called as if sensing my reticence.

I put the doubtful thoughts on the back burner with the full intent of exploring them later. Thus far, Michael hadn't given me any real reason beyond also being a werewolf to doubt his sincerity. I hesitated in the doorway, foot poised to step into the hall at the sudden, alarming realization that I was literally trusting a man I barely knew with my life.

My teeth sank into my bottom lip as I cast an anxious glance toward the living room. A second later, my foot came down. So far, Michael was the one with the answers and that meant I would have to keep trusting.

The beauty of the park easily eclipsed my bleak thoughts and effortlessly pushed aside my persistent doubts. Winter was finally beginning to relinquish its hold on the landscape and fresh sprigs of green peeked out from barren branches. Even the breeze carried a tantalizing promise of change right around the corner.

I sucked in a lung full of air and spun in a circle, arms out wide, while Michael's laughter swirled around me. "What?"

"It's good to see you smiling," he said with one of his own.

"I smile." I frowned.

"It's okay. Most of us find it difficult to be indoors for long stretches of time." He gave his own exaggerated stretch. "It's not easy being confined to the house. That's one of the reasons I wanted us to get out today. Honestly, rain or shine, I'm not sure I could have endured another day." As his arms fell back to his sides with a satisfied sigh, it occurred to me that while I felt like I was under house arrest, as my jailer, he was faced with the same restrictions. Guilt twisted in my stomach at my earlier suspicions.

"Come on." He waved his hand. "Let's stretch our legs."

"I swear if you produce a stick, I'll bite you," I warned. He chuckled and led the way down a dirt path next to the tree line. I sprinted to catch up and fell in step beside him. "Truth be told, I expected you to do as much that first night." The admission flew out of my mouth accompanied by an almost immediate burn on my cheeks.

"You have absolutely no idea how tempting it was," he chuckled. "But I figured I'd be in enough trouble once you learned the truth." He glanced at me out of the corner of his eye.

My face burned hotter as I recalled my behavior that night. I cleared my throat. "Do you come here often?"

He shrugged. "Not really. I'd rather go over to Raven Rock."

"Why didn't we do that today?"

His grin was downright roguish. "Let's just say I'm not typically presentable when I go. You haven't lived until you spend a whole weekend out there."

I thought about how tan he was and the noticeable lack of tan lines. My exhale caught and I started to choke.

"You alright?" He turned as if to start patting me on the back.

Unable to bear the compounded humility, I waved him off and tried harder to school my thoughts from wandering to places they had no business being. Thankfully, he let it go.

"You know what? I'm sure you're probably tired of the

exercise by now, but this is kind of a great place to really test your nose."

"You can't be serious. Can't I have one day off?" I bemoaned.

"Nope, now focus. Tell me what you smell."

I gave him an exaggerated eye roll, which earned me a laugh and I couldn't help but smile. Aside from the weirdness of it all, this was shaping up to be an almost normal day. Obviously, my definition of normal had changed.

He was still waiting expectantly, so I rolled my shoulders and concentrated. I inhaled deeply, sampling the breeze curling around us. Right off, I smelled Michael, his scent deep and musky beside me, the woodsy undertones sparking memories of home and a forest that felt friendly rather than threatening. I pushed the dominating scent away and searched for something else.

"I can't believe I'm sniffing things like some dog," I mumbled under my breath, not thinking about the fact that Michael would be able to hear it. Laughter instantly bubbled out of him, shattering the little focus I'd attained. "Shut up. Don't make fun of me."

He only laughed harder, clutching his side as he gasped for breath. "I haven't heard anything that funny in ages."

"It's not funny! Stop laughing," I griped, shoving him for good measure. "Besides, how am I supposed to smell anything with you standing right there?" I let out an aggrieved huff when his laughter refused to abate. "Fine, be that way," I said and ran a few steps away.

"Wait!" he called after me.

I ignored him and closed my eyes to eliminate any other distractions.

Within seconds, his scent was once again dancing at my periphery. "I'm sorry. I'm not making fun, I promise. It's just..."

"Shh." I held up a hand. and he instantly went silent. He waited patiently as I struggled to pin down what had caught my attention. The eerily familiar scent taunted me like a word hovering on the tip of your tongue.

I focused harder and an image of a medium-sized pond with gray-feathered occupants came to me.

"Geese!" Without a second thought, I raced toward the source.

"Where are you going?" Michael asked, hot on my heels as I dove into the trees.

"I've been here before," I said over my shoulder.

A second later, I burst through the foliage and the oasis I'd stumbled upon weeks ago opened up before me. Sure enough, the geese were swimming lazily around the pond with a few waddling on the shore. It was almost exactly as I remembered it.

"You've been here?" Michael asked as he emerged from the trees, not half a step behind.

"Yeah," I said, walking towards the water confidently. "This is where I ended up that second night."

"Good grief, no wonder I couldn't find you."

I shrugged and kept walking.

"Sara, wait," Michael cautioned. "Geese aren't exactly known to be friendly, especially to wolves."

I looked down at his hand on my wrist and smiled up at him. "We have an understanding," I said and slipped his grip.

He stayed where he was as I approached the pond and my feathered friends, admittedly a little slower than before. They eyed me skeptically, but didn't panic as I walked right up to the water's edge. I gave them a moment to accept my presence and then reached down to scoop up a handful of water. The cool water slid down my throat and I gave a contented sigh.

"Well, I'll be," Michael said with a touch of awe from his safe distance. "One of these days, you'll have to tell me how you earned the trust of a gaggle of geese."

"Sure thing." I stood and wiped my hand on my pants.

A peek over my shoulder showed him eyeing the geese every bit as warily as they were eyeing him. I debated making a crack about how the big bad wolf was afraid of a few feathers, but managed to keep both the terrible pun and my laughter to myself. Instead, I turned my attention to the clearing at large.

My gaze traveled along the perimeter, noting the subtle differences now that I wasn't looking at it from the perspective of a hunted animal. The trees weren't as tall, the lake wasn't as wide, and the geese weren't nearly as intimidating. I smiled to myself and brought my focus to the hill that had nearly killed me, then followed the tree line.

Amidst the crowded trunks, in spite of the bright light, a dark patch stood out and the fear I'd felt that day sprung back to life. I swallowed my sudden anxiety, no longer interested in playing this game.

"You're right about enough exercise," I said as I turned away from the pond and sinister shadow.

Michael looked at me askance. "Something wrong?"

"I'm hungry is all," I said, affecting false cheer.

He didn't seem to buy it, but didn't protest as we made our way back to the original path and then to the car. We ended up picking up lunch and taking it back to his place to settle in for some more heart-to-heart werewolf talk.

"Did it have to be hot dogs?" I asked, kicking my shoes off.

"You didn't really think I'd let it go?" He laughed as he set down the food and fixings.

The couch gave out a big whoosh as I flopped down and eyed the impressive spread. There was enough for a small party, but like everything else, it seemed that was something I would have to get used to.

"Anyway, I figure we should talk about what you're going to do," Michael said, then devoured a dog in two bites.

"About what?" I asked as I prepped a condiment-loaded bun.

"About what?" he echoed, mirroring me with his second helping. "Sara, there's a reason I wanted you to stay here last night."

My appetite vanished, my mouth went dry, and my breaths turned shallow. The darkness from the woods seemed to grow in my mind's eye, becoming more and more ominous as it threatened to swallow me whole.

"I don't mean to scare you, but he knows where you live, it's not safe for you there." Michael's warm hand engulfed my knee, rooting me back in the present.

"I can't live here. I...I mean, all of my stuff, and then there's work. How am I supposed to..." The jumbled mess of words made little sense to me as they tumbled out.

"I understand and we can figure all that out," he reassured me.

"Why can't I stay at a motel or something?"

"Because I can't protect you there. Please don't fight this. I want to know that you're safe and that I'm close by if you need help."

"I suppose it doesn't get much closer than right down the hall."

He blatantly ignored the cynicism and offered an over-the-top smile. "I'm glad you agree. We can go over and get more of your stuff later."

"But I didn't... You can't hold me hostage like this."

"I'm not." His second hot dog disappeared as quickly as the first.

"Then what would you call it?" I asked, my own dog abandoned on the table.

"Protecting you."

"If you're worried about me being alone, then I can stay at Charline's."

He gave me a reproachful look.

Okay, so I didn't really want to drag her into all of this, but it didn't change the fact that trust or no trust, he was dictating my every move. We were in the twenty-first century for Christ's sake.

"Oh, never mind. I'm not going to win, am I?"

"Nope, might as well accept it."

12

———

LONE SURVIVOR

I stared down at the stuffed suitcase and couldn't help but wonder if I was overdoing it. After all, there was no telling how long—or short—I'd be camped at Michael's. I looked around my room again and thought wistfully of my childhood home tucked up in the woods.

The image of my parents poking fun at each other around the breakfast table came to mind and a familiar longing blossomed in my chest. They'd been nothing but supportive in my desperate attempt to prove I could stand on my own two feet. They'd been my rock and safe harbor my whole life...and they deserved to know the truth.

A small measure of guilt wormed its way into my gut. I'd done nothing to create any kind of permanence here, I'd glossed over how well I was doing before, and now I was outright lying. My sigh turned into a miserable groan.

"Is everything alright?" Michael asked as he walked in to acquire the luggage and me.

"Yeah."

He paused and gave me a look clearly not buying it.

"I always thought when I..." I trailed off, unwilling to admit the truth. That I felt like a failure in my own life. That

127

moving in with him wasn't nearly the hardship it should have been. That he was nothing at all like I'd expected. And that I always thought when I moved in with someone it would be because we were together. Except this wasn't that and it never would be.

"When you, what?" he prompted, suitcase already in hand.

I looked at him while I tried to come up with a suitable replacement. Unsure of what to say, I took a page out of Charline's book. "I always thought when I emptied my closet it would be to replace everything."

He frowned at the admittedly vapid response. "There's no reason you couldn't," he said, then turned and exited.

I gave a silent cry of frustration.

What's the worst that could happen if I told him I was starting to like him?

My mind immediately came up with a slew of possibilities, none of which seemed the least bit appealing. He could laugh. I could be accused of having something akin to Stockholm syndrome. Or worse, he could feel sorry for me, the sad little wallflower with her hopeless crush on someone way out of her league. I followed after him to the jeep, feeling miserable down to my toes.

Life would have been so much easier if I'd stayed a dog.

"Think you got everything?" he asked as we turned onto the main road.

"Yeah," I responded flatly.

"We can always get anything you forgot when we come back for your car," he tried again.

As it was, I was pretty sure the only reason we weren't taking my car now was because he wanted to be able to hold my clothes hostage.

"I know," I said, and turned to stare gloomily out the window at the suburban landscape whizzing past.

"What do you want to do for dinner?" he asked in yet another attempt to engage me.

I shrugged, too lost in melancholy to manage words. He gave up trying to talk and we rode the rest of the way in silence. I walked to the guest room in a muted trance where Michael left me to get settled. While I worked at unpacking my things into the small bureau, my thoughts continued on their merry-go-round of doubt.

The fact that I'm essentially living here doesn't mean anything. This arrangement is strictly strategic.

My hormones didn't care. The smell of Michael was everywhere, soaking into my clothes and skin. My hands and the shirt they were holding fell to my sides as I stared up at the ceiling.

Oh God, how am I going to explain all of this to Charline?

Misery encompassed me as I refolded the same shirt for the third time.

I can't tell her the truth. She doesn't deserve to be dragged into the disaster that has become my life.

I sighed.

I'm going to have to suck it up and tell her the lie she already believes. Michael and I have been seeing each other and things have gotten pretty serious.

She'll love that.

The thought even tasted bitter. I plopped on the bed effectively ruining whatever progress I'd attained. I glared at the once folded clothes that were now on the floor in open rebellion.

"Unfortunately, the power of telekinesis is not among the many perks of being a werewolf," Michael said from the open doorway.

I resisted the urge to transfer the glare and instead closed my eyes and pretended he wasn't there.

"Now, why is it that every time I walk by you look more

and more forlorn? And if I didn't know any better, I'd think that your clothes are magically unfolding themselves."

I cracked an eye to see him leaning casually on the door frame. A flare of anger surged through me at his cavalier attitude. "Why do you think? I've basically had to move out of my house—which I feel like I've barely finished moving into—in order to be under armed guard here. And all because some psychotic killer werewolf is out for blood. My blood," I finished with a huff and flopped back.

The bed shifted beneath me as Michael's weight pressed into it. "Come on, here's not so bad. Is it?" When I refused to respond or even look at him, he changed track. "Now about this 'psychotic killer,' we should probably talk about that."

"What more is there to say? He attacked me without provocation and is foaming at the mouth to finish the job."

"There's a little more to it than that. Get off your butt and join me in the living room for a drink," he commanded, smacking my leg as he got up.

For lack of anything better to do, I followed him to the main room and took what was quickly becoming my customary seat. I expected him to bring me a big glass of something dark. What I didn't expect was that something dark would be coffee. The smell wafted seductively out of the warm mug in my hands. I took a sip and lost myself in liquid bliss.

"How's the java?" Michael asked, joining me.

All I could manage was a grateful "Mm."

He laughed. "I'm glad you like it."

Half the cup was gone before I could detach myself. "So, what are these extra complications you mentioned?"

He took a big drink before answering, "They're not complications, so much as why he's so messed up." I sat forward, strangely eager to learn more about my assailant.

"Proceed, good sir."

He chuckled. "I'm glad to see the coffee is doing its job. You certainly look more awake than you have in the last three hours." I scowled at him. "There's no need to be like that. I understand that none of this is ideal, but maybe with a little more perspective you won't begrudge it quite so much. And maybe you wouldn't fight me so hard on literally everything," he added under his breath.

I chose to ignore the snarky comment and focused on the warmth seeping into my hands from the mug instead.

Michael gave an exasperated sigh and went on with his tale. "You already know that he's a werewolf, or at least I hope you've put that together."

I looked up from the half-empty cup. "You don't say."

"Just making sure you're listening."

My shoulders slumped. "I get that you're trying to help, to somehow make this easier to bear," I said, "but it doesn't really change the fact that I'm hiding from a monster and my life." I hadn't meant to add that last bit, but it was too late to take it back now.

His face softened and I looked away. I didn't want his pity. I wanted all of this to be over so I could go back to my lackluster life.

Is that what you really want?

I shrugged off the undermining question. The truth was, I didn't really know what I wanted, not anymore. I was starting to wonder if I ever had.

A minute passed and Michael's mug chinked on the coffee table. "Something you may not have guessed, is that he was bitten as well."

My head shot up and I met Michael's steady gaze. The lamp beside him lent his features an almost ethereal glow accentuated by a dark cast to his eyes that sent a chill down my spine. "How did that happen?" I asked, my mouth dry.

"Before I get into that, I want you to know that I've been watching you and I truly believe that you're adjusting well."

My eyes narrowed. This was starting to sound suspiciously like yet more important information that he'd conveniently neglected to tell me.

"Not all changes go well, especially when combined with traumatic experiences like..."

"Like mine?" I whispered, an edge to my tone.

He winced. "Well, yes, like yours, but you obviously managed alright since you haven't gone on a violent rampage."

"I take it Mr. Crazy did?"

"*Were* society would call him a mutt," Michael said.

"So, our mutt," the word felt strange, yet oddly appropriate, "he snapped."

Michael hesitated. "It's not very common—not that we have real cases to reference—but yes, there are stories where a change caused people to snap."

"And you're just now mentioning this?" The ceramic mug creaked in my hand as I squeezed it.

He gave it an anxious look and went on. "I didn't want you to be so worried about it that—"

"That I triggered a change," I finished for him. "I've heard all of this before. What you've failed to mention is why I didn't."

He seemed to flounder in his search for words. All of the blood drained from my face as the reason he would withhold such pertinent information floated up.

"It's still a possibility," I asked almost soundlessly. Suddenly, maintaining my gaze seemed impossible for him. "Is that the real reason you've been spending so much time with me? All of the lunches? The outings? Keeping me caged here? You were keeping tabs on me!" My voice rose with each accusation.

"No! No, Sara, that's not why. If I truly thought you were a danger to yourself or anyone else then..." he trailed off and I guessed the rest.

"You wouldn't have slowed down when you hit me on the road."

Despite the faint light, Michael was starting to look a little green around the gills. "You're here, because I don't want him anywhere near you," he said softly.

I was at a total loss as to what to say to that, so I set my mug down and leaned back into the cushy embrace of the couch. "I guess it's too late to worry about it now, right? I'll either eventually go off the deep end or I won't." The sardonic comment was maybe a hair melodramatic. "Is this a risk for all *weres*?" I asked, trying to steer the conversation back on track.

He looked up hopeful. "Yes. Certain *weres* are more susceptible to it, but it's a reality that all of us face. Enduring something that traumatizing every month takes a toll; not everyone can manage it."

I nodded my understanding. "So, what's our guy's deal?"

"From what I've been told, there was an upheaval in a northern pack. I don't know the full story there, but the gist of it is that some of the members split and started to go after humans. You need to understand, even if they hadn't murdered innocent people, they risked exposing the pack, exposing all werewolves. That alone is a crime punishable by death." He paused to make sure I grasped the gravity of his words.

It wasn't like I had any intention of going after humans and I definitely didn't plan to out myself as a werewolf to rest of the world—not on purpose anyway. I swallowed thickly and nodded again.

"Naturally," he continued, "the pack devoted all of their efforts to hunting them down. Unfortunately, several people were slaughtered before they could put a stop to it."

His word choice brought to mind horror movies of people being attacked by wild animals and mauled to death. Layered over the imagery was my own indistinct memory of blood and pain. I gave an involuntary shudder.

"One of the rebels was found attacking a group of humans. News reports say they were homeless, but the truth is unclear. The only thing that *was* clear from the report, was the massacre that was left behind. What police didn't know was that the pack was able to catch the rogue and one survivor."

"So our guy is the rebel?" I asked, a little confused at the twists in this tale.

He shook his head. "The rebel was sentenced to death for his crimes." I swallowed hard at the finality in his voice. "I know it sounds harsh, but werewolf justice has to be swift and merciless by necessity. Packs can't risk exposure and mutiny is never tolerated."

I grabbed a folded blanket from the back of the couch and wrapped it around myself. But the cold I felt was deeper than even the thick fabric could touch.

Michael rolled his empty mug between the palms of his hand. "Anyway, they nursed the survivor back to health. As you know, that didn't take long and by that point, there was nothing else to do but wait for the full moon to see if he would change."

"Obviously, he turned," I interrupted from my cocoon.

His mouth twisted in a wry smile. "Honestly, everyone always believed the tales of turned *weres* were nothing more than ghost stories. No one really knew if he would change or not." Michael paused. His gaze flicked up to me and back down again.

I heard what he wasn't saying.

"They thought he'd die."

He nodded sadly. "Until then, he was welcomed into their society much as any *were*. He seemed to get along well enough, though he did have volatile outbursts that grew more frequent as the moon approached. Again, that wasn't wholly unheard of, but with him being bitten not born, they weren't sure if that was the normal-they-knew or something they should be concerned about."

"Clearly it was the latter."

His eyebrows rose in silent agreement. "By the time they found out, it was too late. The night he changed, he slaughtered ten *weres*, including women and pups barely old enough to change. In the chaos, he was able to escape. They hunted him for weeks until he passed out of their territory. Since then, he's been plaguing the east coast, never staying in one place longer than it takes to kill."

"How do you know any of this?" My voice sounded hollow even to my ears.

"The second he crossed territory lines other packs were notified. The Vermont pack shared every bit of information they had about him, which arguably wasn't much."

"Why haven't the police been more involved? This is the first I've heard about a serial killer on the east coast."

Michael's gaze was steady as he met mine. "Do you normally follow animal killings?"

My jaw dropped. It wasn't possible that no one hadn't noticed anything. Then again, the EMTs had asked me about a dog, not a monster.

"As far as anyone can tell, this is the longest he's stayed in one place and the closest we've come."

My voice shook as I asked the only question that really mattered, "Why me?"

"It's been suggested that he might have been killing long before he was a *were*, that maybe he didn't snap, but was always this way. The *were*-gene only emphasized what was already there. If that's true, then it's likely his MO has stayed the same. And his targets," he added quietly.

The cold reached deeper to freeze my core. I would have given almost anything for Michael not to continue.

"He typically targets young, single women without any apparent connections."

I shook my head, desperate to deny what he was saying.

"You're the only one to survive," Michael whispered.

The world around me fractured. "I'll never escape that night, will I? Not ever. It wasn't random, he came for *me*. And he's going to keep coming and coming until I'm dead, ripped apart and bleeding out." I choked back a sob. Thankfully, Michael didn't try to comfort me, I doubted I could've handled anyone's touch at that moment. Gradually, I pulled myself out of the downward spiral, fighting tooth and nail to focus on my current state of safety. Finally, I asked, "How did you know to be there that night?"

The look on his face said it all.

"You didn't," I answered for him.

The guilt on his face deepened. "I'd picked up his scent a few days before near the office and had been tracking him."

"How did you do that?" I may have had plenty of practice identifying people I could see, but nothing like what he was suggesting.

"Previous packs have managed to collect samples like scraps of clothing. The pieces have been spread around so anyone would be able to sniff him out. When a report came in of a similar attack in Wilmington, I was sent a piece." He gestured to the table that held the mail I'd sifted through what felt like a lifetime ago. "Once I recognized the stench, I started tracking him. I'm so sorry I didn't get there sooner, Sara. If I hadn't wasted so much time trying to figure out where he was staying, I could've realized that he wasn't wandering aimlessly and the scent by the office wasn't a coincidence—he was stalking his prey."

"I need a drink." What I needed was to drown out the realization that someone—no, *something*—had been following me for heaven only knew how long, while I mindlessly went about my life.

Soon enough, a tall glass that smelled strongly of whiskey replaced the forgotten mug. I downed the whole thing, grimacing at the burn that spread like fire across my chest. An attempt to talk turned into a cough. I took a fortifying breath and tried again.

"If he knows where I work, then why hasn't he attacked me there?" Ice rattled in the now empty glass.

"The office is too public."

I refused to mention that the parking garage was substantially less so or that there were literally a thousand other places he could've pounced. "Why hasn't he followed me here?" I asked. *How safe am I really?*

"He's probably working on it and even then, I'm a fully grown, male wolf, he won't want those odds. He's a coward," Michael spat.

"You don't know that!" My cup shattered against the wall in an explosion of ice and glass. Michael's gaze never left me, he didn't even flinch.

"Sara, it's okay, you're safe here. I won't let him hurt you," he said as he reached out for me.

I flung up an arm to ward him off. "No, Michael, you don't know that it's safe and it's too late for you to be making promises about not letting him hurt me. It's too late," I sobbed, finally losing the battle to keep it together.

He reached out again. This time he succeeded in wrapping me in his arms, which despite my earlier claim, did feel safe. Unable to muster the energy to push him away, I collapsed into the embrace and cried out my fear in body wracking sobs.

I didn't remember Michael carrying me to his room, but that's where I woke when he came to tell me that it was time to get ready for work.

13

THE DATE DEBATE

I'm just going to tell Charline we're seeing each other. The visual part is true enough, even if the romantic involvement isn't.

Oh god, she's going to ask questions. She'll want details...and feelings.

I groaned. While I had plenty of both, none of them were liable to help the situation. Michael was my self-imposed guard dog and no amount of wishful thinking was going to change that.

What if she ferrets out the truth anyway?

My stomach sank even further if that was possible. At this rate it was going to be sitting beneath my office chair.

What am I going to do? I have to tell her something.

The distinct aroma of baking wafted into my cubicle. I glanced up with a plastered smile on my face that immediately slipped when my gaze landed on my friend. Red rimmed puffy eyes that didn't hold a stitch of makeup, and equally colored a nose that looked like it had been rubbed raw.

"Charline, what's happened?" I gasped.

"Oh, Sara," she sobbed, "It's Ted. I think he's...he's..."

She paused to blow into a wrung-out tissue. "I think he's cheating on me," she finally finished.

"That's not possible." She sniffled, though her watery gaze refused to leave the floor. "Charline, he couldn't. This is Ted we're talking about." I stood and wrapped her in a tentative hug.

"That's what I said!" she wailed, pulling away. "But then there was that bitch Stacy."

"Who?" I asked, at a loss, passing her a fresh tissue.

"The blonde one in Accounting," she spat before giving her nose another good blow.

"Oh. Right," I responded, still clueless.

"She said that Ted was always hitting on her and trying to get her to go out with him and that one of these days she might even say yes, because she'd 'heard things.'"

"What sorts of things?" I asked.

"I don't know! I didn't ask. I just ran. It took everything I had to make it to the bathroom, and I barely did at that." She blew her nose again which was starting to resemble a very large cherry.

"You don't really believe her, do you, Charline?"

She sniffled.

"Come on, you know Ted better than anybody," I tried again with no better results. "Charline, he wouldn't do something like that to you." I paused to give her a chance to say something. When she didn't, I went a different route. "You know what you need to do?"

She looked up, bleary-eyed but hopeful.

"You need to talk to him, straighten this whole thing out," I said with all of the optimism I could muster.

"Sara, I can't. It's so embarrassing." She stood there wringing her hands now that the tissue was completely disintegrated.

"Yes, you can." Her eyes widened at my tone, but she

didn't dispute the assertion. I met her uncertain gaze and softened my voice. "I'm sure he'll understand, Charline. Give him a chance to clear this whole mess up."

She nodded almost imperceptibly. It was progress—not a lot—but progress.

"Besides," I said, "she probably said those things to be vindictive, because she's jealous of you." I patted her on the shoulder for added reassurance.

Whoever this Stacy is should be counting her lucky stars that Charline is too busy being out of sorts to take her out back and beat her.

"You really think so?" Charline asked with barely a quaver.

"Of course, I do. Now you go get cleaned up and don't worry anymore about it until you talk with Ted." I was dubious whether or not she'd take the advice given her current state, but somehow that shallow reassurance seemed to satisfy her.

"You're right," she said, straightening up. "I'm sure Ted can explain why she would say such things."

I nodded in agreement though I seriously doubted it and helped her on her way, giving her one last hopeful smile before she left. She never even noticed Michael walking past.

Michael's perplexed gaze followed her until she turned a corner and vanished from sight. "What's up with her? She's a mess," he said, turning back to me.

I narrowed my eyes and scowled at him. "She thinks Ted might be cheating on her with some blonde in Accounting." My heart went out to Charline. She had the worst luck with men. While Ted may not have been my personal favorite, he'd stuck around the longest.

"Wouldn't surprise me."

I punched him in the arm.

"What? He's the kind of man that wouldn't know a good thing if it bit him on the nose," he responded defensively as he rubbed his arm.

"You don't like him, do you?"

"No, I generally try to avoid him. He looks like a weasel and I bet he smells like one too. Given some of the rumors I've heard about how he treats people in his department, I'm astounded that Charline gave him the time of day."

I shook my head. Michael was right, Ted did kind of resemble a weasel, and my one chance to test the smell theory hadn't worked out. But if I had to guess, I suspected Michael was right about that as well.

"Charline always said those were rumors. Considering her tenacity in acquiring gossip, I believed her, though I confess I've never really liked him either."

"She needs someone who can keep up with her," Michael added.

I nodded in agreement. "Perhaps I should have said something sooner."

"Why didn't you?" Michael asked, his forehead creasing in a sudden frown.

I shrugged. "I never really thought it was my place. It wasn't like *I* was dating him. She is her own woman and has a right to date whoever she wants."

"But she's your friend. Friends are supposed to look out for one another. That includes if you think your friend is dating a jerk," Michael pointed out.

I stared at him in shock, then groaned. "I'm the worst friend ever."

"I don't know about the *worst*," Michael teased.

"Don't make fun of me. My best friend has been dating someone I totally thought wasn't good enough for her and I never said a word. Now she's heartbroken and miserable. And you know what?" Michael raised his eyebrows in silent inquiry. "He's probably out chasing tail on the side," I spat.

"And the wolf-isms come out," he laughed. I clapped a hand over my mouth and groaned again. "Don't be like that, it was bound to happen eventually."

I dropped my hand. "Well at least I didn't do what I was planning to do when I saw her next," I said.

"Which was what?" Michael asked, leaning on the cubicle wall.

"I was going to tell her that we're seeing each other, to stave off the inevitable whispers, but I didn't have the heart."

"You should have told her anyway. It probably would have cheered her up a little."

I threw my head back. "I really am the worst friend."

"You're here for her now and that's what really counts," Michael reassured me.

I looked down to where his hand was gently massaging my shoulder. "So, what are you here for? Don't I see you enough?" I asked as I took a step away from the contact and pretended to order some files.

"I was curious where you wanted to go for lunch today. Unless you think you should have lunch with Charline instead."

"No, she's planning to talk to Ted. Knowing her, she won't wait until after work. So unless she pops back by to say otherwise, I'm all yours," I said, flopping back into my chair.

"I like the sound of that," Michael said with a wicked grin.

I stared into the mirror and smoothed the purple fabric that wasn't in any way wrinkled. The satin underlay clung to every minuscule dip and curve my body possessed, giving the illusion of a figure.

This thing is barely more than a nightgown.

I thought wistfully of a red dress tucked away in my closet. While it was a daring crimson, it wasn't nearly so revealing.

I don't know what I'm stressing about. It's not like this is a for-real date, no matter what Michael says.

After one last self-conscious brush of fabric over my hips, I retreated to the guest room.

This is ridiculous. I'm changing into jeans. I never should have let Charline talk me into buying this stupid dress in the first place.

Guilt washed through me. I considered calling her and following Michael's advice to tell her about us. Given her situation with Ted though, I couldn't bear to bring up anything resembling a relationship with her, even if it was a fake one. A low whistle that reminded me of a cartoon caricature cut through my rambling thoughts.

"Don't patronize me," I said, slipping on the last heel. I wouldn't have bothered at all, except the dress would have looked even more ridiculous in anything less.

"Who's patronizing? You look good enough to eat," he said as his eyes roved over me from head to toe.

I tucked a wayward strand of hair behind my ear and tried not to think about how many girls had tumbled into his bed from that look alone. After a deep breath, I raised my gaze up to meet his and ignored my pounding heart. Unsurprisingly, he looked incredible in a deep green button down and slate gray slacks.

"If you're going to tell wolf jokes all night, then I'm staying here," I challenged.

"I suppose I can keep the others to myself," he said with a chuckle. "But you really do look amazing."

"Is there anything to eat before we go? I'm famished," I added, ignoring the compliment.

"I thought you might be." He gave me another quick once over before leading the way to the kitchen.

I shook my head, thankful for the excuse of food, and followed after him. As I entered the living room, he scooped up a platter from the counter and spun around to face me with what proved to be an enormous plate of pigs-in-a-blanket. I narrowed my eyes at him as he worked diligently to suppress a smile.

"Would you believe me if I told you it was all I had?"

"No. And it really is a shame that I'm allergic to sausage," I replied sadly as I delicately poked at the horrific pun.

His smile faded. "Wha—?"

I took advantage of his distraction and shoved three pigs in his mouth. Laughter burst out of me at the look of astonishment on his face. My breath came out in a wheeze as I clutched my sides. He chewed vigorously and swallowed, then promptly threw one at me. I caught it out of the air and popped it in my mouth.

"Nice," Michael exaggerated.

"Shut it. Now how about you take your bad jokes, sit that down, and share," I said, walking over to the peninsula.

"My jokes aren't bad, just unappreciated," he grumbled.

"We wouldn't be going another fancy-schmancy place where I'm liable to make a scene, would we?" I asked as the last little pig disappeared, barely even scratching the surface of my newfound hunger.

He laughed and shrugged into a coat. "Fancy, yes, but a little less on the schmancy side. More importantly, they're rumored to have the best steak in town."

"Do you keep a list or something?" I asked, plucking my own coat from the back of the couch and joining him at the front of the house.

"Maybe." He opened the door and I gave him a wry look as I walked through. Less than twenty minutes later we pulled up at our destination.

Sullivan's was indeed a superior steakhouse and never one that I'd envisioned myself being at, least of all with a man that looked like Michael.

"You really know how to charm a girl," I said, taking another bite of bloody steak swirled with fettuccine.

"Typically, from you I would assume that was sarcasm, but by the way you're annihilating that steak, I'm leaning more towards sincerity."

"Aren't we the pot calling the kettle black." I gestured at his plate with my knife.

"I don't know what you mean," he replied as he casually popped the last bite.

I smiled at how carefree it all was. Like at the house, we were relaxed and ourselves, without any of the pompous airs and anxiety that usually accompanied a legitimate date.

This evening isn't turning out so bad. He's goofy. I'm sassy. Werewolf stuff aside, it's almost like we're friends.

My libido tried to speak up, not in the least bit interested in a platonic relationship with this man. I shoved it down, determined not to ruin a good thing.

After dinner, Michael suggested we get some ice cream and meander about. The park we found ourselves in wasn't too unlike the one we'd visited before. Sounds of nightlife filled the evening, rebelling against the last cold snap before spring. I laughed to myself at our unique choice of treat that didn't at all fit the weather.

"Having a good time?" Michael asked, steering us down an unoccupied path.

I smiled as I captured a renegade drip of chocolate. "You could say that. I still think it's silly that we're eating ice cream when it's technically winter."

He shrugged. "I was in the mood for Rocky Road. Why? Is the cold bothering you?"

"Of course not." Truthfully, I probably would have been more comfortable without the coat.

The conversation drifted off as we continued our meandering. A light breeze ruffled the hem of my dress before moving on to tease the budding leaves.

"So, is this all werewolves do—eat?" I asked.

He laughed as I figured he would. "No, werewolves do lots of things."

"Like what?"

"Like..." He looked up into the deeply purple sky as if searching for examples. "I don't know. Listen to music, cook, work in the marketing department of a major firm," he said, dropping his head to meet my gaze with a smile.

"Oh really?" I teased as I smiled back. "And what else?"

"Go for walks in the park, howl at the moon."

I barked a short laugh that turned into a smaller series of giggles.

"I'm kidding. Well, mostly kidding," he amended. "Now let's see, what else? Read books, write poetry, ask out pretty ladies. The usual activities."

I turned to face him, my eyebrows raised. "That last one seemed specifically sexist."

He laughed coming to a complete stop and meeting my gaze. "I can't speak for other werewolves. I only know what I like to do."

"Ah," I feigned surprise. "I've heard about the pretty ladies." I made to continue our walk, but his fingers wrapping delicately around my wrist pulled me up short. I turned back to look at him and took in his oddly serious expression

It was only meant to be a playful comment.

Before I could apologize for the unintended slight, he said, "Don't believe everything you hear."

I blinked at a loss for an appropriate quip.

"Besides, I'm really only interested in one pretty lady these days," he added.

My breathing shallowed as I struggled to think of something to say, anything at all that would put us back on even ground.

Before I could come up with anything, he took a half step forward, leaned down, and kissed me. He settled a warm hand on my waist while the other came up to cup my face, emphasizing the gentle pressure of his lips. Shocked, I dropped my cone to the ground. The crunch as the waffle cone smashed against the concrete snapped me back to reality and I pulled back.

"What are you doing?"

"What does it look like I'm doing?" He countered with a hint of laughter and made to lean back in.

"Why?" His brow furrowed at the sharpness of the question.

"Because I like you," he said, looking even more confused.

"Since when?" I fired back, at a loss for how this evening could have turned so quickly.

"Since—" He cut himself off. "We've been on like eight dates."

"Those were lunch. And the other was for show. You said so yourself." He had. Hadn't he?

"You didn't think they were real?"

The tone of his question made me hesitate before responding. "Of course not. I figured you were calling them dates to get back at me for Charline." The words left a sour taste in my mouth, but that didn't make them less true.

"Charline hasn't said a word. If anything, she's probably

the reason there hasn't been so much as a whisper about us in the office."

"But you at least have heard some of her comments," I insisted.

"I promise you, I haven't. And what would it matter if I had?"

"What would it matter?" I scoffed.

"Sara, extenuating circumstances aside, I really like you. I've enjoyed spending time with you. I thought you did too."

I shook my head as my hormones screamed at me to believe him. But I couldn't. No matter how much I wanted to, people like Michael didn't waste time with people like me. I should know, I'd spent my whole life trying to figure out how to *be* one of those people.

"I did. I do." My words were as jumbled as my thoughts. "Ugh, this is so confusing."

I don't like this joke. It's not funny. Isn't my Stockholm Syndrome bad enough?

"What's confusing about it?"

"Everything. You're you and I'm me."

"Yeah, that's kind of what I like about it." He reached out as if to pull me back.

I shied away. "You don't get it. You're gorgeous and successful and interesting. I'm nothing. A meek little mouse. A wallflower no one sees. People like you do not date people like me," I tried to explain while fighting back tears.

This is so much worse than the prank Carter played on me in high school.

"I've never heard anything so absurd in my life," Michael countered.

"Well, you wouldn't, would you?" I snapped.

"Sara, even if you don't believe you're beautiful, you're witty and smart and all manner of other things," he said, refusing to back down.

I quickly turned away before he could see the tears threatening to well up. "I'm going to find a hotel tonight," I said, my voice quivering.

"Damn it all, you insufferable woman."

His hand encircled my arm and yanked me back towards him. He dominated my mouth with a kiss that swallowed my gasp.

Something inside of me that wasn't afraid took control. My fingers tangled in his shirt as I was lifted to my tiptoes. Heat curled from my bruising lips to touch all the deepest parts of me, making me tingle, and tighten, and ache. The kiss grew wild and more demanding, pure passion, raw and powerful in its intensity. And I wanted it. I wanted all of it.

"You taste great, like chocolate and starlight," he whispered into the heat-fogged night when we finally broke apart for breath.

All of my previous arguments seemed to have been seared away. I smiled in the dark, not really thinking about the fact that he could see it. "As long as it's not rabbit."

Who is this brazen woman?

"Much, much better than rabbit," he replied, his voice deep and husky. His mouth closed over mine again and the unbearable ache spread.

"We should probably head back," I whispered, my breathing ragged.

"You're right."

14

HEAT OF THE MOMENT

The door had barely closed behind us before I was swept up in another fiery kiss. I'd never experienced anything like it or my own eager response. Every sensation heightened almost to the point of stimulation overload. The cool wall pressing into my shoulders created a delicious contrast to the heat of Michael pressing against me. The satin fabric caressing my flesh emphasized his rougher hands.

I ran my fingers through his thick hair and across his broad back, reveling in the feel of his muscles shifting beneath the touch. His fierce kisses moved first to my jawline, then my neck. I gasped when his hand slid up my thigh and heat surged through my core.

Eyes closed, I leaned my head back, arching into him. I wasn't in control of what was happening. My body clearly had its own agenda, forcing my doubts to take a back seat. A heated growl vibrated through my chest where his lips traced the line of my collarbone, hot and needy and a little terrifying.

The world glitched.

Another growl echoed between my ears and rocked me

to the core. Teeth grazed my neck and my stomach twisted. Terror swam like ice through my veins. My vision blurred, no longer able to distinguish reality from the world of agony consuming me. Fear saturated every cell. But fear of what, I couldn't remember. There was only the overwhelming desire to stay alive.

I tried to shout for help, desperate to understand what was happening to me, but there was only that savage growl in my ears.

My fear sharpened into a bright point of pain, blinding me to everything else.

Teeth flashed in the moonlight. My arm jerked and spasmed sending out waves of nausea. Red glistened wetly on concrete. An aching numbness dominated my legs. Pain defined my being, dragging me into the merciless light. It flickered once and went out.

I finally found the escape I sought as I collapsed into darkness.

When I came to, the bed was soft and warm beneath me, though every inch of my body ached, like when I'd been sick with the flu for two weeks straight. A yawn cracked my jaw as my body insisted on wakefulness.

Ten more minutes.

I rolled over in pursuit of dissipating dreams of sunlight and an open field. Geese swam in a pond while birds chirped from high up in the trees. I looked up into a perfectly blue sky and the ground fell away.

My body gave a violent jolt at the sudden sensation of falling. The impact of hitting the ground rippled through my body, emphasizing the pervasive ache. My nails scrambled for purchase on the floor as I tried to get my bearings or at least my balance.

"Sara?" a voice said from somewhere above me.

I froze. Slowly, I lifted my gaze up to find a bleary-eyed man peering down at me.

"Sara. Calm down."

I shook my head. Big mistake. The room titled and swam, adding to my disorientation.

"Focus on me, Sara," the deep voice insisted.

My eyes squeezed shut.

"Sara..." A creak of the bed suggested that its occupant was now moving towards me.

My eyes flew open in panic to confirm this. I mentally screamed at my body to move, but it refused to obey. As his foot lowered to the floor, I finally managed an awkward, backward shuffle. Elation surged through me then promptly died when I backed into the wall.

The man lowered himself to his hands and knees, his dark hair falling in short waves around his face, then inched closer. Shushing noises blended almost perfectly with the near-deafening sound of blood rushing in my ears. My breath came in short pained gasps as I struggled and failed to catch it. The soreness in my body took on new levels as every muscle tensed in anticipation.

He shifted closer until he could reach for my face. I craned my neck, searching for an escape I knew wasn't there. My nails slid across the floor in a useless attempt to get farther away. Firm hands wrapped around my muzzle and forced me to look at my captor. His eyes bored into mine and my own widened in response. My heart faltered in my chest, refusing to beat.

"Sara, try to remember."

Remember? Remember what?

"Shit, the change was too abrupt; you didn't have time to adjust."

Change?

"I'm going to let go now. Don't panic."

With exaggerated slowness he released my face. Tension coiled in my legs. He slid back slightly and a clear passage opened up. I darted forward and fell once more into darkness.

The scent of summer pine wrapped around me in a comforting cocoon. I could almost see the dappled sunlight drifting through the branches. A deep inhale brought all the scents of home and something else. I opened my eyes and found not leaves, but finely woven navy threads. A groan drifted out of me. The ache from before was virtually gone, leaving in its wake an embarrassment that would have normally set my face blazing.

Thank God for small mercies.

I shifted and realized the reason Michael's smell was so intense was because my head was currently being cradled in his lap. A gentle hand landed on my head and brushed the fur back.

Maybe it was all a dream. I never actually changed back. Werewolves aren't real. I'm not one and neither is Michael.

I sighed contentedly into the remarkably soothing touch.

"It's okay, Sara. I'm here."

In five words, my beautiful fantasy went up in smoke. If Michael knew I was Sara, then that meant everything else was real too.

How is it possible to screw up so royally? We can't just be friends, so I have to sabotage everything else too?

I shifted in an attempt to slide off of the couch, but he thwarted me by encircling my middle in an iron grip and I whimpered in defeat.

I can't even retreat gracefully.

"Oh no you don't, not again," he said, and released me to resume petting my head. "You have nothing to be upset about. Believe it or not, your sudden change in a heated situation is not that far out of the ordinary. I realize your circumstances are a little different, but you need to accept that these things do and will happen. I was worried that I'd hurt you more than anything. And when you woke up and couldn't remember..." His hand paused mid stroke.

I glanced up at him.

"Don't scare me like that," he said softly.

I whimpered again for lack of a better way to express myself.

"Please don't be upset. I promise, what happened to you is perfectly normal. Come to think of it, that's probably why most young *weres* are discouraged from dating humans. Control is something that has to be learned, it doesn't happen overnight."

I looked away from his well-meant assurances and moved out of reach. It was mortifying enough that I'd changed in the middle of the hottest make-out session of my life, but having him make excuses for me was worse.

"Sara, please," he said, letting me go.

I continued to retreat until I huddled at the far side of the couch in my own personal bubble of misery.

He gave a sigh that mirrored my own hopeless state. "Okay then. What do you say we start working on that control?"

My ears perked forward and I looked at him out of the corner of my eye, curious despite myself.

"You heard me. I'm not going to sit here and let you wallow, you're stronger than that."

I let out a huff of disagreement.

"Nope. No arguing. Get off your rump. You're changing

back," he said, then reached over and pushed me off the couch.

It was only by the grace of my newfound reflexes that I didn't land in an uncoordinated heap. I straightened up to my full three-foot-five and glared at him.

He affected a look of pure innocence. "What? You were taking too long."

My glare instantly morphed into a glower.

"Look, we could wait around for you to decide to do it on your own, but I don't think you have that many sick days left."

I narrowed my eyes.

"Don't look at me like that. It's past time you started working on control."

Okay, he had a point, but we both knew I hadn't a clue how to go about it on purpose.

"I'm going to talk you through the process, then give you some space." He paused a moment to let what he was saying sink in, before continuing with said instructions. "The first thing you're going to need to do is try and relax. Yes, I know, easier said than done considering what is about to happen, but it's kind of important. If your body believes there's danger, the wolf won't let go. You'll have to put aside your fear if you want to accomplish anything. Clear your mind."

Easy for him to say, he grew up with this nonsense. It's not like he's only just learned that werewolves are freaking real.

"Stop making that face or it will get stuck that way," he teased.

I huffed again.

"Seriously, Sara, lighten up. Now where was I? Right. Once you relax," he paused and gave me a very pointed look, "then you're going to focus on what it's like to be human. Think about sensations—how does the world feel from that perspective? Once that is fairly set, try to move towards it."

I blinked.

"You look confused."

Understatement of the century.

"Okay, what about this? Try to remember how you were feeling the first time you changed back. All you need is to get the first couple dominoes going, the rest will take care of itself. Ready to give it a shot?" he asked way too optimistically.

I immediately began shaking my head.

"Well, it doesn't really matter if you are or not, because you're going to anyway."

I loudly blew air out and he gave me a no nonsense look in return. With what dignity I had left, I followed him down the hall and to the guest bath. He stepped aside to let me pass into the pristinely kept space. My paw hesitated on the threshold, but with Michael cutting off the only exit, there was no choice but to forge ahead. My nails clicked on the white tile as I padded into the room. The soft yellow glow made the space almost serene.

"I'll give you a chance to do it on your own first. Remember what I said." He gave me an encouraging thumbs up before closing the door.

This is absurd. I can't do this. I'm a failure as a human and now I'm a failure as a werewolf.

I laid down on the cool surface and prepared to wait indefinitely. There was simply no way to convince myself I wanted the agony of the change, even if it did mean I would be human again.

For all the good that's doing me.

Time continued to pass with nothing more remarkable than an itchy nose. To my surprise, Michael did not come check on me.

He better not have left.

I lifted my head from my paws and stared at the very round, gold-finished door knob.

Not a chance in hell I'm opening that without hands.

I sighed in despair and dropped my head. The tile between my paws glistened brightly, polished enough that I could see my reflection. Looking at the image, I could almost believe it was me. The hair was the same color brown, if anything, it was more vibrant. Even the lines of my face resembled that of my human one, though that might have been a stretch. But my eyes, my eyes were distinctly human and undeniably mine.

A mental image of myself locked into place, truer than any thought. My abdomen clenched and the world turned inside out and upside down all at once.

I will not throw up on the floor.

The thought came viciously coherent despite the torture clawing its way across my body. Nails splayed on the tile, stretching to impossible lengths. Ribs gave a sickening crunch as they caved inward. I cried out as my knees buckled and sent my kneecaps crashing into the tile with an audible crack. My skin burned and itched everywhere. The only thing that prevented me from tearing it off was the disjointed state of my hands.

After an excruciating length of time, the pain faded to mere echoes. My breath came in harsh gasps that reverberated off the small, tiled space. The door opened with a creak of hinges that was more like a scream to my over-sensitive ears.

"Are you alright?"

I glanced up at Michael standing in the doorway totally unconcerned by the fact that I was naked. "Can I get some water?" I croaked, the words barely more than a whisper of air.

He disappeared without another word. While he was gone, I focused on trying to stand. My sweaty hands slipped on the slick tile and I bit back a cry as my knees were reintroduced to the unforgiving tile.

I took a deep breath and tried again, this time putting less weight on my hands and using my core to pull myself upright. My legs wobbled beneath me, already unaccustomed to the bipedal way of life. I reached out to grab a folded towel and skidded. My arm flailed out and met with the counter in my attempt to prevent another fall. I ignored the new throbbing pain and adjusted my grip so the Formica surface could steady me.

By the time Michael returned with a glass already wet with condensation, I'd managed to wrap a towel around myself and was stable enough that I wasn't worried I'd fall if I took a step.

"Thank you," I said as calmly as I could.

He opened his mouth, no doubt to inquire after my well-being, clearly having noticed my fresh bruises and the several broken tiles.

"I know you want to talk about this, but I want to shower first. I feel..." Words failed and gestures fell short.

He simply nodded and left again.

The water was harsh at first, nearly blistering even after I turned it down, but it quickly became a steaming blanket of comfort. While lost in the fog, my thoughts wandered back to how I'd gotten into such a horrible position. The embarrassment was almost enough to make me never want to leave the bathroom.

I sighed and ducked my head under the pounding spray. That had been my chance. A chance I hadn't even known I had. He'd never want to touch me again after this. And who could blame him?

When I met Michael in the living room, I'd made a sort

of peace with my humiliating display. Against my better judgment, my gaze wandered over to the wall by the door expecting to see blood and torn fabric like when I'd returned home from my first shift. But there was nothing, not a single trace of my change or of the dress I'd been wearing.

Mental note to self: stop investing in dresses, they're clearly bad luck.

"Before you say anything, I want to apologize." Michael's words caught me off guard and I swung my gaze back to him.

"What for? It's not like you're the one who freaked out."

"I lied," he said, dropping his gaze to the floor.

"About what?"

Oh God, here it is. The truth about that stunt he pulled in the park. He never meant any of it.

"I said I'd give you privacy, but I was right outside the door the whole time," he went on.

"Michael," I started, then stopped. It wasn't what I'd feared, but I failed to see what the issue was. After all, I'd been the one who apparently couldn't enjoy being in the moment.

"I realize I shouldn't have done that, but after this morning, I was worried, and..."

"Michael, stop, it's okay. I understand," I emphasized.

He didn't look relieved.

"Honestly, it's a little comforting to know," I tried again.

"You don't get it." An emotion I didn't understand thickened his voice. "The change is a really personal thing, it's when we're at our most vulnerable. What I did was a serious violation of trust. I mean, occasionally there are exceptions, but they're rare and usually involve permission or at least some sort of understanding. I realize that werewolf etiquette might be a little beyond you right now, but that's no excuse for my behavior. I know better," he finished then turned away and flopped onto the couch. His head hung in his hand, his fingers twisting in his hair.

"I don't really know what to say, Michael, except, you're right, I don't understand how everything works, but what's done is done. And quite frankly, I need you to stop feeling guilty, because I would like to talk to you about what happened."

He lifted his head so I could see his brown eyes peering back. He still looked sullen, but didn't try to resume apologies.

"Thank you. Now, can you explain how it works? I know you sort of walked me through starting the change, but what exactly is happening? And don't worry about sugar-coating, I think I'm a little past that," I added with a small smile.

He let out a large sigh and finally dropped his hands. "It's definitely not a pretty process. The only reason we survive at all is because we have super-accelerated healing."

"Okay, I can understand that. What else?" I prompted.

He shrugged and took on an almost scholarly tone as he proceeded to break down every gory detail from breaking bones to ultra-sensitive fresh skin. I nodded along, appreci-ating that he didn't hold back even when the explanation was gruesome. When he finished, he knotted his fingers together and leaned forward to rest his forearms on his knees.

"And eventually, I'll be able to choose when all of this starts?" I chewed my lip a moment then met his patient gaze. I'd asked before, but after what had happened, I wasn't sure how much faith I had in the answer.

He stood and grabbed both my hands. "Sara, you will master this and I will do everything I can to help."

"Will it always hurt?" I asked barely above a whisper.

His expression saddened. "You'll get more used to it as time goes on."

It was the answer I expected, but that didn't make it any easier to hear. I removed my hands from his grasp and wrapped my arms around myself as if somehow it could keep me whole while I was so clearly falling apart. This was my life now, assuming I stayed alive long enough to live it.

15

———

A REAL RUN

Michael assembled his duffel with a precision that spoke of years of practice. I glanced at my own which had not received the same level of care. I'd had a whole week to brace myself for this, but I didn't feel any more prepared than the first time. Okay, maybe a *little*.

"How long will it be before I don't have to change at the full moon?" I asked as he zipped his bag shut.

He let out a sigh that sounded a bit like resignation. "Resisting isn't easy. Even with years of practice, it's rarely foolproof."

"So, I should definitely clear my calendar?" I quipped. Sarcasm, I could handle. Turning into a wolf in less than three hours, not so much.

"Yeah, you might want to consider it," he said with a laugh.

"Werewolves should get extra sick days," I grumbled. *I'm definitely running low.*

"It's usually only a problem when the moon rises early. Typically, you'll be able to go to work that day, change later in the evening, then return to work the following day."

I stared back at him in amazement as it fully registered that he truly had been doing this his whole life.

"What's that look for? I'm serious, unless the moon rises in the middle of the day, you're pretty much in the clear," he added.

"That's convenient." Between both of my experiences, I was shaping up to be an utter disaster as a werewolf.

"Sara," Michael said as his fingers landed lightly on the side of my face.

Electric awareness surged through every cell. I wasn't sure whether to be relieved or disheartened that he hadn't made any attempt to resume intimacy between us over the last week. I swallowed past the sudden lump in my throat and met his steady gaze.

"I will be with you every step of the way. You don't have to do this alone." His thumb stroked across my cheek, leaving a trail of tingles in its wake.

The air in the room suddenly seemed thinner as if somehow, I was standing hundreds of feet in the air as opposed to a little bedroom in North Carolina.

Maybe it wasn't a one-off. What if he really does want to be with me and the dates aren't excuses to give me bad news?

A part of me still believed the only reason I was even staying at his place was because he felt responsible and that everything that had transpired was actually a product of guilt—reverse Stockholm, if that was even a thing. But then, there was the way his hand held my face, like he was balancing a feather on the tips of his fingers, and the way his brown eyes seemed to be searching mine for the answer to a question we both were asking.

I should say something.

Before I got the chance, his cell phone vibrated and shattered the fragile moment. He dropped his hand to silence it. "That's our cue. Time to hit the road."

My face burned, emphasizing the cold absence of his touch. I looked up through my lashes as he slung the duffel over his shoulder as if nothing had happened. My rebelliously optimistic heart sank.

I'm his project, nothing more.

"You ready?" he asked, even though he knew I already was.

"Yeah," I said quietly and followed him out of the house. As we approached our ride, I stalled. The bright yellow Jeep sat completely open to all of the elements. "You took the sides off."

"It's a beautiful night. There's no reason we shouldn't enjoy all of it." His bag made a decisive thunk in the back and he held out a hand for mine.

I scurried the last few feet and handed it over so that it could receive the same treatment. Once the bags were secure, he turned to look at me wordlessly. I tucked a loose strand of hair behind my ear and folded my arms as if the barrier could somehow protect me from my own feelings of insecurity. He continued to stare without uttering so much as a syllable. Finally, he looked away and I let out the breath I was holding. We walked around to our respective seats and buckled in. Within moments, the engine roared to life, signaling that we were officially on our way.

In my continued pursuit of avoidance, I focused on the drive itself. Gradually the stoplights and green street signs gave way to a county road with scarcely any traffic to be seen. Open highway and giant trees quickly swallowed suburbia and the city skyline.

If I didn't know better, I'd think we were headed to my parents' place.

After a while of appreciating the breeze gusting through the open cabin I asked, "How far are we going?"

"It's about an hour out of town. This time of year, the

park isn't too busy. Even then, we'll need to swing wide to make sure we go to the far side. All in all, I'd say we have another forty-five minutes or so."

"Right, don't want any adventurous campers stumbling across a pair of werewolves."

He gave me a look out of the corner of his eye.

"What?" I asked.

"If you're thinking about backing out, it's a little too late," Michael said as he navigated the Jeep down the county highway.

"I know, I know. If I chicken out now, I'll never gain control," I lamented, yet again trying to steel my resolve.

"I was going with it's almost dark and we'd literally not make it back anywhere safe before you change."

Cold spread across my face as all of the blood drained from it. I gripped the side door hard enough to hear the plastic strain over the wind.

Michael glanced quickly in my direction and added, "But that too."

My mouth twisted into a sour scowl as I glared at him.

"Sara," he sighed, "you have to do this sometime. You can't be afraid of this your whole life—this *is* your life now. Besides, doing it out here will feel better, feel right. Trust me." He gave my knee a friendly pat.

I took a deep breath and released my death hold on the door. He gave me a reassuring smile, then carefully maneuvered down a dirt road that looked like it hadn't been used in the last decade. The scent of pine hung heavy on the breeze. Shadows played on the ground as we slipped past trees determined to persevere against the harsh bite of winter. Here and there fresh growths of green could be spotted, but they were gone too fast to see more than a blur.

An eerie awareness of the approaching night permeated my skin. I scratched absently at my arm and shifted several times unable to find a comfortable position while I stared out at the deepening twilight. Michael glanced repeatedly in my direction at each movement, but neglected to comment.

By the time we parked, the sun sat like a giant red ball on the horizon. Michael immediately got out and walked around to grab our bags.

I stayed seated until the last remnants of vibration from the vehicle dissipated. The ominous sun glowed like a fiery harbinger of doom between the rows of pines. Each passing second bringing the day closer and closer to the end.

I swallowed back the acid inching its way up my throat and slipped out of the Jeep. The door clunked shut loud enough to startle me and several nearby birds. I looked up from my cringe to see Michael eying me speculatively. I quickly straightened up and re-tied my hair in a tight tail. He zipped the keys into an internal pocket of his duffel, then slung his bag on before tossing me mine and waltzing towards the tree line.

I fumbled the catch and made it two steps before stopping. I whirled to look at the Jeep and called after Michael. "Aren't you worried about someone stealing it?"

He looked back, his gaze swinging from me to the Jeep and back again. "Not really."

"But anyone could walk up and—I don't know—hot wire it or something," I insisted.

A smile played on Michael's lips. "Do you see any potential thieves around? We literally drove to the middle of nowhere to be as far away from people as possible. If they're that motivated to steal my truck, they're welcome to it. That's what insurance is for," he said. Then with laughter in his eyes, he turned and disappeared into the darkening shadows.

"It was a fair concern," I grumbled to myself.

"You're stalling!" Michael's voice called from far ahead.

I let out an "Eep" and scurried to catch up.

He led us on a path that aimed deep into the forest. Twigs and other dry things snapped under foot while the night wrapped around us. As the light died, my senses focused on other things. Squirrels scrabbled against bark as they found their way home. Tiny feet and their tiny steps whispered on the breeze. When an owl hooted overhead, all the scurrying stopped for a heartbeat, then resumed with renewed purpose.

I spun around at each minuscule sound in search of its source. My duffel switched from shoulder to shoulder, never lasting more than a few seconds in any one position. I rubbed my arms, though I wasn't cold, and did my best to keep up with Michael who was virtually silent compared to me and the rest of the animals. Each step clawed at my nerves, heightening the anxiety I'd been fighting since before we left the house, until it was all I could do not to shriek and bolt back to the jeep.

"That's it. This is as far as I go." My bag landed with a muted thud on the leaf strewn ground. Something scratched my face and I ripped out a stray twig along with my pony-tail. "You've dragged me heaven only knows how far into these creepy-ass woods and I'm done," I snapped, my chest heaving as unexpected anger flowed through me.

Michael stood a good ten yards ahead of me, but he was by my side in an instant. "I'm sorry, I should have given you a better idea of what to expect. We don't have to go any farther. Here's fine," he said, scooping up my duffel.

Guilt flashed white hot through me at my unprovoked outburst. I shook my head and held my arms. "No, I'm sorry. I know you wanted to get deep into the woods..." Abruptly, I realized I was shaking. It didn't take a genius to know it wasn't because of the cold. I looked up at Michael as fear took root.

"You're going to be okay," he said calmly. "Take a deep breath and try to relax."

I nodded and he stepped away. My first attempt stuck in my throat, but I managed the second and another well enough. I placed my hands on my knees and focused on one steady breath at a time. Slowly, the feeling of someone sitting on my chest eased. While I worked on not collapsing, Michael checked out the area where we'd stopped.

"We need to get ready," he said as he completed his circuit. "I normally prefer more cover, but here should be fine."

At the sound of a zipper, my head snapped up. His jeans slithered to the ground leaving his legs as bare as his chest. He snatched them off the ground and folded them along with the shirt.

Stop staring.

While this wasn't technically the first time I'd seen Michael naked, it didn't diminish the sight. My pulse slowed as I raked my gaze shamelessly over his naked body. The last remnants of twilight reached out to caress every sculpted inch of him and there was no denying that even in a human shape, he looked like he belonged out here.

I doubt the same could be said of me.

Abruptly, he met my blatant gaze and gave me a wink. I choked on my latest steady breath and almost fell over. He gave me one of those carefree smiles that came so naturally to him, then promptly disappeared into the trees, presumably to hide his clothes.

I waited an eternity for him to come back. With each passing moment, my measured breathing became harder to keep in check. My hands flexed repeatedly as I paced in place. My steady breaths turned into harsh pants. As a last resort, I tried counting to ten, only to discover that making it past seven was near impossible.

How long does it take to bury a damn duffel?

The barest crunch of leaves reached my ears. I jumped, realizing a fraction too late that the sound had come from the same direction Michael had vanished. "It's about freaking time," I snapped. "Now how am I supposed to hide my bag? Is there some kind of protocol? Are some leaves better than others? Do I need to involve dirt?" My slew of inane questions stopped as I finished turning around.

At the edge of the trees stood a very, *very* large wolf. My mouth went dry and my heart pumped furiously. The dark creature sat and cocked its head to the side. A fresh bout of anger seared away my sudden fear.

"Seriously? Are you trying to give me a heart attack? And what happened to me changing first?" He barked and I gave another involuntary jump. "Stop that." I took a deep breath and rolled my shoulders in an attempt to ease the tension gathered there. The motion did nothing.

I can do this.

Not like I really have a choice.

I dismissed the bitter reality check and focused on doing what I should have been doing while I waited for Michael to return. My shirt came off less than gracefully, quickly followed by an equally awkward attempt to remove my pants. In retrospect, removing my shoes first probably would've helped. I looked up, finally bare to the elements, expecting to see Michael laughing at me. To my surprise, his back was turned.

I shoved my things into the duffel and walked over to where he sat patiently waiting. Once I was by his side, he led me over to where his clothes were concealed, then walked me several yards away to where I could hide mine. When I was satisfied that they were sufficiently hidden, I returned to the area where we'd stopped. He was waiting for me in the small clearing. He held my gaze for a moment, then silently turned and padded out of sight.

Okay, I can do this. It won't be that bad, and it'll be over quickly.

Who am I kidding? This is going to be awful.

I looked up at the purpling sky and spied the first stars twinkling to life. Michael had told me how to be human again, but had neglected to say how it went the other way. I tried to remember what it was like to be on four legs instead of two, what my tail felt like, how everything looked and sounded, but I kept coming back to when I was a wolf, I wasn't me—wasn't human.

Maybe I can get Michael to growl at me.

I dismissed the idea with more reluctance than I cared to admit, but the idea had merit. I couldn't only remember the mostly good things.

The fear of that first night as I ran for my life spread through me. Streaks of light zipping past as I ran faster than I'd ever been able to before. The pure smell of water and the strange way it tasted. Crashing through trees and leaping high enough to fly. Pain that defined every breath, each step more determined than the last to survive.

A telltale spasm jerked my abdomen.

My breath fogged as I gasped at the pain. Knowledge of what was happening did literally nothing to ease the transition. If anything, it made it worse. Now, I was waiting for the sickening feel of my ribs caving in and then pushing back out in a different shape. Waves of nausea poured over me, threatening to swallow me whole.

I clutched my stomach with claws that pierced the sensitive skin and looked up in search of peace. White light encompassed my world as the impossibly large moon filled my eyes. A shudder wracked my body as I continued to stare, completely enraptured. Then the change began in earnest.

Time became a blur, an hour, fifteen minutes, a few seconds, it was hard to say. When it was done, I lay there panting. Once my breathing steadied, I pressed my front paws into the earth. They sank slightly as I maneuvered myself off of the ground. My legs quivered, but didn't buckle, while my ear twitched as the muted whisper of leaves shifting tickled it. I stared into the trees in search of the culprit.

Michael.

I lifted my nose to the air to confirm my suspicions. The light breeze carried with it the woodsy scent I associated with him and a heavy dose of musk. A shiver rippled through me and I took a step forward. At my movement, a patch of darkness detached itself from the rest and made its way towards me. Despite enhanced vision that defied normal perception, it remained an amorphous shape.

I tensed, a sudden bout of human fear leaking through my confidence. The inky form got closer until it solidified into the wolf I'd seen earlier. As he approached, it occurred to me that this was the first time Michael and I had been wolves together or that I'd seen this side of him. The moon shone on his glossy coat, helping to distinguish him from the shadows.

He walked forward, dipping his head past mine. The heat of his breath slid past my protective coat to caress the shielded skin beneath. I gave a shiver at the peculiar, yet oddly intimate sensation. Michael took a step back and I met his eyes. Impossible as it was, I knew he was smiling his usual grin and I couldn't help but return it. The night around us filled with sounds and smells I'd never associated with the woods before, yet this moment was still, expectant.

Without warning, he spun around and bounded into the

trees with barely a crunch of leaf to betray him. I raced after
him. All awkwardness was forgotten as I soared through the
foliage, weaving in and out of the dense undergrowth. The
wolf knew exactly what to do, so I let her.

My body bunched and stretched as I covered ground at a
brisk pace, staying behind Michael. With every pound of my
paws on the earth I got closer and closer to the wolf inside.
It was through her eyes that I could see this world was not
all black and moonlight. Michael's coat was dark, but not
indistinguishable from the night. The trees weren't dead,
they were waiting, their breath held in anticipation of
spring. The world wasn't quiet, it was bursting with activity.
And I was part of it all.

Suddenly, the shadow I was chasing disappeared. I
skidded to a halt and searched the moonlit night. My ears
swiveled in search of my companion and only found tiny
creatures going about their evenings. A vise tightened
around my chest as fear began to take root. A twig snapped
and I jumped to face the source.

Without any other sound to betray him, Michael burst
through the undergrowth and barreled into me. I let out a
grunt and swung an accusatory glare at him. He huffed a
laugh and danced on all four feet, looking for all the world
like he was prancing in place. I cocked my head to the side
and he dropped his to rest between his paws. I huffed my
own laugh. His tail, which was sticking straight up, wagged
slightly. When I didn't respond, he rolled his eyes, then
closed them and placed a paw across his face. I yipped a
laugh.

He can't possibly be serious.

He cracked an eye at me, then promptly closed it.

Oh shit, he's serious.

My gaze swept over the forest surrounding us in search
of a decent hiding place. I chose a direction at random and

ran as hard as I could until the sight of a hollow amidst some roots got my attention. My pace slowed as I approached to make sure it wasn't inhabited. Seeing that it was available, I made myself comfortable. It was a tight squeeze and by the time I settled down, the distinct sound of another large animal approaching was thudding through the ground.

My breath slowed and my body tensed. I fought the impulse to peek out and stayed frozen. The thuds got closer and my breath stilled altogether. Then they moved along, leaving me alone and undetected. I barely didn't bark in triumph.

A moment later, that victory was forgotten as a muzzle shoved into my hiding place. I yelped loud enough to raise the dead and snapped at the intruder. The muzzle vanished and I began the arduous process of removing myself from the cramped space. When I finally emerged, I gave myself a hearty shake.

Michael stood there, tail-wagging, apparently quite proud of himself. I blew air through my nose, making it clear that I didn't appreciate the rude treatment. He huffed and walked in a circle, then stopped to look at me, tail wagging. I stared back. He gave a short bark and I caved, rolling my eyes as he had done before. He danced excitedly as I laid down. I gave him another eye roll before closing them. In a whisper of air, he was gone.

This is ridiculous. I don't even know what number to count to. Ugh. One Mississippi, Two Mississippi, Three Mississippi. Right, that's enough of that. Surely he has enough of a head start.

I stood back up and immediately began sniffing the ground in search of which direction he'd taken. The deep musky scent wrapped in pine sprung out of the backdrop of other scents. With an inward snicker, I took off, but after a few yards, lost it. I yipped in frustration and retraced my steps to find it again.

This time, I didn't barrel off, but took my time and only lost it twice before it finally got stronger. I warily approached a set of bushes large enough to hide a wolf of Michael's size. The fact that it was a probable hiding spot made me distrust it all the more, especially after the merry goose chase I'd been led on.

I placed each step carefully, barely shifting the leaves beneath me. My breath shallowed with only the icy fog to betray it. Even my heart seemed to slow so that the solid thump was barely even audible to me. A hush fell over the night as my legs coiled, prepared to spring.

A sharp bark behind me, sent me sprawling. I curled up in a mortified ball as Michael crowed his triumph. He let out a small whine, which I ignored. Then another louder one followed by a snout nosing my side. When I didn't react, he pushed hard enough to roll me. I snapped at him and he danced out of reach.

He gave a soft bark. I stuck my nose in the air and looked away. He made another low whine deep in his throat. I glanced at him out of the corner of my eye to see that his tail had fallen and even covered in fur and not remotely human, he looked discouraged. I barked loud and short. Instantly, his tail came back up. I stood up and he dropped to the ground. My tail wagged and he closed his eyes. Then it was my turn again.

The game continued until we came across a stream to drink. The chill liquid slid over my tongue and quenched my thirst. I lifted my head, enjoying how the cold traveled down my throat to pool in my belly. Michael bumped my side and I looked over to see his muzzle glistening in the white light. His eyes flashed yellow as he turned to gaze off into the underbrush.

I cocked my head and listened intently. My ears strained to pick out one sound among many. Then I heard it. A small scurry followed the muffled thump of two large feet. No sooner did I identify it, than Michael was off. I surged after him. By the time I caught up, there was streak of gray darting haphazardly in front of him. The moment I saw the long-eared creature, something deep inside came to life.

Abruptly the rabbit switched direction and doubled back to race straight at me. Unprepared for such a move, I came to a full stop. The creature darted between my frozen legs and I looked up in time to see Michael almost collide into me. He veered at the last second while I braced for impact. When he almost immediately returned, I knew it was too late, I'd lost it. The belief was further emphasized when he made a noise deep in his throat that was part huff, part growl.

I hung my head in shame. My perfect opportunity, and I'd choked. After a minute, Michael walked up beside me, pressing his weight into me as he passed. I looked up at him hopefully. Now that rabbit was off the menu, and rather than start our game up again, Michael led us on a slow walk through the forest, strangely reminiscent of our human stroll through the park. It was a nice change of pace that let me appreciate the night and the wonders it held.

After a while, I realized we were heading back to our clothes. We reached mine first and Michael continued on to his own. Now came the real test. The moon still flowed hot in my blood, but if I was ever going to have any modicum of control, I had to do this. I focused on how the world looked and felt when I was human, on how I looked and felt.

Like before, nothing happened. I shook my ruff out and thought about what it was like not to have fur. Despair threatened to creep in when the change finally took hold. I took a deep breath and did my best to ride out the tide of unadulterated pain that threatened to drown me. Time dragged by while my body twisted into unnatural positions in pursuit of one right one.

When there hadn't been any pops or cracks for a while, I pushed up to my feet. A faint breeze brushed against my fresh skin, feeling more like water than air. After a night in fur, it felt wrong to be in nothing but skin. I quickly began searching for my clothes. Leaves and twigs scattered at my touch, but no duffel was forthcoming.

They have to be around here somewhere.

Frustrated, I straightened up and spied Michael walking towards me. His duffel hung carelessly in one hand, the contents threatening to spill out, but not a stitch graced his body. My heart hammered against my ribs as a flush burned its way across my bare skin.

"Would it have killed you to wait a minute?" The words came out hoarse, but gained strength.

His only response was to rake his eyes over me hungrily. It may have been dark, but I didn't need enhanced vision to see that he liked what he saw.

"Sara," he said at last, his voice deep and husky.

I swallowed hard and shifted my weight from one foot to the other. He mirrored the movement, using it to bring him closer. The breeze shifted and I found myself downwind. The smell of earth, pine and what could only be described as desire swirled around me. The wolf inside crashed against the logic that this was a bad idea with enough force to frighten me. She wanted what she wanted.

He took another step closer and I took a nervous one backward.

"Michael, I...I..."

I don't know, I wanted to say. I'm scared. We've been down this road before and it only ends in catastrophe. This is the moon, it isn't real. But it was too late, he was already in front of me. I flinched when he moved a sweat-soaked strand of hair away from my face. The haze cleared slightly from his eyes, though the nearness of him wrought havoc on my senses. The wolf continued to fight against my doubts, pushing relentlessly to get her way.

"You're not likely to change again so soon. I doubt you have the energy for it, especially since you're so new." His words were soft and calm, but they also held a promise.

I searched his face. I wanted him so much it hurt. It wasn't just the wolf. *I* did. But there were still so many doubts. What if this is an effect of the change? What if this is a one time, heat-of-the-moment? What if someone finds us? What if he changes his mind?

Of all the insecurities racing through my mind, only one made it out. "Is it safe?"

"I'll never let anything happen to you," he said and his mouth closed over mine.

Every sensitized fiber of me reacted. Any reservations or doubts that had accumulated were washed away by an undeniable wave of desire. I reached out for him, hungry for more. The instant our bodies touched I became fire. My skin was still hypersensitive from the change and everywhere his hands glided a new inferno leapt to life. He pulled me in tight, his groan bordering on a growl. For a split second, my human mind and my new wolf heart were at odds.

I pushed him and the indecision away. "I trust you."

His eyes seemed to simultaneously burn and soften as he caressed the side of my face. I licked my lips, tasting him there. He stole a sweeter kiss that stroked its way through me, warming everything in its path. I moaned into him and the night took the sound.

As he lowered me to the ground, I didn't care that we were out in the middle of the woods. If he wasn't worried, then neither was I. When I looked up at him from my new position, he seemed to be soaking in the sight of me laid bare beneath him. Instead of the warm blush that I would have normally had at being so appraised, all I could feel was the moonlight on my skin and humming in my veins.

I reached up and pulled him down, snaring him with a kiss the moment he was within reach. My lips healed as fast as they bruised while my fingers traced every inch of him I could reach.

Need burned in my veins, blinding me to anything but him and this moment. He rolled us and leveraged his new position to run his hands down the length of my back and cup my ass. I threaded my fingers through the downy hair on his chest as I shifted to kiss along the side of his neck. He let out a choked groan when I sucked a hickey into his collar.

He snatched a hungry kiss that seemed to echo my desperation then nudged me into a seated position where I straddled his waist. I flattened my hand on his chest and lifted my hips so I could guide his hard length where I wanted it most.

"Wait," he said as his fingers delicately wrapped around my wrist.

"What's wrong?"

"We don't exactly have protection."

I floundered for a way to get what my body ached for and still be smart. "What about the pill?"

"Not really sure how well that would hold up to were-wolf genetics." His crooked smile somehow banished the hiccup of uncertainty and set every butterfly known to man fluttering in my stomach, maybe even a few moths.

"Then what?"

"Like this." Michael placed his hands on my hips and gently brought me back down so that his erection nested between my thighs, then encouraged me to move.

I put my hands on his chest and gave an experimental roll of my hips. The ache turned to sparks as I rubbed myself along the length of him, shocked at how much stimulation the move created without him entering me.

He took a shuddering breath that edged on a moan as I ground myself against his erection. The cords of his neck stood out as he fought to keep from thrusting up and finishing claiming me. His hands flexed on my hips until his right hand drifted between my legs. The pad of his thumb teased at my already sensitive bud and my movements became more erratic as I approached the precipice of release.

Moonlight seemed to pour out of me as I tripped over the edge and fell into ecstasy. I continued to chase my fading bliss as Michael finally moved with me. His hands returned to my hips and I quickened my pace, eager to see him lose himself as much as I had. When his hands shook, I knew he was close.

I lifted off of him slightly, leaned down, and kissed him. Our tongues tangled together while my hand wrapped around his length. I used the moisture trapped between us and stroked him, keeping my grip firm. A few slow strokes later, his breath caught and he released into my hand with a groan.

"Fuck," he growled as he continued to come undone.

"That was the idea," I said with a cheeky grin.

His head fell back to the earth as he let out a full body laugh that shook me and threatened my precarious perch. I couldn't help but join him, feeling lighter than I had in years. Half-imagined dreams paled in comparison to the reality of this moment. The things that had held me back vanished and we laughed in our bliss with only the full moon as our witness.

16

THE TWISTED TRUTH

Exhilaration and contentment hummed through me as I lay on the forest floor. A heavy mist hung in the air, obscuring the canopy above, punctuated by spears of golden light. Even without a stitch on, the chill didn't touch me. The dense foliage beneath us made a pillow softer than any bed and the sweet chorus of birds was all that broke the hush of the morning.

"Amazing, isn't it?" Michael's soft whisper drifted beneath the melody. He squinted up at the canopy. "We should probably gather our things and start making our way back." He trailed his fingers lightly along my side and a wave of goose pimples rose in response.

I let out a small gasp and his gaze flicked up to mine. A smile played on his lips while his hand caressed the exposed flesh. He leaned down to steal a kiss that had me arching into him for more. My soft sigh of disappointment chased after him when he released me and cast another quick glance at the distant canopy.

I followed his gaze and squinted. "How do you know how late it is?" The most I could discern was that it was morning, but that had more to do with the mist and logic than any supernatural indication of time.

"Years of practice," he said as he stood. Cold rushed in to take his place and I shivered. He held out his hand to help me up then gave it a not-so-subtle shake when I didn't immediately take it. "Come on, day's a wasting." I frowned and accepted the assist.

"You surprise me," I said as he passed me my things.

"Oh? Why's that?" he asked, reaching back into the leafy pile.

I shrugged and removed the fresh set of clothes. "I would've figured you for a morning snuggler."

He pulled me in close, hampering my ability to right my shirt. "And normally I am, but we slept later than I'd planned." He nuzzled my ear and a shiver that had nothing to do with the cold swept through me. In its wake, heat sprung to life. "I guess we had a harder night than I thought," he added with a playful nip.

I giggled and worked my hands free from between us. My fingers twisted in his hair as I brought his mouth down to mine, eager to feed the hunger he'd awakened. Apparently, that was yet another aspect of being a werewolf that Michael had failed to mention, not that I was really sure how one brought up supernatural stamina in casual conversation. I kissed him deeper and pressed my body against his.

Michael's arm tightened around my waist, crushing me against his chest. My pulse raced in anticipation even as a twisted note of logic weaseled its way through the fog.

He's right, we should get going.

Then again... It is the weekend.

I smiled against his mouth and pulled on his bottom lip. He groaned softly in response. "We should really go," he repeated.

"I don't see the rush," I countered and kept his head captive.

"Don't get me wrong, I love that you feel at home out here—I really do—but someone lost dinner last night."

It was my turn to groan. Now that he mentioned it, ravenous hunger clawed at my insides. I frowned and stole another kiss, determined despite the hollow pit in my stomach. The warmth of his hand spread across the small of my back and I melted into the sensation.

A sudden sense of wrongness invaded my warm, fuzzy feeling. My ears strained to find some explanation for the inexplicable alarm. I pulled away from Michael, abandoning my quest, and brought a hand up to stop his inquiry at my abrupt withdrawal. A second of complete silence dragged by.

Cold washed through me.

"Michael, the birds. Where are the birds?" I whispered, too scared to do anything louder. His eyes locked onto mine and the fear tripled. The urge to run as fast as possible saturated my limbs. Only Michael's iron grip prevented me from bolting. The conflict of motion had me vibrating in place.

The logic that running was a terrible idea, did nothing to quell the desire to do exactly that. My breaths faltered as I fought to prevent myself from shifting. Michael held a finger up to his lips and I stopped breathing altogether.

The thunder of a snapped twig echoed through the forest and the silent birds took flight in a cacophony of noise. Michael yanked me forward, nearly ripping my arm from its socket. I stumbled the first few steps, then found my balance. Once Michael was sure I was following, he released the appendage and we raced for all we were worth straight for the Jeep.

Branches whipped across my face. Rivulets of hot blood streamed over my cheeks. Thorns and briers ripped out hair. Despite the accumulating wealth of injuries, I kept running. By some miracle, I avoided tripping or crashing into any trees. I desperately wanted to look back to see if anyone was following, but didn't dare. Then the bright yellow of the Jeep was a beacon before us.

We're going to make it.

I caught the flash of keys in Michael's hand. Right as a sigh of relief hovered on my lips, a dark blur launched itself from somewhere deep within the shadows. My feet skidded in the damp leaves, losing their traction as I attempted to come to a complete stop. I careened forward into a disastrous crash that rolled me several more yards.

"Michael!"

He turned at my scream in time to be hit head on by the blur. Their combined momentum threw them into the shadows. Then he was up again and sprinting for the vehicle. "Get in the Jeep!"

I struggled to my feet and stumbled the last few yards. Michael launched himself into the driver's seat and slammed the key into the ignition. The engine roared to life, nearly sending me into my suppressed change. He jerked the car into gear and tires whirred on loose foliage. The wheels found traction and we lurched forward.

Our assailant landed on the hood with a terrible screech of metal, a monstrous, half-changed beast of horror, and my scream drowned out the straining engine. Legs that would never straighten dug clawed feet into the rent hood. Fur sprouted in patches across the grotesque body twisted into a shape that violated nature itself. Pointed ears rose high above his head that pivoted at odd angles as he struggled to maintain his grasp. Blood dripped down newly grown razor-sharp fangs to color the ropes of saliva hanging from a mouth never intended for fangs.

Yellowed eyes swiveled to look at me with a sickening

promise of violence. In slow motion, his mouth split in a sadistic smile too large for his face and I knew exactly how a deer felt before the jaws of death closed around its neck. I stared into eyes seething with hate and my breath went shallow as memory took hold.

My scream pierced the night as dagger-like teeth ripped into my leg, cutting through skin and muscle to scrape bone. I turned and beat at his snout with one hand while I tried to drag myself away with the other.

Chips of paint caught beneath my fingernails. The beast snarled and pulled me back. Loose grit seared my skin. My hand flopped to the concrete as the stoop drifted further out of reach.

Terror gripped me, not just of the pain, but of those eyes.

I knew those eyes.

The tires squealed as the Jeep swung wildly and the answer that had been within reach slipped through my fingers. I mentally scrambled to get it back even as I clung for dear life to the jeep as it bucked wildly over exposed roots and divots in the ground.

The attacker's head swiveled to fixate on Michael. The hair on the back of my neck stood on end as a mangled claw ripped free of the twisted metal and rose up. His savage growl promised retribution. The Jeep slammed to a halt and sent the mutated *were* flying with a screech of tearing metal. Tires whirred once more and the jeep launched backwards.

I reached out reflexively to steady myself against the violent shift in direction and the dashboard disintegrated beneath my touch. I stared down in absent shock at the plastic fragments coating my hands. Then we were back in drive and careening through the forest.

It wasn't until we had been on the highway for a good thirty minutes that I dared to look over at Michael. His fingers wrapped around the steering wheel tight enough to turn his knuckles white while he stared down at the asphalt with an intensity I'd never seen from him.

"Michael," I rasped.

His eyes barely twitched in my direction. "That was him."

"You're bleeding."

Like me, he was covered in scratches and bruises from our flight, but he also had a set of claw marks running the length of his arm. He looked down as though he hadn't noticed they were there in the first place, then finally looked at me.

"Oh, Sara."

The empathy in his voice stripped away the last of my strength and hot tears ran heedlessly down my cheeks, turning my filth into bloody mud. He made as if to reach out to me, then replaced his white-knuckled grip on the steering wheel.

We burst into Michael's house and I only had one thought. "I swear, I knew him. I looked into his eyes and *knew* him."

Those green eyes flecked with amber would haunt me until the day I died. My duffel skid along the wood floors to thump into a distant wall.

Michael's sigh could've been for the potential damage to his house or it could've been from my assertion. Judging by his attitude, I was leaning towards the latter.

"You don't believe me," I said, furious down to my toenails.

"I'm not saying that, but let's be reasonable," he said, calmly placing his duffel beside the armchair.

I crossed my arms and narrowed my eyes at him.

"Before you get defensive, all I'm saying is that it stands

to reason that you've seen him before, especially if he's been stalking you as long as we suspect."

My shoulders slumped. I didn't know what was worse, some faceless beast wanting me dead or someone I'd met face-to-face wanting to kill me so bad he was willing to do it in broad daylight. Despair threatened to turn me into a puddle of helplessness. I forced the thoughts away and focused on my anger, since it was the only thing keeping me upright.

"How? How did he know we were there? We were in the middle of the woods for Christ's sake!" I threw my arms out as I paced the living room. "Did he follow us from here? The office? How long has he known where I am?"

"Sara, calm down."

"Don't tell me to calm down!"

Deep down, I knew what he was really saying—that I was dangerously close to working myself into a change. Quite frankly it'd only been a few hours since my repressed change and it probably wouldn't take much to send me over the edge. However, that logic did nothing to diminish my panic.

"Sara, please." He reached out.

I flung my hand up to ward him off. "Don't touch me."

His face fell, as did his hand. "At least sit down." He gestured at the couch.

"How can I sit? He could burst in here at any moment." My arms flailed wildly in conjunction with the outrageous statement. What should have been an exaggeration was all too likely. "He's probably making his way here as we speak. This is hopeless. Why did I think I could outrun him?" I squeezed my eyes shut and shook my head, fighting vainly against the despair so determined to swallow me whole. "He seems to know our every move, but we don't know anything about him."

"We know some things."

"Like what? His name? What he looks like? How he managed to find us in the middle of nowhere?" I screeched.

Michael made as if to reach out again and thought better of it. Part of me wanted the consolation, another part was positive that if he touched me, I'd tear his arm off.

"I can't be here right now. I need to go."

Michael nodded as if he understood. "Then let's go."

"Without you."

Tension filled the room as he stared back at me in silence. For a second, I thought he would argue. For another, I wanted him to. Then it was gone. I squared my shoulders and glared back defiantly.

"At least take the Jeep," he said, tossing me the keys.

I debated arguing the impracticality of driving something that clearly had been through hell, but that required too many words. I snatched the keys out of the air without responding. The door slammed home behind me and I was already dialing by the time the engine turned.

I needed space. I needed advice. I needed Charline.

"Hey," I said when she picked up.

"Sara? What's wrong? You sound awful." She didn't sound so hot either.

"It's just...just..." Just what? What could I possibly tell her? That a homicidal maniac that just so happens to be a werewolf is after me? "Just guy issues. Can I come over?" I asked.

"Oh honey, if you're looking for a place to be sad, this is definitely it." By the end of her morbid statement, she dissolved into tears.

Ted.

Guilt swam hot in my belly. "I'm on my way."

Ten minutes later, Charline answered the door, eyes red-rimmed, puffy, and wide with surprise. "That was fast." I could have smacked myself for forgetting how much closer Michael's place was than mine.

"I sped—and maybe ignored a few traffic laws," I offered in explanation.

She nodded, not disputing it, and stepped aside to let me in. As I stepped over the threshold, I couldn't help but notice the condition of my dear friend. Flour covered her in bursts of powdery white, not a speck of makeup could be found on her face, her hair hung limp and lifeless from a low pony, and she wore jeans. The absence of a dress alone was cause for concern.

I wrapped her in a tight hug. She wheezed at the pressure and I relented, realizing too late that I could've hurt her. "Oh, Charline, I'm so sorry," I said quickly, terrified I might have cracked a rib or something.

"It's...fine." Her voice quivered, betraying the lie.

"No, it's not. I've been so absorbed in my own guy problems that I forgot that you're dealing with some pretty big ones of your own." I pulled away to look at her. "Have you made cake yet?"

"Three," she sniffled.

"In that case, I think it's time to break out the wine."

She simply nodded and allowed herself to be led back into the house. I pulled up short as we stepped into the kitchen where dessert seemed to be the theme for the day. Cannoli, éclairs, and cream puffs dominated the table, along with two perfectly decorated cakes, a plate of chocolate chip cookies and...

"A Bundt cake?"

"I wanted to see if I could do it. I'm working on angel food and divinity now." She shrugged as if that was no big deal.

No one would be able to tell if Charline was a werewolf. It would be stranger if she wasn't surrounded by food.

"You should really start a bakery," I said, my voice tinged with awe. She shrugged again and poured two glasses of Moscato. I pulled up a seat at the island overflowing with treats and encouraged her to take one as well. "Stupid question, but how are you holding up?"

She visibly composed herself before answering. "He came to get all of his stuff Friday after work." She paused as her voice cracked. I diligently restrained my surprise. She took a shaky breath and tried again. "He got his things and brought my stuff from his place." She gestured through the entryway to a box by the front door that looked to be over-flowing, then slid me a slice of cake.

"Forget him. I never liked him anyway. Please forgive me for not saying something sooner." That earned me a shadow of a smile and a noncommittal shrug. "You really are way too good for him," I added. "You're beautiful, talented, and interesting." That earned a laugh. "Honestly, I'm surprised that he lasted this long."

She looked up at the frank comment. To my surprise, she didn't seem upset. Astonishing me further, she said, "And you know, I don't think he liked my cooking either."

I barked a laugh and she coughed a fragile one, followed by several stronger, albeit small ones. I casually tucked away the empty bottle and poured from the second she'd so help-fully already opened. A third slice of cake made its way onto my plate as she topped off her own glass.

Charline took a sip from the dangerously full glass then turned the mixer back on. The beaters whirred gently, whisking the sugary concoction into smooth mounds. After a silent minute of watching the mixture, she turned off the machine and looked up at me with sorrow brimming on her lashes. "I know he had his flaws. But, Sara, I really thought we'd make it."

I patted her hand before sampling the current project

and promptly moaned in appreciation. "I'm serious, Charline, you have to open a bakery. You're depriving the world." She completely ignored me as she unlatched the bowl from the mixer and spooned its contents into a pan. As it found its way into the oven she started talking again.

"I'm in my thirties now and who is going to want that? They all go younger. Ted certainly proved that." Her face scrunched as if she'd smelled something bad then almost instantly fell. "I can't compete with some vapid twenty-year-old who only wants shiny things and sex. I want a home and stability and children." She spun on me unexpectedly and I almost choked on what was left of the second cake. "That's another thing, he didn't want kids. At all. Ever. Who doesn't want kids that much?" She gave me a look like I was supposed to know the answer.

I pushed the empty plate away and prayed she didn't notice the shortage of confections. "Forgive me for asking, but if that's the case, then why did you stay with him?"

"I don't know. I mean, I loved him and I guess that insecurity..." I gave her a doubting look. "Hey, underneath all of this fabulous hair there's plenty of insecurity," she asserted, complete with accusatory finger. "Enough about my problems. What's going on with you?" she asked as she removed her apron with a flourish.

Unsure of what to say, I stalled for time by pouring another glass and then relocating to the living room. I chose a comfy chair and settled in with my wine and snagged cannoli. "Honestly, I don't know," I finally said.

"What do you mean you don't know?" She leaned down to turn on a lamp, then went to shut the blinds.

"Exactly that. I have no idea what's going on with us." I shifted in the chair not sure how to go on. "Things have become kind of awkward recently." I sagged defeated into the cushions. Outside, I could hear the crickets picking up their evening tune and even the birds were starting to quiet down.

"Did you drive here in Michael's Jeep?"

I looked up, startled by the unusual question. To my horror, Charline stood at the window, staring out at the street. I gave an inward groan at the stupidity of parking right out front. "Yes."

"Why?"

"Because, Michael insisted."

"Insisted, that's a funny thing to say. Why would he do that?" she asked, peering through the blinds in confusion.

"Because a homicidal werewolf is after me."

All of the air suctioned out of the room. Charline turned to face me in slow motion, her eyes wide. But her surprise was nothing compared to the shock that had to be plastered on my face.

"Oh my god, you're not kidding."

Of course, I am. That's ridiculous. Werewolves aren't real.

The words were there, but nothing was coming out. I sat like a lump, unable to provide any logical argument.

She sat down hard on the chair adjacent to me and speared me with a look that demanded answers—good ones. "Sara."

"I...I didn't mean to say that," I fumbled.

"No shit. You're not exactly prone to flights of fancy. And although it could be the wine, you're nowhere near as tipsy as you should be after two and a half bottles, not to mention you ate two whole cakes." I withered beneath her intense scrutiny. "You know, it'd be much easier to write it off if you didn't look so damn guilty. What's really going on?"

"You won't believe it. Even if you try, you won't. I barely believe it and it's happening to me," I said in a barely intelligible stream.

"Only one way to find out. Spill."

"I'm a werewolf." The unbelievable statement fell into silence. Her face twisted into a frown, while her mouth opened and closed a few times without any words coming out. I swallowed and waited.

She narrowed her eyes at me and stayed that way a long moment before finally saying, "Maybe you should start at the beginning."

I took a deep breath. Despite my intention to sugarcoat the tall tale, out poured the unfiltered truth. "You know my dog attack?" She barely had a chance to nod, before I was going on. "Not a dog. Actually, a serial killer who's also a werewolf. He bit me and now I am too, not a serial killer, just a werewolf."

"How could you possibly know that? I mean of all the things," she said as she sank back into the chair, disbelief clearly written on her face.

"Aside from the fact that at the last full moon I turned into a wolf? Michael."

That threw her for a loop. "Michael?"

"Yeah, he's also a werewolf, only he was born that way," I clarified.

"Sara, this is all..." She shook her head in time with the words.

"Impossible? I know!" I shouted and she jumped. "Every morning, I wake up, and before I open my eyes, I pray it's all a dream, but every time I still wake up at Michael's."

"Why are you at Michael's?"

"I've sort of been staying with him," I admitted, twirling the stem of the empty glass between my hands.

"Okay...story please," she prompted.

I glanced up at her and back at the glass. "You remember those days I missed last month?"

"Yeah..."

"That was my first change," I said quietly. "Somehow, I

got stuck. Long story short, he hit me with his Jeep and I ended up at his house."

"He hit you? With his car!"

I met her righteous fury with a level look. "Jeep," I corrected. "Anyway, when I finally changed back..."

"You called me," she filled in.

"Right."

"Are y'all seeing each other at all?"

I winced at the undercurrent of betrayal. While I may not have gotten around to telling her we were together, I clearly hadn't done enough to disabuse her of the notion either.

"Sort of. Well, now, anyway. I think. Maybe not," I finished unconvincingly. My shoulders sagged and I put the wine glass down before I could accidentally snap it in two. "Anyway, the real problem is the killer wants to finish what he started. That's why I've been staying at Michael's, so he can basically be my bodyguard and because the killer already knows where I live. But all of it was for nothing."

"How do you mean?"

"Yesterday he found us in the woods and tried to kill me again." I clutched my hands together. "Charline, I don't know if I've ever been so terrified in my life. I wasn't alone. I was supposed to be safe. He promised to keep me safe," I hiccupped. "But I wasn't. And now things are awkward between us. That's why I drove Michael's car instead of mine, so the killer wouldn't think I was alone," I finished out of breath, unshed tears stinging my eyes.

The silence dragged by filled only with crickets and tense anticipation.

"Sara, honey." She reached out, and unlike when Michael had reached out to console me, I didn't flinch away.

"So, yeah, this is my life now," I said, meeting her gaze with a watery one of my own.

"I really don't want to believe you, but your attitude suggests that it's all true. Or at least you think it is," she qualified. I opened my mouth to argue, but she held up her hand. "I like to think that you're not off your rocker and for the most part, you seem sane enough," she said with a small smile.

"Oh, Charline." I launched myself across the space between us, almost breaking my empty glass in the process. "Thank you so much for not freaking out and thinking I've lost all my marbles," I said, making sure to hug her more gently this time.

"Who said I'm not freaking out?"

"What?" I released her and slid back.

"Sara, there's a serial killer after you. Werewolf aside, it's still a serial killer and you've already almost died."

"You said it was always clear that I'd survive." Of all the things to surprise me, this shouldn't have been it, yet her words shook me.

"I lied," she said bluntly. "It was nothing short of a miracle."

My stomach sank. "That means that the werewolf curse is what saved my life," I said more to myself. I looked back at her, she seemed equally unnerved by the explanation.

Had it really been that close?

The skepticism of the nurses and surprised optimism of the doctor suddenly became much more profound. "Thanks for lying I guess," I said, averting my eyes.

"It seemed like the thing to do." She gave my hand a reassuring pat. "Now that we've covered that, you have a long way to go to helping me believe all of this."

"I thought you said you accepted it?"

"I'm maintaining it as a possibility."

I frowned at her. Tonight had already turned into an

emotional roller coaster and I wasn't really up for defending my reality.

"Don't look at me like that. Come on, even you have to admit it's pretty far out there."

I nodded in defeat, recalling how I'd fought Michael on the topic despite having already turned twice. "What do you want to know?"

"For starters, what can you do? Can you do it now, so I can see?" she asked, eyes wide with hopeful wonder.

"Um no." Her face fell in obvious disappointment. I rolled my eyes and sat up straight. "Eventually, I'll be able to change when I want, but for now it's mostly with the moon."

"Mostly?"

"Well, it's also whenever I panic and freak out. It's very inconvenient, but I'm working on it." I focused on the ground, hoping she wouldn't want me to explain further.

"I guess I'll have to settle for you telling me about it for now. And I want the real story about you and Michael." I flinched at the blatant accusation in her tone.

We stayed up well into the night. Me telling her everything and her doing the best she could to take it all in.

17

─────

KISSES THAT BURN

I woke up in Charline's guest room to the tantalizing smell of breakfast. I followed my nose to the kitchen where I found my host surrounded by a cornucopia of breakfast food.

"How do you have all of this food in your house?"

"I plan ahead," she responded, matter of fact.

"For what? The apocalypse?" She gave me a look. "Still upset?" I asked.

"Well, yes. But I also got to see that werewolf appetite first hand last night."

"Duly noted and appreciated. By the way, have you seen my phone?" I glanced around in pursuit of the errant device.

"Um, I think it's by where the cookies were last night." She gestured in the vague direction of the breakfast table. Where the cookies were was now a heaping stack of pancakes and sure enough, my phone—dead. By the time I located a charger and my phone had enough juice to be turned on, Charline had finished cooking.

"Oh shit," I said as the screen finally came to life.

"What?" she asked as she removed her apron and hung it on a peg.

197

"I have twelve missed calls and almost as many voice-mails—all from Michael."

"Oh shit."

Despite my trepidation, I immediately called him.

"Where the hell have you been!" The shout crackled with static. "I've been looking for you everywhere. I drove, I changed, I called. What's the point of a phone if you don't use it?" I winced and looked over at Charline in silent apology.

"I've been at Charline's. We were talking and I left my phone in the kitchen. It got late and I thought it would be safer to stay. I didn't realize my phone had died until this morning." When he didn't respond, I tried again. "I'm sorry." Still nothing. "Michael? Michael?"

"What's the matter?"

"It cut out." I looked down at the phone that very clearly read as no longer connected to the call. "I don't understand."

"Is it charging? Maybe it didn't have enough power," Charline guessed.

"Maybe." I double checked the cord to make sure it was plugged in all the way on both sides. Sure enough, the connection was secure.

"You could try turning it off and taking out the battery." I frowned at her. "Or not." She threw her hands up and walked away to deal with the beeping oven.

With a defeated sigh, I settled for simply restarting it. I was about to try calling him again when I heard a thunderous knock at the door. Charline and I exchanged nervous looks. After a brief moment of hesitation, she went to check it out. While I couldn't see the door, I could hear everything fine, including the very loud voice that definitely was not Ted.

"Where is she?" Michael demanded.

"Now calm down. It was an accident..."

"I want to see her. Now."

I scurried to my feet, prepared to meet my maker. Michael launched into the kitchen like hell itself was on his heels. His gaze encompassed the kitchen in one blistering sweep. I swallowed as anxiety took hold. When that fiery look landed on me, I shrank inward.

Maybe it would have been better to hide.

He stalked towards me and I stepped back only to run into the table. My voice shook as I held up a hand to stall the inevitable. A feeble protection in the face of such wrath.

"Take it easy, Michael. I…"

He ignored the impediment and grabbed me in a hug tight enough to send all of the air whooshing out of my lungs. "Thank the moon you're okay. I've been so worried. All I could think was that…" He failed to finish and squeezed tighter. "I never should have let you leave." His hand stroked my hair as he buried his face against my neck. "You could have told me you were coming to Charline's," he added, softer.

"Michael," I wheezed, "my ribs." He immediately released me and I had barely enough time to drag in a ragged breath before his mouth crashed down on mine. "Mm," I mumbled in surprise. My toes barely scraped the ground as I was swept up in the unexpected embrace. One of his hands slipped into my hair and pressed my mouth harder against his. I gasped at the fierceness and he took the opening to deepen the kiss.

Fire raced through me, heedless of the fact that I was standing in someone else's kitchen. He eventually released me to stumble back to the table. I leaned against it for support, more than a little light headed.

"Wow. I want a man to kiss *me* like that," Charline said from the entryway.

I sank into a chair, which was about the only thing I

could manage. Michael's hand drifted from my head to rest on my shoulder where it stayed as if to reassure him that I was really there.

"Sorry for bursting in here, Charline," Michael said, not sounding nearly as winded as I felt. "I didn't mean to frighten you," he continued. "I..."

"I know. You were worried. Now that you're here, you might as well join us for breakfast. I should have enough for two werewolves."

Michael's head whipped around to face me. I waved weakly and glanced past him at Charline who was scowling at him despite her proclamation of understanding.

"She told me all of it and quite frankly it's getting harder and harder not to believe." She shook her head and pulled another plate down.

"I can't believe how much better I feel now that Charline knows." The bed creaked in protest at my unceremonious fall. "You don't think she'll—you know?" I quickly dismissed the doubt. "No, of course not, silly of me to even think it. But it's such a relief. Don't you think?"

The bed shifted as Michael joined me. "Mmhmm," he mumbled.

"That was enthusiastic." I lifted up to my elbows so I could look at him. He met my gaze, but didn't comment. I let out a groan and flopped back down. "I suppose it's not really a big deal for you, you already have people who know and accept you."

"Yeah," he said softly, without any real conviction.

I wonder what that would be like, to have a whole bunch of people know and not care.

"Michael? You're being awfully quiet. You're not still

upset, are you?" I asked, this time sitting all the way up. "I told you I'm sorry. I really didn't mean to worry you."

"I suppose I'll get over it," he said as his fingers danced lightly across my cheek.

"What are you doing?" I asked, breathless. Rather than respond, he pulled my tee so he could place a kiss on the exposed shoulder. "Oh." I cleared my throat, which had constricted at the sudden onrush of heat. I hadn't really been sure what to make of the display at Charline's and now this was adding to the confusion. "I thought. I mean. I didn't realize..." I trailed off. He placed a kiss on my jaw and my heart skipped.

"What did you think, Sara?" he asked, his voice low and husky, his lips barely brushing my skin.

"I...I'm not sure."

"Did you think that the other night was meant to be a one-night stand? Or maybe you thought it was because of the full moon." The warmth of his hand burned against my thigh.

"I guess," I squeaked as he slid his fingers under the hem of my shorts. His resulting chuckle made my insides quiver.

"Oh no, Sara, I've wanted you for months." He placed a kiss on my neck and I gasped at the faint feel of teeth. "Maybe longer," he whispered, his breath hot on my increasingly sensitive skin.

"Define months."

"Let's see," he began as he lifted my shirt up and placed a trail of hot kisses across my stomach. "You wore a blue top with green stripes and gray slacks your first day. Your ass looked great in those by the way. Don't suppose you still have them?"

"My first day? That was over two years ago."

"Guess that makes it longer," he mused, undeterred in his attention.

"If that's true, why didn't you say anything before?"

He let out a soft sigh that was punctuated with a gentle kiss. "Things were complicated," he finally said as his nose trailed along my abdomen.

"And now they're not?"

He stopped and looked at me. There was so much in his eyes, the expected heat and surprisingly, sadness. "Yes, things are still complicated. More now than ever. But I..." His odd explanation stopped midway. He leaned forward and pressed his lips against mine.

"You what?" I whispered, determined to have answers no matter how much my body wanted me to shut up.

"I can't be this close to you every day and not touch you," he said at last. Where I expected at least a small, teasing smile, there was a firm line.

Worry seeped past my curiosity. "What aren't you telling me?" I searched his eyes for any hint. "What are these complications?"

"It's not important now. They're my complications and I'll deal with them when the time comes."

I opened my mouth to demand a better explanation only to have my words dissolve into a moan as his heated touch slid further up my thigh. He captured the sound with a kiss that sent what was left of my thoughts scattering.

"I can tell you one thing for sure," he said, returning to my middle.

"What's that?"

"I'm not letting you out of my sight again," he said, his words bordering on a growl.

"We'll see about that."

He gave a throaty laugh that sent delicious tingles emanating from where his mouth touched my flushed skin. Heat continued to travel up my torso until his lips found mine once more. The kiss had a tenderness to it that brought back pleasant memories of our brief time in the woods. I tangled my fingers in his hair as the sweetness started to burn.

He broke our kiss to sit up where I helped to relieve him of his shirt. I wasn't sure when mine had been abandoned. While his arms were busy with the garment, I stole the opportunity to run my hands over his chest. Craving more, I added my own kisses. He moaned and his fingers slid into my hair. He pulled me away and recaptured my mouth with an unforgiving kiss that tasted of need. Mindlessly, we ditched the last of the clothing separating us and resumed our fevered exploration.

Before he could settle back into the leisurely kisses he'd been blanketing me with, I pinned him to the bed and began my own leisurely stroll. He caressed my sides as I worked my way across his torso. His chest hair tickled my face and I stole a moment to rub my cheek against the softness, pleased with the rumble it elicited from Michael.

I refocused my attention and licked at each nipple followed by a light bite that made him hiss. Humming with satisfaction, I scooted further down and took his erection in hand. He groaned and I glanced up to find him watching me completely enraptured. I gave him a wicked smirk and held his gaze as I slowly lowered my mouth to his tip.

I swirled my tongue around the head, appreciating the hint of saltiness teasing my tongue. Michael's lids fluttered as he struggled to keep his eyes open. I gave his length a leisurely stroke then wrapped my lips around him. His fingers white-knuckled the sheets while a groan that shook the bed fell out of him.

"Full moon at midnight!"

While I had no idea what the hell that meant, the breathy way he said it was more than enough to convince me I was on the right track. I swallowed him deeper and sucked with renewed vigor. When his hips threatened to buck, I laid my hand flat on his hip and held him still. His next moan bordered on a whine.

"Stars. Shit. Fuck. I'm gonna come."

I pulled off with a pop and stared at his heaving chest while he panted for breath. "Please tell me you have condoms."

"I didn't," he said, instantly dampening my sex high. He chuckled, undoubtedly at my crestfallen expression, and tugged me up his body to claim me with a toe-curling kiss. In a heartbeat, he'd reversed our positions again. "Which is why when you left yesterday, I borrowed your car." He reached out and pulled open the drawer of the nightstand. His hand dipped inside and emerged with a small handful of rubbers.

I huffed a laugh and shook my head. "Tease."

"I haven't even begun to tease," he said huskily as he lowered his mouth, bypassing my lips to suck lightly on my neck. I squirmed with impatience, but he simply chuckled and moved to my chest.

A sharp cry escaped me as he sucked my breast into his mouth and twirled his tongue around the nipple. He relinquished his hold long enough to give me a toothy grin, then switched to the other breast while his fingers trailed down my quivering stomach to tease my entrance. The pad of his thumb rubbed with confidence along my clit until I was physically aching for more.

I dug my fingers into his shoulders and valiantly tried to stave off my orgasm to no avail. He nipped at my overly sensitive nipple and pressed harder and I came with a shuddering moan. My release was still washing through me when he slipped a finger between my folds, then two. He curled them at exactly the right angle and a second orgasm crashed through me with reckless abandon. I groaned loud enough to wake the neighbors as I clenched around him. His thumb danced lightly over my bud as he slowly slid his fingers out and back in.

I whimpered at the onslaught of pleasure. "Michael, please."

"You sure?" He curled his fingers again and my entire body jerked. "I think I could coax another couple out of you yet."

"I'm sure," I panted. "I'm really, really sure."

He rewarded me with another throaty laugh and stole a kiss before rocking back on his heels and reaching for one of the condoms. I watched his movements with an eagerness I hadn't felt in years. And thanks to his insistence on waiting to use protection, I knew it wasn't because of the full moon; this was all me.

He leaned down and snared me with a kiss that hovered between slow and desperate. I curled my arms around his shoulders while his tip teased my swollen entrance. He broke the kiss and looked at me, his deep brown eyes filled with a tenderness that terrified me. Then he pressed forward and I forgot about everything else.

We moaned in unison as my body welcomed him, pulling him deeper and squeezing tightly. I wrapped my legs around his waist and he began to move, slow at first then with increasing tempo until our bodies were slapping together and the sound of our panting breaths filled the room. I moaned and raked my nails across his shoulders as another orgasm rolled through me.

"Stars, you're tight," Michael panted, his pace faltering. "I'm not gonna last."

I tightened my legs around him, lifting my hips off the bed and sparking the start of another wave of release. "Then come for me."

Michael's fingers dug into my thigh as his thrusts

became more erratic. He groaned deep in his chest as he gave a final stroke and came undone. He shuddered through his release until he caught his breath and fell forward to snare me with a sweeping kiss that spread an entirely different wave of heat.

"I think you've ruined me," he said with a huffed laugh as he disposed of the condom.

We took turns cleaning up in the bathroom and taking care of other necessities, then flopped on the bed, twisted sheets and all, in satisfied exhaustion. We lay intertwined, our fingers tracing the map of our skins.

I sighed contentedly and snuggled closer. "Mm," I hummed. "Why can't every day be like this?"

"What? With you disappearing and leaving me beside myself with worry? Yes, of course, can't imagine why not," he said with a laugh that was low and warm.

"I told you I was sorry, and I am." He placed a gentle kiss on my forehead and gave me a squeeze. I glanced up at him through my lashes to find him looking right back as if searching for something. Our conversation from earlier drifted back to me.

He's hiding something, something important.

Before I could bring it back up, he leaned down and gave me a lingering kiss that left my lips tingling.

"So, this is a thing now, huh?" I asked quietly.

"This is definitely a thing," he growled. The next kiss was far from sweet.

18

DAVID

*Beep*Beep*Beep*

I silenced the alarm with a decisive smack then twisted around. To my amazement, Michael was still asleep. I reached out and brushed the dark brown locks from his forehead. He grumbled in his sleep, but otherwise didn't move.

As carefully as I could, I slipped free of the sheets. My hands reached towards the ceiling in a long luxurious stretch that arched my back and pulled at muscles that were sore in all the best ways. I gave a satisfied groan and dropped my arms back down.

Impressed that I'd awoken first, I left him to snooze a while longer. I stretched again in the living room then padded over to the sliding door. The blinds had been left open, offering a spectacular view of the backyard.

My own breath steamed on the glass and I drew a smiley face. Satisfied with my handiwork, I shifted my gaze back to the yard where the faint pink of sunrise was starting to make the foliage blush. Bare branches hung down low over full, resilient shrubs in manicured chaos. Unlike my yard,

Michael's had no fence and butted right up to the forest itself.

My hand hovered over the handle, my fingers a mere snap away from unlocking the door. I chewed my bottom lip as the human reality of needing to get ready for work battled with wild impulse to streak into the trees with abandon. The sun inched a little higher while I struggled with indecision. I glanced over at the clock to see how much time I had to kill when a flash of light outside caught my eye.

I immediately returned my attention to the yard. Whatever it was glinted again in the increasing dawn. I strained to bring it into focus. Stripped branches became flush with barely distinguishable growth, shrubs morphed into young trees, and there amidst the denser greens were two luminescent orbs of gold.

My heart leapt to my throat, nearly strangling the scream that tore free. My calf bumped the edge of the coffee table and I careened backwards to land in a truly spectacular crash. I stared in horror at the yard beyond occupied with no more than the early light of dawn.

"What is it?" Michael asked, suddenly standing beside me.

I ripped my gaze away from the glass to meet his alarmed one. His hair poked up in random directions and his face still bore the imprint of a pillow.

"Sara," he snapped and terror renewed its grip on me.

I shot a panicked look at the door where the lawn remained empty.

"What is it?" he repeated as he strode over to the door.

I swallowed hard. "I saw him."

"I don't see anything." He glanced briefly back at me. "Are you sure?"

"Michael, I saw him. I swear. He was here!" I scrambled to my feet and joined him.

"Okay, I believe you." He gently squeezed my hand and I let out a relieved breath. "I'm going to go out and sniff around."

"Do you want me to lock it behind you?" I whispered. He shot me a look. Right, because glass and a locked door would stop a determined werewolf.

He released my hand, then stepped out into the crisp, morning air, the only sound to betray his leaving that of the door clicking shut. Rather than head straight for the back, he veered off to the side, disappearing from sight.

Fear clawed at me and I pressed against the door to keep sight of him. The cold glass leached the warmth from my hands as I scanned the space. I finally spied Michael gliding around the perimeter like a ghost. He made two complete circuits before coming back to the house. I moved aside and rubbed my arms in a vain attempt to dispel the chill that had nothing to do with the temperature.

The sliding door snicked shut behind him. "He's gone now." He sighed and ran a hand through his hair, worsening the already prominent bed-head. His gaze caught mine.

"What? Why do you look like you're about to give me particularly bad news?" I asked, barely containing the impulse to break down right there in the living room.

Whatever he says, I can handle it.

"This isn't good." Those three words stole all of my false confidence and I whimpered. "He knows where we are. If he's bold enough to come here..." He left the statement unfinished.

I swallowed and fought back the tears already burning my eyes. "What are we going to do?"

"You're going to get ready for work, and I'm going to make a call."

"You can't be serious," I argued.

Michael shook his head and grabbed my arms, but the

gentle touch didn't match the concern clouding his eyes. "He's not likely to return this morning. He was probably staking the place out." On that horrible note, he released me and strode off to retrieve his phone.

Despite my frazzled nerves—or perhaps in spite of them—my stomach growled. I prepared breakfast by rote, mindlessly fixing enough for both of us. When Michael returned from his mysterious call completely dressed, we traded places in silence. What was there to say? We'd been found. All our hopes of safety had blown away while we slept.

The drive to work held no more conversation than breakfast. Michael pulled into an open space and as the engine died, silence reined once more. We sat a moment in the increasing tension, then quietly got out and went our separate ways.

I stared at my computer screen and its blinking prompt to enter my password. Beside the monitor sat a stack of folders in desperate need of attention. I picked one off the top, opened it, then closed it again without reading anything. It rejoined its fellows and I picked up a magnetized paperclip holder. The contents spilled onto the desk in a small series of clicks.

My mind flashed to the sliding door clicking shut a few hours ago. I squeezed my eyes shut.

If he's willing to walk right up to Michael's house, then what's to stop him from waltzing right into the office or snatching me from the parking garage?

I tilted the holder towards the desk. Two paper clips flew up.

Why can't he just leave me alone? I never asked for any of this.

A blue paper clip shot up to join its fellows, bringing the chain to a staggering five clips.

There has to be something I can do. I feel like a chicken sitting in a pot waiting to be boiled.

Images of the gruesome creature from the woods came to mind. His warped face twisted into a snarl. Ropes of saliva hanging from jagged teeth as if in anticipation of tearing through my flesh. Spittle flecking the windshield as he raged on the other side of the thin barrier. A shudder ran through me as I realized once again how close I'd been to death.

If he'd walked up on us sleeping. If I hadn't heard the birds... Oh God, how long was he out there?

I slammed my head down on the desk. Paperclips scattered and a distinctive groan emanated from the surface. I quickly sat back up and checked to make sure I hadn't cracked the desk in two.

I need to think about something else.

I shook my head to dispel the darkness. I conjured happier thoughts. Sunlight warming my back. A light breeze kissing my face. Michael's arm resting across my hip.

He's hiding something from me. Who did he call this morning?

The answers to my nagging doubt weren't in my cubicle. More pressingly, I needed to make sure I didn't work myself into a change.

Focus on the good. Hands gliding over smooth skin, spreading a deep heat. Wonderfully kissable lips, tasting every inch of me. Moonlight sinking into every pore. Michael's teeth gently nipping, fingers sliding around my inner thigh. A gasp as he...

"Sara."

I jumped in my chair and the wheels squealed in protest.

"Jesus, Bob, you scared me half to death." I clutched at my chest.

Bob raised an eyebrow at my theatrics, but offered no empathy. "I need you to run down to HR and pick up a report."

"I'll get right on it," I mumbled.

"Oh, and Sara, you might want to look into getting your nails done." He gave my hands a very direct look before returning to his office.

Since when did Bob care about the state of my nails? I glanced down to find eight deep gouges marring the surface of my desk. I hurriedly examined my hands. Nothing seemed out of place, but the rents in the desk suggested otherwise.

I grabbed several folders and spread them over the latest development in my abilities. Once I was satisfied the ruse sufficiently covered the evidence, I quickly made my way to HR, intentionally taking a route that avoided the marketing department.

"Where are you off to in such a hurry?" Charline's voice followed after me.

I pulled up short. In my distraction, I'd walked right past my destination. "Oh, hi, Charline. Sorry. Bob sent me to pick up a report."

She scowled. "How many times do I have to say it? You need to tell that man to go take a flying—"

"Yeah, I know," I quickly cut her off. "And quite frankly, I'm closer to it every day. However, today is not the safest day to get into it with him." I gave her a pointed look.

She immediately sat up a little straighter and glanced around before leaning closer and whispering, "Did something happen?"

I sighed. "I don't even know where to start. Best not to talk about it here. I want to get through this day in one piece." I grimaced at my own word choice. Thankfully, Charline let it drop with nothing more than a concerned expression.

"Shannon has the report. I think it's something about interns. I wasn't sure who the lucky department was going to be, but it looks like you'll be pulling babysitting duty," she said in an attempt to add levity.

"Great," I groaned. "That's the last thing I need." I rubbed my forehead, temporarily forgetting that those nails had recently put holes in a desk.

Charline's eyes softened in understanding. "I'm sorry, sweetie, I really am. If there's anything I can do…"

"No," I shook my head. I didn't want to drag her into this anymore than I already had.

"Well, the offer stands. I have an idea though," she said, brightening back up.

I dropped my hand and looked at her. "If it's shopping, I'm out."

She gave me a wry smile. "No, it's not shopping. Though I personally don't see what you have against retail therapy. Do you think we could get together and hang out? No shopping, I promise. I need—a bit of distraction."

You and me both.

"When were you thinking?" I asked aloud.

"How about Wednesday? I think I can survive until then," Charline quipped with an added eye roll for emphasis.

"Wednesday night?"

"No, Wednes*day*. The office will be closed for the electrical upgrade." When I didn't respond, she added, "They're upgrading the lights? Sara, it's been posted for over a month."

"Shit. You're right. I totally forgot."

She threw up her hands and leaned back in her chair

with a huff. "I swear, not a damn soul around here reads the memos."

"I've been a little caught up. Anyway, Wednesday sounds great. We'll get out, do something fun." The image of a poster on the message board came to mind. "I think there's a fair in town."

"That would be awesome! I don't know the last time I went to the fair. Ted doesn't like them, says they smell, and you know how he feels about crowds, so we never..." she trailed off.

I laid a hand on her arm. "All the more reason to go. You're too much fun to keep cooped up." While her smile seemed forced, I could see the light trying to peek through. "More importantly, what are you going to wear?" I quirked an eyebrow.

Her eyes widened. "I hadn't thought of that." She spun back around and furiously scribbled on a notepad.

I suppressed a laugh and made my way down to Shannon's office. "Hey, Shannon," I offered by way of greeting as I strode in. A loud thump resonated through the floor and papers flew into the air, creating a miraculous windstorm of perfectly typed pages. "I don't suppose one of these is the report Bob needs?" I asked, snatching a few out of the air.

The rest of the papers finally cleared enough to make out a wide-eyed Shannon sitting on the floor. "All of them," she squeaked.

"Oh my God, are you okay?" I dropped the papers and rushed over to help her up.

"I...I never even heard you," she stuttered.

"That's my fault. The door was open, but I should have knocked."

I helped her back to her feet and she looked about the room, taking in the cyclone of disaster. "Oh."

"Let me give you a hand."

Between the two of us, we made short work of the mess. By the time we were done, she was back to her normal, business-like self.

"He'll need to review and sign these. This stack needs to be archived and tagged for next quarter. And this is for you." She placed a much smaller packet on top of everything else.

"What is it?"

"You didn't know? PR is getting an intern."

I barely managed to stop the groan. For a split second, I seriously debated taking Charline's advice and telling everyone to go take a flying fuck off the roof, then it dawned on me that she would probably have to file the report. With a resigned sigh, I shuffled out of the office, viscerally aware of what it would look like if I dropped the towering stack.

I skulked through the office like I was in some sort of adventure video game, cautiously making my way through the maze of cubicles, each junction potentially fatal to my precious tower. I craned my neck around the last corner before I would have the relief of a straight shot. Coast clear, I eased myself into the walkway.

Slightly more relaxed, I glanced around at people going about their business, completely unaware that a werewolf was in their midst. My gaze passed over the entrance to the marketing department and I did a double take. In my attempt to take the safest route, I'd unintentionally ended up in the one place I was trying to avoid. Naturally, Michael was headed straight for me.

"Hey, Sara, what are you doing here?" he asked with a smile.

How can he be so calm after what happened this morning? We could've died and he's going about his day like imminent death is nothing to worry about.

He eyed my ludicrously high pile of paper. "Please tell me we're not getting another intern."

I rolled my eyes. "No, that would be my privilege. If you don't mind, I really should be getting these to Bob."

"Let me give you a hand. I was actually on my way to see you."

"Why?"

A cloud drifted across his face. "Because I wanted to talk with you."

I could have kicked myself. We'd already established this was a thing.

So why am I still second-guessing everything?

I leaned a bit to let him take off the top half. "What did you want to talk to me about?" I asked as he fell in step beside me. Naturally, now that I had help, the way back to my desk was miraculously obstacle free.

"I figured it might be a good idea to get someone to give us a hand with our... problem."

My mouth hung agape while I stared back at him in wonder at how he could casually talk about being hunted by a serial killer werewolf in the middle of the office and not bat an eye.

"What?" He waited for me to shake my head, then continued unperturbed. "Anyway, an old friend of mine is in town with work for a few weeks. I invited him over for dinner tonight. You'll be able to meet him then."

"Is he... like us?" I asked, clearing papers off my desk to make room for the stack he was holding.

"Yes, he too is awesome," he responded. I looked up in time to catch his signature wolfish grin. "What happened to your desk?" he asked.

My gaze snapped down to the claw marks scarring the desk, that I'd incidentally revealed when I'd made room for the new reports. "Nothing." I deliberately placed his stack over the marks, my face burning.

"Okay... All joking aside, yes, he's like us. If anyone can help us out, David can."

"Is that who you called this morning?" I asked.

His face seemed to pale and darken at the same time and an unusual sour scent that brought to mind feelings of anxiety with an almost intangible undercurrent of fear tinged the air. I frowned at the results of the subconscious dissemination.

That can't be right. Michael isn't afraid of the mutt. So, what has him looking like he's been given a terminal diagnosis?

Michael cleared his throat to play off his delay in responding. "Anyway, David is a great guy. I trust him. He won't let anything happen to you."

I leaned against my desk, nearly toppling over the recent additions and crossed my arms. The sense that he was hiding something reared up stronger than ever. Rather than pursue what might end up being a very loud conversation, I chose a different track. "How long have you two known each other?"

Michael shrugged, his lips lifting in a half smile and some color returned to his face. "We grew up together. We...uh...haven't spoken a lot recently, but I'd still count him as one of my best friends, more like a brother really."

This was an interesting ripple. Someone from Michael's past. Perhaps this David would be able to shed a little more light on the mystery that surrounded Michael.

"Oh good, you're already here," Michael said as he ran the last few steps to the elevator and pressed the already lit call button.

"I was beginning to think I needed to send out a search party. What took you so long?"

"Max." The way he said it did not invite additional questions. I held my peace as he pressed the button again and tapped out a mindless rhythm on his thigh while staring transfixed at the red floor number.

"Is everything alright?" I asked.

The elevator binged and the doors slid open. They hadn't even fully receded into the wall when Michael grabbed my wrist and tugged me inside, his other hand already mashing the down button.

"I told David to meet us at my place after work."

"Kind of figured that," I quipped.

He let out a huff of frustration. "David's generally pretty prompt. I was hoping to get to the house earlier so I could...clean."

I frowned. "He's your friend, I'm sure he'll understand if we're a little late. Besides, your place is pretty freaking spotless."

"Yeah..." he replied unconvincingly.

The elevator arrived with a thud at our destination and Michael launched out the doors. Rather than risk another rebuke, I made sure to stay hot on his heels. There was zero pretense of small talk as he shifted the car in gear and we raced to his house, only narrowly obeying traffic laws.

The Jeep whipped into the empty drive then lurched to a screeching halt. I glanced around to see if maybe our anticipated guest had parked somewhere along the street, but there were no out of place cars there either.

"Where is he?" I asked.

Michael rolled his shoulders and stalked towards the front door. "Maybe he got lost," he mumbled as he double checked his phone.

"Are you sure he knew where to come?" I asked, in an attempt to be helpful.

"He has the address."

"There's no need to be snippy," I said as I closed the door behind me. "Seriously, what's going on? You said you two were friends. Why are you acting so wound up?"

"I haven't seen David in a long time," Michael said, staring at the device in his hand like at any second it was going to impart very bad news.

I narrowed my eyes. "How long?"

Michael glanced up at me briefly. "Twelve years, give or take."

"Twelve years!"

A knock rattled the front door. Before the sound could dissipate, three more came in rapid succession. My throat tightened and I took a nervous step back.

"Who-who is it?" I whispered. My gaze darted between him and the only barrier that stood between us and whatever was on the other side. Michael squared his shoulders and reached for the knob. Everything seemed to slow down as the door swung inward. I held my breath as I took in the behemoth of a guy dominating the threshold.

"I thought you'd never get home," the behemoth's voice rumbled.

The words themselves weren't inherently threatening, but the gravel tone had me frozen in place with only the tiniest inner voice chanting at me to run.

"Where the hell—"

The backlit shadow moved forward, grabbing Michael and cutting off his question. "I've got you!" the voice growled in triumph. Michael's own menacing growl rolled out as he pushed against the stranger. Despite the force Michael was exerting, the intruder advanced deeper into the house.

I quickly scrambled out of the way as Michael continued to grapple with an opponent larger than himself. The struggle brought them to the ground with a loud thunk that shook the furniture. Their growls intensified as each wrestled for the upper hand.

Panic raced icy cold in my veins. My middle clenched in time with their collective thud into the coffee table.

The dying sun shone unhindered through the open door, fierce and unforgiving, the red light like blood on the wooden floors. My breath came in short, strangled gasps as my heart pounded sickeningly. Furniture screamed against wood. A cup fell to the floor with a loud crack and caught the light as it rolled across the room.

My mind raced back to the fateful night on my front porch. I staggered back, unable to see, and ran into a wall. My trembling legs gave out and I sank hard to the floor. The sharp contact jolted my senses. The haze of red cleared to reveal Michael's trashed living room and two bodies locked in violence.

Run.

Fight.

Every hair on my body stood on end at the demand. My spine cracked in a way it was never meant to and my head slammed against the wall. "No, no, no," I moaned. "Not now." Through the haze of building agony, I could make out two concerned faces. Confusion briefly eclipsed the pain.

My mind struggled to chase down the thought, but it slipped away.

I can't stay here.

I couldn't remember why, but I did remember that there was a bathroom around the corner. I pushed through the pain and crawled in the desired direction. Shapes moved in my peripheral as a fresh wave of agony washed over me, giving my blinded senses the last push they needed.

I lurched forward and careened around the corner. My shoulder smashed into the wall. Blinding white stars exploded in my vision as I pushed the last few steps to the bathroom. I slammed the door shut in time to cover my scream as I collapsed.

The static of white noise filled the silence until it separated into two distinct voices.

"Mother of the moon!"

"I'm sorry Michael, I shouldn't have come at you like that."

"No, it's my fault. I didn't think. That's something we've done since we were kids at the House." Michael didn't sound alarmed at all. That meant the other voice probably belonged to David. The David we were expecting.

Fury whipped through me. Fury at changing in a cramped space; for Michael not warning me; for my ruined clothes; and most of all, at myself.

A tentative knock was followed by a concerned voice. "Sara?"

I spun to face the door. Something rumbled inside me, starting deep down and turning to thunder. Michael's surprise permeated the barrier. I felt powerful. I wasn't afraid, I could fulfill my threat.

I'm no one's victim.

The growl faded as I distinguished the sound of retreating steps.

"How is she?" David asked, his tone teasing.

"I think she wants some space."

"No shit. I thought you were going to need backup."

"Shut up, David."

"Seriously, the look on your face. I haven't seen that since Alpha..."

"Just help me straighten this mess and get dinner ready."

The sound of movement suggested that they were doing exactly that, but I could still make out David's quiet laughter. A muted thump punctuated the otherwise quiet and I could all but see the pillow fly across the room to smack

David. I waited until I heard sounds in the kitchen before I began the arduous process of trying to change back.

I will change back. This is my body and I'm in control.

Without me interfering, my body anticipated what it needed to happen. The process was excruciating, but bearable.

Sweat slid down my freshly turned body as I stood. Though the force of my shaking threatened to send me tumbling back to the ground. I gripped the counter with slick hands and waited for the tremor to subside. I briefly contemplated grabbing a towel, but dismissed it given the sensitivity of my new skin. The exertion of two changes made me feel weak. I doubted I'd be able to make it across the hall, let alone indulge in modesty.

I stumbled into the door. It vibrated in its frame and I looked up to the ceiling. It took me two tries to turn the knob before I got the door open. I took a tentative step into the hall and stopped as black spots swam across it. A glance to the side showed that my noisy exit had attracted Michael's and David's notice. I dared either to make a comment with a look. They stayed quiet as I crossed the hall to the guest room.

"Are you sure she was bitten?" The question drifted in as the door closed behind me.

I slumped to the bed.

"—don't want to hear it David," Michael said.

My ears perked up at the tone.

Why does he sound upset?

"I'm just saying—" David started.

"I know what you're saying," Michael cut him off.

"I know things are different now. I can't keep quiet. Your scents—"

"David, please. I'm begging you. One problem at a time."

I frowned at how defeated Michael sounded.

What are they talking about?

"What would you have done if I hadn't been alone? What if Alexander had come instead?" David's last question sounded almost like a threat.

"Mother of the Moon. Is he here?" The fear in Michael's voice pushed me to dress faster. Why was Michael afraid of this Alexander? I nearly fell as I caught my foot in my pant leg and almost missed David's response.

"No. And I hope you realize the position you've put me in."

"I know." Michael's words were said so softly that I almost didn't hear them.

"Maybe it's time to come back. Let go of the past."

"I can't do that. What I am..." I strained to hear the rest of the statement, but all I got was a resigned sigh.

"It doesn't have to be this way." David's voice bordered on pleading.

My hand hesitated on the handle as I paused in my rush to join them. *What am I thinking? I can't barge in and demand to know what they're talking about.* I clenched my fingers and chewed on my lip as I faced the reality of eavesdropping on what was possibly a very private conversation.

Fuck. I'm going to have to pretend like I didn't hear any of it.

My heart sank. I was a terrible liar.

I threw off the doubt, determined to fake my nonchalant attitude and opened the door.

Michael and David looked up at me from the dining table. I joined them and launched into my abbreviated, albeit blunt, introduction.

"Let's try this again. Hi, I'm Sara Sheppard. I was attacked by a serial killer who turned me into a werewolf. You must be David," I finished and held out a hand. Now that I wasn't freaking out or blinded by sunlight, it was clear to see that David bore no resemblance to the mutt. He had a carefree air about him, that combined with his physique and sandy hair reminded me of a surfer.

David laughed then leaned over to snatch me in a bear hug that squished the air out of my lungs. "I like her, she's feisty," he said as he released me.

I wasn't sure what to make of the appraising look that Michael gave me and couldn't help but wonder if it had something to do with the overheard conversation. Before I could pursue it, David spoke up.

"I hear you're an undervalued genius in the PR department where big fluffy works." He gestured at Michael with his thumb. 'Big Fluffy' gave a snort, but didn't take the bait. I chuckled, more eager to talk with David and see what else I could learn about Michael.

"I don't know about genius. I'm mostly a glorified personal assistant and all around go-to girl for the department head. Officially, I'm a Junior PR Consultant," I quipped. "What about you? Michael says you're in town for some work. What do you do?"

Michael averted his gaze at the question and excused himself from the table.

"I'm the Senior Foreman for Wolfsbane Construction. Thankfully, I don't have one of those boring desk jobs like someone we know." David gave me a wink. "I like to travel, move around, and follow the action."

My smile at his silliness dissolved into a frown. "How do you know Michael has a desk job? I thought you two hadn't seen each other in a while." David's happy expression slipped at the same time the dish Michael was carrying clattered to the table.

"Don't let David fool you. He's a homebody through and through. When he's not on a job, he spends most of his time at the House, and only occasionally deigns to enter the real world."

David shrugged, not disputing the correction.

"What project are you working on anyway?" Michael asked, spearing a chicken onto his plate.

"Mm, you know that high-rise on Pine and May? I'm overseeing renovations. It'll keep its historic looks outside, but the interior will be a gallery and office space," he supplied around a mouthful of food.

"You always did like fixing things," Michael commented. David gave him a knowing look and Michael focused on his plate.

"What was it before?" I asked before things could get any more awkward. Another large bite of the delicious chicken made its way into my mouth. I had to consciously avoid swallowing my piece whole.

David launched into an explanation while Michael stacked three more not-so-small pieces on my plate.

I interrupted David to stop Michael from adding more. "Don't you think that's a bit much?"

"We're typically pretty hungry after a change. It takes a lot out of us, especially if there isn't much time to recuperate between," Michael explained.

"Oh." Heat crept up my neck as the embarrassment I'd been ignoring pushed to the surface. I dropped my head to study the heap of chicken while I poked at it with my fork.

I can't wait for the day I'll finally be out of Wolf 101.

"Right," David said, clearing his throat and downing his second glass of water. "Think it's time we got to the bottom of this." I looked up in time to catch Michael give David a barely perceptible shake of his head. "I have to know, man," David said quietly. Michael's hand fisted around his fork, but he didn't respond.

"Have to know what?" I asked, my voice rising slightly.

David turned to face me with what at least appeared to

be a genuine smile. "Maybe *you'll* be more inclined to fill me in on what's going on and what you're doing here."

I looked at Michael for guidance and found none. "I-I thought Michael told you... The *were* who attacked me keeps trying to finish what he started. It's safer—or it was—to be here."

David's sudden laughter startled me and set my nerves on edge. "Not about the mutt." Michael rolled his eyes which only encouraged David to laugh again. "No, I meant what's going on between you two." He leaned forward to rest on his elbows and looked me square in the eye.

My flush from earlier returned with a vengeance at his downright menacing smile.

David left me to my floundering and rounded on Michael. "If I didn't know any better, I'd say you're becoming a believer. Though I can't help but hope to the stars that you're not."

I looked at Michael curious what David meant, but only found Michael glaring daggers at David.

"Or is it too late?" David asked softly.

My gaze darted between the two of them. "Is there something I should know?"

Neither of them said a word. The staring match continued and the tension in the room doubled. At any moment, one of them was going to launch across the table and we'd be right back where this evening started. Not sure if I was quite ready to test my new resolve for control, I scarfed the last piece of chicken and stood, rocking my chair hard enough that I had to catch it to prevent it crashing to the floor.

"How about a drink?" I asked and made a grand show of gathering the dishes.

Without a word, Michael got up to prepare the drinks. By the time everyone had one, it seemed that we were done with the death glares and suspicious prods for the evening. We caught David up with Michael doing most of the talking and mercifully leaving out anything too personal.

"So let me get this straight. Michael stumbles across this guy's scent by chance somewhere around where you two work. While he's trying to figure that out, you're attacked at your house. A month later, he comes back to finish what he started. Then y'all are attacked at the next moon in the woods and he follows you here?" David asked in summary.

We both nodded.

"Something isn't adding up," David said with a scowl. For a hot second, I was afraid he was going to dig deeper into some of the obvious omissions.

"What do you mean?" I blurted.

"Why did he wait?"

I let out a silent sigh of relief. "Maybe he couldn't find me. I mean I was moving around a lot. First, my extended stay at the hospital, then getting lost in suburbia, and ultimately ending up here."

"He's right," Michael said, though he didn't look pleased about it. "Even if it did take him a while to realize that you were alive, it wouldn't have taken him that long to track you. And what about before your first change?" Michael added.

"I never really thought about it," I admitted.

"You know what I think?" David wagged a finger at the two of us. "He's enjoying the stalk." My dinner threatened to revolt at his words. It never occurred to me that he could be toying with us—with me. "All his previous assaults have been quick, right?" David continued, oblivious to my silent freak out. "This is the first time he's been able to enjoy the same kill multiple times, though I imagine he's getting a bit frustrated by now. Are you okay, Sara? You look a little green around the gills."

I gulped my whiskey and soda a little too enthusiastically and coughed against the burn. Michael smacked David.

"Ow. What?"

Michael glared at him.

"Oh. Stars, Sara, I'm sorry. Sometimes my tongue gets ahead of my brain."

I tried a more sedate sip to calm my lurching stomach. "No, you're right, we have to look at the facts. I can't afford to get emotional about this, not anymore."

Michael's warm hand pressed into my back, offering silent comfort. David didn't comment on the gesture, but instead gave me an encouraging smile.

"So, what's the plan?" I asked.

Michael withdrew his hand as if suddenly conscious of where it was. "By David's logic, the best thing to do would be to draw him out. Make him come to us on our terms. This hide and spook business is getting old."

I nodded in whole-hearted agreement.

"Preferably start with someplace public," David said. "Somewhere he feels he can blend into the crowd, but won't risk an attack."

"There's a fair in town and we're off Wednesday due to some office maintenance," Michael proffered.

"About that—" I began.

"Perfect! We can have some fun and hopefully turn the tables on this mutt," David said with a face-splitting grin.

"But—" I tried again.

"Let's not get too ahead of ourselves," Michael cautioned.

"Don't get your tail in a bunch," David said.

"That's great, except I already made plans," I blurted before they could talk over me again. They each turned and looked at me like I'd grown a second head. "I'm already going to the fair with Charline," I clarified.

David glanced at Michael. "I don't mind. The more the merrier."

Michael looked less sure. "I suppose it would make sense to turn it into a group thing," he conceded though he sounded reluctant. "It would look less like his prey walking around with bodyguards."

I groaned none too quietly.

"What?" Michael asked.

"Charline is going to kill me."

19

THE FUN HOUSE

"I cannot believe you." Charline's glare could strip paint and hadn't relented once in the twenty minutes since I'd picked her up.

"How many times do I have to apologize? Look, it was a little unexpected. And it wasn't like I didn't try to tell them we had plans already."

"I needed a girls' day. Emphasis on *girl*. Now I'm being usurped by your stupid boy-toy and his dopey friend."

"He's not dopey," I countered, though having known him less than twenty-four hours, I'd no idea if that was true or not.

She glared at me over her crossed arms from the passenger seat. "Honestly, Sara, I can't believe you'd do this to me. Ever since you and Michael have gotten together. Whatever happened to sisters before misters? You know I need this time. I need a distraction. Not to be surrounded by extra gooey stuff."

"I get it, okay? You're mad. But the fact is things have gotten more complicated and Michael had to call in a favor. This isn't exactly something I wanted either." I brought the car to a halt in the crowded parking lot.

"Fine, I'll concede that having an armed escort was unavoidable. But keep the lovey-dovey stuff to a minimum," she ordered as we made our way to the entrance.

"I think you're giving our relationship more credit than it deserves." She opened her mouth no doubt to continue arguing, but I cut her off. "Michael said they were already here, so keep an eye out. He promised to stay near the ticket pavilion."

Charline's mouth snapped shut, but she diligently began searching the crowds with me for our unwanted companions.

"See anything?" I asked after an unsuccessful few minutes.

"What?" Charline responded absently.

I glanced at her, but her attention remained focused on something ahead.

"I wonder who that is," she mused aloud as she smoothed the fabric over her hips. Personally, I thought the bright yellow sundress was too flirty for a trip to the fair, but I shouldn't have been surprised that a down and single Charline would dress to the nines.

I waited impatiently for the latest herd of people to move so I could see who had captivated her. When the way cleared, it revealed a tall man with broad shoulders. "That's David," I said, impressed that she'd spotted the two before me.

His sandy hair caught the light and his big smile looked as though he'd just finished telling a joke. He wore casual jeans and a red shirt that accented his impressive physique. Michael stood next to him, shaking his head but smiling. My stomach gave a little flutter of happiness to see him in better spirits after the awkward dinner.

She spared me a disbelieving look. "Maybe today won't be a total loss after all." She checked her hair, which was perfect, then sauntered over. They barely had a chance to register our arrival when she introduced herself. "Hi, I'm Charline," she said, oozing charm.

You'd never know she's going through a rough breakup.

David turned his beaming smile on her. "Pleasure to meet you. I'm David. I hope you don't mind too much my crashing the party."

"Not at all," she quickly responded.

I looked at her. Was it my imagination or did she sound breathless?

"Do you like fairs?" she asked as she twirled a finger around a large, red curl then tucked it behind her ear.

Someone nudged me in the ribs. I looked up to see Michael grinning like a kid. "Hey."

"Hey yourself. You haven't been waiting too long, have you?"

He glanced over at David and Charline beaming at each other like a couple of miniature suns. "Not too long." The back of his hand brushed mine, but he didn't take it; instead, he shoved both hands deep in his pockets. A sadness I hadn't anticipated welled up at the loss. "What do you want to do first?" he asked the group at large.

"Ooh, I know!" Charline piped up. "Let's do the Sizzler first." She didn't wait for alternatives before taking off. With a laugh, David followed, leaving me and Michael scrambling to catch up.

The ride itself was ludicrously small and left me to doubt whether or not it could hold all of the people it claimed without falling in a heap of metal. The machine ground to a halt after spinning its patrons every which way and we stepped forward.

"I'm not sure about this," I said nervously.

"Don't be such a wuss. It's nothing." Charline launched out the gate to snag two adjacent benches. "You can sit with me, David, that way Michael and Sara can be together." David shrugged and joined her, snapping down the metal safety bar.

"After you," Michael said with a gallant gesture. I rolled my eyes and took the proffered seat. He sat down and pulled the bar across.

"What happened to the real reason we're here?" I asked as the ride slowly began to rotate.

"David and I talked about that. It needs to look believable if we're going to draw him out and there's nothing to say we can't enjoy ourselves."

My retort died in a screech when the ride unexpectedly flung us out towards the onlookers. The sound of straining metal rang in my ears as the mechanisms struggled to pull us back.

We spun into the center only to be thrown out again. My white-knuckled grip on the bar did nothing to prevent me from sliding into Michael with enough force to bruise a hip. His laughter rolled out around me.

A glance across the way showed both Charline and David also laughing as they slid around on the slick bench.

Finally, the ride began to slow, forcing us in gradually decreasing circles, while I continued to cling to the mockery of a safety bar.

"I haven't been on one of those in ages," David said as he helped Charline out of their bucket. She laughed and gave a response I didn't catch.

"You can let go now," Michael whispered.

I glanced up to see him barely containing a grin. I released the bar to find two perfect imprints of my hands. He raised his eyebrows, but didn't comment. I extricated myself and stalked towards the exit.

"Y'all are ridiculous," I exclaimed as I neared my companions.

"Don't be such a spoil sport. It was fun." Charline bumped David who nodded his agreement.

"You mean to tell me you couldn't hear how that contraption sounded like it was going to fall apart at any moment?" I asked in disbelief.

"I didn't hear anything," Charline said while David shrugged.

"It sounds a lot worse than it is. Perhaps we should stick more to the games," Michael suggested. Charline pouted, but David nodded in agreement after Michael gave him an almost subtle hint to check out our car.

Charline pouted for all of a second then moved on. "The Sizzler really is the only one worth riding anyway. David, what do you say we try that arm at one of the throwing contests?" She may have mentioned his arm, but her appraising look hadn't stopped there.

"You're on," he said with a grin, then they were off.

"Those two are a mess. I forgot how much David can be like a little kid. I guess not that much has changed, though he's probably three times the size he was when I saw him last."

I swiveled my disbelieving stare at Michael. "You mean to tell me that man used to be smaller?"

Michael laughed. "Even *weres* can have late bloomers. Anyway, what about Charline? I mean, I knew she had a bubbly personality, but I had no idea she was such a firecracker."

"It didn't help that Ted suffocated her personality. I don't think she realized how bad it had gotten until he was gone." Seeing her so full of life and unapologetic freedom made me feel guilty for not saying something sooner. "You know," I began as we followed after them, "I think that breakup might have been the best thing for her."

"I'm inclined to agree."

"Good grief, what is this made of?" Charline asked beneath the weight of an obnoxiously large pink bear. "Isn't stuffing supposed to be light?" David casually relieved her of the fluffy monstrosity. "There's no way we can carry all of this. Besides, it's not like we need them," Charline added, eying the rather impressive accumulation of stuffed prizes.

"Are you sure? You could always take them home and put them on your bed," David teased. Charline drew up to her full five-foot-ten and squared her shoulders.

"He's gonna get it now," I whispered to Michael.

"Grown women do not cuddle with stuffed bears," she said, the words dripping with indignation.

To his credit, David took the rebuke in stride. "Good point. In that case, none of these need to make it back to the car."

"What will we do with them?" I asked, impressed that he hadn't faltered under her scathing reproach.

David looked around a moment, then smiled. He took the pink bear over to where a little girl had lost her Go Fish game. The girl's face lit up as she accepted the stuffed creature easily twice her size.

"David, that was beautiful," Charline cooed when he returned, sounding like her heart was melting like ice cream on a hot day.

"All of these games are rigged anyway. Look at it as righting an injustice. What do you say we find homes for the rest of these, then get some more?"

We'd given away the last of the prizes when stomach grumbles started up loud and clear. The guys left to acquire some much-needed refreshments and snackage while we commandeered a picnic table. Charline very pointedly remained in sight, giving the occasional wave to David.

"This is great, Sara. I don't know the last time I had this much fun. Sorry about razzing you so hard this morning."

"It was understandable given the circumstances."

"So..." she dragged out. I glanced at her. Her eyes widened as she leaned over the table conspiratorially. "Is he —you know—one of you?" she whispered.

My mouth fell open and much like a fish, no amount of opening and closing it was making words come out.

She sat back with a satisfied smirk. "I'll take that as a yes."

"But..." I floundered, not sure if I was supposed to keep other werewolf identities secret. Once again, the intricacies of werewolf etiquette eluded me. Throwing caution to the wind, I abandoned hope of any decent denial and went with it. "Yes. Those complications I mentioned earlier? Consider him the cavalry."

"You won't hear me complaining. When I asked for a distraction, I had no idea how well you'd deliver. I've never dated a werewolf before. Not that I'm aware of anyway. Maybe Billy in third grade..." she pondered to herself. "Anything I should know?" She flashed me a smile very much her usual, confident self.

I smiled back at her, glad to see her lightening back up to the person I'd met two years ago. Then a sudden thought almost stole all the happy. Did *weres* date humans? I'd never thought to ask, but it made a little sense that they didn't in light of Michael's own confession of liking me and doing nothing about it.

"Everything alright?" Charline asked.

"Umm," I began awkwardly.

I really need to learn more about werewolf culture.

Before I could ruin Charline's fun, Michael and David returned laden with food and began spreading the loot across the table. As David took his seat beside Charline, he gave her a very thorough once over which she dutifully pretended to ignore. I shook my head and grabbed something at random.

"You okay?" Michael asked, leaning in close so he could whisper.

"Yeah, it's just...I've never been on a double date before," I admitted.

Both David and Charline looked up from laughing with each other. In the blink of an eye the entire mood shifted. Michael looked at David. David looked at Michael. Charline looked at David. Then as quickly as the tension appeared it vanished.

"Then we'll have to go on more," David said, giving Charline a wink.

Beside me, Michael relaxed slightly. David caught his eye again, but neither said anything about the unusual exchange. Rather than dwell on it, I focused on eating and appreciated being at a table full of friends.

While I didn't really know what to make of David, I felt a kinship with him that made me want to count him a friend anyway. Maybe it was Charline bridging the gap or maybe Michael, but I wasn't about to ignore the inherent trust. As for Michael, whatever we were or would be, I hoped I would always be able to at least count him a friend. Charline laughed and her infectious joy spread around the table brightening all of us.

When was the last time I felt this at ease?

Something stirred deep inside of me. It took me a moment to recognize it—anger. I was furious that this mutt, this animal, had taken my life hostage and expected me to dance to his malicious tune.

If it's the last thing I do, I will never be someone's victim again.

I didn't know who this new Sara was, but I'd been

looking for her my whole life. She was strong and confident, or at least mostly confident, and wasn't going to stand aside while others pushed her around.

Maybe the wolf isn't so bad.

Maybe it's not the wolf.

The counterintuitive thought struck me as odd. I'd never been this easy or outgoing before. It had to be the wolf. She was the one constantly threatening to send me into a frenzy. But deep down, I knew the truth. I could have easily snapped and gone on my own homicidal rampage or melted into a mess with or without the attack.

"Sara."

I glanced around to see Charline looking a bit impatient. "What?"

"Welcome back to Earth. I was saying that David volunteered to take me to the fun house, which I know you hate. So, you and Michael should wander around and meet us at the end."

I looked at Michael, not really sure if it was safe or wise to leave David alone with Charline.

Michael shrugged. "I say let them. I could go for a casual walk." He squeezed my waist and I squeaked. "That sounded like a yes to me. You two have fun and try not to get into too much trouble."

He gave David a serious look and I took the opportunity to spare one for Charline as well. She rolled her eyes and the two of them raced each other towards the funhouse entrance.

"Come on, it's you and me now," Michael said.

He helped me off of the bench and chose a direction at random in complete disregard of Charline's suggestion. We walked in silence, meandering our way through the slowly thinning crowds until we found ourselves alone behind a strip of rides and tents.

"Are you having a good day?" he asked when the noise cut down to a dull murmur.

"Yes," I said with a laugh.

"Why is that funny? I think it's a great thing."

"It is, it is. I was thinking about that—how nice today is and how I haven't really been this relaxed in a while. Nothing against our time together at the house," I quickly added. He raised a skeptical eyebrow, but let me continue. "It's nice to be outside. Where I can stretch my legs and breathe fresh air, even if it is tainted with exhaust and trash."

"I know what you mean. Humans are nasty creatures." I punched him in the arm, then allowed him to wrap that same arm around my shoulders. "I'm glad you're enjoying yourself," he said, rubbing my arm. "I don't mean to keep you cooped up or be overbearing. I...I just want to keep you safe."

We walked a little farther in quiet, turning to continue our way behind another strip of mechanics supporting the small carnival rides.

"You know, I've actually liked you for a while, Sara," Michael said, breaking the silence.

I looked up at him. "You may have mentioned something to that effect. Though I'm not sure how much I believe it."

"Believe it," he said with a squeeze for added emphasis.

"Then why didn't you do anything about it before?"

His face fell. "My life is complicated."

"So you said. But so is mine," I countered.

Sorrow clouded his features. "There are rules I have to live by. Rules that mean I have to be very careful with who I get involved with."

"So, what you're saying is that all of the rumors about you sleeping with half the office aren't true and you're *not* an incorrigible flirt," I teased.

He laughed. "The flirt part may be true, though mostly unintentional."

"Sure it is," I poked.

"But the other is purely fabricated. I've had partners, but not nearly as many as everyone wants to believe. Truthfully, before all of this, it'd been longer than I care to admit," he said, guiding us around a generator.

I snorted.

"Seriously. I know that the whole *were* thing kind of forced us together, but I wanted to get closer to you. I went through all kinds of scenarios, including accidentally knocking down your lunch, so I'd have to take you out to make it up to you."

I couldn't help but laugh. The idea of Michael having to stoop to such a juvenile meet-cute was preposterous.

"You laugh, but that was an actual plan at one point. There was even a time when I was afraid you and Bob were a thing." He shuddered. "That was awful." I gave him a scornful look and he reached his free hand up to stroke my cheek. "You're a very private person, Sara. I wanted a chance to get to know you. I had this feeling that you were worth getting to know."

My face warmed beneath his touch. Instead of commenting on the blatant blush, he planted a soft kiss on my nose and gave me an unexpected twirl. Laughter bubbled up and I did another spin on my own. When I stopped, his eyes widened with surprise. He shoved me hard and I stumbled a few paces.

I regained my bearings right as a metallic bang shook the immediate area. A high-pitched squeal of white noise split the air and the world vibrated in time with the deafening sound puncturing my ears. To my surprise, no one rushed to investigate.

I blinked repeatedly and covered my ears to muffle the

persistent sound. Without the ringing, my vision finally focused on the scene before me. Michael lay atop a heap of twisted metal, all that remained of a generator. As if the sight of viciously sharp metal curled around him wasn't terrifying enough, a horrifying creature, straight out of a nightmare perched on his chest. Then the smell hit me.

The twisted scent of wrongness clogged my senses. Nails screeched on metal and Michael cried out. The familiar clench started in my middle. I restrained it, but didn't try to shove it off as I ate up the ground separating us. When I landed on top of the *were*, my nails were sharp enough to pierce skin. I willed them longer and used my momentum to roll us away. I released him mid roll and sprung to a crouch.

Blood poured down from the mutt's shoulders. His face was such a mess of contortions I couldn't even distinguish his eyes. Nothing about him was natural for a *were* or a human. He moved as if to renew his assault on Michael and I maneuvered to stay between them.

Pain lanced through my jaw as it shifted to make room for teeth not intended for a human mouth. He took another step forward. I flexed my claws and growled, showing more than enough teeth to back up my threat. Uncertainty flashed across his misshapen face. I lowered the growl another octave and shifted my weight, ready to lunge.

He gave a final glance toward Michael, then with a snarl, the mutt turned and vanished. I waited a couple of tense seconds, scanning the area to make sure he was truly gone, before racing to Michael's side.

Blood coated everything. It flowed freely to saturate what remained of Michael's clothes and dripped with abandon onto the dead grass. I reached out to try and staunch the wound. That's when I remembered my hands weren't exactly hands. I glanced around in alarm and thankfully found not a soul in sight.

I closed my eyes and took a deep breath. Calming my body wasn't easy with so much adrenaline rocketing through it, but with a couple steadying breaths, I could feel my claws shorten. Another deep breath.

Don't retch.

My fingers shrunk to normal length. Another deep breath. My jaw popped painfully and I tasted the metallic tang of blood. I spit it out with lips that felt human enough.

I took one last look at Michael and ran. Maybe it wasn't right to leave him vulnerable, but he needed help and I couldn't give it to him. I needed to find David.

Clouds of dust wafted up around me as I skidded onto the main track of the fair. All I could do was pray that I looked mostly human. Smells wove like braids amidst the stalls of games and fair food, the scents of the carnival we'd jokingly commented on, now nauseatingly clear.

I spun around in search of a heading, becoming more agitated with each pass. How was I supposed to find anyone in this chaos? Then a familiar scent caught my attention. The unique mix of spices and baking stood out like a breath of fresh air against the stink of sweat and fumes. It wasn't much of a leap to pick out David's which seemed to swirl around hers and had a distinct *were*-ness to it.

I dove into the crowd, swerving around people as I raced along the trail. It was beginning to feel as though they had crisscrossed the whole fair when I finally caught sight of them. They turned to look at me, smiles on their faces, when I skidded to a breathless stop.

"Well, what?" Charline's sharp tone snapped me back to reality.

"Michael needs help."

"Where?" David asked. No other questions.

"This way."

We cut straight across the fair, barely excusing ourselves as we forced people out of our way. I didn't have the patience to be polite, all I could see was red-tinted metal shining in the afternoon sun.

"Oh my God," Charline gasped when we emerged behind the tents. I'd hoped that he would've healed more, but it would take more than a few minutes of super healing for the gash showing bone in his shoulder to seal up. If anything, he looked worse. Rips covered his clothes and flesh without distinction.

My mind flashed to teeth cutting through my arm while a street light flickered. I shook my head. I didn't have time for that.

"Charline, get some water and towels," David ordered. "Sara, come over here and give me a hand."

Charline barely hesitated before spinning on her heel to pursue her task. I, on the other hand, approached with caution.

Explanations of what happened spilled from my lips. "I don't know how we didn't smell him. I know Charline said to meet you guys, but we were talking and sort of wandered off. One minute everything was fine and we were laughing, then there was a horrible noise. My ears still hurt. I didn't check to see if he was breathing. The mutt left, but I don't know where he went. I'm sorry, I didn't know what else to do. I know it was dangerous to leave him, but..."

"Sara." David's firm tone immediately ebbed the flow. "This wasn't your fault. We knew this could happen. In fact, we were planning on it. We shouldn't have split up, that's on us." He indicated the severely injured Michael and himself. "Help me get him up. We should be able to get to the cars through there."

I looked at him in disbelief. "Will I develop a sixth sense

to know where the car is? Because that could come in handy."

"Not quite. I noticed this line of trees and more specifically, those stalls, when we got here," David said, matter of fact.

I narrowed my eyes.

"It's my job to pay attention. You didn't think he wanted me here so I could keep your lovely friend company, did you?"

Thoroughly chastised, I moved to help.

We carefully maneuvered Michael into a seated position. An awful squelch filled the air as we pulled him free of the devastated generator. I forced the bile in my stomach back down and envied David his calm.

"There you are, Charline. Good, you found some towels. Let's clean him up a bit, maybe we can attract a little less notice. We'll stick to the trees just in case. Can you grab my truck and pull it up right there? It's a white pickup," he elaborated as he pointed over to where the trees and the stalls abruptly ended.

The distance yawned before me.

How are we going to get him all the way to the car without anyone noticing?

Charline accepted the keys and immediately began running towards the parking lot. While she was definitely pale, she too was exceptionally calm. I glanced over at David and the resolute set of his mouth.

Why am I the only one freaking out?

We were almost to the edge when Charline pulled up in a large white pickup, the tires squealing to a stop. David did a thorough sweep of the area for any potential witnesses, then we began the arduous process of getting him in the truck. Michael let out an agonized moan as we situated him in the passenger seat and strapped him in so he wouldn't fall over.

Charline hopped out and grabbed my arm. "Come on, Sara. We'll follow in your car." David shot her a look. "It's not far. You should be able to keep an eye on us from the cab." David gave the tiniest of nods and let her pull me away. She guided us over to my car and made sure that I was buckled before tearing off after the truck.

20

———

SURVIVAL INSTINCTS

"Do you think he's okay?" I asked as we stopped at yet another red light.

Charline glanced at me. "I'm sure he's gonna be fine, sugar." The heavy dose of Southern did nothing for my anxiety.

"There was so much blood. How can there be that much blood in one person?" The distinct image of metal dripping crimson dominated my vision. I squeezed my eyes shut, but the gory vision remained.

"We're almost there," she said, rather than address my concern. My vision cleared enough to recognize we were entering Michael's neighborhood, then fuzzed back into smears of gray and green.

"Do you think he's awake yet?" I asked in a near whisper.

"I don't know about that, but he's not in the truck anymore."

"What?" I turned my attention to the white—empty—pickup parked beside us. My fingers fumbled at the seat belt determined to hold me captive. I pulled relentlessly at the clip with no success.

How is it I can destroy a dash with my bare hands, but I can't get out of a fucking seatbelt?

"Get me out of this thing," I growled.

"Take it easy. Let me help." She reached over and the belt clicked.

I launched out the door before the strap was completely clear. Drops of red staining the concrete caught my attention and I sprinted the rest of the way to the door. It opened without resistance to an empty living room. My ear twitched as it caught the sound of a faint groan and my stomach twisted itself into knots.

Please be okay.

I made my way with halting steps down the hall to the main bedroom. The door stood open, offering a clear view of David helping Michael into the bed. Michael might have been awake, but he looked awful. I was amazed that David had managed to bring him inside by himself.

"Do you think he'll be alright?" I asked in a whisper as I tiptoed into the room wary of making too much noise.

"I'm trying to get him settled without making any of the wounds worse," David responded as he adjusted another pillow.

"I'll be fine. Stop treating me like a baby," Michael retorted, smacking away David's helping hand, then violently shook with a series of coughs.

"You look pretty bad," David said. "And sound worse. It's going to take a while to get back up to speed after a fight like that."

"Do werewolf scratches take longer to heal?" Charline asked as she set down several waters.

David ran a hand through his hair as he straightened. "Yes and no. *Were* on *were* is one of the most brutal assaults that we can endure. Whether that's because of some *were* gene that makes the attacks more lethal or simply because the attacks *are* more lethal is a toss-up." He looked over at me. "You've seen how rapidly we can heal and how that healing can save someone, but it isn't a cure-all."

I looked away. Fingers brushed my wrist and my attention instantly refocused on Michael. "What is it, do you need something to drink?" I asked, already reaching for a glass.

"You changed." His face took on an absent expression. "You controlled your change," he elaborated, ignoring the proffered water. "You fought him off. I was blindsided. He came from upwind. But you...you stopped him." A hint of awe touched his voice.

"I...it...I didn't know what else to do," I floundered.

"I'm so proud of you."

"What?" I asked at the unexpected praise.

Michael lunged forward to grab me. The air went out in a whoosh and by some miracle the glass I held didn't shatter on the floor. As abruptly as the hug started, he was being pulled away. "Ow. Get off of me. I can hug her if I want. Stop mothering me," Michael said as he fought with David.

"How long do you think it will take him to get back on his feet?" Charline asked.

"I'm right here," Michael griped. She patted his arm absently.

"He should be able to return to work in a couple of days, but I wouldn't push it. From what I can tell, most of the gashes are pretty deep. He needs rest."

"I'll be fine," Michael insisted.

"I'm going to drive Charline home," David declared. "I'll be back in a little while. You two try to get some sleep. I won't be long." He spared us each a look before leaving.

The moment the two were gone, Michael's mask of

bravado fell. His breathing became more labored as his body struggled to heal wounds that would've killed anyone else. He lay unmoving as if all the fight had gone out of him and in an awful twist, I knew exactly what he was feeling. I was intimately familiar with this kind of agony.

"You can stop staring," he coughed. "I can practically hear you worrying."

"Michael, you shouldn't talk." He shifted and I caught the pained groan he tried to suppress. I placed a gentle but firm hand on his shoulder. "You got knocked harder than I thought if you think I'm going to let you out of bed."

"Ouch, I don't know what hurts more, my shoulder or my pride."

"Don't be a baby, I didn't press that hard." I pulled up an armchair and brushed his hair back from his sweat drenched forehead. "Be honest. How do you feel?"

He gave a strained chuckle. "Kind of like I was attacked by a homicidal werewolf."

I flicked his forehead.

"Ow. Have you no sympathy?"

I narrowed my eyes at him and he let out a shallow sigh.

"Fine. In all seriousness, I hurt like hell. That mutt really did a number on me. I can't believe I'm saying this, but I think I'm going to have to call in tomorrow. And before you suggest it, you're not, you've already missed too much. Besides, what would the office gossips say if we both missed a day?" He winked and then winced.

"Considering one of the biggest office gossips already knows the truth, I'm not really all that concerned. Besides, I doubt anyone would make the connection that the two of us might be playing hooky together."

"Why do you do that?" He reached out, but stopped.

"What do you mean?"

"You assume that no one would put the two of us together. Why?"

"We've been through this. You're you and I'm...me." I failed to see why that was so hard for him to understand.

"What does that mean? Sara, you're amazing—before the bite and after. Why can't you see that?" His gaze clouded with concerned confusion and probably a concussion.

"Because there's nothing to see," I said, anger flashing through me. It was a fact, it had always been a fact. He was the guy always at the center, the one everyone saw, the one everyone always wanted to be, and I was wallpaper, never noticed, never missed. I was just me, just Sara.

"That's not true. You've got to stop belittling yourself. Why can't you see the person I see, the person everyone sees?" He attempted to roll on his side and cried out.

"Stop moving," I insisted. "This conversation can wait."

"No. Not until you listen. You're an incredible person. You're full of life, and curiosity, and a passion that I nearly forgot."

I shook my head. "That's the wolf, it's not me."

"For the love of the moon, you can't keep blaming the wolf! It doesn't change who you are."

"Except I wasn't any of those things before I was bitten," I countered, my anger spiking again. "Can we have this argument when you're feeling better?"

"Why can't you believe that you're special? There's a fire in you, and the only one trying to put it out is you."

"That's not true." My lips pressed into a thin line. Somehow hearing someone say it out loud was so much worse than only feeling it inside.

"Yes, it is."

"Stop. Michael, please just stop," I begged, but my pleas went unheard.

"It's a terrible thing to say, but sometimes I'm grateful I got the call to hunt down this mutt. You saved my life, and I'm not just talking about today. Yes, I know I've found my way to the heart of office gossip as a flirt and who knows what else, but I've never been with someone who made my breath catch like you do. I'd do anything to keep you safe, even risk—"

"Michael, stop. This isn't the time for this. You need to rest. You need to..." The tears welling in my eyes were quickly joined by a lump in my throat that silenced me.

"I can't pretend anymore. Stars know I'll pay for that, but I can't."

"What are you talking about? Pretend what?" I asked, terrified of the answer.

"I love you, Sara, you have to know that by now."

"What?" I asked, the word as numb as my lips.

"I know it's wrong to be glad that you were bitten, but I am. You're the best thing that's ever happened to me and if I have to sacrifice everything, then I will."

"I can't do this." I vacated the chair and made a beeline for the door.

"Sara, wait!" he called after me before his voice was stolen by a massive coughing fit.

I spun around to see him hanging half out of the bed. "What are you doing!" I moved back to his side and helped re-situate him. "Are you out of your mind?"

"I'm sorry. I didn't mean to..." He squeezed his eyes shut. When he opened them again, they were clearer, but not by much. "I can barely think straight. Everything hurts. I don't want to argue with you, Sara. If it takes walking into the office and making a public declaration, then I will."

"That's not funny."

"It's not meant to be. I care for you, more than I've cared

for anyone in a long time. And while I can't understand how you can't see how special you are, you need to know that I do. I believe in you and I pray to the moon that you learn to believe in yourself too before it's too late."

His words struck a nerve that I tried very hard to keep buried. I licked my lips unsure of how to respond in a way that wouldn't result in me having a total meltdown. "If I promise to stay, will you stop trying to get up, and rest?"

His features relaxed slightly, but the fear and sorrow in his eyes didn't fade. He gave me a small nod and looked away.

A fresh wave of guilt tightened around my chest. With a heavy sigh, I carefully climbed in beside him. He cast me a surprised glance, but said nothing. We sat in silence, the weight of everything he'd said heavy between us. I'd never had anyone call me out so thoroughly on my lack of self-worth, not even my parents. It had defined me since I was little. Since I'd learned the truth about who I really was: no one.

I, Sara Sheppard, was no one.

I slid a little closer to Michael. I hoped one day his words would be true, but I feared they never would be.

I sat up, clawing for air. Sweat drenched every scrap of fabric around me while a humid heat clogged my lungs. Careful to not disturb Michael, I crawled out of bed. I peeled off my clothes and let out a grateful sigh at the cool kiss of fresh air on my bare skin.

A wave of panic shattered my relief as I registered the source of the ungodly heat. I scrambled back to Michael's side and stared down at his unmoving form as if I could will a fever to be visible. I pressed my fingers against the smooth skin of his forehead, then snatched my burned hand back as cold flooded through me.

No. This can't be happening. Werewolves don't get sick.

I fought back my rising panic and strained to hear him breathing. A faint rasp tickled my ears, shallow, but there. Momentarily reassured, I pulled on the nearest thing that wasn't soaked, which happened to be a shirt of Michael's. Not bothering with anything else, I ran down the hall, sending up a silent prayer that Charline hadn't charmed David into staying the night. A quick glance in the guest bedroom showed that David had not succumbed to Charline's wiles. I woke him with a violence that bordered on hysteria.

"Wha—?"

"Michael has a fever. He's burning up." Cold swept through me with renewed vigor at the blank look on David's face.

Oh God he doesn't know what to do either.

In a heartbeat, his mouth set in a grim line as he threw back the covers, then strode down the short hall. I blinked, realizing I'd been left behind and spun to follow, nearly crashing into the wall in my hurry to catch up.

"Should we take him to a hospital?" The darkness swallowed my feeble question.

"That probably wouldn't be a very good idea."

"Why not? I was at the hospital."

He looked at me clearly at a loss. "You hadn't turned yet. How are we supposed to explain this?" He peeled the cover back and I gagged. Michael's bandages were a mess of sticky fluids, including what was clearly blood seeping through, and surprisingly hair. The stench of decay wafted up to fill the room with cloying sweetness.

"Why is he like that?" I held a hand to my mouth and fought down the bile threatening to rise.

"I don't know," he said shakily.

I stared at him as he dug deep for a solution.

Finally, he fisted his hands and squared his shoulders. "I'm going to make a call. In the meantime, try to clean him up. That much, I do know." David swiftly exited the room, leaving me all alone with the sensory onslaught.

I finally absorbed the instructions and flicked on the lamp. Michael and the putrid mess that covered his chest looked even worse in the light. Before I could wuss out, I gathered hot water, towels, antiseptic, and a hand towel to tie over my nose and mouth. When I returned with my supplies, Michael hadn't so much as twitched. I took a deep breath that I instantly regretted and systematically began removing the ruined bandages.

They clung with sickening stubbornness to the rancid wounds. The long scratches across his chest glared red and angry in the low light, the gaping wounds oozing a greenish pus. I peeled back the bandage barely covering the deepest slash and found the source of the matted hair. It was growing out of the wound.

Fortitude escaped me. I ripped the cloth from my face and vomited in the wastebasket I'd brought for the bandages. I glanced up as David entered the room still on the phone, likely alarmed by the sound of dry heaves. His face went very pale as he took in Michael's wounds in the lurid light.

"Yeah. Wait a sec." He scrambled back out of the room, his voice gaining strength the farther he got from the horrific sight.

Steeling myself, I regained control of my body and returned to the task at hand. As I cleaned, Michael's words from a couple of hours ago came back to me. 'You stopped him'. But I hadn't, I hadn't saved the man I'd come to care so much about, who was showing me there was more to living than waking up and going through the motions.

I choked back a sob.

The scuff of a foot on the hardwood alerted me to David's return since my sense of smell was completely shot. I couldn't help but wonder if I'd ever be able to smell anything other than the rot of infected flesh.

"Please tell me you have something," I rasped.

"We have a theory, but I have no idea how we're going to put it into action."

Tears streamed unhindered down my face as I looked back at him. "What do we need to do?"

He took a deep breath and pointed to the matted hair. "You see this? It's like part of his body is trying to change. We need to get all of it to change."

"How are we supposed to do that? Is he even strong enough to change? It could kill him."

"Yes, it could. But he is definitely dying now." He looked back at me as if willing me to believe that it would work. "It's all we've got," he whispered. The silence stretched. The seconds ticking by like pieces of Michael's life slipping through my fingers.

"How?" I finally asked.

"We need to trigger his survival instinct. If he feels threatened enough, the wolf should take over and force a change. Like when you..." He looked at me sideways.

"Like when I freak out. But Michael isn't afraid. Simply growling at him isn't going to work."

"No, but threatening his mate might." My face scrunched in confusion. "Sara, you have to know, he'd do anything for you," David said quietly.

That was the problem, I did know. That was what had gotten us here in the first place. I nodded my head, not trusting words.

David's hands closed around mine. "I need you to be strong, Sara. It has to feel real."

I nodded again.

"This could be really dangerous," he cautioned. "If the mutt is nearby, we could be in a lot of trouble. I hope the neighbors aren't feeling especially helpful tonight." Then, without any other preamble, he turned and left.

I tried to squash the growing hopelessness and sudden fear. David hadn't exactly said how he intended to accomplish this impossible, potentially deadly goal. I suspected he'd left it that way intentionally.

I don't care what it is, as long as it works.

I reached over and turned off the light. I couldn't bear to see Michael like this. Despite enhanced night vision, the room seemed exceptionally dark without the lamp. Despair seeped into my bones devouring the tiny spark of hope David had created.

A long, shrill, howl echoed down the hall. The hair on the back of my neck rose in response to the piercing sound. I knew that howl—I'd run from it in my nightmares every night since I'd turned—it was a hunting howl. And there, at the back end, as it trailed off, a note of victory—he found what he was looking for. My stomach clenched.

No. I will not change. I will be strong for Michael. I couldn't save him before, but I can now.

I stood and turned to confront the threat. He twitched beside me and I glanced down.

He can hear it too.

Hope bloomed inside my chest. Then a low growl emanated behind me. My happy feeling evaporated. I swallowed hard and turned back to the doorway. Logically, I knew it had to be David—prayed that it was—but all I saw was the flash of teeth. For once, it wasn't my mind playing tricks on me. These were real teeth catching the almost nonexistent light in the room as their owner launched across the space separating us.

I screamed as we fell to the floor. My surprise battled with the trauma that was trying to overlay the two experiences. I was in a bedroom. No, I was on a sidewalk.

It's just David. It's just David.

The mantra repeated itself over and over in my mind. I pushed against the heavy form only to have my arms fold beneath his weight. His savage growl merged with the memory of deafening thunder. Teeth grazed my shoulder. I flinched and something deep down tried to take control.

I can't change.

A scream ripped through me as jagged teeth tore into my arm. In a split second of pain came clarity as instinct took over with a vengeance.

Not again, never again.

Claws sprouted and I used my free arm to swipe at my assailant. The nails dragged into flesh and the teeth relinquished their hold. Injured arm cradled to my chest, I swiped again and again at the darkness, blinded by pain and rage, my own growl rolling out to fill the night.

Not ever again.

Something slammed into the wall. I stopped blindly swinging and looked up. The beast I hoped was David sat five feet away staring at the bed, heedless of the blood beginning to mat his right side. The contrast snapped me back to my senses.

I lurched to my feet and the room swam before I regained my equilibrium. Michael bucked on the bed and his head thumped hard into the headboard. I'd never seen anyone go through the transformation, not even myself. A sense of morbid curiosity consumed me. I watched fascinated as his legs cracked and bent the wrong way. I willed my feet to carry me out of the room, but they refused to move. I needed to know. I noticed that David wasn't leaving either. He needed to know too. Would Michael live?

Each pop of bone and sinew squeezed my heart. I could see why people chose to change in private. It wasn't just the obvious, that it wasn't exactly a pretty sight, there was something more. The change made you vulnerable, caught between the battle of selves fighting for dominance and ultimately being weaker than both.

David lingered another minute then padded out of the room. When he returned, it was on two legs instead of four. I barely spared him a glance, absorbed in the awfulness that was the change. David may have been confident in Michael's survival, but I was not.

Michael's transition ended with him disappearing under a mat of bandages and bedding. I strained to hear the sound of a ragged breath or faltering heartbeat, something, anything to know he was alive. A faint whimper drifted up from the tangle of bedding. I lurched forward, scrambling to remove the ruined sheets.

"Sara," David's whisper urged caution. Another whimper.

With slightly more care than I'd started, I removed the shredded bedding. The figure beneath filled the bed, larger than I remembered and infinitely more fragile. I didn't care if he would instinctively lash out, I reached out to him. He flinched and whimpered again, but otherwise didn't move.

"David, turn on the lamp. He's so dark I can't see anything."

A soft light bloomed behind me. I took a moment to let my eyes adjust, then set to the very careful task of checking Michael over. Parts of his arm and shoulder had the look of raw, new skin with next to no fur. That was promising, if a little disturbing.

I shamelessly used soft, comforting sounds in order to

roll him a bit so I could see his chest. The gashes there hit me like a slap in the face. My strangled sound made Michael twitch and brought David rushing over.

"What is it?" he asked in a harsh whisper.

"They're still there."

David took a moment to perform his own inspection. After a minute, he let out a huge sigh. "But he's not really bleeding anymore and what blood there is looks healthy." In a true test of my squeamishness, he gently put my fingers in the little blood that had leaked out of the wounds and held it up to the light. Red. A bright, perfect red.

"Let's put a temporary bandage on them and let him get some rest. The change did what it needed to, the infection is gone and for now, he'll be okay."

I nodded and pulled out the fresh gauze I'd acquired earlier.

"Let's give him some space," David said once we'd applied our haphazard bandages, including a smaller one for the quickly healing punctures in my arm.

"But..."

"He needs rest and no distractions. I can smell your anxiety," David emphasized.

I conceded and picked up the wastebasket filled with the putrid remains of his previous bandages as well as the ruined sheets. Once the trash was triple-bagged, I joined David in the living room where he'd already acquired us some water. I sipped it, knowing my body needed it, but not really appreciating it. We sat on the couch in silence to wait for dawn. The hours dragged by and my eyelids grew heavy.

I didn't remember falling asleep, but there I was, an awkward sleepover mess of tangled limbs with David on the couch. He looked like he was stirring as well, but what had woken us? A soft shuffling noise made my ear twitch.

Logically, I knew I should be more concerned about a

strange noise, but exhaustion kept the alarm muted. I cast a drowsy glance towards the hall then bolted upright much to the discomfort of David.

"I see how it is. I'm out of commission for one night and you're already moving in on my girl."

David waved away the accusation, more concerned with untangling himself.

"Mi—" I began.

Michael held up his hand to stop the onslaught of concern. That simple movement alone betrayed his true state. I could clearly see the tightness in his face, his hand shaking as it supported him against the wall, how he wasn't putting any weight on his leading leg. My heart constricted, but I held my tongue. Meanwhile, David extricated himself from the couch and stretched his arms above his head. That's when I realized he was only wearing boxers...tight boxers. Heat flooded my face and I quickly adjusted my attention.

"So, um, how are you feeling?" I asked Michael.

"That's all I get?" he teased. My attempt at a smile faltered. His laugh sounded painful. "No hug? No kiss? I almost died."

I bounded up, thankful that I didn't immediately face plant, and went to him.

"Easy," he whispered in my ear as I cautiously wrapped my arms around him.

"I'm glad you're okay. Well, mostly okay. How do you feel?" I asked again.

"I suspect better than I have a right to. Do I want to know how bad I was or how I'm alive at all?" I looked back at David who really didn't seem to care at all about his state of dress or lack thereof. He simply shrugged and made his way to the kitchen.

I gently guided Michael to the now vacant couch. David

placed a glass of water within easy reach as Michael slowly lowered himself, using me as a support.

"How much do you remember?" I asked.

"I can remember the fair—most of it anyway. I know we were split up when the mutt attacked us... Behind the tents?" I nodded and he continued. "I remember landing on something and a bang, but it's hazy." He glanced at me sideways, but didn't say anything. I could almost make out the surprise and was it—pride in his expression? "After that, it's all fog. I don't remember how we got here. I don't remember what the wounds were or how extensive. Only...pain, a lot of pain."

Before I could say anything, David reached out. His hand looked so healthy compared to Michael's. "Suffice it to say, it was bad. All that matters now is that you're recovering. You're alive and you have your very brave partner to thank for it."

Michael stiffened beside me. I glanced over at him, curious if he remembered any of our conversation after David and Charline had left. He met my gaze with a look that bordered on hunted.

David's voice cut through the mounting tension. "You will have plenty of time to stare into each other's eyes after all of this is over. Right now, we have a mutt to sort out."

I shifted my focus to David. "You're right, we need a plan of action. I'm tired of running, of always looking over my shoulder. I've been so caught up in simply trying not to be killed that I haven't been able to really absorb any of the new, amazing things in my life. I think it's time this fucking son of a bitch got a taste of his own medicine."

Silence met my declaration. I glanced at each of them in search of a reason for the inexplicable lack of response. Michael looked at me like I was a victim of the alien body snatchers while David seemed to be appraising me with a new level of respect.

"What?"

David barked out a laugh. "Eventually, the wolf brings out the mettle in all of us. You can go ahead and shut your mouth, Michael. Your dreams of a meek partner are gone." Shaking his head, David made his way down the hall past us, shouting back, "Clothing, food, and then plans."

In silent agreement, Michael and I made our way back to his bedroom. With each step, the tension between us increased. Between our conversation last night and all of David's strange comments, not to mention Michael's even stranger reactions, I was more lost than ever.

"I've never had dreams of a meek partner, nor have I once thought of you as meek," Michael said as my head popped through a fresh shirt.

"I didn't say anything," I responded as neutrally as I could. David's words had cut a little too close to home.

Michael sighed. "It's written all over your face, etched in your body language, and edging your scent. Stop looking at me like that, it's called paying attention. I may be half dead, but I'm perfectly capable of being observant."

"We should have enough food for breakfast," I said, ignoring his comment. "We might need to get a little creative though, you're due to go to the store." I made an exaggerated show of looking for my shoes.

"Sara, look at me."

I kept searching.

"Sara, please."

I dragged my gaze up to meet his.

"You're not meek, you're reserved."

"Then what was that surprise for?" I asked a tad aggressively.

It took him a moment, then a smile spread across his face. "I don't think I've ever heard you curse."

"What do you mean? I curse all of the time."

"Not around me." He finished dressing and walked over. "I always knew you could be bold. Honestly, I've been waiting for you to trust me enough to show me that side of yourself." He moved a loose strand of hair out of my face. "It's nice to see you finally do."

21

CHARLINE'S BIG PLAY

I didn't even jump when Charline's voice materialized out of thin air in my cubicle. "Are you planning to sit here all night or are you coming to the store?"

"What do you mean?"

"I'm going to the store with you."

I looked at her blankly, the words not registering.

"David called," she prompted. "Apparently, you two have eaten Michael out of house and home."

"You're coming?" I echoed.

Her sigh of exasperation could have won an Oscar. "Obviously. It's not like all of you are up to the task of carrying things." She quickly hurried on before my face could crumble much further. "Besides, I told David I'd cook for everyone tonight."

And there it was—her big play. I dared David not to fall madly in love with her after one of her all-out home cooked dinners. His werewolf stomach didn't stand a chance.

"Don't look at me like that."

"How am I looking at you?" I tried not to laugh, but my humor covered the words.

"Quite frankly, you have an evil grin. It's almost like you're implying that I'm up to something."

"Aren't you?" I elbowed her gently.

"Oh hush." She waved away my subtle nudge. "Now, are you guarding the office tonight or can we go?"

I looked at the clock for the first time in what must've been hours and shot straight out of my seat.

"Wow, you're fast." Charline's note of awe was wasted on me as I scrambled to get the hell out of there before they really did lock us in.

We were virtually the last cars left at the office and trailed each other back to Michael's. Once there, we switched cars and all piled into David's truck.

"Are you sure you're going to be alright?" I asked Michael for probably the hundredth time in as many seconds.

"Would you quit your worrying? If I didn't feel up to it, then I would sit out." David and I looked at him, not buying it.

Charline intervened, preventing me from asking yet again. "If we don't get going, then there won't be enough time for dinner." The threat of no dinner at all proved suffi-cient motivation to get all our tails into gear.

Michael gave David directions to the store he had in mind. As he navigated the streets, I couldn't help but wonder how one smuggled out such exorbitant quantities of food on a regular basis without raising suspicion. I'd never have considered a trip to the grocery an eventful outing, but that was before I needed to buy enough rations for a zombie apocalypse.

As it turned out, the trick to not looking like an apoca-lypse prepper when you went shopping for mass quantities of food was to have more than one grocery store. The solu-tion was so simple.

In his defense, Michael managed fairly well for the majority of the excursion, though he didn't pick up much. Time was helping, but I worried it wasn't enough. I remembered my own healing process and realized how much I'd started to take for granted.

"Does anyone have a meat preference?" Charline's head popped up at the end of the aisle.

I'd been so absorbed in not watching Michael that I had no idea what aisle we were on, though the fullness of the cart suggested we'd been down quite a few. Michael shook his head in answer to her question.

"No? Okay then," she said and disappeared again.

I was no more prepared when she instantly popped back up. "Jesus Christ, Charline, quite doing that. You're going to give me a heart attack."

She gave me a face. "Don't be so dramatic. Has anyone seen David? I want to make sure he doesn't have any allergies either." Abruptly someone hoisted her in the air from behind.

"None that I'm aware of," David said and Charline gave a squeal of delight at realizing who had hold of her.

"*She* seems to be feeling better at least," I mumbled under my breath.

"Please don't make me laugh," Michael whispered back after a strained laugh.

"But I wasn't trying to."

"What are you two lovebirds whispering about over there?" David asked, setting Charline back down. She immediately began straightening her dress, the picture of propriety.

"About how much we're looking forward to dinner," Michael responded casually. You almost couldn't hear the edge to his voice. I glanced from him to David, but David made no indication that he'd heard anything out of the ordinary.

"In that case, I have everything I need," Charline declared. With that, we made our way to the checkout.

"Looks like quite the party," the young attendant commented, his eyes completely riveted on Charline.

"Gotta feed the hungry masses," she replied flippantly.

The young man smiled then noticed David staring directly at him. His smile faltered and he picked up the pace. We loaded the groceries in the truck without further fuss and began the drive back.

While Charline became a one-woman cyclone in Michael's kitchen, the rest of us put our minds to the task of how to hunt the hunter.

"What I don't understand is how we're supposed to get the jump on someone who seems to always be three steps ahead of us," I said, more than a little exasperated with our lack of progress.

"You'd been trying to sniff out where he was staying. Did you ever get close?" David asked Michael.

"Maybe, but I feel like I was being led by the nose instead. I'm not even sure if he was staying in one place. As far as we know, he was living a nomadic lifestyle when he was turned. We don't know how deep those habits go. Were they a product of situation or choice?"

"You told me that he'd probably killed people long before he was bitten," I said. Michael gave a slow nod, obviously not sure where I was going with this. "I'm assuming that no one found any traces of him near his previous killings. I feel like we should err towards choice," I finished.

"I don't follow," David said, then drained the last of his wine.

"He chooses to be homeless. Why would he risk

someone eventually identifying him? Roughing it would be a breeze, especially, now that he's a *were*. He could stop in an alley or side street and no one would think anything of it."

"Maybe," David interjected, "but Michael's scented him before. Wouldn't he have stumbled across our guy's trail by now if that was the case?" David's logic took all the wind out of my sails.

I wracked my brain for anything to explain how neither of us had picked up on his scent around the office or in the parking garage. Then it hit me. "Perfume." The two men turned to face me with curious expressions. "I mean cologne. He's hiding his scent."

Michael made a face. "It would have to be some pretty potent stuff," he said with a defined note of skepticism.

"What if he's not using a man-made smell?" David suggested. My face screwed up in confusion.

"Rosemary."

"What?" I asked, twisting to look at Charline. She had a smudge of flour on her nose and impatience shone in her eyes.

"Do you have any more rosemary, Michael?" she asked again.

Oh, right. Dinner.

"The refill is on the top shelf of the cabinet by the fridge," Michael responded before returning to the conversation. She gave a distinct sound of satisfaction and resumed her chaos of cooking.

"He must be doing something, otherwise Michael would've ferreted him out by now," David concluded.

"He has to sleep sometime," Michael said. "Anything he would use to mask his scent would eventually wear off. I think Sara's onto something. The creature we've seen in the past doesn't exactly have stellar hygiene and what clothes he wore, looked beyond ratty," he added. His vote of confidence made my heart swell.

"Then that's how we'll find him. We'll use his own vagabond habits and routines to ferret him out," I said, finally daring to hope.

"We can check popular haunts, and hell, unpopular haunts. The places most people try to avoid," David contributed, now fully on board.

"I know you're not talking about my cooking. You haven't even had it yet." Charline's statement edged dangerously on a dare. "At any rate, dinner is ready." There wasn't even the pretense of preamble before we rushed the table.

"This looks incredible, Char." David looked up at Charline with something akin to wonder. I'd never heard anyone call her that, at least not on purpose, but she didn't seem to mind.

She clapped her hands together to get our attention. "Tonight, we have roast beef, with onions, garlic mashed potatoes, roasted carrots, fried okra, lemon-pepper grilled corn and for dessert, a blueberry cobbler with fresh whipped cream." I'm pretty sure all three of us were salivating before she got to the corn.

David clearly missed the challenge in her eyes as he was too busy staring at the extravagance before him. I gave Michael a sidelong look and was pleased to see that he too was trying to keep quiet laughter to himself.

David is doomed.

Dinner didn't contain much talk beyond satisfied eating sounds. By the time we were ready for the cobbler, Charline already had cups ready to go with coffee. It wasn't even her house and yet, she was the quintessential hostess. Without a word, both of the men got up to clear the table then started cleaning the dishes. Charline and I decided to take our ease on the sofa while they finished.

"I've never seen anything like it," I whispered to Charline as we watched the two make short work of the mess.

"I know. That's definitely something I could get used to."

I gave her a look and she shrugged. I shook my head and returned to my coffee.

When the guys were done, they joined us in the living room. Once they sat down with their own cups, our earlier conversation resumed as if it had never stopped.

"The real question is, how are we going to canvas all of the rundown places in the city without arousing suspicion or having him get the jump on us again?" David asked as he looked at the bottom of his empty cup. When he returned, it smelled of something a bit stronger than coffee.

"We could always leverage our lunch breaks to take 'casual' strolls," Michael proffered.

"Yes, but that would limit you to within range of the office. And what if the weather decides to be uncooperative?" Charline asked.

This was all well and good, but I'd been mulling something over in my mind throughout dinner. "I know we all want to pounce on this right away. Trust me, I'm more than eager to be done with this whole mess once and for all, but let's face it, none of us are really up to taking him on right now. David is still getting the lay of the city, I'm exhausted, and Michael is in no condition to be tackling anything right now. We need a chance to recharge." I held up my hands to stall the building arguments. "I know, I know. We were talking about not running around anymore, but I'm not suggesting we run away. I think we should use the weekend to regroup." I looked pointedly at Michael who clearly wanted to argue.

"And what are you suggesting we do? Here is obviously not the safest place anymore." David's words rang out a truth no one wanted to admit.

"Exactly," I agreed. "We should get away. At least give Michael a chance to heal in peace without being worried that a rabid werewolf could come barreling in through the sliding doors at any minute." Charline shot the glass a furtive glance. No one had mentioned to her that he'd already been here once before.

"My parents live a few hours away. They've been asking to come see me since I got out of the hospital." I thought of the last few voicemails. "I'm worried they might show up to verify I'm alright for themselves. I thought it might be nice to go see them instead. It would give us a chance to relax and I could ease their concerns. Not the best plan, I know, but you need rest," I said, giving Michael another pointed look. "And I won't risk their lives because they decide my excuses aren't good enough and show up like bait at my currently unoccupied house."

Charline's look said it all. *She* hadn't even met my parents.

"This has potential," David said.

"What do you mean?" Michael asked, giving no hint as to how he felt about the idea.

"We could make it look like we've called it quits and skipped town. It'd give me a chance to scope out more of the city and you a chance to recover. Plus, if he doesn't think you're here, he basically has to start at square one. Sara, can you take back roads to your parents'?"

I snorted then nodded. The whole way was basically back roads.

"Good. I already have a place to stay for the job I'm working he couldn't possibly know about. To be safe, I'll check in on Char to make sure he doesn't get any ideas."

Charline positively radiated delight at the prospect. I looked at Michael. Everyone else seemed to be on board and he still hadn't said a word for or against.

"What do you think? I know it's a bit soon to be doing the whole meet-the-parents thing, but I really think this is for the best. You need more time," I said with all the confidence I could muster.

His smile crinkled his eyes. "I would love to meet your parents."

22

RUNNING AWAY

I'd never been so anxious to call my dads in my life. The phone rang harsh and metallic in my ear. I turned the volume down, then had to do it again.

"Sara?" The man's voice on the other end of the line held warmth and love as well as an edge of concern.

"Hi, Dad." My voice warbled and I struggled not to burst into tears.

Keep it together.

"Sara, sweetie, is that you?" Another voice came on the line. "We've been worried sick. Why won't you let us come see you? I swear to all things holy in this world, if you don't give us a better reason than last time, I'm getting in the car before you hang up."

"Easy, Tom. Calm down. Let the poor girl speak." A disgruntled huff drifted through the static-filled line.

"Hi, Daddy. Before you two have go at me, I wanted to ask a favor."

"Anything, love," they chimed together.

"I was hoping I could come home for the weekend. There's a lot I need to catch y'all up on and I think it would be easier in person."

"Love, you don't ever have to ask if you can come home." Peter's voice held all of the gentleness and understanding a daughter could want, or at least, I hoped that was understanding.

I swallowed. Now for the hard part. "I'll be bringing someone with me. His name is Michael."

The line went eerily quiet and I immediately saw how werewolf hearing could be a burden. Majority of the room was painfully aware of the dead silence dominating the line. I could practically hear my parents exchanging looks miles away.

Peter's voice finally broke the awkward silence, "We would be happy to have you and your guest. I'll make Tom put in a little extra effort into straightening this place up." I made out a faint thump through the line. No doubt, Tom had taken offense to the implication that his cleaning was sub-par. "When should we expect you?"

"We'll be leaving first thing after work tomorrow. If we don't run into any traffic, we should be there by dinner."

"We'll be ready. Can't wait to see you, honey. And Sara, please be careful."

"Yes, Daddy." The call ended and I stared down at the blank screen. I let out a breath of air. Of course, it wouldn't be that easy. I'd never brought anyone home before and their reaction to my inclusion of a man on this trip was telling.

"This is perfect. You two can pack tonight and be ready to go without ever coming back to the house. I'll pack my things as well in order to solidify the illusion." David's confidence strengthened my conviction that this was the right play.

I gave Charline a hug and thanked her for the glorious meal before following Michael down the hall. Michael gave me space to be lost in my thoughts as we gathered our things. He silently tossed me the same duffel I'd used when we last changed.

I checked my sigh and scooted clothes around to make room, then reached down to grab my shoes. When my hand didn't immediately meet the expected resistance, I looked down.

"Everything alright?" Michael asked, seeing my confusion.

I popped my head up. "Yeah, my shoes must be in the other room. I'll go get them."

"Your tennis shoes?"

"The house is kind of in the middle of the woods. Appropriate footwear is definitely a must."

"Oh." He looked pleasantly surprised.

I finished stuffing the bag and walked out of Michael's bedroom to retrieve the wayward sneakers. The question was, which other room? On a whim, I glanced in the guest room and found them sitting neatly by the wall. David had to have done that since I was pretty sure I'd tossed those in here. As I picked them up, I heard hushed voices.

Curious, I padded closer to the living room and peered around the corner. David stood talking to Charline by the front door. He trailed a finger down her cheek and she bloomed a dusky pink as he said with a low laugh, "Dinner was incredible, Char. I don't think I've ever had a meal quite like that."

"I'm glad you liked it," she responded, her eyes downcast.

His finger made it to her chin and he tipped her head up so their eyes could meet. "I very much liked it." He gave her a gentle kiss.

A warm hand slid along my waist and I nearly fell out of my hiding place in the hall. Guilt burned on my face as I turned to face a speculative Michael. He raised an eyebrow and I gave him a nervous smile and a shrug. Officially busted, I retreated back to the bedroom.

We didn't talk about the intimate scene we'd witnessed or what it might mean. Eventually, the soft sound of the front door closing drifted down the hall. I smiled to myself and zipped my bag closed.

Michael simply shook his head before asking, "Is there anything else besides appropriate footwear you think I'll need?"

"No, we likely won't venture far from the house and we are only going for a couple of nights. I'll warn you though, my dad might insist on separate rooms."

Michael's eyes twinkled. "I can be quiet." The comment caught me off guard and my face burned furiously. True to his words, I didn't hear him step closer and got another surprise when he stole a kiss.

I cleared my throat. "Would you focus?"

"I am focusing."

"You know what I meant," I said as he snaked an arm around my waist and pulled me close. "Are you done packing?" I tried again.

He kissed the side of my neck and I sighed. "I was done when I found you in the hall."

"Oh, so..." I cleared my throat. "Do you have any questions about this weekend?"

Finally, he relinquished me, stepping back. He removed the duffels from the bed and placed them by the door. "Tell me about your parents," he prompted as he took a seat on the bed.

"Well," I said joining him, "they can be a little eccentric."

"Like how?"

"Honestly, there's not really a way to describe it—you kind of have to see it first hand to get it. On paper they seem perfectly normal and then you meet them." I rolled my eyes and was rewarded with a chuckle. "They have also been madly in love pretty much their whole lives, so be prepared for extra gooey." My jaw cracked with a yawn.

"Extra gooey, huh?" He repeated his arms circling around me.

"Mhmm," I mumbled sleepily.

"I can be extra gooey myself." He placed a row of tender kisses that trailed from my jaw to my shoulder as if to emphasize his point. "Maybe you should warn them."

I sighed with contentment and burrowed deeper into his embrace. "Sure...first thing...in the morning." I barely got the words out before slumber officially dragged me down into its depths.

I launched out of bed when the alarm went off, more energized than I'd been in days, maybe weeks.

"Someone's excited," Michael laughed, tossing off the covers.

"What? I like my parents and it's been a while since I've seen them. Also, for the record, I've never brought anyone home before." I lingered long enough to see his face go sheet white, then I dashed into the bathroom. While our reasons for visiting my parents had nothing to do with our relationship status, it didn't stop the anxiety determined to turn me into a nervous wreck. Despite all my doubts, I wanted my parents to like Michael and I wanted them to like *me*. I'd changed, I only hoped it wasn't too much.

Once at work, I drowned myself in menial tasks to fill the time. I conquered the stack of folders waiting for me, finished the Bigsley report, and filed the internship paperwork. When I ran out of busy work at noon, I made my way over to Charline's desk.

Charline's bold red curls bounced as she leaned back and eyed me. "Well, isn't this an interesting reversal. Aren't I normally the one who comes and bothers you?"

"What can I say? I finally caught up with virtually everything since I was out, and now I have nothing to do. Only seemed fair."

"Touché. While normally I would cherish the distraction, regrettably, I'm under a deadline and can't visit." My enthusiasm evaporated. "I'm sorry, Sara. I can chat for a little bit, but *someone* filed their internship paperwork and now I have to deal with that."

"Oops."

She waved it away. "It seems like you're pretty excited about going home."

"Yeah, I can't believe it's been two years. Before I moved to Raleigh, I'd never been away longer than a few weeks and that was summer camp...which I bailed on halfway through."

"So..." she prodded.

"So, what?"

"Sara, honestly. What did your parents say when you told them you were bringing Michael? Do they know about Michael? Do they know about anything?"

I plucked at a loose thread on my blouse. "You heard me tell them I was bringing someone... But no, they don't know the rest." Charline's eyes widened to the point I feared they'd fall out of her head. "I know, I know. I probably should have mentioned at least some of what's been going on to them, but you don't understand, they would—"

"Drag you back home?" she offered.

"Worse. They'd be beyond supportive and I would end up running home with my tail between my legs."

"You have a skewed sense of family," she said, narrowing her eyes.

"I know."

"Oh shit." Charline sat up and immediately became hyper-absorbed in the paperwork on her desk.

"What?" I asked, looking around for the source of her shift in behavior.

"Thank you for clarifying, Sara. I'll make the adjustment and send you the update about the new hire's start date and any paperwork they may need to fill out."

"Uh, sure. No problem," I replied, spying Brianne making a round of the HR cubicles. Her air of self-importance swept the area before she sauntered off to harass someone. "She's gone now."

"I swear that nosy busybody has it out for me. You'd think all I do is sit around and gossip all day." She threw her hands in the air.

"Guess I'll leave you to it then."

"Sorry, Sara," she said, before turning back to her color-coded folders. I was making my way out of the department when she said over her shoulder, "You know, lots of people leave early on Friday, especially if they've cleared their queue." She angled her head so I could make out the wink.

I raced off to the Marketing Department. After nearly colliding with no fewer than three people, none of whom appreciated my abrupt appearance in their path, I found my quarry.

"You know, I don't think I've ever seen your office." Michael looked up in surprise and I gave him my best wolfish grin. "It's nice," I carried on, "at least you have a door."

"Please don't tell me we're getting the intern after all."

"No, that's definitely us. I just turned in the last of the paperwork."

He rolled away from his desk and I took it as an invitation to sit on it. He smiled back at me. "What brings you over to these parts then?"

"Oh nothing." I fiddled with the pens on his desk.

"Okay."

"How are things going? Getting a lot done?" I asked, beginning my fishing expedition.

"I suppose. Of course, things are going a lot better now." He slid a hand up the back of my calf and I almost lost my precarious perch.

"Michael," I hissed under my breath.

His grin turned positively wicked. "You can always close the door if you're worried about people seeing us."

I rolled my eyes and crossed my legs. "Like anyone would think much of it."

He dropped his hand and turned his attention to some papers in danger of falling to the ground. "So, what's up?" The clipped question bore none of the playfulness from a second ago.

"I was wondering if you'd be able to wrap up sometime soon and we could blow this popsicle stand early."

His eyebrows shot up. "A bit eager, are we?"

"Didn't we cover this earlier?"

He glanced around at the desk. "Truth be told, there's nothing here that couldn't wait until Monday. Most of the more pressing deadlines have already passed and the others aren't my responsibility." He took in my borderline manic grin and laughed. "Okay, okay. Give me an hour to straighten this up and I'll meet you by the elevators." I frowned and he amended, "Okay, half an hour."

"Much better." I hopped off of the desk and sauntered back to my own department.

Thirty minutes later, I had an immaculate desk, an array of color-coded paper clips rainbowing across my desk, and one very sad attempt at an origami frog. I left a sticky note on Bob's empty coffee mug and scooted out. Odds were, he wouldn't notice, but just in case, the note seemed prudent. It wasn't until we were strapped in the Jeep and I was bouncing with anticipation that it occurred to me that I probably should have left a list of the finished tasks as well.

Michael shifted into drive and that was the last I thought of it. I guided him out of the city veering us northwest until we hit the more obscure county roads.

"Should we call to let them know we'll be early?" Michael asked.

"I was wondering that." A glance at my cell showed the tiniest of bars fading in and out. "Damn."

"What?"

"Reception is already shot." I squirreled the useless device away. "It'll be fine."

"If you say so."

I opted to ignore his bleak tone in favor of conversation. "I know we've already talked about it, but I thought we could use this time to go over our problem."

"What exactly were you wanting to discuss?"

"I don't know. I feel like we should know more than we do. How is it that no one has any idea what he looks like? If he's been doing this for years, then someone has to have seen something."

"We have the scraps."

"But smells can be masked. That still isn't a guarantee."

"I suppose you have a point. Enough perfume and you can't smell a damn thing."

"Exactly. Not to mention, we've seen him twice now and we still don't know what he looks like." Michael rolled his shoulders and stared straight ahead. "I know a name isn't any better as far as identification," I continued, "but at least it would be something."

"I don't know what to tell you." The comment put a severe damper on what had started as a good mood.

"So," I said, dragging it out until Michael glanced over. "Charline and David. Thoughts?"

He laughed, the strain of it barely noticeable. "I honestly don't know who I'm more worried about."

"What do you mean?"

"No offense, but Charline is definitely a handful. She's going to give him a run for it. But I don't know, David comes with his own quirks."

"Like what?"

"For starters, he's always been on the lookout for *the one*. He can be a little intense about it."

"You say it like there's more to it than the usual hopeless romantic business."

Michael shifted in his seat. I couldn't tell if it was discomfort at the wounds or the turn in conversation. "Some *weres* hold the belief that there is one true mate for everyone—a soul mate if you will. Since David was a pup, he's believed that someday he'll find his true mate."

"That explains some of his weird remarks. What about you? Do you believe in the one-true-mate philosophy?" I asked it jokingly, but his response was serious.

"I razzed David relentlessly about it while we were growing up. I viewed it as a fairy tale that parents told their children to keep them from being irresponsible. The idea that you could meet someone and instantly know that you wanted to spend the rest of your life with them is ridiculous." His fingers tightened around the steering wheel. "That's not how real life works and it's foolish for him to be so stubborn about it."

The intensity of his words set me aback. Granted, I wasn't sure how I felt about what David had said, but Michael's conviction bordered on angry. "Is that what his comment to you was about the night he came to town? Whether you were becoming a believer?"

He deflated right before my eyes. "Yes. He's determined that one day I'll learn the error of my ways and will likely lord it over me until the end of time."

"I'm pretty sure that's what best friends are for."

He looked at me surprised, clearly not expecting such a lighthearted answer. I smiled at him and nearly missed our turn.

"Oh, take a right up here. We're almost there."

"Have you told them anything?" Michael asked, guiding the jeep down the narrow turnoff.

"Anything about what?" I really didn't want to have to admit that they knew literally nothing about him beyond that he was coming with me.

"About being a werewolf."

"Right. No, they don't know anything specific about the attack or anything after."

"Well," he prompted.

"Well, what?"

"Are you going to tell them?"

"I feel like I should, but how many people are you supposed to tell? We never did talk about my slip up with Charline. Both of them," I amended.

He chuckled. "That was probably inevitable. I don't know how she does it, but she could put a priest to shame in getting confessions."

"Isn't that the truth," I mumbled.

"As for the rest, information should be on a need-to-know basis."

"So, you *don't* think I should tell my parents?"

"On the contrary, I think you absolutely should. They're your family and deserve to know the truth. Plus, it will make future visits a lot less awkward when you don't have to constantly come up with explanations for behaviors people might find odd."

"Run into that, have you?" I poked.

"Maybe once or twice. It was very different when I moved to Raleigh. Adjusting to life outside of the pack wasn't easy. Then again, it wasn't really optional either." He snapped his mouth shut, but before I could inquire more, he said, "This must be it."

23

GHOSTS IN THE ATTIC

My parents' three-story Queen Anne style house appeared before us in all its eccentric glory. The dying light blinked in gabled windows nestled beneath steeply pitched roofs highlighting the asymmetrical design.

A deep sense of longing arose within me as I took in the historic home that had somehow withstood not only the passage of time, but being swallowed whole by a determined forest. It was behind those vine-covered walls that I'd first come to know love at the hands of two doting parents. I could think of no memory that didn't have at least a touch of happiness or joy. *This* was home.

I never should have kept them away.

Who knows, maybe if I hadn't been so blindly stubborn, then none of this would have happened.

I absently swiped at a renegade tear and glanced over at Michael. As the car lurched to a halt, my anxiety returned, twisting my stomach into an unpleasant knot.

"You grew up here?" Michael asked, sparing me an incredulous look.

I unclicked my seat belt. "Yeah, why?"

He shook his head as he opened the driver side door.

"No reason. A little surprised is all. Kind of reminds me of where I grew up."

The unexpected tidbit immediately caught my attention. "Oh? How so?"

He took a second to appreciate the view. When he looked back at me, sadness clouded his eyes. "No reason. Forget I said anything." The door closed with a metallic thud.

"But..." I began, twisting around to chase the answers he was withholding. That's when I noticed the claw marks on the hood.

Crap! How could I have forgotten about those? That's not going to comfort my parents at all.

I looked to the front of the house as the front door opened and my parents stepped out onto the porch. I swallowed down my burst of nerves and slipped out to join Michael at the rear of the Jeep. They appeared to be waiting for us, but there was no telling how long that would last.

Thanks to enhanced vision, I could clearly see Peter's sturdy grip on Tom's arm. Seeing them standing side by side gave me another thought. I grabbed Michael's arm to get his attention and prevent him from finding out before I had a chance to correct my oversight.

"I forgot to mention something earlier."

"What is it?" he asked as he passed me my duffel.

"I have two dads."

"Yeah." Of course, he would have heard them on the phone when I called. "Is that what you were so nervous about?"

"Not exactly."

"Then what?" he asked, pocketing the keys.

"Remember how I said I've never brought anyone home?" Michael missed a step and I bit my knuckle. "Yeah, probably should be interesting."

"That's putting it mildly."

I grimaced at his tone and fell in step beside him. We walked in silence until we stood mere feet away from the two men who'd raised me. Rather than wait for things to get awkward, I launched into introductions.

"Michael, these are my parents. This is Peter." I gestured to the man with a shock of red hair that remained vibrant despite his age. "And this is Tom." To my alarm, Tom's blond hair seemed to have gotten grayer in the two years I'd been away.

"It's a pleasure to meet you both," Michael said with a smile as he extended his hand to shake each of theirs in turn.

"And you as well, though I confess, it would've been nice if Sara had given us a little more to go on besides your name," Tom said smooth as silk. Peter shot him a look that Tom blatantly ignored. The scent of anxiety stung the air as he held Michael's hand hostage.

"I assume you two are dating?"

Michael hesitated and I floundered. I was so unprepared for this. Was there a right answer? And who was supposed to answer it? Was it a question?

Peter rescued us all when he cleared his throat. Tom dropped Michael's hand, but the steel in his eyes remained. "What do you say we move this inside?" Peter suggested.

Michael followed hot on his heels, while Tom ushered me inside with a look that said words were coming. Tom was very good at words and if the scene outside was anything to go by, they promised to be a doozie.

"Do y'all mind if I excuse myself to the restroom?" Michael was no fool, he knew trouble when he smelled it.

"Not at all," Tom replied, his intense blue eyes never straying from my face.

"Why don't you use the one upstairs, it's right across

from Sara's old room. I've refreshed the linens," Peter added. I dropped Tom's intense gaze to stare in shock at Peter.

"Sounds great. Thank you, Mr. Sheppard," Michael replied politely before retreating to the stairs that he promptly took two at a time, abandoning me to the mercy of my unblinking fathers. I shuffled my feet and tried not to look as guilty as I was sure I did. After another moment, Michael could clearly be heard moving around on the second floor.

I'd gathered my nerves to start explaining myself when two pairs of arms encircled me. It wasn't the bone-crushing embrace I'd become accustomed to, but it was pretty close. Then, abruptly, I was pushed away.

My dad's eyes bored into me. "What were you thinking?"

"Why didn't you call? You're more important than some trip," Tom said practically on top of Peter.

"What's really going on?" Peter's question cut to the quick of everything. Tom flashed him a brief look.

"And who is that?" Tom demanded to know. "You've never mentioned you were dating, and neither of you seemed too sure about it at the front door."

I swallowed past the dryness dominating my mouth. We'd been here all of five minutes and I already felt over-whelmed. "I've mentioned him before."

Tom's eyes narrowed and Peter scowled. "The only men I've heard you talk about were your pig of a boss and the office heartthrob," Tom responded.

Peter's scowl dropped and he glanced toward the stairs. "No," he said in awed disbelief. I shrugged my shoulders and gave them an awkward smile.

"No," Tom echoed, catching on. "*That's* the office hottie?"

"He is attractive," Peter noted. Tom smacked his partner in the chest, while I turned redder than the poppies that grew in the garden. "What? I have eyes, Tom."

Tom frowned. "Sometimes I wonder why you ended up with me. You clearly have a type."

"Yes, I do, and even after forty years, he still sleeps like some deranged octopus," Peter responded without missing a beat.

Tom's mouth hung open in search of an adequate response. Meanwhile, I covered my face. How much worse was it going to be when I told them I was a werewolf if I couldn't even convince them I was dating Michael?

"Sara, why didn't you tell me your house is haunted?" Michael asked as he ventured back down the stairs.

My head spun in the effort of following the dramatic shift from the conversation I'd been having with my displeased parents. "Because it's not."

"I'm pretty sure I didn't imagine the ghosts upstairs, and besides," he scrunched his nose, "it smells funny. No offense."

"It smells like home and it's not haunted."

"Yes, it is," three voices said together.

I spun around to face my dads. "What do you mean it's haunted? I've never seen anything."

"Sure, you have, sweetie." Tom wrapped his arm around my shoulders and gave them a gentle squeeze. Gone was the terrifying figure that had greeted us at the door. In his place was the wonderfully goofy man I'd called Daddy for the last twenty-eight years.

Peter chuckled and added, "Who do you think your imaginary friends were?" I stood there plainly flabbergasted. "Remember Helga?"

"Helga? I haven't thought about her in over a decade."

"Oh, she won't like that at all," Tom said with a smile tugging at the edge of his mouth.

"That's not funny, Daddy."

Peter rolled his eyes at Tom's blatant mischief. "She's a ghost."

"She hates your dad by the way," Tom whispered in my ear, though not quietly enough for Peter not to hear. He frowned and shrugged his shoulders, lending credibility to the statement.

In yet another shift that left me reeling, my dad dropped the topic of ghosts in favor of the one more likely to make me squirm. "Let's have a seat at the breakfast table. I think you've put us off long enough."

"I believe you owe us quite an explanation for your behavior," Tom added as he led the way down through a passage to my right. I glanced back at Michael who simply shrugged before following after them.

Once situated, I launched into most of the sordid tale. I had to repeat parts of the haphazard story as I wandered and skipped through it. In the end, their only reaction was the wide-eyed shock plastered on their faces.

"So, yeah, I'm a werewolf now." They both frowned at me and I fought the urge to squirm beneath their collective stare.

There was little doubt in my mind which parts they'd taken issue with; though, much like Charline, they seemed to be handling the werewolf part pretty well.

"In case it wasn't obvious, I am too," Michael added. They seemed less than impressed and still angry.

"If it hadn't been for Michael, I probably wouldn't have made it."

Peter slammed his glass down and I flinched. It was rare to see him upset, but I'd done it. "I swear, Sara. Did it ever occur to you to reach out? I know you wanted to focus on being independent, but this...this is ridiculous. You insist on keeping me and Tom at arm's length for the better part of two years and then, when something happens, you still keep us at bay. Why?" The anger and hurt in his voice twisted in my chest.

"I was confused and then everything happened all at once. I'm not saying that's an excuse. It wasn't smart. I made a mistake." Hot tears streaked freely down my cheeks. So much for keeping it together.

Tom rubbed his temples. "I don't understand. Do you hate us that much?" The question cut me to the quick.

"No! I don't hate either of you. If anything, I was afraid I'd end up back here."

"You know we wouldn't do that to you. You've worked so hard to get that job and build a life for yourself. Hell, you're even dating." Tom gestured to Michael. It didn't seem like the best time to point out that was also a product of nearly dying.

"I wanted to prove that I could handle it."

"This isn't something that anyone is expected to 'handle' on their own. That is what family is for, what *we're* for," Peter said, reaching out to take my hand. As his fingers closed over mine, his eyes widened briefly and he shot a look at Tom before returning his concerned expression to me.

"I know that."

"Then why? And I'm not talking about everything you've told us." Tom glanced between Michael and me. "Why haven't you let us come see you? You've barely talked to us in the last two years. Are you ashamed?"

"Of course not," I responded vehemently. "I was tired of being everyone's burden. Poor Sara doesn't have any friends. Poor Sara stays in her room all summer. Poor poor Sara. Going to Raleigh was supposed to be my chance to become the person I wanted to be, not the person I was. And when I failed miserably, I didn't want you to be disappointed in me."

"We could never be disappointed in you," Tom said. Both Peter and Michael mirrored Tom's shock. I'd never said out loud how much of a failure I believed I was.

"Well, you should be. If I was more social, then I wouldn't have been home alone and none of this would have happened."

"Sara, that wouldn't have changed anything. He was following you before that," Michael said in some misguided form of comfort. My parents immediately picked up on the detail I'd very intentionally left out.

I rounded on him. "Oh? I was under the impression that he was in the habit of stalking weak, vulnerable women." Michael's mouth fell open. I turned back to my parents. "There's that too. It wasn't *just* a werewolf, it was a serial killer. So, yay, miracle I'm alive." I shoved back from the table and Michael reached out for me. I evaded the comfort, trying desperately not to dissolve into a full-blown meltdown complete with wracking sobs and a snotty nose.

"Honey we wouldn't have made you come back home, if that's what you were worried about," Peter offered quietly with a reassuring nod from Tom.

"I wasn't worried that you'd make me come back, I was worried I would. That I'd give up and run home, too afraid to try again," I said through hiccups. "Since the day I left, my life has been one disaster after another. I have one friend, no prospects, and I still haven't finished unpacking. I'm a failure. I always have been and I always will be."

I shook with the force of the bitter tirade. My efforts at keeping the blowout at bay were not proving to be very successful. Michael's gaze became an inescapable weight that made me want to crawl into a hole and never come back out.

True to form, Peter noticed it as well, because he decided to give me the out I needed. "I think that's enough for one evening. You two have had a long trip and an even longer few weeks. Why don't you get some rest tonight and we can pick up tomorrow?"

Tom looked at him incredulously. "Peter," he said, his tone of disbelief evident.

"Tom," he replied, giving him a level look.

Tom soured, but didn't pursue the argument bubbling beneath the surface. After a few tense moments, he gave up his scowl and turned back to me. "Well, you're here now. No matter what you think, you're not a failure and you will not be running back home. Come on, give us a hug and then get some sleep."

I let out a breath, relieved that I'd have a modest reprieve before the grilling resumed. With a strong sniffle there was no point in hiding, I did as requested, carefully squeezing them both and earning myself some mussed hair.

"It's nice to meet you as well," Peter said. "I trust we'll get to learn a little more about *you* tomorrow."

Michael's smile faltered at the look in Peter's eye. He quickly bid everyone goodnight and started the trek upstairs. I gave my parents a smile then hurried to join him, though I wasn't looking forward to what might be waiting for me after my outburst.

"Your dads are nice. They really care about you. I'm sorry for slipping up about the homicidal part," Michael said as soon as I entered the room.

"It's done."

"Sara, please look at me. I'm sorry. Growing up, I told my family everything."

"Well your family is werewolves, so it's a little different," I snapped.

"Was. My family *was* werewolves."

I abandoned my study of the floor to look up at him. "What?"

"My parents died during a hunting accident when I was thirteen." Anger and bitterness laced the dire statement, flashing across his face like lightning.

"I'm so sorry. I had no idea."

His eyes held a hardness I'd never seen before and for the tiniest moment it was like he was looking through me instead of at me.

"What aren't you telling me?"

He blinked and quickly averted his gaze to glare at the wooden floors. "All I'm saying is, human or *were*, your parents are here for you." His fingers played with the fringe of the quilt folded on the bed. "So, you really didn't know your house was haunted?"

I welcomed the blatant shift in topic. "No. I mean, hearing some of the things they said, it makes sense, but it doesn't feel any different to me."

"The way I understand it, not everyone is sensitive to them. Strange, considering they're your parents."

A sharp spear of pain lanced through my chest at the cavalier statement. "I'm adopted, Michael. I'm not related by blood to Tom or Peter. I was abandoned as an infant and they became my family."

His face fell, but there was something in his eyes that suggested pieces of a puzzle were falling into place. I gritted my teeth and turned my focus to my own duffel. So what if we were both orphaned? It didn't mean anything. His parents hadn't willingly given him up.

"Anyway, there have always been tall tales about this house and anyone who's lived here. My dad—Peter—says that when he came here, everyone was convinced that my Great Aunt Alice was a witch. But she passed away long before I came into the picture." My hands tightened around a bundle of clothes. "It never occurred to me that any of the stories might be true." I unclenched my fingers, leaving the ruffled stack where it was. "And I've never seen any ghosts that I can recall, no matter what they say." I straightened, having finally run out of air.

"Guess that makes me more sensitive than you."

"That's right, you're Mr. Sensitivity, with all the feelings and making fun of your best friend for believing in soul mates." I nudged him and smiled lightly, grateful that we weren't going to plunge into my childhood issues.

His laughter faded and he put down the clothes he'd been unpacking. "Are we going to talk about this?"

"About what?"

"When your parents asked if we were dating, you froze."

"I don't recall you giving an answer either. Besides, it felt like a trap." This also was starting to feel a bit like a trap.

"Fine, I'll give you that. But what about what we discussed on the way here?"

"Charline and David?"

Instead of answering, he asked a different question. "You know, you never answered your own question."

"Which was?"

"Do you believe in love like that? In soul mates as you put it?"

Here I thought I'd dodged a bullet only to stumble into a minefield. "The only love I've seen like that is my dads'. It doesn't take much to realize they were meant to be together. I've heard pieces of their journey and if anything can make you believe in soul mates, that can." I paused, not too sure where to go from there. "I mean, but that's different. That kind of love doesn't happen all of the time. Not everyone is fated to be with one person. I can see their love, but I never expected that for me."

"Why don't you think the world will happen for you? You act like you're on the outside of everything looking in. If the last few months have done nothing else, you should know by now that you're not a spectator, the world happens to you, not around you. Bad things yes, but also good things. Unless you don't think this is a good thing." He motioned between us.

I flinched back as if the gesture had struck me. A reaction that did not go unnoticed. I sank onto the edge of the bed with a groan, my mind reeling with a thousand different thoughts.

"But I *am* a spectator. I always have been. Aside from the last couple months, nothing ever happens to me. I was abandoned by a well in some nameless town. The fact that I was adopted by Tom and Peter is the most remarkable thing about me. It's everyone else who's interesting, who has incredible lives."

"Sara." My name hung in the air, a desperate plea to understand something that I myself didn't. In its wake, silence fell heavy and awkward.

"It doesn't feel real," I finally said. "So much is happening. This isn't my life. I'm not even sure half of the time if I'm not actually in the hospital having some drug-induced dream."

"*I'm* real, Sara. *This* is real. But I need to know now if you don't want it to be."

"Why is this something we have to talk about now? Haven't I been through enough without having to run this gauntlet too?" The words snapped out of me and I instantly regretted them. He'd opened up to me about his past and now he looked as if I'd slapped him. I groaned and held my face in my hands. "I'm sorry, that was uncalled for. What's wrong with me?"

"*Nothing's* wrong with you." The gruff response held none of the tenderness I'd become accustomed to, he was talking to me like a grown woman because that's exactly what I was.

I sat there at a loss for what to say. When I didn't answer, he did it for me.

"You don't have to say anything tonight. You're right, a lot has happened. I can understand how it could feel a bit much. I noticed the room across the hall is made up as well. I'm going to sleep over there tonight." He swung the open duffel onto his shoulder and walked out. He paused in the doorway and said over his shoulder, "But I do need an answer." Then he was gone.

I sat there alone, tears sitting heavy on my lashes, unable to find my voice. I *did* want it to be real, but the fear that it wasn't clawed at me without mercy.

24

LET'S TALK ABOUT US

I switched my clothes from the day before to give the appearance of freshness and walked over to the hall bath to wash my face, but the cold water wasn't the shock I needed it to be. The mirror revealed that I looked as bad as I felt.

I strained to see if I could hear anything from the other room—the one Michael had vanished into—but was rewarded only with silence. I hung my head, giving it up and trudged downstairs, uncertain of what kind of reception would await me.

"Morning," I announced as I entered the kitchen.

"Good morning, sweetie. How did you sleep?" Tom asked as he turned to help Peter with a plate of bacon. He placed it at the breakfast table next to a precarious tower of pancakes. He noted my look. "As usual, your dad has taken having a guest as an opportunity to show off." I didn't have the heart to tell them this was nowhere near enough food. I'd have to sneak a snack or two later.

"I heard that," Peter replied over his shoulder. The pan gave a wonderful sizzle as he added sausage. "So, little one, how did you sleep?"

"Not very well." They exchanged a knowing look. "I don't suppose either of you has seen Michael this morning?"

"He was down here when I came in to start breakfast," Peter said. The grease popped and he quickly devoted his attention to the pan.

"Where is he now?"

"He asked about the woods," Peter responded as I sat at the table. "Even asked if I would mind if he took a stroll before breakfast."

We all looked out the windows at the woods that came up as close as they dared to the house. No more than fifty feet from the back door, trees closed in like they were closing ranks. Many people had gotten very lost in those woods, including apparently Tom. Not that I had any fear that Michael would get lost, more a fear that he would want to be.

Tom sat next to me and wrapped an arm around my shoulders. "Sweetie, what's going on between you two?"

"Oh, Daddy, I think I've really messed things up."

Moments later, Peter joined us at the table steadily loading my plate with the various options. "Well let's hear it. One of us is actually good at relationship advice. You can decide which one at the end."

I sighed and picked up a fork.

"You can start with whether or not you two are actually dating," Tom deadpanned.

"I noticed he slept in the guest room," Peter added.

I flinched. "That's hard to explain."

"It's really not." There was zero forgiveness in Tom's tone, not that I could blame him after keeping them in the dark about everything else.

"I don't know. No. Yes? It's all a muddled mess."

"Why don't you try starting at the beginning," Peter suggested as he took a seat.

I took a deep breath then let it out in a defeated huff. "After the attack he began this crusade to get to know me. It was weird and out of the blue. He kept asking me out, but they always felt like pity luncheons. You know? Turns out, he was really working up the nerve to tell me what I'd become. Except he didn't. Not in time anyway."

"What do you mean?" Tom asked.

"I'd no idea what was happening when I had my first full moon. The change is awful and I thought I was dying. When I came to, I panicked and blindly ran across town. Through a series of several horrific events, the least of which was nearly being run over, I ended up at his place."

"The universe has a way of giving us what we need when we need it," Peter said, giving my hand a squeeze. He and Tom shared a look.

I pulled my hand back. "This isn't destiny or fate, Dad. It was a horrible tragedy that nearly killed me, still could, if we're being honest. Besides, there's nothing sweet about why I essentially had to move in with him. Michael is basically my jailer. Everything that followed was for show." I paused. "Until it wasn't. I knew I would fall for him, for the image we were creating."

"So, you *are* dating."

"Daddy!"

"What? It's an honest assumption."

"If we are, I don't feel I can trust it. Yes, I really like him and to hear him tell it, he's liked me for a while." I quickly dismissed telling them about what he'd said during his fever, it seemed stupid to share something I didn't believe myself. "But what does any of that mean? I have all of these new senses and instincts and urges. I don't even know how to process most of them."

"Urges?" Peter asked flatly. Tom smacked him.

"It seems to me that he truly liked you before any of this started," Tom began. "Yes, I know what you said."

"Why are you so convinced that he can't like you beyond all of this?" Peter followed up.

"Because the whole situation is beyond outrageous."

"What you have to decide is if you like him outside of these exceptional circumstances," Tom said.

Peter nodded knowingly and for the briefest moment I could have sworn my old imaginary friend, Helga, was sitting at the table also nodding sagely along. I blinked and she was gone. Clearly lack of sleep and ghost stories were getting to me.

"Sara, you're smart, resourceful, and beautiful. Now I know at least two of those are subject to parental bias, but I've seen the way he looks at you. I don't understand how you can't see it too."

I slumped in my chair. "Why is it so important to label everything now? I need time to absorb what's happening to me."

"Then tell him that," Tom said. "People can't understand what's holding you back if you don't tell them." Peter looked down at the table and Tom reached out to place a comforting hand on his shoulder without looking away from me.

"I always wanted a love like yours." My words drifted like a light wind across the table.

"Destiny or not, all love must be fought for. Love may feel like magic, but it's faith and perseverance that makes it happen," Peter said, looking back up.

"You don't have to decide your entire future in a couple weeks," Tom said. "There's always time."

"It doesn't feel like it," I grumbled.

"Then stop wasting it."

I'd already torn through several yards of underbrush before I stopped to consider the futility of my current search tactics. Morning sunlight fell in dappled patches tinged with green. Growing up, I hadn't been afraid of the woods, but I hadn't been altogether fond of them either. I didn't know them as well as my dad, who'd spent his childhood roving them and learning every path and pebble. But I had other talents I could use besides an inherent knowledge of the area.

A quick glance back towards the house revealed nothing but dense foliage. Without delay, I stripped down, not bothering to hide my clothes. I took a deep breath and started the change. For once, there was nothing to fight.

Incredible how much acceptance alone eased the transformation. The pain was still excruciating, but I wanted to get to the other side and I had complete faith that I would be alright once I got there. I stole a few moments to adjust to the growingly familiar form.

My pads barely whispered against the dense layer of fallen leaves as I made my way back to the edge of the forest. Beyond the foliage, the Sheppard ancestral home arose both familiar and strange to dominate the horizon.

I lowered my nose to the ground and walked along the line of trees where they abruptly lost their battle to Peter's strict boundary. Picking out a woodsy scent in the woods seemed like an impossible task, until I found it. Michael's smell was indeed very similar, but there were nuances that I'd never appreciated before, like the undercurrent of leather and jasmine or that it made me think of an autumn afternoon. With the scent solidified in my mind, there was no question which way he'd gone.

Michael's scent meandered across clear-cut paths in favor of more unchecked wilderness. I abandoned the path, trusting my senses to guide me. The constant flood of new and conflicting scents ensured that I went slowly lest I lose the one I was following. I knew without a doubt that if I lost it now, it would be swallowed by the myriad of smells and I'd never be able to pick it back up again.

The sun hung almost directly overhead when I found him sitting on a large boulder that looked like it had been there for at least a century. It sat in a small clearing that had enough space between the overarching canopies to allow a full circle of light to stretch out on the ground next to him. He lifted his head, recognizing that I was near, but otherwise didn't move.

I doubled back a short distance and returned to my human form. When I walked out into the clearing, I was still coated in a faint sheen of sweat that quickly cooled in the chill air.

"Hey," I said, suddenly nervous.

Michael stared at me completely nonplussed by my nakedness. "I'm impressed. I didn't think you would change."

"Why wouldn't I? This is what I am. I won't deny it anymore." I chewed my bottom lip a moment before giving voice to something I'd been reluctant to admit to myself. "I'm actually becoming quite proud of it." My words sent a ripple of surprise through him that I could almost smell.

"Why are you here, Sara?"

"You're missing breakfast." He gave me a look. "Fine. I wanted to apologize."

His ears seemed to twitch, but that could have been the product of a hopeful imagination. When he didn't say anything, I took a step closer.

"This has been really hard for me."

"I know it's a lot, but—"

"Would you let me finish?" I cut him off.

His mouth snapped shut, a huff of air misting in front of him.

"I'm not talking about the werewolf part."

His eyes widened in surprise.

"I'm talking about us." When he began to say something, I held up a hand. "You don't get it. Yes, my parents are wonderful, I love them dearly and they are pretty much my whole world. But when I found out at fourteen that I was adopted, it did something to me. I went from being a care-free kid to being a shell without an identity. I recognize how silly that sounds, but it doesn't change that that's exactly what happened. Who was I if I wasn't theirs?"

The breeze shifted, causing the dappled light to play across his face. He continued to sit quietly waiting for me to go on. This was everything I'd never been brave enough to admit to myself and now I was saying it out loud. It was every bit as hard as I thought it'd be.

"Then you came along. I don't know if you were telling the truth about how long you've liked me and quite frankly it doesn't matter. What I do know, is that I've had a crush on you since you sauntered into the PR department with market projections two years ago."

Surprise flickered in his eyes.

I gave him a crooked smile. "You're kind of hard not to like." My grin slipped. "As I got to know the real you, that changed. I'm not even sure when. Then you were attacked and you told me..." I couldn't finish.

The dark tan of his face colored slightly.

"Yeah, that. With everything else going on, it was a lot to take in. I'm not saying I don't or that I can't return those feelings. All I'm asking is for time to figure them out. I need to understand myself—the old and the new—before I try to give it away to someone. Can you give me that? Can you give me time?"

The silence stretched around us. My new senses picked out the sounds of tiny scurrying feet and the smell of pending spring in the air. The slight breeze tickled my bare skin, reminding me that I was completely naked. I gave an involuntary shiver and tried not to overthink his lack of a response.

"So, what you're saying is, you like me."

My sound of pure exasperation startled several birds into flight. When the noise and the leaves cleared, Michael had abandoned his perch and was standing in front of me.

"Is that all you heard? I'm kind of baring my soul here."

"I heard all of it. You're right, all of this is going really fast, even for me. There are so many things you don't know. Things I need to tell you, but..." His words trailed off as he brushed a thumb gently across my cheek.

I blinked at him, holding my peace.

"I'll try to slow down, but I can't make any promises. I meant what I said, I'm in love with you. Stars help me, I have been for a while. But as dangerous as I know that is, I can't stop." His fingers danced along my cheek to tuck a strand of hair behind my ear as his eyes searched mine. "Think you can put up with me while you decide if I'm worth loving back?"

I gave a strangled cry of frustration. "I never said—"

"I know, I know. I'm teasing you," he chuckled.

"You have to be the most infuriating man I've ever met."

"And you're probably the most stubborn woman I've met. That's part of why I love you." He leaned forward and pressed his lips against mine.

I didn't argue. I wanted this, wanted us. The gentle kiss deepened as he placed his hand on the back of my neck.

"Let's go for a run," I suggested breathlessly. He gave me a look. "Give me a little credit. I know I can't change again so soon."

He smiled. "And where are your clothes, my brazen werewolf?"

"Somewhere else," I replied wickedly before racing towards the heart of the forest. The crash of leaves behind me suggested he was hot on my heels.

25

20 QUESTIONS

When we returned to the house, shadows stretched like fingers across the garden. There was no comment about our extended absence, only welcoming waves. What *was* worth noting was the truly impressive amount of food prepared for dinner.

"Wow, Dad, you've really outdone yourself."

"Smells amazing, Peter."

"Not to say that Tom is right, but I do rarely get an opportunity to show off."

As if summoned by his name, Tom came in to gather dishes. Michael and I eagerly began helping. After spending hours running, we were both in need of a substantial meal. That aside, it was a far different quantity than what I'd seen this morning.

"Hey, Daddy, that seems like an awful lot of food."

"Surely you didn't think that we would be idle while we waited for you two to return from your...romp in the woods."

Color surged up my neck in a wave of heat to cover my face at the very noticeable pause before romp. Someone coughed behind me and I turned to see an equally embarrassed Michael. Tom spared a look for each of us and returned to the kitchen.

"Oh, Peter, my love, the children are wondering about the sudden presence of so much food." Dutifully, we followed him back into the kitchen, though there wasn't much left to retrieve.

Upon our entry, Peter turned. "Surely you didn't think we'd be idle until you returned from doing heaven-knows-what in the woods," he said in a near perfect echo of his partner. The heat in my cheeks intensified. "Come on, Sara, you're a grown woman and from what we've looked up, werewolves aren't exactly shy."

"What you looked up?" I squeaked.

"It seemed prudent to try and understand a little more about your new life. Granted, a lot of what we found was pure nonsense, and some of it was downright disturbing, but some things remained consistent." Peter gestured at the plethora of food.

I could easily picture the two of them huddled around Tom's computer with horrified expressions at the images that would inevitably pop up under the search: My daughter is a werewolf. I groaned, too low for them to hear, but not low enough to escape Michael.

"If you want, I'd be more than happy to answer any questions you have."

The rest of us looked at him. We all knew how likely those questions would be to escalate from modest curiosity to outright invasiveness.

"I'm serious, I won't take offense to any question you ask. Plus, it will be another learning opportunity for Sara."

I grabbed Michael's arm tightly. He shot me a questioning look as I addressed my parents. "Will you excuse us?"

"Dinner in five, young lady."

"Yes, Dad," I responded quickly before dragging Michael into the hall.

"What was that about?" Michael asked the moment they were out of sight.

"Are you out of your mind?" I hissed.

"Sara, it's only fair that we answer as many of their questions as we can. It's a *good* thing they want to understand." Michael glanced back toward the dining room at the scrape of a chair. "It'll be fine," he offered reassuringly as he laced his fingers through mine.

I shook my head and tightened my fingers around his. "I know they have a right to know, and I love that they want to be supportive, but you have no idea the kind of blanket permission you gave them."

He leaned in and placed a kiss on my forehead. "Have a little faith."

Easy for you to say, you don't know my parents.

"This is gonna be one hell of a dinner," I mumbled, then squared my shoulders and let Michael lead us into the dining room.

Mercifully, we were given a chance to eat before the game of Twenty Questions began. Peter and Michael cleared the table while I helped Tom set out the dessert options, cookies and a chocolate cake from the bakery in town. Once everyone settled back down with their plate of decadence and a cup of coffee, it was clear the blessed delay was at an end.

Michael set his fork down, cake untouched, and addressed the elephant in the room. "I'm assuming that from your research you surmised that werewolves have a slightly larger appetite. By the way, dinner was wonderful, thank you."

A small smile tugged at Peter's mouth. "You're welcome."

"Showoff," Tom snickered. Before the conversation could degrade into their usual banter, Michael spoke up.

"I confess, I haven't searched 'werewolves' recently, but I doubt much of it was more than gore and teenage fantasy." Tom and Peter shared a look that confirmed my worst suspicions as to what they'd found. "In light of that, I'm anticipating some interesting questions. Now, who wants to go first?"

There was the smallest of interludes before the volley was set loose.

"Does silver kill you?"

"What are your abilities?"

"Do you turn into a wolf or something kind of like a wolf?"

"Do you have a pack?"

"Do you have an alpha?"

"Is your bite lethal?"

"Does wolfsbane do anything to you?"

"Do you have any special powers?"

"Are you only a wolf at the full moon?"

The questions came so fast, I couldn't distinguish between who asked what. Many of them were expected, but some I'd never considered. Like what the heck was wolfsbane? Michael, however, refused to be ruffled and took the questions in stride, providing answers almost as fast as they could come up with questions.

"Anything trying to kill you usually will, silver is no exception, but no, we aren't allergic to it. We turn into a larger version of a wolf. To the untrained eye, we're indistinguishable from our cousins. We can turn virtually any time, but almost always at the full moon. Call it myth, call it biology, we just do." He hesitated a moment and glanced briefly toward me. "I have a pack and an Alpha. Yes, our bite can be lethal. Think of it more like if you're not allergic, then you might turn into a werewolf."

"Is *biting* a common practice?" Peter said the word with such disdain that I had to actively try not to shrink into my chair. I could practically see Michael's hackles rise. Tom reached out a hand and placed it on Peter's arm. He blinked and shook his head. "I'm sorry, that was out of line."

"No. I gave my word that I wouldn't be insulted." The feel of him betrayed his words. My dad's words had truly cut him. "Before this whole mess, I couldn't tell you of the last time I'd heard of anyone being bitten. We weren't altogether sure if a bite *would* turn someone. We know better now." He took a deep breath noticeably calming himself. "As for wolfsbane, I know it's a poison, but other than that I don't know if it has any particularly adverse effects on us. We have enhanced senses and strength." He glanced at me and laughed. "But please don't ask for a demonstration." Tom immediately frowned.

"Come on, Daddy, you didn't really expect us to change right here." His look said that he'd hoped. "It's not a pretty sight." I hesitated then pushed forward with the truth. "It hurts." Michael reached out a comforting hand. I gave it a light squeeze and met my parents' sympathetic gazes. "It gets better with practice, but that doesn't make it fun to do or to watch."

Michael came to my rescue, sparing me the concerned looks that were now firmly plastered on my dads' faces. "Typically, when we go out to shift, we find a private spot in the woods to put some clothes and change before joining others in the group."

Tom cocked his head to the side. "Well, that answers another one of my questions—do your clothes change with you? It's right up there with whether you indulge in both forms."

"Daddy!"

"Tom."

"What? It's an honest question. And don't tell me it hadn't occurred to you, Peter. This is our baby girl we're talking about. I want to make sure everything is consensual."

Michael fought a sudden coughing fit, while Peter shook his head in scorn and I wished I was anywhere else.

"We do maintain our senses, logic, and memories," Michael finally managed. "There's no reason it shouldn't always be consensual."

"Right, I think that's enough questions for one night," I said, desperate for an end.

"Not quite," Peter said.

Anxiety rushed to replace my embarrassment.

"Now that we've gotten some of those out of the way," Tom picked up. Some? How many were there? What more could they possibly ask?

"We have a few about you personally," Peter finished, spearing Michael to his chair with a look.

He swallowed. "Okay. Like what?"

"Like, what are your intentions with our daughter?" Peter asked, his face deceptively neutral.

"Well..." Michael's gaze slid towards me.

This is my fault. If I hadn't made such a scene this morning this wouldn't be happening.

"Are you experienced?" Peter added before Michael could formulate any kind of response.

"Dad," I scolded. He ignored me.

"When was the last time you got tested?" Tom asked. My mortification found new depths.

"Tested for what? She's already a werewolf," he said defensively.

"We don't know what else you could give her." My mouth hung open in shock at Tom's total lack of shame.

"I've had all of my shots, if that's what you're implying."

"How many partners have you had? How many *do* you have?" Peter asked. I was officially redder than the poppies and Michael didn't seem to be faring much better.

Once again, before he could answer, Tom spoke up. "Are the rumors true?"

Peter turned a confused look to Tom. "What rumors?"

Tom leaned towards him and whispered, "I don't know. Just go with it." They both turned serious expressions back to Michael.

This is not happening.

"How close are you with your family?" Tom asked and all the blood drained from Michael's face.

"Nope, that's it for you two. Michael has been more than cooperative with your wild questions. We're going to bed," I declared, standing for emphasis.

"I think you're right," Michael said as he mirrored me. "But I need a shower first. Those woods are no joke. I would love the opportunity to explore them properly sometime instead of getting lost."

I choked on air, thankfully my dads seemed to miss it. Tom was clearly sore that Q&A was over and Peter was busy telling Michael where the spare towels were.

I ventured upstairs and milled about my room picking up trinkets that seemed to belong to another life. The music box with its frozen ballerina. The macaroni necklace curled on the dresser. A medal for academic achievement.

"Thinking back to simpler times?" Michael asked from the doorway.

"I'm not even sure I recognize those times anymore. So much has changed. I've changed. No pun intended." He laughed anyway. Judging by the sudden reappearance of his things, I assumed that I would not be spending another miserable night by myself.

"So that was—intense," he said as the duffel flopped on the bed.

"That's one way to put it. It felt like we were on trial, and none of the questions were even directed at me." I shook my head.

"I hope they don't start up again in the morning. I like Peter and Tom, I really do, but there's only so much I can take." He sounded lighthearted, but I'd seen his face.

"I'm sorry about that, in all fairness, I did try to warn you not to give them free rein. Though I didn't anticipate how far over the line they'd go," I added with a wince.

He shrugged. "They're being parents. It's their job to look out for you."

I snorted and snagged my pajamas off the dresser. "I, for one, am in desperate need of hot water and soap. If you need anything, I'll be in the shower." He nodded and continued to rifle through his duffel bag.

The steady patter of water hitting the tub echoed in the small space. Steam rolled around the room, curling up the walls in long tendrils and fogging the mirror. The sound and mist wove together to create a quiet that embraced me like a hug. I took a deep breath, inhaling the vapor, and relaxed into the white noise. The perfectly scalding water hit my skin and tight muscles loosened. I closed my eyes and gave my body a good stretch, the exhaustion of the last few days seeping out of me with a relaxed sigh.

The harsh screech of the curtain being pulled back cut through the muffled quiet. My scream stuck in my throat as a surge of adrenaline set my pulse racing. Steam was sucked through the sudden vortex to be replaced with cold rushing in to fill the void. My feet slipped on the tub as I took an involuntary step away from the mist-shrouded figure standing before me.

"G-ghosts aren't real," I stuttered.

A hand came up and I shrank against the chill wall behind me. It waved in the air creating swirls of steam in its wake. "Of course they are. But I'm not one. Or at least not yet." A circle of rapidly closing mist framed Michael's smirk.

I sagged against the wall and quickly straightened back up. "You scared me half to death, Michael!"

"You said if I needed anything you'd be in here."

"Oh? And what do you need?" I couldn't see much of him due to the curtain and rolling steam, but I fully expected that he was naked.

"Isn't it obvious?" He stepped into the tub. "I need a shower."

His answer was so unexpected that I barked out a laugh, then immediately clapped my hands over my mouth.

"What? I'm not allowed to bathe? I know I'm an animal, Sara, but that doesn't mean I don't like to be clean." He took a step forward, bringing him irresistibly closer to me and to the water.

I scooted back enough to let the water create a partial barrier between us. "And I suppose it was too much to wait your turn?"

"I did say I was taking one first. Besides, what if you used all of the hot water?" He slipped his hand around my waist and tugged me closer so that said water cascaded all around us.

"What else is a possibility?" Being coquettish was new for me, but I was inclined to think I was doing a damn good job if the low rumble that came from his chest was any indication.

High on steam and daring, I spun around so my back was pressed against him and deliberately bent to grab the soap. A strangled moan escaped him and his fingers dug into my hips. I wiggled for good measure before standing straight again.

I turned my head to look at him over my shoulder. "Everything okay? I know it's tight."

His only response was to pull me hard against him and capture my mouth. My free hand reached back to caress his head and urge his kisses deeper.

When he finally broke the kiss, we were both breathing heavily. He tipped my nose with his while he glided his hands over my slick sides. "There's a very real possibility I've fallen madly in love with you, Sara Sheppard."

"That so?"

"Yes," he growled, spinning me around to face him again.

I held up the bar I'd acquired and had to bite the inside of my cheek to keep from laughing, "Would you like me to help wash your back?"

"Oh, you think you're funny," he said, his eyebrows raised. "You can definitely help me with something and we won't be needing the soap."

"No?" I attempted to say, but it came out as more of a gasp when he tweaked my nipple.

"No."

He cupped my ass and lifted me. I wrapped my legs around his waist and dropped the soap in order to grip his biceps as he pressed me against the wall, then slid his entire length into me in one quick thrust. He buried his face in my neck and my moan ricocheted off the tile as he nipped and sucked at the tender skin. I tangled my fingers in his hair while the wet slaps of our skin competed with the white noise of the water cascading around us.

Electricity danced through my veins and tingled in my fingertips as I met him thrust for thrust. He moved to kiss me again and I hungrily devoured his mouth, sucking on his tongue until he moaned and his pace faltered. We broke apart and exchanged labored breaths for a moment, then he thrust hard into me. I cried out in pleasure as my body tightened and my climax crescendoed like an exploding firework. Michael yelled obscenities as he followed shortly after.

"You're incredible," he said, his voice husky as he rested his forehead against mine.

"You're not so bad yourself." My cheeky response earned me a chuckle.

"Where have you been my whole life?" he whispered before pressing his lips against mine in a soft kiss that made my insides tingle as much as my orgasm had. A happiness I'd never really believed could be mine, floated through me, warm like a summer breeze and filled with promise. I couldn't even bring myself to care that we'd made enough noise to raise the dead, not to mention my parents.

***

Sunday dawned bright, clear, and unforgiving. By the end of the day, we'd be back at Michael's, once more at the mercy of the horrors that awaited us.

"Awake already?" Michael purred in my ear.

"No."

He chuckled at my denial.

"I don't want to be anyway. I'm not ready to leave."

He let out a sigh. "I know what you mean. But we can't hide from this, not forever. You lived. The next target might not be as lucky."

I let out a groan. "Don't remind me. Besides, that's not what I was referring to."

"Oh? Then what?" His hand slid warmly across my

middle, the touch both comforting and a bit possessive. "I've missed my parents and this place."

"We can always come back after. I'm serious about exploring those woods. Can you imagine how much fun it would be during a full moon?"

"We'll have to live long enough first."

"We will," Michael reassured me, his arm tightening.

"How are you feeling? I know last night—well, yesterday in general—wasn't really conducive to healing."

"I wouldn't trade yesterday for anything." His fingers trailed up my side until they could trace my cheek.

I stared into his eyes wondering for the millionth time how I'd gotten here. "You didn't answer the question."

"You're insufferable."

"And you're evading."

"What would it take to convince you I'm fine?"

"For starters," I began, but he silenced the pending argument with a kiss thorough enough to steal my breath. "Michael, I'm serious," I tried again.

"So am I," he replied, not dissuaded.

"My parents are probably awake."

"Mhm," he mumbled as he trailed kisses across my jaw.

"Peter at the very least, if not Tom too."

"Speak of the devil," he murmured into my neck before giving it a playful nip.

My confusion only lasted a moment, then I made out footsteps making their way to our door. I waited until they should have been close enough to allow their owner to knock.

"Good morning," I said clearly and was rewarded with a soft thud, most likely from a jump of surprise. Michael and I giggled quietly.

"I see how it is. You get fancy new hearing and now you

want to use it for evil, scaring your poor old dad." Tom's voice was notably affronted. I didn't have a chance to respond before he went on. "Breakfast is hot, and please dress before you come down. I see pajamas are apparently out of the question, due to the total disregard for which they are strewn about the bathroom." With that, he made his way back towards the stairs.

I turned to look at Michael, my eyes undoubtedly the size of saucers and he laughed. A whopping ten minutes later, we took our seats at the breakfast table. I ate in sullen silence, thoroughly miserable about having to leave.

"What's the matter, Sara?" Peter asked.

I sighed, my gaze searching both my parents' faces, and admitted to myself how much I'd missed them. "I'm not ready to go."

"Do you really have to? You could stay here for a while longer." Tom's words, while optimistic, were unrealistic.

"I'm out of sick time. And besides, hiding here won't make our problem go away," I said, echoing Michael's earlier statement. "Plus, what if he tracks us here?" I shook my head at the horrible image of that monster tearing through my family. "I couldn't do that to you."

"We're not exactly defenseless, little one." Peter's words rang true, but paled in my mind compared to what I knew would be coming. Tom gave Peter a look and he didn't pursue it. I had no delusions. This broken creature would never quit until he'd finished what he'd started or was stopped—permanently.

"We understand that this is something you need to face. You know your dad and I will be here for you no matter what. I mean it, if you need anything, anything at all, you better call," Tom said, his tone both stern and supportive. "As for you, Michael, you seem like a decent person. You hurt my baby girl though and you'll find out the hard way that I am not the gentle one in this pair." Tom's not so veiled threat visibly shook Michael.

I gave my dad a beseeching look. Peter's only response to the plea was a gesture that very much suggested I was on my own.

Time continued to slip through my fingers with blatant disregard for my own desire that it remain frozen. I looked first into Peter's light green eyes and then Tom's speckled blue ones. I hadn't even left yet and I was already homesick.

"I promise not to be such a stranger anymore. We'll definitely be back. That is, if it's okay?"

"You're both welcome anytime," Tom said to me. Out of the corner of my eye, Peter leaned closer as if to say something to Michael. I strained to hear what it was, but Tom was still talking. "Now, promise to call when you get back. And I want regular updates this time." He waved an admonishing finger while I nodded dutifully.

"Yes, Daddy."

He smiled and produced a rock candy as if by magic. I gave a squeal of delight. Michael turned to face us as I clutched my prize with the exact same enthusiasm I had since I was three. "Don't worry I've got one for you too," Tom said. "I would ask you which color you would prefer, but I'm afraid you're stuck with red."

"Why is that?" Michael asked.

"Because the blue is my favorite," I said, waving the stick of crystalline candy. "I haven't had one of these in ages." Michael laughed at my childish exuberance. "What?" I asked through a mouthful of sugar.

"Nothing," he said, turning back to my dads. "I want to assure you both that I will do everything in my power to keep her safe. We do have a little help. I don't think we mentioned it before. I have a friend in town that I've called to give us a hand. His name is David. I've trusted him to have my back since we were kids and Sara has proven several times now that she's not some damsel in distress. Your daughter has turned into quite the fighter." My face heated at the unexpected praise from Michael. Pushing for a more pleasant line of goodbyes I spoke up.

"When everything settles down, I'd really like y'all to come visit. I think it's about time you see where I live and where I work. And you have to meet Charline, you're going to adore her."

"We would love to, sweetie," Peter said as he wrapped an arm around Tom.

26

PLAN OF ATTACK

I stood in the doorway of Michael's Craftsman house and wondered when I'd become so comfortable here. Familiarity washed over me as I took in the living room and kitchen already filled with so many more memories my own bungalow couldn't boast.

"Here you go," Michael said as he passed me my duffel then turned to secure the door."

"Thanks." My fingers tightened around the rough handle and I set off down the hall.

"Don't even think about going into the guest room," Michael called out from the front of the house right as my foot crossed the threshold of said room.

Once more in the main bedroom, I heard his voice again, this time too indistinct for him to be talking to me. "Who was that?" I asked when he joined me.

"I let David know we're back. He'll be over later." His bag landed with an audible whoosh on the bed. "Is everything alright? You've been pretty quiet," he asked, his voice tight as he stepped closer.

"Everything is real again."

"Things are going to be different this time." He moved a

strand of hair out of my face and cupped my cheek. "We have each other and we *will* conquer this. Together."

A nervous smile spread across my face. This whole us-thing was still pretty new, but I liked knowing I wouldn't be on my own.

"What do you say we make the most of our time while we wait for the cavalry to return?" Before I could respond, he leaned down and gave me a playful kiss that sent heat all the way down to my toes.

His duffel fell to the floor with a thud as his mouth sealed over mine. I arched into him, while my hands ventured beneath his shirt to caress the planes of his back. He moaned into me as I dug my fingers into the small of his back, encouraging him closer. We toppled backward to land on the bed and I wrapped my legs around him. Heat passed through me in wave after wave to settle between my thighs. His mouth shifted to my neck and my legs tightened around him, prompting a deeper groan.

The doorbell rang. We both froze, then looked at each other and burst into laughter at our joint expressions of guilt. "We're worse than teenagers," I said as we quickly put ourselves back in order.

"I fail to see what's wrong with that." Michael brushed his lips across mine in a brief kiss before slipping out on silent feet to answer the door.

I took the opportunity to take stock of my attempts to organize myself. My clothes were rumpled, my hair reached wildly in all directions, and a distinct flush stained my cheeks.

Shaking my head, I splashed cold water on my face and pulled my hair back into a pony then wandered out to see who I assumed would be David. To my surprise, Charline was with him.

"Hey!" An enthusiastic embrace accompanied her

cheerful greeting. She gave me a brief squeeze then put me at arm's length to give me an appraising look. "Your holiday seems to have done wonders for your disposition."

"Well, I'm looking at things a bit differently now."

"I can tell." She gave me a wink and sauntered off to the kitchen, two brown bags in hand. "How are your parents?" she asked over her shoulder.

I took a seat at the bar as she unloaded goodies. "I hadn't realized how much I missed them. I'm planning to invite them down when all of this is over. Then you can finally meet them. I know you're dying of curiosity," I added.

She feigned shock and put a bowl of sweet potatoes and a peeler in front of me. "So, did you tell them?" The room stilled.

I glanced back at Michael. "Of course I did. They have a right to know."

"I think that's swell," Charline said as if the awkward pause had never occurred.

I started peeling potatoes as Michael told David, "Her house is haunted." I spun back around to address the ridiculous stories Michael had decided to share, but didn't get the chance.

"It is not. How do you know?" David asked, sounding eager to be proven wrong.

"I'm serious, her house is totally haunted. Her dad told me so."

"Yeah, but did you see a ghost?" Both of their eyes were wide, filled with a mix of mischief and wonder.

I turned to Charline who was equally intrigued. "Do boys ever grow up?"

"I think some of them grow up quite well." She gave David an appraising look and I couldn't help but wonder what mischief *they'd* been up to over the weekend.

"I swear I almost saw one, you could practically smell them. It was kind of like damp electricity."

"No way," David said and I rolled my eyes at Charline who did her best to cover a giggle.

"Is it too much to ask for time to absorb one supernatural impossibility before being forced to accept another?" I asked as I tossed the last potato in the bowl.

"My mama always said things come in threes. So, I'd say you're due for at least one more," she said with a shrug then swept the finished sweet potatoes away.

"I really wish I could accept things as easily as you seem to," I said with an envious sigh.

"It's called faking it 'til you make it, dear. There's not a damn thing I can do about any of it except smile, so that's exactly what I'm doing." True to her words, Charline flashed me a dazzling smile, then promptly slid the pan of oiled potato chunks into the oven.

The remnants of another delicious Charline masterpiece vanished before we reconvened in the living room. The friendly chatter faded as the reality of our situation settled between the four of us.

David leaned forward in his commandeered kitchen chair and rested his forearms on his knees. "I'm assuming we'll pick up where we left off."

I shifted in my corner of the couch and Michael moved to place a reassuring pressure on my back. David's gaze flicked to him at the motion, but said nothing and Michael didn't remove the gentle touch.

"Anyone?" David prompted.

I swallowed against a sudden tackiness in my throat. "We'll start hunting the hunter, and hopefully find where this killer is holed up." I sat up a little straighter. "I know it's not the best plan—certainly not the safest—but let's face it, we've got to do something."

"Our last scheme didn't exactly work out," David pointed out.

I shot him a glare. "We already know how dangerous it could be scouting in the city. The real question is, how do we want to tackle this? Will we go in pairs? What time during the day? How far out do we need to search?"

"That last one is tough. Most of the attacks have happened far away from the office, but we would be remiss to assume that he isn't keeping tabs on it. After all, that's where I originally picked up his scent." Michael's words sent a shiver down my spine and Charline's fair skin paled to a ghostly white.

"You know, I think you might really be on to something," Charline said. I looked at her, amazed at her recovery. "It stands to reason that he's probably somewhere really close to the office," she continued. "I mean, don't most stalkers like to be close to their prey? Somewhere they can keep tabs on their comings and goings? Since Sara stopped being at her house and then vanished for a few days, the only place he could be relatively certain she'd return to would be the office."

My jaw dropped in amazement at Charline's glorious execution of logic. Why didn't I think of that? I looked at the guys. Why didn't they think of that?

"What? Y'all can stop looking at me like that. I'm not *all* hair. Besides, now that I'm helping, the least I can do is contribute."

David choked on his drink.

"What?" she asked innocently.

I reached out to place a hand on the armrest of the loveseat she'd curled up in. "Charline, this isn't your fight. It's touching that you want to help, but I can't let you put yourself in danger because of me."

She gave an indignant huff. "I'm not going to sit back

twiddling my thumbs while the rest of you risk your lives. I refuse to be idle when someone I care about is in danger." She met each of our worried looks with level determination. "Look at it this way, it'll add unpredictability to the rounds if the people and pairs are constantly changing. Also, I think it should be done in pairs, since no one bothered to ask me. I've seen enough horror movies to know that splitting up rarely works out well for those involved, and it would be too obvious if we all searched together."

I had the sneaking suspicion that no matter what we did, she'd somehow get involved. While I was worried, David was borderline apoplectic. Michael kept shooting him glances and appeared to be on the verge of saying something more than once, but he held his peace.

As I looked around, Michael's words came back to me.

I'm not alone.

The thought should have comforted me; instead, it left me nauseated. At least two of these people genuinely cared for me and they were putting their lives in danger to protect mine.

"We need to practice intentionally triggering my change," I blurted into the stillness. Amazed eyes swiveled in my direction. Welcome to left field.

"What?" Michael sounded as lost as he looked.

"I need to learn how to properly defend myself. I can't keep reacting to my situation," I elaborated. "Something tells me the usual tactic of 'play dead' won't work and I refuse to be the reason any of you get hurt."

"What are you suggesting?" David asked.

I could almost see the gears turning in his head. If I wanted to be able to fight, Charline would want to as well.

Much to my surprise, Michael answered. "We already know that in tense or potentially violent situations Sara's survival instincts trigger. The wolf takes over." He looked at

David for a long minute. Anxiety slithered coldly down my spine as their silent exchange continued. David gave the barest of nods and Michael continued. "We're going to have to beat that out of you." I gave an involuntary shiver at the ominous statement and its blatant threat of violence.

David's voice cut through the blanket of tension. "No, Charline, you cannot help. No, you cannot be present. And no, this is not up for debate." David never looked at Charline, but I stole a glance. The hurt on her face sent a pain through my chest.

Michael's words were softer. "This isn't going to be pretty or fun. It'll be painful and exhausting." He swallowed hard. "And there's a very good chance you won't like either one of us by the time we're done." The hollow words seemed to open a chasm between us despite the fact that neither of us had moved.

Charline glanced between us, no doubt sensing the tension. "I think I'm gonna call it a night. What with work and everything." She made a grand show of gathering her things and I met her by the door.

"I'll see you tomorrow," I said.

She gave me the briefest hug. "Good luck," she whispered before stepping away. She glanced back at David who undoubtedly had heard and scowled at him. "I don't need an escort." In complete disregard of her statement, he gave me a tiny nod and followed her out anyway.

I waited until they were in their respective cars before rounding on Michael. "What the hell was that about?"

He took a deep breath and let it out in a sigh. "I hope you know what you're asking," he said, not addressing my concern, then turned and made his way to the bedroom.

I followed hot on his trail, growing angrier with each step. "I've asked you to teach me how to defend myself and the people I care about. What's so wrong with that?"

"What's wrong with that?" he echoed. "You don't know what that will entail. Conquering your triggers will be torture. Literal torture. There's no other way. And you're standing there like it's nothing, like you won't hate both of us by the time we're done. Assuming we succeed."

"Do you want me to stay broken? Is that what you want? To always be a danger to those around me?"

"You're not broken! You were traumatized. It's entirely understandable to need to work through the ordeal you've been through."

"And what happens if I freak out in public one day? It's not like I can go downtown and see a psychiatrist about this."

He threw his hands up and turned away.

"And who's to say that all of this constant fear doesn't eventually cause me to snap? I won't be a monster, Michael. I won't be him." My entire body shook, not from the onset of a change, but from pure human rage. "I'm tired of being ruled by my instincts, of constantly succumbing to my base emotions. I'm more than an animal."

The anger in his body softened to something that smelled like defeat. He sat on the bed and cupped his head in hands. "If only I'd found him sooner, none of this would have happened."

"We've been through this. That wasn't your fault, none of this is your fault."

He looked up at me and the sadness in his eyes was enough to drown in. "What happens next will be. I can't be gentle. You need to know that. If we hold back in any way, it won't work."

I nodded in agreement and wrapped my arms around him. "I wish we could've stayed at the house," I whispered.

"Me too."

"You're telling me that all you've got on this guy is a smell?" Charline's voice bounced off the brick and concrete walls that rose up on either side of us to reach towards a distant strip of blue. All of the alleyways we'd been down so far looked much the same and this one was no different.

"Pretty much," I said as I slid into the lead. Just because she refused to be benched didn't mean I'd intentionally put her in harm's way.

"That's some B.O. But seriously, nothing? I mean, haven't you seen him like three times now?"

"I don't really need the reminder, Charline. And in case you forgot, I was kind of being attacked all three times."

"Fair point."

I rolled my eyes and tried not to think about how all of the noise we were making was likely ruining our chances of finding anything.

She nudged a loose bit of trash with her toe. "I feel like we should have more clues by now."

"This isn't a Nancy Drew novel."

"I know that. Maybe I should start putting a list together of the details."

I wasn't sure if she was talking to me anymore, but the last thing I wanted was to get grilled about my numerous near-death episodes, so I changed the topic. "So, you and David."

"What about me and David?"

"You two seemed pretty cozy the other night. What did you get up to while Michael and I were out of town?"

"Nothing."

I glanced at her out of the corner of my eye. "Doesn't seem like nothing."

"You know, I think I saw a deli back a short ways. Why don't I grab us something?"

I stopped and stared at her. "You really don't want to tell me."

"I just think actually getting lunch would help make all of this look a little more believable. Don't you?" She spun around without waiting for an answer and left me staring after her in disbelief. I shook my head and went to lean against the wall while I waited. A second look at the slime-covered bricks quickly changed my mind.

"To hell with it, I might as well go with her. It's not like I'm doing anything productive out here," I said to no one in particular.

Something tickled my senses as I stalked past one of the countless side streets we'd encountered. I slowly backpedaled to the entryway and stared down the narrow passage.

Sour tendrils of a scent curled in my nostrils and my nose twitched. A deeper look down the alley revealed no more than slim shadows and miscellaneous piles of trash. I took a hesitant step forward, sweeping my gaze over any number of things that could be the source of the smell that had caught my attention. I hazarded a few more cautious steps before I paused and glanced over my shoulder. I shifted my attention back to the narrower off-shoot that somehow seemed that much gloomier by contrast.

The sudden clack of shoes on pavement had every hair on my body standing on end. I took a deep breath, simultaneously trying to calm down and not identify their owner. If I lost the faint whiff I was following, I wasn't liable to redis-cover it.

"Find something?" The whispered question startled me so bad I almost lost the scent anyway.

"Good grief Charline," I hissed. "You scared the crap out of me."

"I was only asking if you smell something."

"One of these days, I hope to be as cavalier as you about all of this. Not so much as a blink when asking whether or not, like a bloodhound, if I've caught the scent of our target."

She shrugged, causing the plastic bag in her hand to crinkle loudly in the nearly silent space. "So did you?"

"Yeah, I think so." Her eyes went wide and I gestured for her to stay behind me as we inched forward together. My frustration increased with each step as the smell remained elusive. We were well down the alley by the time it got stronger. Then another smell emerged, powerful in its rank intensity. I cautiously turned a corner and ran right onto a homeless man.

Charline and I let out a joint screech and the man bolted.

"Oh, God, what's that stench?" Charline asked from behind her hand.

"I suspect it was that gentleman we scared out of his nap."

"Please don't tell me that's what we've been following." She blinked back tears at the overpowering stench and took a step back.

"No, there's something else here." I choked back bile as I carefully moved matted blankets and grime encrusted cardboard with my foot.

Charline whispered words of scorn behind me, but I persisted. I pulled back what I thought to be the last layer, uncovering an old army jacket that had seen better days.

"He was here." I waved a hand behind me, not taking my eyes off the garment for fear it'd vanish the moment I blinked. "Give me the bag."

She reluctantly passed over the plastic bag that had

previously housed the sandwiches she now cradled in her arm. I placed the threadbare item carefully in the thin container, doing my best not to let it touch too many other things.

"Do you think that will work?"

"It's the best we've got. And I have no desire to bring any extra scents home with us." I tied the bag tight and for reasons that eluded me proceeded to replace the items I'd moved.

———

"I cannot wait to stop touching this thing. I feel like I could take ten baths and still smell it," I said when we returned to the familiar bustle and noise of the office.

"I'm not saying bleach should be involved, only that you might want to consider it." I chuckled at Charline's extreme suggestion.

"Come to think of it, I'm not really sure how well werewolves stand up to chemicals."

"Shit." Charline's sudden expletive caught me off guard.

"What is it?"

"We have company." She gestured towards our destination. Above my cubicle wall, I could make out two heads.

My hiss caught the attention of the nearest cubicle's occupant. "I knew we should have said something."

Charline gave a groan beside me. "This should be fun."

I took a fateful step into their line of sight and held up my hands in what I hoped was a placating gesture. "Now before you start—"

Michael's hand encircled my arm and he dragged me the rest of the way into the small space. "What the hell were you thinking?" His harsh whisper immediately had my hackles up.

"I was thinking this was the plan," I hissed back. His frown deepened. "Remember the plan? I was there. You were there. We were all there." My sweeping gesture encompassed our small party. "And we *all* agreed on it."

"We didn't agree to you two traipsing off without a word about—"

"This isn't the place for this," I cut him off. "Besides, in case you hadn't noticed, we found something." I tossed the bag to David who snatched it out of the air with ease. He gave it a not so discreet sniff then scrunched his nose and put the offending item at arm's length.

Michael's searing gaze never shifted from me. "I don't give a damn what you found. You could've gotten yourself killed."

"Eh-hem," Charline fake coughed in an attempt to get Michael to temper his increasing volume.

He shot her a look and David intervened, gently pulling him back. Judging by the fire in Michael's eye, I was a little surprised he didn't bite him for his trouble.

"Look man, relax. They're fine. They're back, they're safe. And she has a point. Granted, a little more communication would've been nice." He spared Charline and me a look before returning his attention to Michael. "Sara didn't do anything the pack wouldn't have expected."

Storm clouds brewed on Michael's face. "You weren't so okay with this ten minutes ago."

David's mouth fell open. "That's different. She can't defend herself like Sara can."

"What's this?" Challenge laced Charline's question as she crossed her arms beneath her breasts and tapped her foot, the perfect image of dignified outrage.

"Char," David tried. Her blistering look should have left burn marks on the wall behind him.

I quickly interjected before she could unleash. "Yes, I

know we should have told you we were headed out, but it wouldn't be much of a divide-and-conquer if all we did was tail each other around."

David gave a resigned sigh. "I guess we'll convene about it later. I know we didn't cover this before, but I think that whenever we aren't out searching, we should stay together as much as possible. Create the illusion that we're traveling in a pack instead of the suicide missions we're currently operating."

Michael's scowl seemed permanently stamped on his face, David was clearly digging a hole he had no hope of getting out of, and Charline looked like she might miraculously sprout claws.

"Fine, but I'm tired of cooking at Michael's. After work, we meet at my house. I imagine you can remember how to get there on your own?" Pure Southern hostility undercut the question. Without another word, she made her way past the blockade, magically not touching either of them, and vanished into the bustle of the office.

I, however, did not have the luxury of storming out of my own cubicle, so I did the next best thing and blatantly ignored them. After suffering several seconds of feeling like there was an itch between my shoulder blades, I spun to face them.

"Don't you have somewhere to be? A job that involves bossing *other* people around?"

David wisely didn't respond and slipped quietly out of my office.

"And as for you," I said, turning to Michael, "I wasn't aware you'd transferred departments."

His jaw tightened and a muscle twitched in his cheek.

I raised my eyebrows. "Are you the new assistant I keep telling Bob I need or do you also have somewhere else you need to be?"

Michael's eyes flashed and he stalked off in sullen silence.

I counted to thirty before I dared breathe a sigh of relief. I knew it had been a mistake to not leave a note. The only mercy from the whole interaction was that David had taken the revolting bag with him.

That's it, I'm going straight to Charline's after work. Do not pass Go, do not collect two hundred dollars.

No sooner did I have the thought, then my phone dinged. I looked down to find a message from Michael. My hope for an apology shriveled at reading the ominous text.

<Come to the house before dinner.>

27

TRIGGERS

A strangled sound of indignant rage stuck in the back of my throat as I shook the steering wheel, barely remembering to check my strength before I snapped it clean off. I removed my white-knuckled grip and tried again at a steadying breath. Finally, I looked up at the Jeep parked in front of me. A chill slithered down my spine as I took in the driver side door swaying in the breeze.

"Oh no." I scrambled out of the car and raced towards the house.

My feet stopped dead on the threshold and my heart tried to do the same. The front door swung into the shadowed interior, its crimson paint a disconcerting match to the glistening liquid on the wooden floors. I took a ragged breath and stepped into the gloom, the sun back-lighting me made it impossible to focus my night vision.

Maybe I should close the door so I can see better.

Even half paralyzed with fear, that sounded like a terrible idea. I took another nervous step. The shadows thickened enough to let me make out the state of the room. The coffee table lay shattered. The couch sat on its side. Pillows and papers covered the ground in haphazard chaos.

When I didn't find a body, I let out a breath I hadn't realized I'd been holding.

"Michael?"

A low growl emanated from the darkness.

I fought the reflex to squeeze my eyes shut while every fiber of my being screamed at me to run. Thankfully, some rational part of me recognized that impulse as the exact wrong thing to do. I slowly turned to face the threat. Indistinct shadows danced along the ground and the menacing sound rolled out once more.

My heart pounded, the rushing of blood in my ears drowning out the world. As if sensing my dread, the growl came again an octave lower. At the same time, a small sound of pain emanated from deeper in the house, slicing through the noise to stab into me.

Michael.

I scarcely dared to breathe as my foot slid a fraction forward in the direction of the tiny sound. A soft scrape of claw on wood raked across my nerves, unnaturally loud in the small space. I attempted another cautious step and found no purchase.

My body lurched forward as my foot unexpectedly slipped several inches farther than I'd intended. Teeth flashed in the amber glow of the setting sun and my instincts won out. I bolted, not out the door, but deeper into the house.

Weight barreled into my side, sending me careening into the toppled couch. An exposed leg punched into my gut and I gasped. Serrated teeth ripped into my arm. Bright spots of light exploded across my vision doing nothing to illuminate the world around me. I screamed and the wolf inside fought to take control.

I scrabbled uselessly along the ground. Cold seeped into my core as my vision blurred red. The nearly impossible task of fighting off a wolf three times my size compounded with my own inner struggle not to shift. With mounting terror, I realized I was losing both battles.

My nails scored the floor under me as the beast dragged me deeper into the house. Desperate, I pulled back on the captive arm. The pain crystallized and I almost bit off my tongue to stop the scream from tearing free. His growl echoed off the walls and inside of my chest. My fight not to change moments from being lost, even as I recognized I'd die before I finished.

Light blasted to life around me. Through the haze of pain, Michael swam into focus. He stood in the kitchen, arms crossed, a look of disappointment clouding his face.

"Enough."

Confusion briefly eclipsed the pain. Then my arm fell to the ground. I looked down at the appendage in wonder, amazed to find minimal damage as opposed to shredded flesh. My gaze transferred to my attacker who sat staring at me with unblinking eyes.

"David?" Once I said it, I knew without a doubt, it was true.

He immediately slunk off to change back. Now that my fear no longer dominated my senses, I could clearly distinguish his scent as well as Michael's. Another scent, however, was noticeably lacking—the iron smell of fresh blood.

"You tricked me." The slap of sound did nothing to faze Michael's mask of apathy.

"You were warned."

"I wasn't warned that I'd be deceived into believing you were dying!" That earned the tiniest of a flinch.

"You needed to believe it." I could scarcely hear the words over the roaring in my ears.

My anger from earlier returned in full force as I fumed in silence. After several tense minutes, I shifted to a seated position, but stayed where I'd been dragged while I tried to get a grip on my seething rage.

"None of this will do any good if you don't feel there is real danger. You know and trust both of us," David said as he returned to the grisly scene.

"We had to get creative." Apparently, apathy could be transferred to words as well. I glowered at Michael.

"Let's try to break down the areas that could stand improvement." At David's words, I transferred my harsh look. He remained unaffected. "First off, you walked blindly into what you believed to be a hostile situation."

I opened my mouth to protest.

"You didn't use any of your senses, wolf or human," Michael said.

"You should have been able to tell right away that it wasn't blood and that I wasn't the mutt," David expanded.

"Zero common sense," Michael added without a hint of mercy.

"Now wait a minute," I cut in.

"About the only thing you did do right was not turn," David finished.

"I wouldn't go that far," Michael corrected, indicating my hands, the making of claws already turning them from soft to sinister.

I gave an exasperated cry and stood up. "I'm done with this. I'm going to change clothes. One of you jerks can explain to Charline why we're late."

Charline Montgomery did not abide rudeness and made no secret of it when we made our entrance. "Well, it's about time y'all got here. What took you so long?" No one bothered to answer or make eye contact. "Whatever, have a seat, the table is set. I'm going to grab another bottle of wine."

I looked up at the mention of 'another' realizing that she already held a sizable glass for herself. Silence dominated the table as we all took our seats and picked at our food. Finally, I couldn't take it anymore.

"Dinner is lovely, Charline. Thank you."

"Of course, it is, though you'd never know it by all of your attitudes. What the hell happened this afternoon?"

I stifled a giggle. So much tact in so few words. My unusual outburst seemed to surprise the guys more than Charline's bold demand for an explanation.

"We started Sara's training," Michael said with the same level of apathy as earlier.

"Get over it already," I snapped. "If anyone has a right to be upset, it's me. I'm the one that basically got ambushed in the one place I'm supposed to feel safe."

Shock exploded across Charline's face.

"But that's what I asked for, it would be ridiculous of me to hold it against either one of you. I'm moving on and so should you."

David dared to look hopeful and Charline was obviously exercising some serious willpower in holding back questions. Michael still hadn't blinked.

"Seriously, enough. You made your point this afternoon. Lesson learned. Now please, can we move on?"

"Anyone need more wine?" Charline asked. David's laughter burst into the room. "What?"

"Nothing, babe. Yes, I could do with some more wine. Would you like some help bringing in dessert?"

"What makes you think there's dessert?" We all looked at Charline. "Oh, alright, there's dessert. Get off your keister and give me a hand." They both got up to retrieve the promised sweets, giving me and Michael a moment to ourselves.

I reached over to him, but stopped short of taking his hand and waited. Time stretched until he finally took the peace offering and looked up at me, sadness filling his eyes.

"Michael, I don't understand why you're struggling with this. You know it has to be done."

"I hate resorting to such extreme measures. You should have all the time in the world to overcome your triggers."

"But we don't." Doubt flitted across his face like a shadow, gone as quickly as it arrived. I smiled and gave his hand a gentle squeeze.

"Finally! It's about time you two made up." Charline's exclamation caught us both off guard and our hands blasted apart. "Honestly, there's only so much I can take. You two are constantly swinging from one extreme to another, make up your mind already. It's getting painful for the rest of us."

David's laughter floated behind Charline, but his expression seemed to mirror Michael's concern.

Stepping into Michael's place hours after I'd been led to believe it was a murder scene instantly put me on edge. I raised my nose to the air as Michael followed me inside. While I wasn't expecting another teachable moment or an attack, I had no intention of being caught unawares again.

Michael stood by the glowing lamp, watching me as the soft light pushed against the night. "What do you smell?"

That simple question evoked memories of when all of this seemed so much less serious. A small smile tugged at the corners of my mouth as I recalled sitting across from this man at a deli being made to list all the scents of the day.

"What?" he asked.

My smile broadened. "It smells like home." Surprise flickered in his eyes. I closed the door behind me and walked towards him then reached up to cradle his face. "It smells like you. It smells like us."

The hint of a smile lay like a shadow on his face. His

gaze shifted to the top of my head as he followed the path of his hands as they smoothed my hair back.

"What are you thinking?" he asked quietly.

"That we should go howl at the moon."

His hands faltered in their ceaseless rhythm. A chuckle got stuck in his throat, but would not be denied.

I stepped back. "I'm perfectly serious. I haven't gotten to do that yet."

The dam broke and tension drained from his body as laughter rolled out of him. When he finally caught his breath, he pulled me back close. And there he was—my Michael—complete with that smile that never really seemed to fade.

"I hate to break it to you, but there's a new moon tonight, nothing to howl at." More laughter tugged at his mouth.

I stretched to my tiptoes and placed a tingling kiss on his lips. "Then what shall we howl to?"

In lieu of a response, he captured my mouth with a fierce kiss. "I'm sure we'll think of something." My toes curled in delight at the smoky promise. I smiled harder. "You like that?" His voice dropped low enough to be a purr.

"Mhm," I hummed and stole a quick kiss then took advantage of his ease and slipped his grip. "But you'll have to catch me first."

To my immense satisfaction, I didn't react to the low growl that emanated from him beyond to feel heat rush through me. Michael's eyes flashed yellow as he lunged over the couch. I gave a squeal of delight and circled back around, doing what I could to keep something between us. He immediately swiveled to follow. A lamp went flying and he almost caught me as I paused to make sure it didn't break.

Fingers stirred the air at the nape of my neck. I yipped in alarm and a short bark of laughter filled the space I'd vacated. My feet slid across the kitchen floor finding no purchase. I spun around to face him almost falling over in the process.

He stood blocking the way, victory plain on his face. "Where to now?" he teased, his breath as ragged as mine.

I may be cornered, but I'm not done.

I charged. He let out a grunt when I barreled into him with enough force to land us both in a tangle of limbs and laughed as I peppered him with kisses. He smelled positively delicious and I wanted to taste every inch of him.

I slipped my nails between his buttons and proceeded to tear his shirt apart with a strength that would one day stop surprising me. He didn't seem to mind as his fingers curled in my own top and jerked it over my head. I helped as I grew frustrated with the rest of my clothing and removed it as quickly as possible.

Hot hands roved over my sides and back, decadent in their lavish attention. I bit his lip then diverted my attention to explore across his chest and down his torso. The shine of fresh scar tissue caught my eye. I leaned down to kiss along each mark, tracing the pearly lines with my tongue as I worked my way lower until the rough fabric of his jeans scratched at my face, another sensation for my heightened awareness.

He let out a strangled cry as I bit down on the button and caught his eye. I cupped his erection straining against his jeans, teasing him through the fabric. He jerked beneath me and let out a curse followed by another tortured moan. I took mercy on him and made short work of the intervening garment. Much as I enjoyed driving him wild, he wasn't the only one aching for a release.

I shimmied between his legs to a more comfortable position and took a moment to admire my prize. I curled my fingers around the base of his shaft in a firm hold and darted my tongue across his slit, then wrapped my lips around him. Any thoughts I'd had of taking my time went right out the window as his deep musk wove around me and addled what was left of my senses.

He ran his fingers through my hair and groaned as I continued. His thighs quivered beneath my hands as he fought to maintain control. I swallowed around him and was rewarded with the most divine whimper while his fingers tightened briefly in my hair.

He reached out and grabbed my arm then tugged me toward his body. I straddled his waist, curling my fingers in his hair as I pulled at his lips. I reveled in the feel of his bare body against mine and wriggled, earning myself a throaty growl that made me ache in all the best ways.

My gasp turned into a moan as he guided my hips and I sank onto him. He shifted beneath me, arching off the floor and pressing deep. I echoed the sound he'd made moments before, whimpering as he stroked the sweetest spot with each thrust.

I looked down into his deep brown eyes and the kitchen around us melted away. We could have been anywhere—in the bedroom, in the woods—all that mattered was him and me.

28

WRONG TURN

"I've made a list," Charline declared as she leaned against my desk.

"A list of what?" I asked.

She gave an aggrieved sigh. "Everything we know about," she paused and leaned forward to whisper conspiratorially, "you know who."

"Must be a short list." Weeks of searching and the most we'd turned up was a handful of old scraps.

"It would be longer if you'd give me more details."

"I've told you everything. He wasn't entirely human when I saw him. I don't know what you're looking for."

"Well, David said that a lot of things transfer over from one form to the next. Like hair and eye color."

"David says, huh?" I poked her leg with my toe.

"Would you focus?" She giggled as she pushed my shoulder.

"All I'm saying is that no one spends that much time with someone they only want to be friends with." She ducked her head to hide the spreading blush behind a waterfall of hair. "You really like him, don't you?"

"Is that wrong? I mean Ted and I just broke up."

I shrugged; relationship advice wasn't really my forte.

"How's the training thing going?" she asked.

"Awful and I'm not getting any better. Maybe Michael was right, it's going to take time."

"And trusting your instincts," Charline and I said together. We both laughed. As the sound died, the cubicle took on an oppressive air.

"We have to find a clue or something. I can't live my life like this."

"We will." Charline squeezed my shoulder. "The searches will turn up something. You'll see."

"Because we've found so much already. Face it, the most we've uncovered are a couple of stale haunts, none of which offer any kind of pattern."

Her face fell.

"You better go," I said solemnly. "I'm sure Brianne has something to say about your report."

Charline nodded and spared me a sad look before exiting.

I closed my eyes and flopped my head back. The last couple weeks had been exhausting. I'd already endured far more heart-stopping terrors than any person ever should and it was definitely taking a toll on my mental health.

I swear, if I get one more prank call about someone dying, I'm going to...

"Good, you're here."

I swiveled my chair around to face Bob with his too-tight button down in a terrible shade of puce.

"Well, don't just sit there. We have a proposal to prepare for." He didn't wait to see if I would respond, merely returned to his office.

I grabbed the phone and dialed Michael's direct line in the office.

He answered on the second ring. "Hey, what's up?"

"Bob commandeered me for a secretarial project. No telling how long that will take."

"Thanks for the heads up. I'll find some way to stick around."

Three hours later, Bob finally released me. I immediately phoned Michael's cell. My foot tapped impatiently while I listened to the line ring. I gave up on the eighth. Angry at pretty much everyone, I stormed off to the elevators. When they opened again, my anger dissipated.

I swallowed and stepped out onto the second deck of the parking garage. My steps echoed against the concrete, each clack making me wince, while I scanned the handful of cars.

It's not far. You walk this garage every day. Michael is here... somewhere.

A can rolled in the distance. The faint metal ping as it collided with a pillar almost sent me into a full-on panic. I took a deep breath that didn't feel fortifying in the least. A shadow shifted. My eyes darted to follow it, but it could've easily been my imagination. I forced myself to keep moving.

Where is he?

Panic slithered through my chest and my pace quickened. I frantically scanned the area, but there was no sign of the bright yellow Jeep. My ear twitched and I zeroed in on the noise that had caught my attention, a faint rasping with an odd wetness to it.

Terror strangled my heart and stole the air from my lungs. Every fiber of my being told me to turn tail and run.

What if it's Michael?

The dire thought stopped me in my tracks. Another wet breath. I shoved my fear down as far as it would go and followed it.

A large white pickup loomed before me. In my distraction, I hadn't recognized David's truck. The rasp came again and I stumbled forward. A sharp metallic tang filled the air and I looked down at smears of red coating the ground. My heart lurched into my throat as I followed the trail around the vehicle to a body—Michael's body.

I let out a stifled scream and barely remembered to glance around before rushing to his side. His labored breathing didn't sound like a lie and the blood everywhere was definitely his. "Michael, can you hear me?" My harsh whisper sounded unnaturally loud in the quiet. "Are you hurt? What do I do?" My panic escalated with each question.

"David?" Froth bubbled at Michael's lips and his eyes refused to focus. As if on cue, something rattled against the ground not far off. I stiffened. There was a grunt of pain, then more silence.

"I'm going to find him," I whispered.

Michael's hand shot out lightning fast to grab my wrist. I freed my hand and quietly began moving in the direction of the last sound.

Out of nowhere, a weight slammed into me. My side screamed where nails bit into flesh. Nausea threatened to overwhelm me as my shoulder crunched into the ground. I bit back a cry and searched for the assailant. The urge to change rose like a wave. I willed my nerves to settle and focused my heightened sense of smell.

Instantly, exhaust leapt to the forefront, as well as David's and Michael's scents. Mixed among them was the faintest hint of *Him*. I scrambled to my feet, ignoring the throbbing ache in my shoulder, and strained to hear anything in the void of silence. Every muscle tensed to the point of pain. Then, the tiniest whisper of nail, of fur brushing against something.

I waited, the agony of it spreading across my body like fire. My only advantage was that he would assume I was frozen with fear.

It worked.

He launched over the bed of the truck, nothing more than a blur of color. I waited until the last possible moment and stepped aside.

Nails scratched along the concrete where I'd been standing not a second before. I turned and slammed all of my weight down. The air whooshed out of him and he went limp, but my victory was short-lived as the clean smell of outdoors with a hint of lumber and dust tickled my nose.

"David!" The wolf beneath me tried to stand and I pushed him back to the ground. "This is way past the line. Using a real injury to make Michael bleed! What if he'd come along? Where would you two be then?"

"Actually," Michael said behind me, "we made a small cut in a place that happens to bleed a lot." I turned in shock to see that he'd already changed his shirt. He gestured for me to release my captive.

David stood and shook himself off before making his way to the truck. The back door already hung open and he jumped inside, never once sparing me a glance. I swiveled my attention back to Michael.

"And how did I do in your asinine test?" The question bounced back, a reminder of the empty space.

"Honestly? Well."

I looked forward to being partnered with David with equal parts trepidation and excitement. On the one hand, I barely knew him, on the other I'd finally get to talk to him without Michael around. We'd been chatting amicably off and on for the last thirty minutes while I built up my nerve. I glanced over at him as we turned down a fresh alley.

"So, um, you and Michael have known each other a long time, huh?"

David gave me a sidelong look. "We have."

"He said you basically grew up together."

"We did." The ghost of a smile played on his lips.

Mustering up all my courage, I went for it. "If you two are such good friends, how come you never visit? He said he hadn't seen you in twelve years. Did something happen?"

David's shoulders tightened and his gaze skittered away from me. "It's complicated."

"Did you two have a falling out?" I pressed.

"Not quite."

"Then what's the deal?"

He rubbed the back of his neck and kept his gaze focused on the ground. "It's not really my place to say. Have you talked to Michael about this?"

"What do you think?" I growled. "If he was any more evasive, he'd be talking another language."

His shoulders sagged and he darted a glance at me. "I get that, I do, but it's not my story to tell."

"Then who the hell is going to tell it to me?"

"I understand that you're frustrated—I've told him repeatedly he can't keep you in the dark forever—but there's no reason to growl at me about it."

Silence came down like a hammer crushing me beneath its weight and I was immensely grateful I wasn't with Charline.

"That's not me."

"Don't. Move." The increasingly loud threat swallowed David's grim command and a figure barely distinguishable from the trash emerged to block our path.

I knew instantly why we hadn't and would never have been able to find my tormentor. I'd been looking for a beast. This was a man. My attacker had always been some faceless monster made of yellow eyes and flashing teeth. But this was a person like anyone else.

He stood shorter than I remembered and he wasn't as lean as I would have expected of someone living on the streets. Hazel eyes peered from behind matted hair that obscured most of his face. Everything about the oddly familiar stranger seemed purposely unkempt from his scraggly beard to his bedraggled clothes.

Recognition scratched at my mind then blasted apart when the pop of sinew and bone filled the narrow alley. A responding echo of the change resonated in me. I struggled to hold the instinct at bay. When his shift stopped, he stood half a foot taller, a grisly mix of man and beast.

"What do we do?" I asked quietly. The creature's eyes, grotesquely human as they were, enlarged at the sound. His growl became more of a snarl and he took a step forward.

"Whatever you do, don't run."

This was it. No fleeing, no hiding, no waking up. My own threat vibrated through me. Almost in chorus, David joined. My body ached from restraining the change; even the slightest give in letting my nails grow to claws might be too much to hold back a full-blown shift.

Our quarry's growl hitched. He took a slow step back. I matched him. He took another. My timbre deepened. His eyes narrowed as his gaze darted between us. Without warning, he turned and ran.

I launched after him. Brick and concrete passed by in a blur of monotone colors. Garbage cans clanged loudly on the pavement. I swerved to avoid them and poured on more speed. Determination fueled my limbs as I gained ground.

Then he vanished.

I skidded past a narrow opening on my right. *Shit.* I doubled back and raced to catch up before he could clear the fence at the far end. In seconds, I crashed into the metal links prepared to vault up after him. My foot wedged into a link and I surged up only to be brought back down. I fought against my captor's hold.

"Sara, stop."

"Let me go! I can catch him," I cried as the mutt's shadow turned a corner and disappeared.

"He's gone," David said softly.

I sagged against the fence, suddenly exhausted.

"We're pretty far out," he said as he released me. "We'll have to hurry if we want to make it back to the office in time."

"Fuck the office."

<hr>

"Where have you been?" Bob shouted the second I stepped in his periphery. "I've been looking for you for hours."

"I wasn't aware," I said through gritted teeth.

"Don't give me attitude."

I nearly choked on my attempt at a calming breath. Oblivious to my struggle, he barreled on.

"Where are the Bigsley reports? They were due days ago. I've been lenient with you in light of your *situation* but there can be no more excuses for this sort of behavior. You are paid to do a job and I expect you to do it."

I stopped shuffling my papers and spun to face him. "My *situation*? If by situation, you mean being mauled to the brink of death and having to somehow wake up every day and live with that terror, then you're even more of an asshole than I thought you were. For your information, *Bob*, this is the first year that I've taken sick leave, or hell, a personal day. And what behavior? I've been late a couple of times since the attack and this is literally the longest lunch I've taken in the entire time I've worked here. Need we revisit the mauling?

"And no, you don't pay me for any of this. I'm a Junior Project Manager and am treated and used—not to mention paid—like your personal secretary. So, grow a pair, give me a raise, and get the hell off my back."

He stood there looking pole-axed.

"Oh, and another thing," he flinched as I whirled back on him, "the Bigsley report has been on your desk for two days."

I spun the chair out, slammed into it, and almost toppled over when I violently swung back to the desk. Adrenaline coursed through my veins, reminiscent of what had spurred me on in the alley. I stared straight ahead and played at pulling up my system. When the air behind me finally stirred, I released the breath I'd been holding.

"How could you be so reckless?" Michael's shout greeted Charline and me as we stepped into the house.

"I wasn't alone, Michael." My purse and keys landed unceremoniously on the entry table with a clamor to match. "What would you have had me do? He was right there. And he *ran*." I looked at David for support. He offered none.

"And what would you have done if you'd caught him?"

I bristled. "I would have fought. Fought like I should have that night."

"You don't need to prove anything," he said.

"That's not what it was about! He ran, I chased. David was right behind me the whole time." I gestured angrily at David, hoping he would finally seize the chance to speak up. Instead, he looked a bit abashed.

"You're fast, Sara, like really fast. If it hadn't been for the fence, I doubt I would've caught up to you."

I stared at him in disbelief. "What?"

"I'm sorry."

The couch groaned beneath my sudden weight and Charline made an indignant sound. She extricated herself and grabbed a slice of pizza from the counter. She eyed it skeptically before taking a bite and offered me one with noticeably more meat. I blindly accepted it, my mind reeling.

"But surely you could have…"

David shook his head. I took a bite, but wasn't sure if I chewed it before swallowing.

"At least we know what he looks like now. Sara, can you describe him for everyone?" Michael asked, appearing to have calmed down a little.

"What are you asking me for?"

"Apparently, David isn't very good at details," Michael said. David shrugged, unconcerned by the rebuke.

"I doubt I'll be much better. He was taller than me. Shorter than you. Brown hair, I think. Might have had a scar, could've been tan, but that could've been dirt. Hazel eyes and covered with hair."

"That's it?" Charline exclaimed "That describes almost everyone I've seen on these outings. Hell, that practically describes everyone I've seen ever. It even sounds a bit like Ted. Well except for looking like he was dragged through a knot hole backwards and of course the hair."

"Have I really blown our best chance to sniff him out?" I groaned.

Charline's arm tightened around me and one of the guys passed me a drink. It smelled like brandy. The vapors burned my nose, but I knocked it back without tasting it.

"I'm so fed up with all of this."

RUNNING IN A PACK

I turned to pace the room again while awareness of the pending full moon itched beneath my skin. "Three whole months and we have nothing to show for it."

"That's not true," Michael said. "Your control is getting better." He gave me a suggestive grin before taking a sip of his fifth cup of coffee. I eyed the mug, shook my head, and turned to walk back the way I'd come.

"Good grief, Sara, would you sit down already?" Charline fussed from her corner of the couch.

"You don't suppose Bittens are prone to being moonstruck, do you?" David asked with a chuckle.

Michael's face soured. "Don't joke about that."

"What are you talking about?" Charline asked.

I finally stopped my pacing. "What's moonstruck?"

"Well, some *weres* go a little batty around the full moon," David supplied.

"I'm going to turn into a bat?" I screeched, then promptly fell on the couch.

"No." I could barely hear Michael's response through David's laughter.

"It's not funny," I mumbled. "I feel like I'm all over the place."

"I mean-"

"You're just anxious from being cooped up," Michael cut David off.

"And being chased by a homicidal psychopath," Charline contributed. I glanced up from my misery to see Michael intensely glaring at his best friend.

"I've been meaning to ask something," I said, changing the topic. "Is it normal to shift like that? Because I don't think I could do it."

David looked at Michael before responding. "*Weres* are no different than people. We all have our strengths, the things that we are innately good at."

"Like what?" Charline asked.

"Like not every *were* can be built like a cement truck," he said with a goofy grin.

"Yeah, with brains to match," Michael added and I snickered.

"You're just mad that you haven't been able to out wrestle me since we were fifteen." When Michael rolled his eyes and returned to his coffee, David let it go and turned to me. "I would definitely say yours is speed. You're faster than a hare in spring."

"Speed, huh? I've never been fast before. I never even ran the mile." I glanced over at my unflappable boyfriend drinking coffee at a time like this. "What about Michael?"

David snagged Michael around the shoulders nearly causing the half-empty mug to go crashing to the ground. "Big fluffy here is a natural born tracker." Michael smiled at his friend's over-the-top praise. "You got something that needs finding, you find a Howell. His whole family was like that. Best trackers this side of the Mississippi. Come to think of it, I'm surprised Alexander waited so long to reach out."

Michael's smile slipped and he shrugged David off. "Oh man, I'm sorry. I didn't think."

"Who's Alexander?" I asked, sensing the tension.

David hesitated. "My boss."

"Like work-boss or wolf-boss?" Charline asked.

"Both," he said flatly while Michael wordlessly retreated to the kitchen. I wanted to ask what was going on, but before I could, David spoke up again. "I think it's time we called it a night. You ready to go?" he asked Charline.

Her mouth hung open. She didn't look the least bit ready to leave, especially now that there was intrigue afoot.

"But..."

"We need to get you packed."

She scowled at David. "I don't see why *I* have to leave town during the full moon. Seems excessive to me. And besides, you won't even..." she continued to talk as David ushered her out of the house.

When I was sure they'd gone, I turned to ask Michael what that was all about, except he was gone. I found him in the main bedroom already in bed. He didn't say a word as I stripped and maintained his silence as I slipped beneath the covers. We lay there for who knew how long in silence before I finally fell into a fitful sleep.

Two days later, the three of us piled into David's truck and began the lengthy drive to Raven Rock.

"I think it might be better if Sara went first after all," Michael said from the passenger seat.

David gave me a sidelong look. "Probably for the best."

"I'm right here." Neither responded. "Hello? Are you two seriously going to talk about me like I'm not here?"

Michael turned toward me, his face deceptively neutral. "If I didn't know any better, I'd say you're excited."

A half-baked retort died in my throat. "Oh my god, you're right."

"There's no need to be self-conscious. I'd be more worried if you didn't look forward to it," David said, catching my eye.

I gave him a small smile. "This should be interesting. It'll be my first with someone besides Michael."

"And I'm sure it will end a lot differently too," David responded casually and my face burned crimson.

"Michael!" I shouted, my embarrassment spreading like a rash, as I reached forward to smack him.

"I didn't say anything."

"That's not what I meant at all." David looked mortified. My arm froze mid-smack.

"Oh," Michael and I chimed.

"What I meant was..." He cleared his throat. "That if our friend does make an appearance, it won't be the usual fun-filled adventure."

"There's no need to sound so melancholy." Michael gave him a shove.

"Yeah, I'm sure we can scare up a rabbit or two," I said. That brought a smile to his face.

"Oh, she's done for," David said.

"What's that supposed to mean?" I asked.

"You haven't even changed yet and you're already dreaming of all the rabbits you'll catch." I stuck my tongue out at him.

"I haven't caught one yet," I corrected him.

David laughed and Michael gave me a knowing look. We joked the rest of the way until we pulled into the same clearing Michael had brought us before.

"Okay," Michael began, "I know we're all feeling the effects of the moon, but we need to be careful."

The reality check had an unpleasant sobering effect. Duffels in hand, we began our trek deeper into the forest.

"Michael, if we go any farther, we'll pop out the other side," David said after an eternity of walking. He dropped his camo bag into foliage so thick it barely made a sound.

"Fine." He nodded to David who began walking away to give us some privacy. "Are you going to be okay?" he asked when David was out of earshot.

"I'll be fine," I reassured him.

"I know you will." He leaned down and snared my lips with a delicious kiss that set my pulse racing, then released me and walked off in the opposite direction with a smirk.

I smothered my own stupid grin and started removing my clothes, then hid everything like before. Once that was done, I squared my shoulders, took a bracing breath, and got down on all fours.

My head hung between my shoulders as I closed my eyes and thought about the moon. I pushed all other thoughts aside and focused on the growing awareness and the primalness it brought. My body shook with a need I finally understood, a need to be more, a need to be free. An image of the moon full and white eclipsed all other thought.

I gritted my teeth and tried to relax as pain radiated across my body. All of my muscles tightened and I panted heavily, resisting the urge to tear at my shifting skin. A fresh wave of pain washed over me and I fell to the ground, losing my perfect image of the moon.

A slight breeze ruffled my fur as I panted into the earth. I shakily got to my feet unsure of how much time had passed. The crisp leaves let out tiny crunches as I trotted off in the direction David had gone.

He laughed when I appeared. "You look happier."

I wagged my tail then left him to his own transformation.

In far less time than it had taken me, David stepped into the clearing, his sandy coat easily distinguishable from the shadows. He sat at the edge and we waited for Michael to join us. Not long later, David lifted his muzzle to the sky and set free a single, pure note. Almost at the same time mine and another voice climbed into the night.

An elation I'd never experienced filled me to the point of overflowing as the song reached for the stars. The sound trailed off and I dropped my head in time to see Michael's darkness walking towards me

We rubbed faces and he nipped at my shoulder. I gave him my own toothy rebuke, and he barked a laugh. Then I turned to see David shamelessly rolling around. I gave a short bark. He popped up, looked around for a moment, then took off. Michael and I plunged into the dense undergrowth in pursuit.

Damp leaves stuck to my paws as I wove around trunks eager to find the lead. In no time at all, I surged past them. I enjoyed my victory by pulling farther ahead, until a whiff of something floated on the breeze.

Rabbit.

I veered and the others followed. A small form rocketed out from under a bush scaring me half to death, but I didn't freeze this time. My claws sank into the soil as I adjusted course. The rabbit zigzagged through the foliage, gave a hop, and vanished.

The others skidded to a halt behind me as I uncovered the burrow the crafty bastard had disappeared into. Disappointment permeated the air like I'd lost dinner despite the fact that we'd eaten before heading out. Between the three of us, we were bound to catch something, but that didn't diminish my dejection.

Giving it up as a lost cause, I turned to find the guys roughhousing. I barked a laugh and stepped forward to join. Out of the corner of my eye, I caught some movement and renewed hope swelled in my chest. Maybe my little friend wasn't so clever after all.

I turned back to the burrow and something substantially larger than a bunny burst forth. A scream tore through the night as razor-sharp teeth sank deep enough into my shoulder to scrape bone. By some miracle, I kept my footing, though I had no idea what had attacked me.

Then I smelled him.

The rancid odor of wrongness clogged my nostrils. Between the pain and the smell, I could barely breathe. The mutt released my shoulder, spinning me around and I stumbled. I tried to regain my bearings, but pain shot up my left foreleg when I put weight on it and I almost crashed face first into the ground. I curled the injured limb against my chest and blinked the tears from my eyes as I took in the scene unfolding before me.

David circled Michael and my attacker, all three growling loud enough to shake the ground. Unlike before, the mutt was fully shifted. Michael snapped at a paw that didn't move fast enough. I limped over in an attempt to cut off any escape route. The rogue's eyes shifted at my movement and his growl deepened.

Michael took advantage of his distraction and lunged, only to soar right past him. The mutt bolted through the opening David was too slow to close. Michael scrambled to his feet and all three of us tore after him, but even with adrenaline pumping through me, I couldn't compensate for my injury.

The others pulled farther and farther ahead until I lost all awareness of them. My shoulder throbbed in time with my heartbeat and my vision refused to hold steady. A howl rose up and I did my best to orient myself to the sound. I managed one stumbling step before it faded out.

It's no use. Even if I figure out which direction, I'll never be able to catch up. Not like this.

I tentatively put more weight on my leg and immediately curled my paw back under my body. With a whimper, I sat in the damp undergrowth, my sides heaving as I tried to control my panic. I looked around at the world that I'd been so excited to explore only a couple hours ago. What had been fun obstacles to swerve around, now stood like ominous sentries. Even my wolf seemed at a loss for what to do.

If I can just find my way back to where we changed.

My body lurched forward with new determination. Each step presented a new challenge. I jumped at every sound, and while the pain in my shoulder had dulled to an ache, it still felt like my arm was going to fall off. I could've howled with relief when I finally stumbled on the clearing.

I stepped clear of the trees and immediately went on high alert. Thirty feet away stood another wolf. Every hair on my body stood on end, the resulting static crackling through my fur. For a brief moment, I forgot about my shoulder. I couldn't smell him, but I knew. I *knew*.

The beginnings of a howl rose in my throat. I quickly suppressed the human instinct to call for help. He'd rush me and my throat would be bare. Pain shot up my arm as I planted my feet. I pushed the agony back and did my best to focus.

His eyes glinted in the moonlight and a chill rippled across my body at his toothy grin. Leaves crunched like death knolls as he walked towards me, each step deliberate and drawn out. The wolf in me wanted to gnash her teeth, rip and tear, while the human wanted to scream in terror. I didn't waste breath on either.

A furious snarl replaced his open-mouthed grin when I didn't react to his scare tactics. The savage growl hit me like a physical blow and despite my best efforts, I flinched. The forest crashed around me and it took every ounce of willpower I had not to react to the deafening noise. The alarm on his face registered right before the world slid into darkness and I collapsed to the wet earth.

I awoke miraculously human again and looked around bleary-eyed, willing the world back into focus. Across the way, Michael and David stood changed and dressed, their voices as indistinct as their images. Belatedly, I realized I was in the back seat of the truck with all the doors open.

"She's awake." An edge of something I couldn't place undermined David's calm.

"How are you feeling?" Michael asked as he brushed sweaty strands of hair from my face.

I blinked at him not sure how he'd gotten there and managed a noncommittal groan.

"Try not to move around too much, your shoulder is pretty messed up," he said softly.

"Mike, I don't see anything. He's long gone by now." David's words reminded me of the danger we were in.

"What happened?" I croaked, my mouth drier than sandpaper. As if by magic, a water bottle appeared. I drank greedily, not caring that I choked on half of it.

"Easy," Michael cautioned, his hand on my hair.

David walked closer, his right leg jerking unnaturally with each step. "You passed out and he ran. And *someone* refused to give chase."

"What would you have had me do?" Michael's question had the sound of a tired argument.

David leaned down to massage his leg without responding.

"What if it had been Charline? Would you have left *her* defenseless?"

David sighed, but said nothing and Michael returned his attention to me.

"What do you remember?"

"How did I change?" Water dribbled down my chin, but at least the words didn't hurt as much.

There was a tense pause. Awe tinged Michael's voice when he finally answered. "You changed while you were out."

"That has to be the smoothest transition to human I've ever seen." David's words struck something within me. I struggled for a moment to identify it and then it hit me like a wall. I felt violated. It must've shown on my face.

"Don't get upset with him, it took us both by surprise." While I could understand that, it did nothing to soothe my ruff.

"How is that possible?" I flashed back to all of the times that would've been helpful.

"I've heard of it, but honestly, I never really believed it." David sounded like he wasn't sure if he believed it now.

"Can we please go home?"

Michael took one last cautionary look around the clearing. "Of course."

30

LONE WOLF

Michael insisted I wear a sling while my shoulder healed. While I couldn't fault the logic, I couldn't understand why the damn thing was taking so long to heal. I shoved my hand beneath my thigh in an effort to stop fiddling with it and blew out a frustrated breath.

"What happened to your arm?"

I glanced over at the inquiry, surprised to find Bob standing at the entrance to my cubicle. "I went for a run last night and fell on it pretty hard. I'm trying not to make it worse." I mentally crossed my fingers and hoped the explanation had enough truth to be believable.

"I didn't realize you ran. Where do you go?"

Maybe I should have lied more.

"It's a relatively new pursuit..." I trailed off, not sure how much detail I should give the story.

"We go running in the state park when we can," Michael's timely answer materialized out of thin air.

Bob took in the image of us standing close together, Michael's hand placed familiarly on my non-injured shoulder. "I would say you should notify HR of your new status, but I suspect HR has already been made aware. In any case, be sure to read the memo in regards to inter-office dating and appropriate behavior."

He glanced down the hall leading to our corner of the office. Sure enough, Charline was making her way towards us. Bob gave us a wink then disappeared back into his office. While I was glad to see we were apparently on good terms, I wasn't sure about this new interest in my personal life.

"What was that about?" Charline eyed the closed door. Before either of us could answer, she turned back and asked, "How's your arm?"

"I see David was unsuccessful in convincing you to extend your holiday," I sighed.

"Quit stalling." Yep, a determined Charline was a persistent Charline.

"It hurts."

"Shouldn't it—you know—have healed by now?" she whispered.

"Bites are a little different." My shoulders slumped at Michael's succinct answer and he gave me a gentle squeeze. "You seem like you're in good hands. I'll see you later." He gave me a quick kiss on the cheek and left me on my own. So much for coming to the rescue.

"He's in a surprisingly good mood, all things considered," Charline said when he walked off. I groaned inwardly. Despite her amazing grasp of everything, she couldn't quite accept the enhanced hearing.

"What can I say? Nothing like an attack in the woods to put things into perspective and bring everyone together."

"I'll say." I raised an eyebrow at the response that clearly had nothing to do with me and Michael. "I'll tell you about everything when all of this is over."

"That seems a little one-sided," I quipped. She floundered a moment, but didn't cave. "I'm assuming you're here because you want the full story?"

"Actually, I'm here to let you know your relationship status has officially been updated with HR. Per company policy you'll be receiving the standard inter-office memo regarding appropriate behavior in the workplace." My jaw dropped and she cracked a smile.

"You're awful." We laughed and I filled her in on as many of the details as I could remember. "It was horrible. All of this training, and never once did it occur to any of us that we should train in the other form."

"At least you all came out alright, maybe a little worse for wear, but you're okay enough to be at work."

I scoffed. "Charline, at this point, I'd probably show up to work dead."

"That's not funny."

"You're right, it's not. But in all seriousness, I'm very glad it's Friday. I need a break." She nodded her agreement then left me to the rest of my day.

***

Saturday did not prove to be the beacon of renewal I so desperately needed, not the least of which because my damn shoulder was taking its sweet ass time to heal. A light rain peppered the windows of Charline's home as we all wallowed in our melancholy.

"Alright, enough of this," I said, breaking the hush.

"Enough of what?" Charline asked, looking up.

"This pity party."

The guys shifted in their respective seats.

"So he got the best of us the other night. What're we going to do about it? Where did we go wrong?" I looked to each of them and waited.

"We didn't work together," David said, leaning back next to Charline.

"We got caught up by the moon," I added, hoping to keep the conversation alive.

"We never trained or even talked about how to react if he confronted us while we were in wolf form," Michael finished.

"We leave Charline out of everything," Charline tossed out. David smirked at her pouty addition and gave her a side bear-hug, prompting an indignant, "Oof."

"Seriously though, how do wolves coordinate in the real world? It's not like they have walkie talkies. He split us up with hardly any effort."

"It's pack instinct," David said. "The Alpha leads and everyone falls in line." He glanced over at Michael who kept his gaze firmly on the rug.

"Well, that's progressive. So, who's the alpha here?" Charline's innocent question effectively sucked all of the air out of the room. Michael shrank in on himself, while David rolled his shoulders.

After a very long pause, David answered. "Michael will take point. This is his hunt after all. Besides, you're his partner," he added with a lopsided grin. His attempt at levity barely made a dent in the otherwise tight atmosphere.

"We need to go back," Michael said into the void.

"Say what now?"

David ignored my question and nodded sagely. "It's the only play we didn't run."

"So, we'll run it tomorrow," Michael said with finality.

"Um, this isn't football. What exactly are you expecting us to do?" I asked. They shared an intense look that seemed to pack an encyclopedia's worth of words.

"Exactly what he said. We're going back to the park tomorrow. Only this time, we're going to practice running as a team." David's piercing gaze slid past me.

I looked to Michael for clarity, but he refused to meet my

gaze and instead grabbed his keys and headed for the door. "I guess we're leaving," I said to Charline.

"Sure, doll. I'll talk to you later." We both glanced at David. Something was definitely going on.

I joined Michael in the Jeep and managed to make it to the end of the street before I exploded. "What aren't you telling me? Why was that so weird? Pack dynamics may be a bit beyond me, but even I could tell that was tense."

He rolled his shoulders, refusing to make eye contact.

"Answer me."

His sigh threatened to fog the windows. "Those questions don't have easy answers and David was being generous. I'm not an Alpha, I'm not even a Beta."

"What are you?"

"I'm..." He paused and his knuckles tightened around the steering wheel. "I'm what's considered a lone wolf."

"Why does that sound bad?"

The steering wheel creaked beneath the increasing pressure of his grip. "You know how some people are considered extroverts and others antisocial?"

"Yeah."

"Those things don't really fit into the pack hierarchy. If you don't have a role, you don't have a pack."

"Okay. Where do you fit in?"

"I don't."

"But I've heard you talk about the pack—your pack."

"We have a loose relationship. An uneasy truce, if you will." He passed the turn for his street. "I don't cause trouble, I come when called, and I do as I'm told. In return, I'm allowed to live outside of the pack." His explanation wasn't making things any clearer. "If I was to even think about what Charline asked..."

"Then what? What would happen?"

He stared straight ahead.

"Damn it, Michael, answer me!"

He finally looked at me, his eyes filled equally with anger and despair. "Then the pack would hunt me down and kill me."

The Jeep lurched to a halt in the drive. He got out and strode with purpose to the door. I followed more slowly, giving him room to breathe. He was sitting on the couch, already at the bottom of a glass that smelled like bourbon, when I came in.

"Is that why you and David got upset?"

He scoffed. "That's not why I'm angry."

"Then why?"

He rolled his head on the back of the couch to face me. "Because of you." Thankfully, he didn't make me ask what that was supposed to mean. "You deserve to have a pack, to know what it's like."

"That doesn't make any sense." I poured myself a glass and sat on a chair, officially more confused than ever.

"You really don't get it." I bit my tongue. "Of course, you don't understand, this isn't your world, not really, not yet." He paused to take another sip. "When this is over, you'll report to the Alpha. They'll accept you, and you'll be pack."

Slowly the pieces started coming together. "But you're not."

"I'm not."

"I don't understand. I'll be with you. That won't change."

He got up to fix another drink. Downed it and poured another. Sadness poured off of him in waves. "Everything will change when you become part of the pack. And I can't —I won't—ostracize you like that." His eyes squeezed shut and he tightened his grip on the glass and it cracked under the strain. "Loners aren't allowed to mate."

"That's twice now someone has used that word like I'm missing something glaringly important. Would you please explain what that term really means?" I strained to keep my increasing volume in check.

"All loners—all loners permitted to live—are confirmed bachelors. To take a mate, a partner, would be considered an open act of aggression. It would be a threat of a rival pack."

"No."

Michael set his glass down hard. "This isn't something you get to opt out of. Packs are not a democracy. You show up and do as you're told or you're cut off. More often than not, the cut is literal."

"I won't let my life be dictated like this. I've lived this long without a pack. What's so important about it anyway?"

He grabbed me by the shoulders. "Sara, you don't get it. A pack is security. A pack is family." A deep longing filled his voice and laced through it all—heartbreak. He slumped to the floor and a sound of anguish barely distinguishable from the thud floated up.

I joined him on the ground and wrapped my arms around him. "We'll figure it out. One life-shattering problem at a time." I tried to bring some lightness, but the desired laugh dried like dust in my mouth.

The doorbell sliced through the fog of dreams. I begrudgingly slipped out of bed to answer it, leaving Michael to sleep. Much to my surprise, Charline greeted me.

"Good morning. Ooh you look rough. But, hey, your arm seems to be doing better," she said brightly. Morning people.

"Yeah. I guess. But what are you doing here?"

"She wouldn't be left behind," David said as he surged past her.

Charline made a face and followed him inside. "Where's Michael?" she asked.

"He's asleep," I said.

David quickly schooled his surprise. "Well go wake him up. I thought we wanted to get an early start."

"No need. I'm up. Sara, why don't you get dressed?" Michael suggested from the hall, looking as terrible as I felt. Without a word, I went to change out of yesterday's stale clothes.

Once again, we sandwiched into David's truck. Awkwardness and tension no one seemed eager to address defined the lengthy drive.

"Is this where y'all come?" Charline asked as she explored a clearing similar to the one where we'd changed the other night.

"Come on, we need to get deeper," Michael stated, then guided the group through the trees. He only went about a mile before he signaled for us to stop. I looked at him questioningly. "If something happens, Charline needs to be able to get to the truck quickly."

"Enough with the stalling. We all know the drill," David said, clearly upset that Charline was here in the first place. I shook my head and wandered off to find a private spot.

My anxiety increased as I stripped down and braced for the change. Trepidation around how Charline would react to seeing all of us—seeing me—kept the change at bay until I managed to clear my mind. It returned with a vengeance, however, once I settled into my new body and padded back. Sunlight tickled my paws as I stood at the edge of the clearing, clinging to the shadows.

"Is that you, Sara?" Charline called as I continued to hover.

I braced myself for the inevitable rejection and stepped into the full light of day.

"You're beautiful," she gasped.

My ears perked forward in surprise then twitched as a cracked twig betrayed David's approach on my right. Michael followed shortly after, stepping up on my left. I hung back while they approached.

"Hello, David," Charline giggled at the lighter wolf. Wisely she didn't reach out to touch him until he bumped into her legs. "Yep. So that makes you Michael. Easy enough to tell with that hair."

I cocked my head to the side. Seeing the two of them in the daytime, I realized how much larger David was than Michael. In human form their height difference didn't seem like much, but shifted, the difference was stark. The question of who should take the lead seemed ludicrous now; my instincts were very clear on who should be in charge...and it wasn't Michael. A belief further solidified after thirty minutes.

Mercifully, Charline had no idea the level of awkwardness unfolding before her as I tripped and stumbled worse than I had my first shift. The three of us did our best to persist until Michael threw in the metaphorical towel and simply sat down.

Without any audible cue, David walked to the center. He caught each of us with a look and we stood up. David gave a short huff and I walked over to sit beside Michael. He made another sound low in his throat and Michael cocked his head to the side.

David shook out his ruff then fell into an easy lope. I merged to join him and together we wove in and out of the trees circling the clearing. I glanced over at Michael who had yet to move and slowed. David pulled up beside me, his frustration evident in the way he kept shaking his head, then gave a short yip and nodded toward the far side.

Understanding bloomed inside me and I took off in a

dead sprint. I bolted past Michael and banked off the sizable pine to snap at a low hanging branch. David barked at Michael. When he didn't move, he barked at me. Michael bared his teeth and a low growl rolled out of him. I stepped forward to intervene, but pulled up short when David snapped at me. Michael's growl dropped another octave as he lowered his head.

I whimpered in confused alarm at the scene unfolding before me and danced in place.

Michael's eyes shifted to me and his growl died. No comment, no bark, nothing, just silent surrender. David's own threat tapered off and he huffed. I cautiously stepped toward Michael, wary of another reprisal, and brushed against him. His soft sound of distress hurt my heart and I glanced back at David who gave me an odd sort of shrug. Is this what it was to be a lone wolf, to have no place?

My jaw tightened with determination and I bumped Michael. When he didn't look up, I bumped him harder. He shot me an angry look and this time I hit him hard enough for him to stumble. He regained his bearings and squared off with me. I brushed the length of his side in an attempt to convey encouragement, then bumped him again. He bared his teeth and I cocked my head to the side, then took a half step forward. When he didn't respond, I dropped to the ground and placed a paw over my eyes. I peeked up at him and finally saw the light of understanding in his dark brown eyes.

I perked back up and yipped at David. He shook his head in obvious laughter then resumed his easy run around the clearing. This time when I fell in line, Michael was right beside me. Together we wove through trees and under shrubs.

I banked to the right and so did he. As I picked the pace back up, he maneuvered to cover my flank.

When I came to a complete stop and he halted as well, looking out into the trees for any potential threats. David gave a short bark of approval and both of our heads swiveled to face him. Michael caught my eye and gave me a toothy grin.

Charline pulled out sandwiches and the three of us eagerly raced off to change.

"I'm glad someone thinks of these things," I said as I joined her on the ground.

"That was incredible guys," Charline commented, handing us each a monster sub. "I had no idea wolves were so graceful. I mean wow."

"It would've been nice to really stretch our legs, but I didn't want to stray too far," David said, glancing at Charline with a softness in his eyes.

She leaned back on her arms, her red waves falling behind her. "What a beautiful sky."

I looked up to see the deeper hues of dusk coloring the horizon. "Guess that's our cue," I said and began cleaning up our picnic.

"Today has been refreshingly uneventful," Michael said with a smile.

"It's nice not being attacked everywhere we go," I laughed.

"You guys are kidding, right?" Charline asked. We piled into the truck without answering. "Right?"

"What do you plan to do once your current contract is finished?" I asked David once we were officially on the road again. Charline leaned forward eagerly.

"I don't know. I'll probably head back to the House, but I might find a reason to come back to the area and stick around." He winked at Charline who positively beamed. "What about you?" he asked in return.

"What do you mean?"

"News travels fast in this circle. I heard about the incident with Bob." Charline at least had the decency to blush.

"Oh, well, I hadn't really thought about it. He hasn't said anything."

"Maybe it's time for a change of scenery," Michael suggested.

"I'll take that under advisement," I laughed.

"And who says you have to stay in this city? You could go anywhere," David added.

Michael's face grayed, but before I could delve into the peculiar expression, something large darted across the road. David swerved and we ran off the highway. The truck dipped and bucked until we came to a dead stop with a metallic crunch.

31

FRIEND & FOE

"Is everyone okay?" David reached back and squeezed Charline's knee while she nursed her head.

"And that's why we wear seat belts," I moaned. "What was that?"

"It looked like a stag," Michael said as he unbuckled and swung the door open. "I'm gonna check out the damage."

"I'll give you a hand." David's buckle released and he exited the cab.

A third click rang out. "I need fresh air."

"You going to be alright, Charline?" I asked.

"I'm fine. A little woozy is all." She carefully extricated herself, mindful of her head. I looked to the front where the open hood obscured the windshield.

I wonder if we'll need a tow.

A hair-raising scream pierced the air. I turned to find the source and nausea enveloped me.

Charline stood at the edge of where the forest threatened the road, her eyes wide with terror. Behind her was the mutt. He stood on two twisted legs, partially transitioned, his hand wrapped around her neck. Time slowed as a rivulet of red drew down her pale skin to pool in the hollow of her throat.

Everything happened at once. A shout came from the front of the truck. I tore at my buckle, heedless of the pain in my shoulder. Broken bits of plastic stuck to my hand as I crushed it. I glanced back up, but where Charline had been now Michael restrained a shouting David. He struggled to hold him in place, shouting something in return, while I sat frozen, staring at the last place I'd seen Charline.

Blood rushed in my ears and my middle violently twisted. I should have been far too exhausted to change—I was wrong. My shoulder crashed into the window and the glass splintered. Leather split beneath the force of growing claws. The springs in the seat groaned in protest, then gave out, causing the cushion to sag. My legs tangled in the belt, ripping it free of its source.

In a record ten minutes, I lay panting on the obliterated seat to the backdrop of David's angry shouts. I heaved myself out of Charline's open door and landed in a riotous tumble of limbs. My side slammed into the truck as I got back to my feet.

At the noise, Michael looked up from where he'd managed to pin David to the ground. Horror spread across his face as he realized what he was seeing. He released David who surged back to his feet and stumbled toward the tree line before catching himself. Michael took a step in my direction. My gaze slid past him to the section of trees where Charline had vanished. He took another step, hands outstretched, and I sprang forward.

A shout rang out behind me, but the sound of breaking twigs and the crunch of fallen leaves swallowed it. I dove into the underbrush, the smell of baking spices clear in my nose. Cinnamon and clove burned a trail as bright as any neon sign and I barreled after them. Around the familiar smell twined a stench of wrongness. I ran faster.

When Charline's scent threatened to overwhelm me, I slowed. I took a wary step and poked my head through some soft underbrush. Directly across from me, not five feet away, Charline sagged against a tree. I searched frantically for any sign of bite marks.

Thin streams of blood covered every inch of exposed skin along with several deep gashes that gushed red. Now that I wasn't so focused on spices, the metallic smell of blood tainted the air. My stomach heaved. She needed help —now. I took a cautious step forward. A dry twig snapped beneath my weight and cracked out like a gunshot in the stillness.

Charline moaned and lifted her head. "Sara?" Her eyes widened with recognition and panic. "You have to go. Run. He's still here. It's a trap. Sara, it's—"

A sharp growl cut off her hysterical warning and she withered against the tree, clutching her hands to her breast. Tears streamed down her dirty face as the beast that haunted my nightmares stepped out from behind her.

Rage burned in my belly. I lowered my head, baring my teeth, and let out a growl that sent Charline scrambling back against the tree. He hovered perfectly poised to reach out and crush her windpipe between his jaws. If she stood any chance of walking away, I'd have to draw him off.

I shifted my weight to run and his gaze darted to follow the movement. Energy coiled in my legs and I willed myself to remain calm. All I had to do was run and he'd follow. I chanced a quick glance at Charline and prayed she'd under- stand, then launched forward.

He slammed into me before my paws could touch the ground. I scrambled to get my legs back under me and teeth sank into my ruff. He leveraged his advantage and threw me.

My back cracked into a tree and I fell to the ground like a ragdoll.

Charline's scream filled my ears and kept the darkness at bay. I pushed shakily back to my feet, determined to lead him away. I made it two steps this time before he used his weight to crush me against another tree. Air rushed out of my lungs in a pained wheeze. I sagged against the bark as he spun away only to return and grab my front leg.

I cried out as he dragged me away from the tree. He released his hold and sunk his teeth once more into the loose skin around my neck. I fought the hold, kicking out with my legs and gnashing my teeth to no avail. He swung his head violently from side to side pulling me from the ground. Acute pain lanced from my shoulder to my injured leg while hot streams ran down my sides.

He tossed me again. This time when I hit the tree, I didn't get up. He walked over to my limp form, a gruesome smile twisting his canine features. Charline took advantage of his distraction and made a break for it. He spun to stop her, his savage growl making her trip and fall.

My eyes widened with horror as he stepped away from me to stop her. Without a doubt, I knew he'd kill her. She was nothing more than bait to lure me out here and he didn't need her anymore. With the last of my strength, I pushed back up to my feet and lunged. My jaws sank into his ruff, but found no purchase. He spun to dislodge me and I tightened my hold.

Tears sprung to my eyes and my jaw ached, but I didn't let go. He growled again as Charline stumbled back to her feet and lurched toward the woods. Distant crashes that didn't match her faltering steps filled the air.

The mutt used all of his weight to slam us into the ground. My skull bounced off an exposed rock and I lost my hold. His head swiveled toward the encroaching noise and he snarled. Fearing a renewed assault on Charline, I barked to regain his attention.

He transferred the snarl to me and advanced. I curled in on myself and whimpered. He was almost on top of me when another crash came behind him. His head jerked up, exposing his throat. I dug deep into the well of my waning strength and surged off the ground.

Satisfaction rolled through me as hot blood poured into my mouth. I shoved the urge to gag as deep as I could and sank my teeth deeper. He yelped and backpedaled, swinging furiously to dislodge me. Try as I might, my hold wasn't enough and when claws tore at my chest and belly, I let go. He returned with a vengeance and I barely rolled away in time.

Jaws snapped on empty air and his furious roar ripped through the forest. His face contorted with rage, foam dripping from his jowls. I struggled back to my feet, determined to buy Charline as much time as I could. Dirt went flying as he launched at me once more. Rather than brace for impact, I pushed forward to meet him head on, my body a missile of muscle and purpose.

My good shoulder rammed into him, causing him to lose the little balance he'd regained. His claws scrabbled furiously, searching for purchase as I used my back legs to kick his out from under him. Growls along with dirt and debris filled the air as we each fought for the upper hand. The wolf within grew to fill every inch of me as I battled for survival. Then, I found my opening.

With single-minded purpose, my jaws closed perfectly around his throat. Fresh blood pooled between my teeth and poured out the sides of my mouth. He thrashed violently and I tightened my hold, sinking my teeth deeper into the sensitive flesh.

A crash stole my attention and I looked up to see a

woman with fiery hair cowering behind a pair of wolves, one a light, sandy shade, the other, nearly the color of night. The dark one took a step forward and I gave a low warning growl. He stopped and lowered his head, but didn't bare his throat in submission. My growl deepened. I squeezed my jaw, causing my prey to whimper. The dark one looked back at the lighter and larger of the two.

He barely had a chance to shift his stance, before I twisted my head. A crunch like so many leaves ready to burn echoed in the early twilight. The lifeless wolf fell to the ground with a muted thud. His blood immediately soured in my mouth. I cast a wary glance at the others and slowly padded away from the corpse to find water.

Leery of his pack seeking retribution, I hastened my steps. I'd gone a fair distance when I caught the faint, crystal scent of my quest. The source turned out to be a small spring winding through the twisted roots of several trees. I cast about for any present danger then lowered my head to drink. The bitterly cold liquid made quick work of the foulness growing between my jaws.

A ripple of awareness shivered down my spine and I glanced up to find the dark wolf from earlier. I hesitated, not sure if he was a threat, then slowly returned my attention to the stream.

Finished with my drink, I went in search of a meal. A stubborn ache in my shoulder was troublesome, but I shook it off and kept going, the dark wolf following after like a shadow. He stayed a healthy distance away, so I let him be.

When the wind shifted and I finally caught his scent, a sense of familiarity washed over me and I stopped to give him a chance to catch up. He hesitated before getting closer. I waited until he was next to me, then returned to my search. With two of us, there'd be a better chance of taking down a deer.

He caught the scent first and slid into the lead. We became nothing more than passing shadows in the growing dark. Hunting with him was natural and I was grateful for the extra set of jaws when I realized the size of the buck. Seamlessly, we drifted apart and circled around to guide our prey to his end. By the time my hunger was fully satiated, complete darkness had descended.

I found a comfortable spot to curl up and appreciate my fullness. The dark wolf continued to mirror my movements and lay down a short distance away.

The hunt had been fairly quick, but my body ached like I'd been running for hours. I struggled to remember what had led to having that other wolf's throat between my jaws, but came up empty. Whatever the reason, he was dead now. I rested my head between my paws and fell into a dreamless slumber.

When I opened my eyes again, the light of dawn drifted between branches overhead, painting the ground a golden glow, and my dark companion was gone. I amused myself awhile by following his trail until I found a path of black rock that smelled of burning things. Interest lost, I wandered back the way I'd come, drifting between trees and trailing small wildlife.

The day passed uneventfully with only the smells and sounds of the forest to keep me company. As the sun progressed across the sky, I grew anxious. Where was my hunting companion? It made no sense to me why I would be worried about a strange wolf, but there I sat, in the last place I'd seen him, waiting for him to return.

I was staring up through the canopy at broken patches of twilight when a scent tickled my nose. My body realigned itself, zeroing in on the source. I searched the shadows, my inexplicable anxiety dissipating like morning mist. A form detached from the trees and stepped into view. All of the anxiety came crashing back two-fold.

The ruff along my spine stood straight up as I took in the two-legged figure that smelled disconcertingly like my hunting partner. I shook my head to change the image, but it remained.

The creature took a cautious step towards me and I mirrored the motion in reverse. We continued our slow dance until he was fully separated from the foliage. He stood there as if made of stone, waiting. The smell of wolf tangled with something almost so subtle as to be lost, not quite fear, something else, something more.

"Sara." My ears pricked forward. His voice was soft, a whisper in the fading light. "You need to remember. It's okay, I'm right here."

Something bubbled at the back of my mind. I stamped it down. Slowly, I closed the gap between us. My body tensed to run as I stretched my neck forward. I kept my eyes locked on him as I reached to get a better scent and hopefully answers. The bubbling sensation returned and I took a final, fateful step forward.

I sat and gazed into his face while he seemed to search mine. I didn't flinch when his hand found its way to my head. The pressure was comforting and filled with affection. His fingers stroked back and the bubbles burst. Sounds and images exploded to life in my mind.

I was sitting in this man's house happy and content. I was running across rivers of black tar and tearing through brush, terror gripping me. I was looking at the moon overcome with awe at the full, white sphere. I had two legs, not four. My name was Sara and his was Michael. We were in a kitchen kissing. He was lying down, torn apart. I was in an office, a parking garage, in front of a house with a blue door. A monster that was all teeth stood in front of me.

Pain wracked my body as something that flashed white in the night tore it apart. I cried out, wanting to fight the flood, but it was too late, nothing could hold back the tide. Images and sensations flashed in rapid succession until the taste of blood filled my mouth.

Something deep inside tore and I collapsed. My body betrayed me as it tried to go in all directions at once. Pain encompassed everything. Then one crystal clear thought emerged: *I'm changing.*

I lay there in a pool of sweat and dug earth, adjusting to this new body. *And it is new. I understand. I remember.* After a few seconds, I pushed up to my hands and knees, then to my feet. My legs shook beneath me as I searched the near perfect darkness for Michael. I found him sitting against a tree a short distance away.

"Michael," I croaked, my voice hoarse and foreign.

In an instant he was by my side and wrapping his arms around me. The embrace burned on my fresh skin, so exposed without the thick layer of fur. I looked into his eyes, which glinted yellow in the night.

"I killed him."

32

INSTINCT

Indistinct voices buzzed like white noise through my sea of darkness. I focused on the static of sound, but clarity brought no recognition.

"What are we going to do?" The high-pitched voice drifted across the ocean of nothing.

"You need to rest," a deeper voice responded, low and full of worry. "I should take you home."

"I'm not leaving until I know she's alright. You've already gotten your way once. I won't be bullied." Fight and exhaustion laced the eerily familiar voice. "You lost a lot of blood, Charline. Remember what the doctor said."

Charline?

I know that name.

"For heaven's sake, I doubt standing here worrying myself sick counts as strenuous activity. She was my friend before the rest of you showed up. I was there the first time she woke up and I'll be there this time."

Friend.

Charline is my friend. We work together.

I like Charline.

"Maybe not the standing, but definitely the worrying yourself sick," the deeper voice argued.

David.

The knowledge fought back as if it was being pulled from some deep pit.

"Michael, help me out," David said.

Michael.

My sea of darkness exploded with blinding light. I blinked against the brightness and a circle of blurry outlines materialized above me. Unfortunately, with sight came sensation. I groaned at the deep hurt that seemed to surpass my physical body to touch my soul. A couple more blinks brought the blurry faces into focus.

"Thank heavens. She's awake." Charline sighed her relief and my gaze latched onto the thick layers of gauze wrapped around her upper arm.

I quickly averted my gaze and sought to get my bearings. From my limited perspective, I made out the edge of the couch, yet more gauze wrapped around my own arm, and an exceptionally anxious David, but no Michael. I eventually found him standing back, clearly trying not to hover and failing miserably. We locked eyes and he stepped forward. I let out a pained wheeze as I maneuvered to sit up

"Easy now." Michael's hands engulfed my shoulders, steady and supportive.

I fought a wave of dizziness as he helped guide me to a sitting position. I closed my eyes against the spinning and didn't open them again until my stomach settled.

"Are you okay? Can I get you anything?" The concern in Michael's voice plucked at my heart. I went to shake my head and thought better of it.

"How long have I been out?" I rasped out, the words barely distinguishable from the rustling of fabric.

"A few days."

I groaned at the impossible task of explaining yet another absence from work.

Charline placed a delicate hand on my leg. "Don't worry, doll, I pulled some strings and made sure you're covered."

I offered her a wan smile and shifted to a more comfortable position. As my hand pushed against the couch, I realized it wasn't the navy of Michael's overstuffed one. "Where am I?"

Concern flashed across Michael's face and he turned to Charline.

She quickly schooled her own alarm and patted my knee. "You're home, sweetie."

My gaze riveted on her fingers covered with scrapes that went up her arm to disappear beneath the hefty bandage. The bruising around them turned her fair skin into a mottled canvas of purple and yellow that climbed like a vine all the way to her face. Her normally vibrant curls were pulled back in a tame low pony, revealing a thin line of scab on her neck. She patted my knee again and I tore my gaze away from the wound to meet her green eyes.

"I'm fine." One of the men grunted, but she ignored him. "I'm more worried about you."

"We thought it might be easier if you woke up in familiar surroundings, so we brought you home." Michael glanced from me to Charline, uncertainty etched in his features.

I looked around, slowly taking in the newly labeled surroundings. "This isn't my home."

Worry crashed over Michael like a wave, clouding his face and edging his scent. His gaze darted once more to Charline. Her mouth hung open as she struggled to find words.

"What's wrong?" I asked.

Both of them looked at me. "We—" A hand appeared on her shoulder.

"Let's give them some space," David said softly.

"But..." Charline looked back at me, her eyes filled with anxiety as David gently steered her from the room.

I glanced back at Michael and it finally clicked why everyone seemed so concerned; they genuinely thought I didn't know where I was. In an attempt to assuage his fears, I looked him straight in the eye and willed him to understand.

"This is not my home."

He blinked and looked away. With a sigh, I reached out and grabbed his hand. He met my gaze once more as he sat beside me, but fear still darkened his eyes.

"This isn't my home, not anymore." I looked around again, taking in the complete lack of personality and permanence. "This place belongs to someone else, someone who has never been part of this world, someone who lived a lifetime ago." The tension slowly drained from his shoulders and I gave his captive hand a gentle squeeze. "Can you tell me what happened?"

"How are you feeling?" he asked instead of answering. I squeezed his hand tighter, sensing a deeper meaning to the evasion

"What happened?" I repeated and he paled.

"The mutt is dead..."

Acceptance resonated inside of me, hollow without attachment. "I killed him."

A riot of emotions played across Michael's face—concern, relief, fear, trepidation—each one fighting for precedent. "Yes." He tried to pull his hand away and I held it tighter.

"What are you not telling me?"

He closed his eyes and took a steadying breath, highlighting the dark circles smudged beneath them. Lines that hadn't been there before emphasized a level of exhaustion that matched my own. The urge to reach out and comfort him, to tell him everything would be alright, welled up inside me, but I remained still. His dark brown eyes focused on mine and the sadness in them broke my heart.

"What is it?"

"Sara." He paused and placed his other hand over mine. "When David and I caught up with you in the woods, you killed the mutt."

"I... know? It's a bit fuzzy, but I remember fighting him." More specifically, I remembered getting my ass handed to me and the taste of blood.

He nodded, but didn't appear relieved. "After you...after you left, the mutt transitioned back to his human form."

I jerked with surprise. "Really?"

"It's normal for werewolves to turn back to their human form when they die."

"I... I didn't realize. So, so now we know who it is—was," I corrected myself.

Michael looked at me with unblinking eyes. "We do."

Trepidation tightened my chest and quickened my breath at the same time a burning need to know ignited inside me. "Who was it?" Michael finally blinked and looked away. "Oh my god, we know them." When he didn't answer, I lurched to my feet. "Tell me who it was, Michael."

Michael slowly pushed his way up to his feet and met my gaze with the same level of sadness I normally reserved for when a relative died unexpectedly. "It was Ted."

Shock exploded inside me to fill the hollow space that held nothing for what I'd done.

Ted? *Ted*? Unassuming, totally bland, totally callous Ted? Who I saw nearly every day, who'd dated my best friend for six months? That Ted?

I swayed on my feet and Michael reached out lightning fast to steady me.

"Sara." Pain saturated my name as it escaped his lips.

I lifted a hand to my head while my mind reeled with the information and the certainty that it didn't matter that I'd killed someone I'd known, had met, had talked to. There was just...nothing. No remorse, no pangs of guilt. Nothing.

I reevaluated the hollow place inside with a desperation that bordered on manic, because I should feel something. But no matter how hard I tried, the knowledge that the monster was someone I'd interacted with, made no difference. I still didn't care. His death meant nothing to me, nor the fact that I'd been the one who'd caused it. I covered my mouth and gasped in horror while tears stung my eyes.

"I know, Sara, it's an impossible thing to accept." Michael's arms tightened around me and he rubbed my back. "To think, all of this time he was right there, someone you knew..."

The words flowed like water, but despite all his good intentions, I felt nothing. My horror deepened. He pulled back when I didn't say anything, confusion stamped on his face.

"Sara, I realize this is hard, but you'll get through it, I promise."

I couldn't take it anymore. My hands came up to forestall the incessant tide of support. "You don't understand."

"I probably understand better than you think." His cajoling tone vanished to be replaced by a seriousness that bordered on expressionless. "Taking a life, any life, is never something that sits easy. It's perfectly understandable to feel the way you do."

"But that's just it," I said as tears streamed down my face, their heat a stark contrast to the cold spreading inside, "I don't *feel* anything." My words seemed to hit him like a train and my concern escalated. Tremors shook my body as fear took root. "Why don't I feel anything?"

"You've been through a lot..." he began, his voice soft once more.

I cut him off, unable to bear assurances that my total lack of guilt or remorse at taking a life would magically appear. I knew with certainty that it wouldn't. "Don't patronize me. I know what I feel and I don't feel anything. He was rabid. He had to be put down. It was a thing that needed to be done and I did it. Is it shocking that it was Ted the whole time? Yes, but it changes nothing about how I feel." My tears turned to sobs. "What's wrong with me? Why doesn't that bother me?"

Michael's eyes softened and he tenderly held my face. "Oh, Sara, my love, there's nothing wrong with you. There are many things in this world that the wolf will always see in black and white, and your survival is one of them. In a kill or be killed situation, why should you feel remorse for defending your life? The wolves in all of us recognized something horribly unnatural about him and the wolf would've had no qualms removing that infection from the world."

"How many things will I not care about anymore?" My voice warbled as I fought back a fresh rush of tears. "Who am I?"

"You're still you, that hasn't changed. You were forced into an impossible situation and you made the only choice you could. You fought. You fought for your life, for your friend's life, for all the women he's hurt and all the ones he could have. You are the person you have always been and I am so incredibly proud of you."

I sniffled and looked up at this man who had somehow become my world. His rich brown eyes, like the color of fresh turned earth, shone with an understanding and compassion I wasn't sure I deserved. And for the first time, the future didn't scare me.

"I love you," I said, surprising both of us. He blinked and then a stunning grin spread across his face.

"I love you too." He sealed the soft statement with a gentle kiss. I breathed in the woodsy scent of him, loving how it was twirled with my own.

"What do we do now?" I asked.

"Now? Now we go home."

The long drive did little for my nerves. It might not have been so bad if Michael had come with us, but that wasn't an option for this particular excursion. After being partners for the last few months, it felt strange to be doing something so important without him. At the sound of the blinker, I swiveled to face David.

"Not long now," he offered and patted my knee.

My focus immediately turned to the window. Lines of trees opened up to reveal a huge swatch of land. There appeared to be an orchard on one side and a forest that refused to be beaten back on the other. And at the end of an obscenely long drive, sat a large plantation-style house.

My gaze slid from the imposing structure to take in the people crowding the expansive lawn. I blanched and shrank back on the seat while David's hand raised in what proved to be a large series of greetings.

"Who are all of these people? Why are they here?" I didn't realize I'd asked the question aloud until he answered.

"They're the pack and they're here to see you, Sara."

My eyes widened in alarm as I took in the multitude of

faces surrounding us. He chuckled and the reassuring pat turned to a friendly shake.

"They're curious. We haven't seen a made-wolf like you in ages, maybe ever. I suspect some of them are here to see if it's true."

I swallowed hard and gave a shaky wave to our eager onlookers. No pressure.

The exceptionally grand house boasted three-story pillars, a crisp white finish, and a sense of importance that dominated the landscape. Whispers and shy waves followed us as we exited David's truck and approached the imposing structure. David pushed open a pair of over-large doors and we stepped into the historic mansion. I braced myself for the decadence that must reside within such a grand house, but where I expected cold opulence, the house emitted a warmth that rivaled my own childhood home.

"David!" A young man with remarkably black hair rushed up and grasped David's forearm in greeting. "You're finally here. What took you so long? Wait, don't tell me. Another long, tearful goodbye? Yet another broken heart?"

"Who knows, Xander, maybe the quest for the one is over."

"No," he responded, eyes wide with disbelief. Before I could make sense of their unusual exchange, another voice rang down.

"You must be Sara."

I looked up to find a stunning woman standing at the top of the stairs, dark hair falling around her light brown face like a halo. She gracefully descended the grand staircase that dominated the foyer, sparing a brief smile for the young man with David.

"I hope you didn't find the drive too long or the welcoming committee too overwhelming. We're a bit off of the beaten path and obviously very excitable." When I failed to find the words to respond to this angel of a woman, David spoke up.

"Sara, I would like to introduce Maria Wolfsbane. And this rascal is her son, Xander."

"It's great to finally meet you. David has told us so much. The things you've had to endure." Sadness wisped across her features before the angel Maria pulled me into a tight embrace. I tensed at the unexpected contact and then the warmth of her hug settled over me.

"Hi," I said shakily when she released me. The boy, Xander, gave a small wave in acknowledgment.

"I realize this is all a bit," she gestured around her, "much. I keep telling Alexander we should tone it down. And believe it or not, we did manage to keep most of the curious onlookers at bay. But like with any family, there is no preventing the inevitable noses from butting in." She gave me a crooked smile and a wink. "Forgive me, you must be tired. Usually, I would let you rest and get refreshed, but I suspect that you're eager to see the end of this journey."

I nodded numbly, unable to form a full sentence.

"Right," she said with a sharp nod of her head, then promptly began walking down the corridor by the stairs. "If you'll follow me, Alexander is in the sitting room. He's been expecting you for some time."

"That's my fault, Maria," David said, sounding a little abashed.

"Ha! I knew it! We can't let you go anywhere," the kid teased as he fell in with us.

"One of these days, you'll get it, and then I'll be the one teasing you."

While they bantered back and forth, I focused on following Maria and taking in my surroundings. Rich artwork and family portraits mixed together along the walls as well as numerous doors and entryways. An aged photograph of several people in front of the House caught my eye and I couldn't help but wonder how long this pack had been here.

Maria made a sudden right and I only barely stopped myself from walking right past what appeared to be an old-fashioned parlor. Almost dead center, a man sat in an over-sized armchair, one of several in the room. He looked up as we entered the room and casually closed the book that had previously held his attention.

His jet-black hair was similar to that of the youth who'd joined us, only it was streaked with strands of silver that mimicked the salt and pepper in his close-shaven beard. At face value, he could've been any slightly grizzled older gentleman, if not for the charisma and command that emanated off of him. I didn't need anyone to tell me that this was the man I'd come to see.

"Come in," he said, his voice firm, but kind. He set his book down and rose to meet us.

As we walked in, movement caught my attention. I turned and my eyes went wide at the sight of Michael standing demurely by the door. My heart landed with a sickening thud in my stomach that I was positive everyone could hear.

"I hope you don't mind our guest?" the gentleman asked, though it sounded more like a statement. When I didn't respond except to keep walking, he continued. "It's wonderful to finally meet you, Sara. From what I understand, you've been through quite the ordeal. I'm pleased to see you've been taken care of."

Is he referencing Michael or David? Why is Michael here?

"My name is Alexander Wolfsbane—yes, I recognize the irony of the name—but what can you do?" His attempt at levity was completely lost on me as I was more preoccupied with not throwing up my road snacks.

"Dad, you really don't have to explain that to everyone."

"I see you've already met my son." Alexander smiled as he looked past me to the young man then returned his gaze to me. The act instantly softened his features, making him look more like a beloved father figure and less like a salty general. Despite my mounting terror at the situation, I instinctively relaxed.

I swallowed and accepted his proffered hand with my sweaty one. "It's nice to meet you too, sir," I managed to croak out.

His face positively shone with welcome as his hand tightened around mine and peace washed over me. I smiled tentatively and squeezed back. His gaze shifted behind me once more and he let go. It was then that I remembered Michael and my anxiety returned two-fold.

Why is he here?

I snapped my hovering hand down by my side as a rising wave of panic joined the anxiety already coursing through my veins. I tried to swallow, but my throat stuck and I almost choked. Unable to stop myself, I turned to follow Alexander's look, all of Michael's warnings about his status in relation to the pack screaming in my mind.

Had David told him about us being together? Would Alexander kill Michael for that? Suddenly, David wasn't one of my favorite people anymore. Or had Michael followed us and been caught? Was he summoned separately for some other offense?

Why is he here?

My heart constricted at the onslaught of possibilities, none of which had a favorable outcome.

"I don't see any reason to drag this out any further," Alexander said and gestured to the back of the room. "Michael, will you please join us? I'm sure you're dying to know why I've asked you here today." My stomach clenched unpleasantly at his choice of words.

This is it, I'm either going to be sick right here on the carpet or change or both.

Michael stepped up beside me and I looked at him out of the corner of my eye, afraid that any more dramatic of a movement would trigger one of the reactions. I stood paralyzed with fear while my adrenaline steadily climbed.

Please don't let me change. Please don't let me change.

I felt more than saw Michael move. Warmth engulfed my hand, instantly grounding me. Michael gave it a gentle, reassuring squeeze, and the tension drained out of me. The slight shift in Alexander's eyes betrayed that he'd noted the movement and my reaction.

"It seems you two have had quite the interesting adventure. I'm rather impressed to hear of your work with Sara in helping her to control her change." Despite my increasing trepidation, I was tempted to return his smile. Alexander sighed. "This is one of the things about being Alpha— everyone is always so serious." He shook his head in obvious frustration. "It's been a long time since you've been to the House, Michael."

"Yes, sir."

"And what do you think?"

Michael shifted next to me. "I'm not sure I understand what you mean."

"The last time you were here," Alexander began to move around the room as he spoke, returning to where he'd been when I'd entered, "we had a very serious conversation. We talked at length about pack and what that means." He reached out to touch the cover of the closed book, gently brushing the aged leather.

"I remember, sir."

Alexander straightened up and walked back to us. He

looked from Michael to me and back again. "I see you finally understand it."

Michael's grip tightened.

"And I think it's time we revisited our arrangement."

My insides twisted, thankfully not with anticipation of the change, but with something equally gut-wrenching —fear.

"I can't very well embrace Sara as pack and have you retain your unique status. I am correct in assuming that you intend to stay together?"

I considered my options. Should I speak? Should I nod? Pack or no pack, I was not about to be separated from Michael. I was going to say as much when Alexander held up a hand to stop me. The act died on my tongue and the words escaped my open mouth as unfulfilled air.

"It's clear you've found the meaning of pack in Sara. I'm genuinely happy for both of you. I can only hope that you can find a way to embrace the rest of the pack as well."

Michael visibly relaxed.

Alexander looked him in the eye. "I'll ask again. How does it feel to be back at the House?"

Michael glanced over at me, that smile I'd fallen in love with plain on his face, and I couldn't help but smile back. "It feels like coming home."

If you enjoyed *Sara's Moon*, you'll love the next book in...
Moons of Mystery

Book One: *Sara's Moon*

Book Two: *Charline's Solstice*

All Charline wanted was happily ever after. Instead, werewolf politics might tear her and David apart forever.

Book Three: *Diana's Eclipse*
Coming soon!

View the series here!
BooksbySBolanos.com/moons-of-mystery

Keep up as the adventure continues...
Want to stay in the loop with all the latest and greatest? Get announcements and specials by subscribing to my newsletter. Sign up now to receive a sneak peek at my current WIP and maybe a few other treats from my paranormal lovelies.

BooksBySBolanos.com/newsletter

Like on FB:
facebook.com/BooksBySBolanos

Follow on Twitter:
twitter.com/BooksBySBolanos

Follow on Instagram:
Instagram.com/SBolanosBooks

Check out the Playlist:
bit.ly/SarasMoonPlaylist

ACKNOWLEDGMENTS

Thanking the people who helped Sara's Moon become a published reality doesn't come close to how much impact these incredible people have had in this endeavor. First and foremost, I want to thank my husband for never giving up on me. Granted, the pep talks started to grate after a year's worth of edits, but his unwavering belief is what saw me through.

From there, I must thank my first true round of beta readers—my family. To take a page out of Charline's book, bless their hearts for reading through that initial hot mess and telling me to my face I had something worth publishing. They definitely lied, but I got there in the end.

Finally, no acknowledgment would be complete without a shout out to my incredible writing community. Melissa, Goose, and Skye I have you to thank for helping me to make this a polished work I am proud to publish. Your eyes for details, brainstorming, and, yes, more pep talks kept me going when I would have gladly thrown in the towel.

I have grown so much as a writer these last couple years and there are countless people I could credit. My mentor,

Annabeth Albert. The incredible WIP-crit group of the Inclusive Romance Project. The local chapter of RWA. And many more. Needless to say, I plan to keep writing and keep publishing. I appreciate every last one of you and can't wait to tackle the next adventure.

ABOUT THE AUTHOR

A genderqueer author, S (she/they) enjoys creating worlds that feel as real as they are fantastical, and doesn't shy away from the darkness that makes the light so much brighter. Her passion for fantasy and the supernatural has given rise to stories where the mystery is just as riveting as the romance.

S is of Cuban-American descent; born in Miami, FL, raised in Mobile, AL. They currently live in Texas, a startling eight miles from everything, as the saying goes. Their two Labradors keep them company (whether they want company or not), and their supportive husband is invaluable when it comes to working out sticky plot points.

Their characters are lively, well-rounded, and reflect the conflicts we all face, albeit with a supernatural twist. Readers can look forward to many stories within the same universe that reach into the past and stretch all the way to the future. Welcome to the adventure!

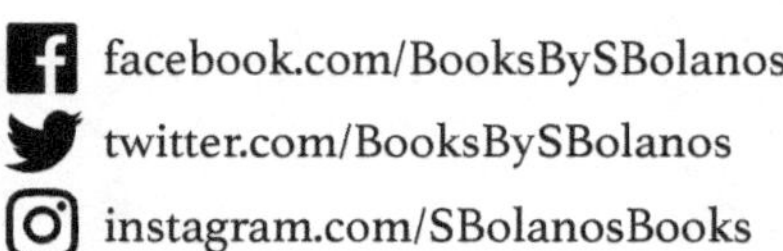

facebook.com/BooksBySBolanos

twitter.com/BooksBySBolanos

instagram.com/SBolanosBooks